PRAISE FOR *THE COORD*
OF LOSS

'An emotion-packed tearjerker.'

Woman and Home

'A thoughtful and sensitive read, well recommended.'

Woman's Way

'We loved this raw depiction of motherhood tested to the limit.'

Take a Break

PRAISE FOR AMANDA PROWSE'S OTHER BOOKS

'Amanda Prowse is the queen of contemporary family drama.'

Daily Mail

'A tragic story of loss and love.'

Lorraine Kelly, *Sun*

'Captivating, heartbreaking and superbly written.'

Closer

'A deeply emotional, unputdown

Red

'Uplifting

Cosmopolitan

The Things I Know

OTHER BOOKS BY AMANDA PROWSE

OTHER NOVELLAS BY AMANDA PROWSE

The Things I Know

AMANDA PROWSE

LAKE UNION
PUBLISHING

Text copyright © 2019 by Lionhead Media Ltd

Published by Lake Union Publishing, Seattle

www.apub.com

Amazon, the Amazon logo, and Lake Union Publishing are trademarks of Amazon.com, Inc., or its affiliates.

ISBN-13: 9781477825211
ISBN-10: 1477825215

Cover design by Ghost Design

Printed in the United States of America

The Things I Know *is dedicated to all the people like me, who throughout their life have always felt that they didn't quite fit. For all those who believe that happy ever after is something that happens to other people. To all of you I would say, 'It only takes one person to show you the magic, and when it happens, you'll know it was worth the wait.'*

PROLOGUE

Hitch pulled the jotter from her bedside table and unscrewed the top of her pen before writing down the thoughts that raced around inside her head. A small act, but one that encouraged the words to stop rolling and helped her think a little straighter.

She had always done it. Some might consider her thoughts and dreams to be somewhat juvenile, but for someone who was born with challenges, a girl who had always lived life a few steps behind her peers, lurking in the shadows, hidden from the shiny, perfect girls who reached for the stars, it was how she expressed everything that was too hard to say out loud.

These are the things I know . . .

I know my name is Thomasina 'Hitch' Waycott.

I know I'm not like everyone else.

I know I was born a little bit different, like someone held the instructions upside down or lost a part when they opened the box.

I also know that words are powerful things and they have weight.

I know certain words have sat in my stomach for as long as I can remember and weigh so much that when I'm in a crowd or I meet someone new they pull my shoulders down and make my head hang forward so I can only look at the floor.

Tard.

Fuckwit.

Rabbitmouth.

I know I want to see other countries.

I know I want to go to New York.

I know I want a boyfriend.

I know I want my own kitchen.

I know I want to paint my nails instead of having them caked in mud.

I know I want to own clothes that are pretty.

I know I want to own sparkly red shoes that I will never get to wear but I can look at whenever I want . . .

What I don't know is just how different I am and I also don't know how I can find this out.

And I know that some days I'm happy and other days I'm sad, but that's the same for everyone, isn't it?

ONE

The two drove back from the Barley Mow in the pickup truck, the dark, shadowy lanes lit in part by the full bright moon that hung low in the late night sky.

It had been a good evening. How Hitch loved Jonathan being home, realising in that moment just how keenly she'd felt the absence of her clever little brother, who had been away at agricultural college for the last couple of years. And now he was back – her entertainer and her protector.

Jonathan, look after your sister!

Her parents had been yelling this at him since he'd been old enough to walk and talk. And that was kind of the unwritten rule: that they looked after each other. Right now Jonathan was drunk as a skunk and it was her turn to watch out for him by driving him home.

The whole evening had felt curiously like a celebration of sorts, as a good night out often did. They had won at pool, beer had been sunk, the jukebox fed with coins, and their high spirits now lingered in the car. Jonathan sat upright in the passenger seat, his face ruddy from too much drink, his shirt unbuttoned at the collar and his breath sour. The windows were rolled down to let the cold night air into the cab of the truck and the sounds of their music out.

'D'you think Shelley might like to go out for a drink with me?' He slurred a little.

'You like Shelley?' This was news.

'Kind of.' He sighed. 'Not really – well, I don't know. I think she's pretty and lovely and straightforward and kind,' he rattled on, 'but you know what it's like, Hitch – around here we can't be too choosy. There's not that many options.'

'You can't go for Shelley just because there's not much choice.' She thought about the nice-enough girl who worked behind the bar and who'd been in her class at school. 'I think that's a bit mean.'

'I would never want to be mean to her – she's fabulous. I just feel like I could go *crazy* here!' he yelled.

'*You* go crazy? You only came home a couple of weeks ago, and actually the way you're shouting like a madman makes me think you're probably halfway there already.'

'Maybe, but I'm twenty-one, Hitch. I want more than this!' He looked up through the windscreen at the wide, dark rural sky. 'Sweet home Whamalama!' Jonathan bellowed, ignoring her point.

'That's not the words.' She sighed.

'I don't care, because I have a secret.' He grinned at her, tapping the side of his nose before drumming his fingertips loudly on the dashboard.

'I couldn't care less if you have a secret.'

'Good, because I'm not going to tell you what it is.'

'Good, because, as I said, I don't care!'

'Good then, because I'm not telling you!'

Some seconds later she let loose the question that jumped up and down on her tongue: 'So what is it then?' She was confident that if he did have a secret it would be nothing of great significance, because she knew practically everything about him.

Over the last couple of years she had devoured the texts and emails he sent from his college digs on the other side of the county. For Hitch, reading about the life he led while learning the business of agriculture in readiness to take over the family farm, it might as well have been on the moon. She would lie in her childhood bed, reading with a smile about the drunken antics of Jonathan and his squad of buddies, who, it seemed, were able to make a party out of the most mundane of events. She pictured the characters he mentioned – Louis, Jasper, Alex, Ben and Big Olly – living her life vicariously through her brother's stories.

She loved her brother and wanted him to be happy, and yet at the same time when she closed down her phone in readiness for sleep, staring at the same walls she'd stared at her whole life, she was left with an ache of envy in her gut for all the things she'd missed out on.

At times like these her mum's words, often quoted, sprang to mind. *There isn't anything out there, Hitch, worth missing. You've got everything you need right here. We love you and you're safe . . .*

The reminder was enough to make her retreat, wary of the ills her mother hinted at – woeful, unimaginable events that might lurk around every corner for a girl like her. A girl who, according to her parents, had arrived in the world twenty-four years earlier with enough ailments to make the midwife wince. Hitch used to imagine the woman's reaction, assuming she must have delivered thousands of babies and therefore understood better than most what the perfect human blueprint might look like. Hitch was far from perfect, her development a little slow and her body a little bent out of shape, and she figured that, with all the things that made her different, those joys that other people took for granted, like love, marriage and being able to wear high-heeled shoes, might be a little out of her reach.

Not that she let her differences hold her back, no sir! With her folded hand, it might take a little longer for her than most to grip things, and early on she had had to work out how to make best use of the misshapen, coiled fingers of that hand, whose movements were a little jagged, but she managed. And her foot, arched on to its toes, meant she walked with one knee raised and a wobble to her gait. It made stairs difficult and the muscles of her foot and ankle ached at the end of a long or cold day, but walk she did – miles and miles across the rough and muddy farm terrain, either in spite of her difficulties or because of them, she wasn't sure. And as for the crude rind of a scar that bisected her top lip, well, that was no more than cosmetic.

Her thoughts churned with what her brother's great revelation might be. Maybe he was one step ahead of the Buttermores and had a cow in mind that might win her class at the county show. Now that would really be something – to beat the golden family, the smug Buttermores, who, while the rest of them lived through feast and famine, always had enough in the kitty to upgrade their equipment and seek sun in faraway places she could only dream of. She liked the idea of triumphing over them, wiping the arrogant smiles from their faces, even if it was only for one day.

Or maybe Jonathan genuinely knew something she didn't. Was Pops finally trading in the rusting old Subaru for a newer model? She squeezed the worn leather-wrapped steering wheel; while a shinier truck might be fun, she'd miss this old girl. They had history. Hitch glanced at her brother briefly and then back at the meandering lane.

'Oh, for God's sake, Jonathan, you're just annoying me now! What is it?'

'Well, if I tell you it won't be a secret, will it?' He wheezed with hysterical laughter, in the way those under the influence did over just about anything.

'You can't say that and not tell me!' she shouted.

'I can't tell you, Hitch.' His tone sobered a little. 'It's too big a thing and you'd only tell Mum and Pops and that will mess things up for me. I need to just do it – just go! Because if I think about it too much, I might lose my nerve.'

'Do what? Go where? You're making it sound so mysterious. God! I won't tell anyone, not that anyone would be interested.' The two shouted over the music, the atmosphere still jovial, if a little charged.

'I promised I'd keep it quiet!' he yelled, before biting his lip. 'And I don't want to jinx things till it's all sorted. I'm relying on a friend, Carter Steele, a guy I know from college, but I want so badly for everything to be in place. I can't wait!'

'So don't tell me then.' She pouted a little, properly irritated now. 'And you're not the only one with secrets, Jonathan.'

'Oh, is that right?'

It was his laughter that caused her tears of frustration to spill over. With her sight blinded, she pulled the pickup on to the verge and jabbed the button to turn off the music.

The silence was sudden, sharp and biting.

'What's going on, sis? Are you okay?' He turned in the seat to face her and she sniffed back the sobs that threatened.

'I . . . I wish I did have a damned secret. I wish I had *something* going on!' She wiped her nose on her sleeve.

'You've got lots going on.'

'Have I? Have I really? What? What have I got to look forward to, Jonathan? It's all right for you – you've been to college, you have friends with names like Carter Steele, but I'm twenty-four and my life is the same as it was when I was fourteen. It's exactly the same! I've just swapped school for work. I feel as if everything is standing still.'

'I think there are a lot of people who would like the comfort of knowing their life is standing still. There's peace in it.'

She was glad that her smart little brother didn't deny the truth of her words, using the soft voice he saved for when she was feeling really sad and he'd do his best to make things feel a little better.

Ignore them, Hitch . . . They're idiots, all of them – what do they know?

'God, Jonathan, *peace*? The quiet strangles me sometimes! And how come *you* don't want the peace of a life standing still?' she asked plaintively.

'It's different . . .'

The two sat in quiet contemplation for a second or two. It was the words he didn't say that rang out the loudest. *Because I have the chance, because I'm not flawed, because Mum and Pops will let me go but they don't like you being out of their sight, because it's just the way it is . . .* She mentally filled in the depressing blanks.

His look of concern, coupled with this rare moment of undivided attention, increased her desire to open up to him, to someone. Digging her nails in her palms, she spoke quickly before the hatch of opportunity closed and she was once again submerged in the darkness of her secret frustrations.

'I love Mum and Pops,' she began, 'but I don't know if this life is enough for me.'

'What d'you mean?' Despite his solemn tone, his eyes lifted in a half-smile, as if waiting for the punchline, and she understood: what other life could there be for her, for them?

'I . . . I . . .' she stuttered. It was so much easier in her head.

I didn't choose to farm; our great-grandparents did! But why does that mean my life has to follow the same path? I like bits of it, but not all of it, and I kind of feel like I'm running out of love for the life and the place, but I don't know what else to do or where to go . . . Who'd give me a job? Who'd want me? And I know Mum and Pops act with love but I feel so caged in that it's suffocating me . . .

'I—' she began, struggling.

'I'm moving away,' he blurted. 'I'm going to America. That's my secret. I'm getting out of here. I'm leaving, Hitch.' He stared at her, eyes bright with excitement.

She felt his words hit her brain like a thump to the chest. 'Leaving?'

'Yeah, going to the States.'

She was breathless, winded by news so big it put her revelation of discontent firmly in the shade. She placed the words she had been about to voice back in the bottle and tamped them down with the stopper, so they rattled around in her thoughts. It was almost unthinkable – a life on Waycott Farm without her little brother? She tried to imagine what this might mean for her parents, who would not only miss him but, on a practical level, would now be a pair of hands short. And what might it mean for her? Jonathan was the sharp snort of laughter over the kitchen table, the one who got her jokes, who played pranks, who sang along loudly to the radio as he worked, the person she locked eyes with when her parents were being unreasonable, her support network and the background noise to her life. The thought of it falling silent was jarring in the extreme.

'Well, say something!' he prompted.

'America?' she managed. 'It's a long way away.'

'Yep, it's a long way away. The good ole U S of A!'

'Are you serious?'

He nodded.

'But . . . but what will you do over there?'

He threw his head back and laughed. 'What do you think I'll do? I have farming in my blood. I'm a farmer! And Carter has told me all about some of the farms out there, Hitch – they sound amazing! Acres and acres of glorious wheat, farms as big as our whole county, and big, blue skies! And neat ranches with horses so beautiful they'd take your breath away.'

'I'm sure they would.' She tried to picture them but could only see the fat ponies belonging to the little girls who lived further along the lane who, led by their mum, trotted along the road with their horses in a slow *clip-clop* that to her sounded a lot like boredom.

'How long are you going for, do you think?' she whispered, thinking ahead to the farming year and trying to suppress the image of a silent Christmas, eight months away, an empty chair at the dining table and one pair of hands short for cracker-pulling. Her parents snoozing in front of the fire, and her without her backgammon partner and no one to lob sweets at across the room . . .

'I don't know,' he said, shrugging and turning his palms up, 'but that's what's so exciting.'

For you, maybe . . .

With a heavy heart she pictured the copy of the *Gazette*, currently folded over and pushed under her bed, with adverts for flat-shares and rooms to let within a five-mile radius of the farm ringed around in red felt-tip. Hitch had chosen them carefully – places that offered her the freedom she craved but were close enough that she would be able to commute comfortably to work each day on the farm. She'd been trying to come up with a plan, not wanting to admit to herself that it was little more than a pipe dream – her wages might just be adequate to cover a small rent, but there would be zero left for food, petrol or anything else, for that matter. Plus, she was pretty certain her parents would veto the idea, hinting again at the woeful, unimaginable events that might bring her harm, were she to flee from under the wing of their protection.

In truth, she'd been aware over the last couple of years that her parents had been treading water, as if everything were on hold, all of them silently waiting for the day Jonathan finished his course and came home for good – meaning also that she could finally, finally, hand over the supporting reins to him and start to live a little. It would be a relief to keep more regulated hours, letting him help out with the early starts, the late finishes and any emergencies, but if he wasn't going to be there, how on earth would her parents manage?

They'll manage because you will help, Hitch, just like you always have . . .

She looked again at her brother, taking in his happy expression. It was, she realised, almost as if his dream came at the expense of hers. She squashed the thought before it really took root.

'Well, say you're pleased for me, excited at least!' His words shook her from her musings. 'This is my great adventure!'

'I'm pleased for you, it's just not what I expected. I'll miss you – we all will.' She winced, seeing her opportunity for a little independence fade away before it had even started.

'You'll be okay,' he offered unconvincingly.

Hitch stared ahead at the dark lane before starting the engine. Fatigue now bit, falling over her like a heavy curtain under which she felt crushed. With his revelation, all the joy of the evening was sucked from the cab of the pickup and thrown out of the window, wrapped in the two words from her brother that had changed absolutely everything: *I'm leaving . . .*

I know that I shall miss my brother.

I know that my mum and dad will be shattered that he's going.

I also know they will try to hide it.

I know he won't think of us half as often as we think of him.

I know life is NOT BLOODY FAIR!

TWO

Twelve months later

Hitch wiggled her stockinged feet on the flagstone floor and rested her bottom on the ancient huge range, letting the gentle heat permeate through her jeans and into her bones. It eased the ache from her left foot and ankle. If there was any sensation half as nice as leaning against the toasty range early on a cold, cold morning, then she was yet to experience it. In fact, the mere thought of it was often enough incentive to pull her out from under her duvet and the soft dip in the ancient mattress in the bedroom, where her breath cut through the chilly air like a knife through butter.

Buddy came over and pushed his muzzle into her palm. She crouched down and lifted his handsome face in her cupped hands.

'Hello, you. Good morning, beautiful boy.'

She placed her head alongside that of the black-and-white collie cross and they shared the moment, just as they did every morning. 'Another busy day, eh?' She loved the scent of him, something akin to warm biscuits.

She stood at the sound of the wooden treads creaking overhead on one of the two staircases in Waycott Farm, the West Country farmhouse in which she had been born. This smaller staircase led straight off the kitchen to the rooms one flight up. On this side of the house each of the bedrooms was strung with sturdy beams that a taller person needed to duck to avoid. Small windows peeped out from the ancient, moss-ridden, sloping red pantile roof, and the whole place seemed to list to the left as if it might tumble, not that anyone seemed too worried by the prospect. The original parts of the building had stood since the late sixteen hundreds. Old sepia photos of her great-grandparents, the upright Walter Waycott and his ferocious wife, Mimi, standing by the front door nearly a century ago, showed the building in a very similar state, and everyone figured that if it was going to collapse into a heap of rubble, it would have done so by now.

Lined with dark wood, the landing and hallways had a feel and smell all their own. Legend had it that the timber had been hewn more than two hundred years ago from boats whose sailing days were done. She sometimes ran her hand over the gnarled, knotty wood around which the house had been built and, closing her eyes, could hear the tales they whispered of journeys over rough and unconquered seas. She could almost smell the salt-tinged breeze through which they cut and feel the slight beat of a heart that pulsed in longing for the life on the ocean waves it had left behind. And she knew how this felt, to be anchored to this place and this building.

The heavy footfall above told her it was the lofty Emery who was up and about. Gathering her long, dark hair over her shoulder, she nimbly twisted a hasty braid and fastened it with a band of red elastic she kept on her wrist before walking to the back door and pulling on her sturdy boots. They were comfortingly heavy, with a thick sole and a sheepskin inner. At two years old and encrusted with mud and the shit of several different animals, they fitted her perfectly, as if hand-made to her exact measurements. In truth, she was so used to wearing them in all weathers that she walked better in them than without. They were familiar, warm and comfortable all at once, and certainly helped correct her awkward, leaning gait, caused by that one damn foot that arched upwards, insisting she walk on tiptoe. She yawned and looked at the clock above the Belfast sink. It was nearly five a.m., time she got out and started gathering before beginning the morning feeds. She heard her cousin's feet quicken their pace on the stairs before he burst into the room. As was his habit, Emery banged his flat fingertips in double time on the beam at the bottom of the stairs and swung into the large, square kitchen, landing with a solid thud on the flagstones.

'Morning, ugly dog. Morning, Buddy!'

She sighed at his pathetic idea of humour and looked down, lacing her boots before reaching for her battered khaki Barbour, as he stood at the sink and sniffed and hawked while running a glass of water. It mattered little that he did this every day. Each morning it made her stomach shrink in revulsion and caused bile to rise in her throat, as if it were the very first time she had heard it. It was yet another way he was so very different from Jonathan and her beloved Pops.

'Do you have to make that noise?'

'What noise?' he said, laughing.

She ignored him, finding his predictable ribbing no more than an annoyance. Emery had been around for over a year, arriving shortly after Jonathan had left for his glorious U S of A, where farms could be as big as this whole county. A quick phone call from Pops and his sister, Auntie Lynne, who'd married an electrician and now lived in the West Midlands, had sent the wayward Emery to help out. Her cousin provided much-needed labour, and here he was, sleeping in Jonathan's bed and turning up for work each day, while never missing a chance to have a verbal dig at her, as if it were his sport or hobby. It had always been this way, ever since he'd first come to stay as a small boy and all the summers since.

Twelve months might have passed, but her cousin was still yet to grasp the fact that his words and jibes slid from her skin like butter off a Teflon pan. There was nothing he could say that was new or inventive, nothing more hurtful than those words that had been spoken since the night she was born.

◆　◆　◆

The story of Hitch's rather hasty arrival one snowy night twenty-five years ago, the first child to a couple in their forties who had long since given up the dream of parenthood, had been told so many times she knew it by heart. It was her mum's party piece.

'Oh my word! She was no more than an itty-bitty scrap of a thing, no bigger than a little pup, and with so many problems the doctor told me to get her christened quick as! And so we did. Shook the moths from the family christening gown stored in the attic and got the job done with barely enough time to pick a name or make a cake. Grandma Elsie poked her head in the crib and said, "*Lord above! What's wrong with that babber?*" And I stared her down and said, "Where d'you want me to start? A little bit of her mouth missing, a weak heart, guts that don't quite work proper, a twist to her toes and a couple of bent-up fingers. We'll be lucky if we still have her here for Christmas!" And then I burst into tears, I did, couldn't quite take it in. But she showed them, that girl of mine! She might be a bit patched up here and there, she won't get any certificate of learning and she won't win any races, but she's a little fighter and no mistake! And we shall treat her like a little lamb whose mum has gone on. We shall hand-feed her and keep her close, out of harm's way! And we have. And we always will, grateful to the Lord above she's still here!'

And this was exactly how she'd always been treated, like a little lamb who needed hand-feeding, a child who was never going to get a certificate of learning or win a race.

Even if she felt like she could.

She'd done her very best to keep up in school, but in the rural environment in which they lived, where class sizes were small, she found herself lumped in with the speedy readers and extroverts, and her lack of confidence meant it was often easier to keep quiet and stay hidden.

And in fairness, the limitations her parents and teachers had placed on her in her early years had made her feel safe. When the other kids at school hadn't wanted to play with her, she didn't blame them, not really, no matter how much it hurt. She could fall back on the knowledge that she was a little bit different, and took comfort from it. There was nothing she liked more than being at home, operating within the boundaries constructed by love and a desire to protect, knowing she would not come to harm. But now those boundaries often felt a lot like prison walls, and the fierce love threatened to suffocate her. She felt the need to stretch her wings, no matter how damaged, wanted to see how far she could wander.

Hitch had always sat in the background, watching life go by and wondering if her thoughts were the right level of thoughts, curious, for example, if arriving in the world as an itty-bitty scrap with a list of things that were wonky was the reason she got so easily distracted. Hitch overheard her grandma say she was no doubt a 'bit soft in the head', a curious phrase and one that interested her enough to try to find out just how soft her head was. Because the truth was there were times when it didn't feel soft at all, in fact, quite the opposite – it felt as if it contained all the dreaming of the universe. If wishes were fuel, she was certain she'd have powered herself to the moon and back and grabbed herself a boyfriend on the way.

Rather than ask the thousand questions that battered her skull, she stayed quiet, close to the farm and to her family, going about the business of keeping things ticking over. And all the while she took the comments, the jibes, the teasing of Emery and his horrible friends, and the supposition of those close to her that most things were a little beyond her, and fashioned them into an armour of sorts.

Teflon . . .

◆ ◆ ◆

'Come on, Buddy.'

She tapped her thigh and stepped out into the cold, dark morning. The chill air cut her lungs and made her cough. She breathed through her nose, loving the autumnal aroma of earth, the slightly sweet perfume of rotting fruit and fallen leaves, mixed in with the scent of real fires, since folk in this sleepy farming hamlet burned wood, oil, coal – anything to keep the bite of cold out and the warmth in.

Hitch made her way across the garden with her unsteady walk, stamping on the frostbitten soil and stepping nimbly in the dark around the raised planting beds in which, when the seasons allowed, her mum grew beans, onions, tomatoes, lettuce, kale, sweet peas and various herbs. With Buddy at her heel, she walked over to the low row of outbuildings which had been converted over the years and now provided a potting shed, a tool shed, a workshop, a tractor shed and a large concrete-floored, metal-roofed building known as Big Barn. She heaved open the barn door with her chilly fingers, sliding it along the wide runner before reaching up for her twin-handled straw pannier, which hung on a hook by the door. She patted Buddy on the flank and shut him inside. He knew the drill by now and made his way to the comfy, battered sofa along the back wall, knowing with certainty that she'd be back before too long.

'Good boy.' She smiled at her beloved companion and headed out to the chicken coop, glancing at the duck pond, where the two Muscovies, Bonnie and Clyde, huddled together. 'I know. It's cold, right? Maybe we should get you sweaters.'

Accessing the henhouse was a complex procedure. In an effort to prevent attack, Pops had raised the coop off the ground so Mr Fox couldn't dig underneath. He had then fashioned a double layer of chicken wire over a wooden frame, and to get in she had to roll one gate away in one direction and the next gate in the other. It was a pain, no doubt, but she had to confess that, despite Mr Fox's best efforts, they hadn't lost a single hen to him or any of his wily contemporaries this last year. She briefly pictured the scene of blood, feathers and carnage that had greeted her last November when Daisy Duke, Mrs Cluck and her friends Daphne, Helga and Little Darling had provided a sumptuous feathery supper for the sneaky fox. It had been a mess and she'd cried great, gulping tears as she scooped up feathers, lumps of bloodied pale pink flesh and the discarded entrails from the remains of his feast. Little Darling and Daphne were intact, perfect in fact, but still dead. This made her dislike Mr Fox even more. To kill because he was hungry and programmed to do so was one thing – she was no stranger to rural life and closer to understanding the food chain than most – but to kill for the sake of it, for sport, was quite another.

'Morning, girls! Hello, lovely ladies, how are we all this morning?' She spoke softly, cooing to them, as she always did, and paused as if waiting for their response. From their quiet acceptance of her presence she assumed that Daisy Duke IV, Mrs Cluck VI, Daphne II, Helga III and Little Darling II were all pleased to see her. They didn't seem too aggrieved that she arrived each day to reach into one of two nesting boxes at the sides of the coop to collect their eggs. She, however, still felt a tiny flash of guilt that after all their hard work, twenty-six hours of making an egg, here she was, ready to snaffle it away with her cold hand and into her straw-lined basket.

'Clever, clever Mrs Cluck!' she would call if the old girl had managed to produce. She'd gone down from four eggs a week to two – not that Hitch would pass this information on to her mum. She remembered the last time she had tittle-tattled on a hen whose egg production had all but halted. Within days, Marion, as she was called, had disappeared, and Marion II had taken her spot quicker than you could say, 'Scrambled or boiled?' Sadly, Marion II had died of natural causes only a month later.

Hitch believed that the more grateful she was for the eggs, the more inclined the gang would be to lay for her. 'Good morning, Helga – no egg today? Don't you worry, my lovely. I'm sure you'll make up for it tomorrow or the day after that. No rush.'

She felt her way around the bedding layer, a mixture of white wood shavings with the sawdust removed and a thin topping of straw. Daphne liked to lay in the small hours, and so Hitch always approached with caution, using her flashlight to scan the ground for the bird before taking a step. It was this kind of attention to detail that the girls really appreciated – respecting them and showing them love. Reaching in, she felt a warm egg and gathered it into her palm.

'Oh, look at this lovely egg – thank you, ladies! That's a beauty. Thank you so much. You have all done so well and I'm grateful. I hope you have a wonderful day and I shall see you all later.'

She winked at Daphne. She knew it was wrong to have favourites, but Daphne, with her fine speckled plume and soft-feathered neck, was so pretty it was hard not to love her a little bit more than the others.

With her usual care, Hitch walked backwards out of the coop and placed the eggs in the straw pannier before going back and securing the double fence. She stood by the enclosed run and gazed down the paddock towards the horizon as the sun began to peep over the curve of the hill. At this moment every day, if conditions were right and she was in time to see it, the wide sweep of the River Severn that formed the natural boundary to their farm lit up like fire, reflecting the early rays of the sun. It was like magic, the very best part of her day.

Hitch took a deep breath and stared out over the horizon. 'I wish . . . I wish . . .'

'What are you standing gawping at?' Emery interrupted from behind.

Hitch closed her eyes. 'I wish that Emery would fall down a deep bloody hole and never come out,' she whispered, opening her eyes in time to see the fire on the water disappear as quickly as it had flared. It was his knack to destroy any moment of joy she could find. She wished he would shove off for good. She was on to him, not as easily fooled as her mum and Pops. Emery wanted the farm, and with Jonathan out of the way he thought it possible.

'Because if it's the case you've got nothing to do, just let me know – there's plenty wants doing in the lower field today and grain wants humping from the storeroom. We could use a spare pair of hands, even bloody useless ones like yours!' he said, chuckling.

'I don't work for you!'

'Not yet,' he said, and winked.

Hitch ignored him and made her way back towards Big Barn to retrieve Buddy and head to the kitchen. Emery's words cut to the quick, but she was confident in her own ability to carry out farm work. She'd learned from the very best – her parents.

Spying a crop of burnt-orange marigolds, a welcome flash of colour in the brown landscape at this time of year, she scooted past and ran her fingers over the soft, puff-headed flowers. She picked one and laid it atop her clutch of eggs. There were two paying bed-and-breakfast guests who had stayed last night. Mr and Mrs Silvioni from New York City.

Noo Yoyk was how the woman had said it. Hitch very much liked Mrs Silvioni's pencilled-in eyebrows, her fancy hair and her gravelly voice. She made Hitch think of faraway places and the movies, and just talking to her was enough in some small way to satisfy her dream of travel.

Buddy settled into his soft bed behind the back door while Hitch took up her favourite spot in front of the range. She heated up the blackened skillet, popping in a nub of bacon fat before putting it on the hottest plate of the range, waiting until it sizzled before carefully laying six fat slices of home-cured bacon in its depths and watching them slowly change colour. At the same time, she cut thick slices of her mum's crusty white cobbler and laid some on the worn round breadboard, along with four pats of Waycott Farm butter and two white ramekins:

one filled with raspberry jam and the other with bitter orange marmalade. When the bacon was crisp, the fat rendered and turned golden, she took two more thick slices of bread and laid them in the fat, watching as they soaked up the flavoured grease and they too turned a happy shade of honey-brown. With the bacon and fried bread kept warm in the bottom oven, she now fried two rounds of home-made black pudding and four skinny sausages while heating a tin of baked beans in the saucepan. Once the coffee was brewed, the teapot warmed and milk poured into a daintily painted pottery jug – by all accounts, older than herself – she set one end of the dark mahogany table in the dining room. A fire blazed in the grate, Pops's handiwork, transforming the wood-panelled room into a space that was warm and homely, with long flames licking the fireplace as logs hissed, cracked and popped their morning greeting.

Hitch placed the loaded breadboard, milk jug, cups, saucers, cutlery and a small green earthenware bud vase holding the single marigold bloom on the table and rushed back to the kitchen.

Her mum came through the back door, fresh from sorting and distributing feed for the limited number of livestock. 'Breakfast on, my love? They want an early start.' Her mum, always too busy for small talk, cut to the chase.

'Nearly done,' Hitch replied, as she reached for the jewel in the breakfast – two fat, freshly laid eggs, still slightly warm, in the base of her palm.

'That's a good girl.' Her mum scrutinised her from the table, looking up occasionally as she scribbled a list.

Hitch took a clean pan and drizzled oil into it before cracking the eggs, watching the shiny yolks gleam like orbs of golden sunshine as they bubbled and cooked against the gloom.

She loaded up two plates with the gargantuan feast and walked through to the dining room, where Mr and Mrs Silvioni had taken seats and were admiring the fire, each with a cup of coffee in their hands.

'Good morning,' she said with a smile.

'Good morning, dear. That's great coffee!' Mrs Silvioni lifted the cup towards her as if in congratulation.

Cworfee . . .

'Do you need a hand with that?'

The woman made as if to stand and Hitch shook her head. With her twisted foot and the fingers on her right side permanently crooked, it was a common misconception that she might need help by those with feet of the correct design and fully flexing digits. Hitch didn't doubt that it came from a place of kindness and a willingness to assist, but it rarely occurred to people that this was her normal, and that since her first breath on earth she had more than figured out how to overcome and adapt.

'I can manage, but thank you.'

'Oh, my goodness, will you look at that breakfast! It's a feast is what it is! That'll keep us goin' till dinner!'

Hitch liked this moment the best, placing the lovingly cooked breakfast in front of guests, watching their eyes widen in desire and their smiles break. It felt nice to be appreciated.

'We're here visiting our daughter. She's at Bristol University, studying Biology.'

Dawtah . . . Their *dawtah*, a lucky girl who got to go to college and to travel to the other side of the Pond . . .

'She's staying in Wills Hall. Do you know it?'

Hitch shook her head.

'It's fancy! Isn't it, Tony?'

Mr Silvioni nodded. 'Uh-huh, real fancy!'

'It is! Like something out of Harry Potter. Do you know it, Wills Hall?' she asked again.

Hitch wished she could give a different answer, as it was clearly of importance to the woman. She shook her head. 'I don't go into Bristol.'

'What, *neh-vah*?' Mrs Silvioni questioned in her nasal twang, and sat back with her hand on her chest, her flame-red nails grasping at the wool of her jersey. Hitch couldn't tell whether this was in shock or in pity.

'No, but I'd like to go and see it. I'd like to go to lots of places. I'd love to travel around, especially to New York. One day. I've seen it on TV and in the movies.'

'Morning, all. Sorry about Hitch – she does like to stand and chat, don't you, love?' Her mum placed her hand briefly on her shoulder and it made her feel like a naughty child who'd inadvertently done or said the wrong thing. Maybe she had?

Her mum continued: 'I'm sure you want to be left alone to eat your breakfast.'

Hitch felt her cheeks flame at the exchange. Despite the sing-song nature of her mum's tone, it still felt like a public scolding, the kind you might give a kid, and not a twenty-five-year-old woman who was capable of looking after a beautiful batch of hens and collecting their magical eggs.

Mr and Mrs Silvioni gathered their cutlery and began to tuck in, but were now a little subdued, as if they too felt suitably admonished at having inadvertently broken the rules.

Hitch walked through to the kitchen sink and ran it full of hot, soapy water before submerging the skillet and pan into its fragrant depths. Grasping the scourer, she plunged her hands into the foam.

'They said they wanted an early start, Hitch. I thought it best to come and grab you.'

'We were only chatting.'

'I know, darlin'.'

Hitch hated the way her mum used a pitying tone, making her feel as though she had once again missed the point.

She heard Mrs Silvioni shout out, 'This is the best – just *dee-lish-us*!'

Hitch smiled. She had made Mrs Silvioni happy and this made her happy.

She studied her reflection in the mottled glass of the windowpane and thought that in the early morning light, with her reflection a little smudged, she looked quite normal, pretty even. Her hair sat over her shoulder in its thick, shiny braid and her chin looked a good shape, her neck in nice proportion to her broad shoulders. But what you couldn't see clearly was the thick, puckered line that ran from the top of her lip to the bottom of her nose, a rather jagged cut where her lip had been stitched by an amateur or impatient surgeon, and her nickname arose because of the resulting hitch to her mouth.

'When they're done, start on the bedroom, can you? We've got a family of three coming in tonight, the MacDonalds, and they'll need the trundle bed brought in for the little 'un,' her mum instructed. 'Can you manage?'

'I can, Mum,' Hitch said, nodding, then set about scrubbing the pan in her hand. *Cworfee . . . Dawtah . . .* she smiled and practised the sounds of New York in her head.

I know that I'm lonely.

I know that the years slip by more quickly each year.

I know that I'm fed up with living on this treadmill.

I know spending time with my chickens is the best part of my day.

I know that I hate Emery.

I know that I'm stuck.

I know that no one will ever love me.

THREE

Hitch cleaned the downstairs of the farmhouse, scrubbing the flagstone floors on her hands and knees with a stiff wooden-backed brush and a bucket of hot, soapy water. Breaking from the rhythm of her scratchy chore, she glanced at the ebonised clock on the mantelpiece. It was a little after three o'clock and she knew she should start thinking about tea and cake in a bit, another food marker that punctuated her day. She'd read once that an army marched on its stomach and she understood – it was the same for farmers.

She rose and rubbed her aching knees before making her way into the yard to tip the bucketful of grubby water on to the flower beds. She then polished the brass grate of the fireplace and quickly dusted the ornaments on the mantelpiece, returning them to the exact same spots where Grandma Elsie and possibly even Great-Grandma Mimi had placed them all those years ago. Running her finger over the once-grand oil painting over the fireplace, which now bore a sooty echo around its slightly battered gilt frame, she smiled at how her family wasn't exactly big on replacing anything, or on change in general. Hence the same furnishings, the same food, the same routine, the same life handed down from one generation to the next, a rural baton greased by the hardship of farming life that made it harder and harder to grip with every passing year.

Lucky Jonathan . . .

She swallowed the thought and the associated spike of envy as soon as it flared. There was no time to think on things too much. Not today, not any day. There was too much work to do.

Always too much work to do.

After feeding Buddy, she browned the lamb in a pan on the stove and lobbed in chunks of onion, carrot, turnip and potato. Along with a handful of herbs and a jug full of stock, she then sprinkled the whole thing with ground pepper and left the stew in the oven to simmer nicely. Next she wheeled the trundle bed from the big closet on the landing into one of the two guest bedrooms. Mr and Mrs Silvioni had seemed like nice people and Hitch wasn't in the least bit surprised to see that they had stripped the bed and folded the linen for her to collect easily. They had also left the bathroom neat and tidy, without damp towels thrown hither and thither, as some were wont to do. This behaviour angered her; she guessed the perpetrators were unlikely to do such things in their own home. The Silvionis had even opened the bedroom window, ridding the room of that morning smell, which wasn't particularly pleasant when it was your own; even less so when it was someone else's.

She took pleasure, as always, in pummelling the pillows; it warmed her, bunching her fists as she knocked the feathers nice and plump, ready for the clean pillow protector and slip. She always thought that pillows deserved special treatment – the things that cradled a person's head and took pride of place on the freshly laundered antique brass bed with its comforting dip in the middle. She ran her fingers over their surface, newly encased in starched white cotton, and smiled. Having straightened the curtains, dusted every surface and made the bed, paying particular attention to the crisp white duvet cover, so that it lay taut and wrinkle free, she placed the vase with the single marigold bloom she had picked earlier on the nightstand.

Hitch made the bathroom shine as best she could. It was easy to achieve an immaculate finish on the mirrors and new copper pipework, but on the Victorian enamelled bath, where the surface had thinned in places, and on the old, dulled brass taps, it was easier said than done. She ran the ancient, clunking vacuum cleaner over the floral-patterned rug, replenished the tea and coffee tray and stood back to admire her efforts.

'Can you get my *dawtah* some *cworfee*?' she asked out loud.

'Who in God's name are you talking to?' her mum called from the landing.

'Myself.' A little embarrassed, she swallowed and tucked stray wisps of hair behind her ears.

'Thought you might have a visitor! Frightened the life out of me!' her mum said, chuckling.

'Who'd visit me, Mum?'

Her mother sighed and gave the embarrassed quick shake of her head that she'd been giving for some years now when she was stumped for an answer. 'This room done, love?'

'Yep.' Hitch stood back to allow her a clear view.

'Good, that's one job out of the way.'

'I thought I'd go and clean the girls out, change their bedding. Have a little chat.'

Again the sigh and short shake of her mum's ageing grey head. 'The girls? You do know they're chickens, don't you?' she offered softly.

I had noticed, yes, mainly because of the feathers and beak thing. That, and they had no opinion on Game of Thrones *when I asked them . . .*

'I just call them that,' Hitch said, staring down at the duster in her hand.

'I know,' her mum said, crinkling her eyes. 'Everything is okay, my love, everything is okay.' She walked over and smoothed the hair from her daughter's forehead, the way she had been doing ever since Hitch was little.

'Louise hasn't invited me to her party, Mummy, and she invited the whole class!'

'Don't cry, my little love. Everything is okay . . .'

'No one picked me, Mum! We had to make pairs for country dancing and I had to do it on my own because no one would hold my hand!'

'Well, it's their loss. Everything is okay, my little one . . .'

'No one's asked me to Prom – I'm not going, what's the point?'

'Don't cry my, little love. Prom isn't all it's cracked up to be. Everything is okay . . .'

'Any chance of a cup of tea?' came the call up the back stairs.

'You all right to go and make it?' her mum enquired, with a look that made Hitch want to scream.

'Sure.'

She stood and watched as her mother muttered beneath her breath, as if offering up a silent prayer, as she trod the creaking corridor back towards the rear bedroom.

Hitch made her way down to the kitchen, carrying the basket of dirty linen to take out to Big Barn, where the washing machine, the tumble dryer with the dodgy door and the ironing board lived. She looked up at the darkening sky, sorry that today there would be no pegging out. It was a job she loved in the summer months or when the weather allowed. In the sunshine she would make her way to the paddock, where a long washing line supported by a slender wooden pole was strung between tall posts across the field. Today, as if burdened by its redundancy, the line sagged forlornly and moved slowly in the saddest dance, taken by the wind. Instead she would be working indoors in the gloom: inhaling the scent of clean cotton; turning over the fresh, warm sheets and towels; folding them with precision and stacking them in a neat pile as the breeze came in through the open window. More than once during such sessions a butterfly or a little bird would fly in and perch on a sill or rafter, watching her at work. She would howl with laughter. 'Who am I – Snow White?'

Sometimes she would put the radio on and have a little bop. But in these colder, greyer times of year, with the farm in the grip of autumn, it was a different story. On certain days the wind whistled up from the river and over the bottom levels, cold enough to strip the flesh from her bones and leave her hands red and aching with the chill, and on those days she didn't enjoy the chore half as much. She put the basket outside the back door.

Buddy loped over and stood next to her, his favourite place to be.

'Hello, my boy,' she said, reaching down to pet his warm flank.

Pops and Emery shucked off their boots and took their afternoon break at the kitchen table, flexing their toes inside their heavy socks. Giving the sigh of the weary, they stretched their aching arms over their heads, turning to draw warmth from the open door of the range as they yawned and cricked their necks. With the *Gazette* spread open between them on the table, they combed articles, following the print with busted, dirty fingernails, enjoying the respite from the hard physical work in the fields.

'All right, Pops?' Hitch smiled at the man she loved, while filling the flat-bottomed kettle and placing it on the hot plate of the stove.

'Not bad, my little lovely, not bad. Mum got any of her cake lying around?' He pointed his nose in the direction of the mismatched cake tins stacked around the almost redundant microwave.

'For you.' She lifted and shook the tins, some now quite worn in places, but heirlooms in their own way. Her Grandma Elsie used to say, '*No cake can be made without love . . .*' and Hitch knew that each of these tins had contained a succession of cakes, while endless tea was poured from the pot, all made with love by her kin. Tea and cake was not so much a treat as part of their working lives. It was not Hitch, however, but her mum who was the baker of the house. She had told Hitch many years ago that one of her essential tasks, as with her mother before her, was to bake for the man she loved. It was a rare affectionate expression from a woman who spoke, lived and stared at her husband as if she were constantly exasperated. But love him she must, as the fruit cake, lemon drizzle, ginger loaf, coffee and walnut or carrot cake, almond sponge, apple and walnut loaf and many others just kept on coming.

Hitch handled the cake tins with care, more than aware that not only had she not quite mastered the art of baking herself but also that she had no one to bake for. There was no man she loved, other than Pops and her brother. Not that she had time for such thoughts today. She rooted around until she found a hunk of fruit cake and cut her dad a generous wedge, placing it in front of him on one of her Grandma Elsie's old green side plates. It was a little chipped and the glaze had worn thin in places, but the fluted gilt edge and exquisite art deco grooves meant it carried the echo of past grandeur and was still a thing of beauty, to her at least.

'That's my girl!' He patted her arm as she put the plate in front of him. She saw the ever-closer creep of age on her dad's skin, and it bothered her, his weather-beaten face, deep furrows etched on his brow from rain, sun and worry. Farming was a risky business and it never seemed to get any easier. It was as if, year after year, they scrabbled in the stones, trying to get a foothold, slipping in the mud as their hands reached for the solid brick that crumbled beneath their touch.

Her whole life long they had lurched from famine to feast and back again. The bed-and-breakfast brought in a pretty sum but, in the grand scheme of things, barely enough to run the oil for the range. It had always felt this way, as if they hung on by a thread, stitching each small sum of money from so many different ventures – selling eggs and fresh-cut flowers, the bed-and-breakfast, cattle, crops, even running tractor repairs – into a patchwork quilt to wrap themselves in as they tried to keep the cold from the door. Every penny went into the coffer that was never even close to full. They lived with the flutter of anxiety in their chests, knowing that one bout of bad weather, one ruined crop, one change in the season, sun or rain arriving too early or too late, and they just might sink into the furrows that surrounded them. They all worked very hard, just to stand still.

Hitch had made a couple of suggestions, which had only raised a laugh of dismissal, if not a titter. 'We could do posh camping – glamping! I've read about it: people pay a lot to sleep in a fancy tent, and we have the space!' She recalled how her mum and dad had exchanged a look that translated as *Oh, bless her!* and it made her want to spit.

'Where's *my* cake?' Emery stuck out his bottom lip like a grotesque toddler.

'I have absolutely no bloody idea,' she whispered, as she cut him a much smaller slice and handed it to him before pouring two mugs of tea, remembering his biting comments of earlier.

Emery eyed his uncle's plate and laughed softly through his nose as he almost swallowed his piece of cake whole.

'Ooh, I got a card from Jonathan!' As if just now remembering it was there, her dad reached into his cardigan pocket, producing a post-card with a picture of Jackson Hole, Wyoming, on the front. He held it up so she could see the rugged snow-capped mountains set against the vast blue sky.

'Ain't that something?' he beamed, as if being in receipt of such a picture was as good as beholding the sight for himself, and maybe, for him, it was.

But not for her.

She wanted to climb those mountains, drink in the sweet, clean air. She wanted to saddle up and canter the paths, walk among the rocky outcrops looking at the trees and the wide-wing-spanned, hooked-beaked eagles that hunted there. She wanted to meet a cowboy and eat beans with him by an open fire where flames flickered against the night sky. There were lots of things she wanted to do, like going to New York and ordering *cworfee* for her *dawtah* . . .

'It says he's got a new job on the ranch; he's going to be a loper.' He held the card close to his face. 'L-O-P-E-R,' he spelled out. 'I think that's how you say it. I don't rightly know what it is, but I know it means he's with the horses morning, noon and night, just the way he likes it.'

'Lucky boy,' Emery snapped, with an air of sarcasm entirely lost on her lovely dad, who only ever wanted to see the best in people, even her.

'He is that, but you know, Emery,' he said with a smile, his big, dirt-encrusted hands now breaking his wedge of cake in two and handing half to his nephew, 'you make your own luck. I do believe that. He works hard, I'm sure – different work to us, yes, and I admit it must be nice to toil with the warmth of that sunshine on your back, instead of frost creeping up your limbs, and living on a fancy ranch sounds lovely, but I know our Jonathan and I know he's a worker.'

Hitch chose not to comment, employing the old adage, ignored by her cousin, that if you had nothing nice to say, then best say nothing at all. She still found it hard to fathom how her younger brother, the ink barely dried on his degree certificate from the fancy Cirencester Agricultural College – their mum and dad had dug deep to make sure he didn't go without while he was there – had then just jumped on a plane to go and work on some stranger's farm for no more than board and lodging, while his family nearly ran themselves into the ground trying to run their own, in the vain hope that one day they might be able to pass the deeds on to him. It was unquestioned, his inheritance, as the boy of the family, the one with the farming know-how that came by way of a fancy scroll and the simple fact that this was how it had always been. Waycott Farm – handed down from father to son.

Hitch didn't care much about that, knowing with certainty that, whether it was Pops or Jonathan who sat at the head of the table, she would always have a place at it too. Whether or not it was a place she wanted to occupy was a whole other story. The simple truth was that she missed her brother. She missed him so much her stomach ached with it.

Her mum, and Pops in particular, still held fast to the notion that he would be home any day to dump his duffel bag in his old room, neck a mug of tea, don his wellington boots, grab the tractor keys and claim what was rightfully his, carrying on as if he'd never been away. Hitch hoped they were right, but to her it was obvious that her little brother was making a life, making memories, becoming one with that breathtaking landscape of the Wild West and planning a future that had no place in it for their muddy little farm on the banks of the Severn. And her biggest fear was that her cousin Emery might just swoop in and take over, and if that happened, she knew her place at the table was far from certain.

She still felt a little let down by her brother, but in recent months and after giving it much thought she knew her feelings were largely rooted in disappointment. *She* was the eldest, and while she yearned to travel, she had never thought to bolt. Hitch had grown up with the belief that they were all in it together, that she was safest working and living within the walls of Waycott Farm and that it was only by working and living as a unit, sharing the load, that they all survived. Recently, however, she'd been feeling the heartbreak of lament, fearing that, as she approached her late twenties, she was well and truly stuck here. This place was her provider, her haven and her jailer.

It was complicated.

Her conflicted feelings over the farm and her place in it had only intensified when her parents saw fit to bring cousin Emery into their home.

The day he had arrived, without fair warning, she'd gone into Big Barn and lain on the battered dog sofa, shivering under Buddy's blanket, despite the warmth of that sunny June day. It was the way he lorded it over her and, in some ways, her parents too – there was no respect, as if he were doing them a favour, when she knew for a fact he was paid a good wage, the only one among them who was. And his board and lodging were free. It was now late October and she had got no more used to having him around than on that first day. He'd always been mean to her, his nastiness wrapped in jokes she found far from funny, and when, as a child, she had complained to her parents, they would tut and tell her he meant nothing by it, he was just a kid! And at the end of the day, he was kin.

Hitch pulled on her beanie and Barbour and whistled to Buddy and the two left the kitchen. She loaded the washing machine in Big Barn and shut in her beloved dog. 'Back in a mo, Bud,' she said, as she made her way over to the chicken coop.

The hens were out in the run, pecking around in the grass and gossiping. Hitch pulled back the fencing gates and made her way inside, wary of her footfall.

'Hello, girls! How are we doing? How are you, Mrs Cluck? And look at you, Daisy Duke – you look very pretty today. And what's this? Ah, who's a clever girl?' She reached down into the nest box and plucked out a fresh egg. 'Helga! You're a marvel. Thank you!' With the egg in her hand, she carefully refastened the fences and walked back to Big Barn with the prize resting in her hand.

She slid back the door and jolted at the sight of Emery sitting with Buddy on the saggy sofa. He was smoking.

'No smoking in here. It's a fire risk.'

'Oh yeah?' He blew a smoke ring into the air. 'What're you going to do? Tell your dad? I'm scared!'

'Come on, Buddy!' She ignored the horrible man as Buddy ran to her. 'Good boy.' She kept her hand on the top of his head, taking comfort from the warmth of his coat as they made their way back to the kitchen. She'd stir the lamb, add the softer veg, season again and then see about setting the fires, ready for lighting later, when the new bed-and-breakfast guests arrived.

She washed her hands, warming them under the hot tap before taking her favourite place at the range, where she stared at the postcard of Jackson Hole, Wyoming, which her dad had propped up on the shelf. She thought of Jonathan and wondered what it might be like to wake each day in the sunshine.

The front doorbell drew her from her musings and Hitch welcomed Mr and Mrs MacDonald, giving them a key to the front door and saying hello to their little boy, who hid behind his mum's legs.

'He's a bit shy,' his dad explained, and averted his gaze, the way some people did. She knew it was done out of politeness, so they didn't stare, didn't make her feel uncomfortable, didn't draw attention to her scar, her face, but the fact that they felt the need to look away at all meant it had the very opposite effect. And in spite of Mr Macdonald's very best efforts, she felt her face colour under his lack of scrutiny.

It made her feel ugly.

Uglier.

Dr Newson had said she might be able to have further surgery, but she was beyond scared – petrified, in fact – remembering perfectly what it had felt like as a kid to wake post-operation with pain from an infection that felt like fire, everyone telling her it shouldn't be that bad, and her screaming at them that it was. Her fear of further surgery was multi-layered – supposing they made her condition worse? And what did it really matter anyway? She never saw anyone important, never went anywhere, never did anything.

Standing now in the bathroom, she ran her brush through her long hair, letting it loose about her shoulders. Next she applied a liberal spray of the perfume her brother had sent for Christmas. It had arrived beautifully wrapped in a fancy box with a gold ribbon. She spritzed her neck and wrists and finally dabbed a little bronzer over her cheeks. Hitch looked back at herself in the mirror and smiled, her hand held over her mouth, before making her way back down the creaking stairs.

'This is proper tasty, thank you.' Pops winked at her and she mopped up his gratitude like a sponge. 'Where you off to, my lovely – somewhere nice?' he asked, as if she had a whole host of options and a whole heap of choice. He sat at the table with her mum and Emery, all devouring the lamb stew, the peppery scent of which filled the room.

'Just up the Barley Mow.' She gave a gentle laugh, as if she ever went anywhere else.

'Are you driving?' her dad asked, spooning the soft lamb and a chunk of carrot into his mouth.

'Yep, I'll take the pickup, Dad, if that's okay? I won't be late.'

'Should think not – you've got an early start, my lovely, and I like to know you're tucked up safe. You know we don't sleep properly until you're in,' her mum reminded her, through her own mouthful.

Hitch glanced at the postcard high up on the shelf and wondered how it was that Jonathan not only got to go to bed at a time of his own choosing without their mum's scrutiny, but he got to do it in another bloody country.

◆ ◆ ◆

She climbed into the ancient, mud-caked Subaru and switched on the engine, letting the cab warm a little before putting the radio on and turning up the volume. She drove the lanes at a fierce speed, shifting up and down the gears with the confidence of someone who knew every inch of ground and every twist and turn in the road. Her heart rate rose at the prospect of meeting someone travelling at equal speed in the opposite direction and knowing there would be neither time nor space to avoid the inevitable. Her thumping heart was accompanied by the booming beat of Kylie that blared from her cranked-down windows.

By the time she arrived at the remote Barley Mow, whose crumbling exterior gave the best hint of the sticky-floored dive of a pub inside, her blood was pumping fast and she was feeling pretty good. She drove the truck to the dark, far corner of the car park before throwing the keys into her handbag. With a final tousle to her hair and swallowing the spike of nerves in her throat, she pushed open the door and let her eyes sweep the place. Several familiar faces turned to look at her as she made her way in.

'Hiya, Hitch, what can I get you?' Shelley asked from behind the bar.

'Half of cider, please.'

'How's your brother doing?'

'Good.'

'You must miss him. I know I do. He was the only decent chap to look at around here! And so polite – reckon that's what a fancy college does for you!'

Hitch nodded and thought that, had Jonathan stayed, Shelley might have been a nice girlfriend for him after all. She climbed on to a high stool and rested her elbows on the bar. A glance in the direction of the pool table told her that Tarran Buttermore and his gang were in. She made out that she hadn't seen their nudges, smirks and comments whispered behind cupped palms. He looked up and smiled at her; she looked away instantly, sending her long hair shivering down her back, but not without letting him see the beginning of her own smile.

The evening, as ever, passed in a haze of chit-chat with Shelley about acquaintances they had in common, swapping small talk and gossip about men and women from school or in the community whose names were vaguely familiar. A long list of people who, according to Shelley, had had babies, got divorced, lost a parent, moved to Australia or, as in the case of Katrina Hopkirk, who was two years above them in school, had got into a fight and been arrested in Magaluf. They were the usual tales and titbits of life exchanged over every bar in every country all over the world and yet, when spoken in her postcode, using names that had been read out either side of hers in the class register, the news felt personal and unique.

It was a little before eleven when the bell rang out behind the bar.

'Time, please, ladies and gentlemen!' Shelley called. 'Not that I can see many gentlemen here, only you lot!'

'Not many ladies either, isn't that right, Hitch?' Tarran stood behind her now. His hot breath sent goose bumps over her skin and the scent of his sweat stirred something deep in her gut.

She looked up at him coyly and swung her legs from the stool before making her way out to the car park. Tarran walked close behind and she heard Digger yell something about a rematch and the boys laughed. Truth be told, she didn't like him or his friends that much, cocky and loud, but she did like the way he looked in his tight jeans and white T-shirt beneath his red-and-black plaid shirt. Jonathan had said once before he left that, when there was little choice, it was easy to gravitate towards any opportunity, and Hitch thought now how true that was – Tarran was the only man who had ever shown any romantic interest in her. Her heart boomed in her chest and her palms began to sweat at the thought that tonight he might just like the way she looked too. Standing on the tarmac, she slowly ferreted in her bag for the keys to the truck. Glancing back at Tarran, she waited, giving him time to make a move.

Her thoughts flitted to that night three years ago when the two had climbed drunkenly up into the cab of the truck and fallen on to the wide front seats, fumbling for zippers, buttons and anything else that at that moment hindered their urgent need for contact. A night that had started with such promise but had ended in shame when, in a moment of distraction, she had tried to kiss him. Tarran had pulled his head back and pushed her chin upwards with the heel of his hand, where it stayed, her head snapped back against the window until he was done. Remembering the way she had felt, like a thing discarded, had robbed her of any confidence.

If he liked you, Hitch, he would have made a move within the last three years, you dummy! Things would have happened, developed, but they didn't. What are you thinking? You don't even like him, not really, you only like the idea of him, of being wanted . . .

No matter how much it upset her, she understood his reluctance, his aloofness. Who would want to kiss someone like her?

Her boldness evaporated and she quickened her pace towards the truck, wanting nothing more than to get home, mortified that she had considered anything else. Sitting in the driver's seat with the hot flush of embarrassment on her cheeks, she looked up at the moon through the side window. It was big and beautiful and she felt herself slip away to a time and place where she was someone else. Someone a man wanted to kiss on the mouth and not simply climb on top of once in the dark, across the front seats of the stinky pickup, where muck and straw lined the footwells, in the dimly lit corner of a pub car park in the middle of bloody nowhere.

In her imagination, that evening years ago had ended differently and Tarran was a different person, a kind one. They had talked, whispered, exchanged affectionate words full of promise, and he had stared at her as if leaving was painful . . .

Looking across the car park now, she watched him climb into the passenger seat of Digger Whelks's car. The two laughed like idiots, doubled over, and Digger punched his friend on the arm before they high-fived. She had no doubt that she was the topic under discussion. Digger beeped the horn three times in farewell and she heard the crunch of gravel under the tyres as he made a speedy exit.

Of course you're keen to get away from someone like me . . . Of course you are . . .

With shaking fingers, Hitch turned the key and started the engine. This time she switched the radio off and drove slowly and quietly with caution along the deserted lanes to Waycott Farm. With only a mile or so to go, she swerved left and pulled the pickup into a layby.

Gripping the steering wheel tightly with white-knuckled hands, she let her head hang down until her forehead touched the leather-bound circle. She sat like that for a second or two, maybe more, before her tears fell like hot rain, cascading down her cheeks, smudging the remnants of her make-up and making breathing difficult as she gulped for air.

'Aaaaaaaaaagh!'

Her cry was loud and unrestrained, the sound of distress, frustration and sadness expressed in the only way she knew how. Out here at this time of night, she knew it would carry, possibly even scare the girls.

But that was just too bad. As her mum had reminded her earlier, the hens weren't girls, they weren't her friends.

They were bloody chickens.

◆ ◆ ◆

'You all right, my girlie?'

It was, she knew, the closest her mum would come to admitting she had heard Hitch crying in the kitchen the previous evening when she arrived home from the pub. Hitch had recognised the soft creak of her tread on the stairs and pictured her hovering in her nightgown on the step, pulling her wine-coloured velvet bathrobe together at the neck, debating whether to come down or stay hidden in the shadows. Her mum had chosen the latter, not that Hitch minded, preferring to face her misery alone, and what could her mum possibly have said that might in any way have thrown light on how she felt? How could she begin to explain her secret desire to seek moments of solace beneath someone like Tarran Buttermore, a man she didn't even really like and who didn't like her, just trying to feel . . . something?

'Yep,' Hitch answered, bending forward as she scooped the soft cow shit on to the wide shovel, dumping it into the wheelbarrow, which wobbled on the cold, concrete floor.

'Reckon weather's picking up – that'll be better for your foot. I know it's uncomfortable in the cold.'

'Yep.'

Immune now to the repulsive stink of the manure, she banged the shovel on the edge of the barrow to free the stubborn lumps stuck to the side.

'We've got one guest in today, a corporate booking, man from London – a banker, if memory serves. You'll get on with the room after that?'

'Yep.'

'You need a hand, my darlin'?'

'Nope.'

Her mum finally walked away and Hitch felt her shoulders sag. She took a deep breath, her stomach folding with embarrassment when she pictured herself giving simpering looks of invitation to Tarran, who had been laughing at her, sharing the joke with his friends. She had woken with sadness on her chest like a weight and a slow chill that started in her gut and spread throughout her limbs. Today she had got out of bed with great reluctance, trying to rid herself of the cold, lingering feeling of nothingness. Her mum was right: Hitch's foot ached to the point of pain and her spirits were low. She had stared in the bathroom mirror, looking intently at the face that stared back, just to make sure she was really there.

Even Buddy, in tune with her emotions, seemed to have lost his playful bounce and had earlier crept by her side across the yard with his head low, ears back, as if able to sense her malaise, so in love with her that her sadness crushed him.

Austley Morton was a small village, and everyone knew everyone else, and everyone went to the Barley Mow, and everyone knew the mouthy Buttermores, and everyone would know that she had put on her perfume, made herself available, only to be knocked back . . . Word travelled fast when there was little else to talk about. Gossip like this was rich social fodder. She shuddered at the thought.

Bending low, she scooped again at the dung, the irritating scrape of the sharp metal shovel on the concrete enough to set her teeth on edge.

She was shivering, despite the fact that her mum was right: the weather was picking up. With the big spade in her hand, she stood briefly at the entrance to the cowshed and leaned on it, looking out over the brow of the fields and down to the river, where the sun rose, touching everything that grew on God's green earth with a golden finger. It was, as ever, uniquely beautiful, fleeting, and all the more moving for it.

She tried to imagine the view that greeted Jonathan each morning, no doubt sun-grazed, snow-capped mountains, shiny, lean horses, white picket fences and that big, big, blue sky! Her gaze fell on the shit-splattered spade in her hand – how could she blame him for trading this for that? It was a horrible realisation that part of her frustration with him and his actions lay in old-fashioned jealousy.

Her baby brother had done it.

He had used his initiative and escaped.

Hitch felt her tears fall and cuffed them away, having learned long ago that crying solved nothing. As a child, no matter how much her sobs soaked her pillow after a tough day, in the morning her foot would still be crooked, her fingers curled and her darn lip just as ugly. Now her body railed against trying to hold back her emotions and she cried hard, long, lingering sobs that robbed her of breath and bothered the calves, who mooed loudly behind her.

She let her head fall on to her chest and found herself temporarily paralysed with sadness. Was this it? Was this to be her life? What was the point in keeping family heirlooms, vintage cake tins, hand-scrawled recipes and deeds for houses if she was never going to have anyone to hand it on to? Would Emery – the ungrateful pig – become the custodian? The thought sent a tremor right through her. How was her life ever going to change when each day was spent on this exhausting hamster wheel? Only now, after all these years, did she fully understand that the faster she ran, the quicker she got nowhere and all that happened was that she collapsed at the end of every day, exhausted and still very much alone, trying to figure out her place in the world. All she wanted – all she had ever wanted – was a chance at happiness, to reach her full potential. That, and the opportunity to have what others took for granted: someone to talk to, someone to love who might love her right back.

Hitch managed to compose herself. She sniffed and raised her head and did something she hadn't done for eighteen years. She looked skyward before closing her eyes and offering up a silent prayer.

'Please, I want something. I want someone. I want more!'

I know that I'm lonely, so lonely.

I know that I'm ugly.

I know that men don't look twice at girls like me.

I know this is how it will always be.

I know that I'm growing weary of it . . .

FOUR

'Hel–lo?'

From where she stood on the brow of the paddock, she heard the voice call out – male, deep, not a voice she recognised, but deliverymen were not uncommon.

Hitch lowered the chicken in her outstretched arms and tucked the bird snugly in the crook of one elbow.

'Hello?' she replied, and was about to make her way across the grass and down towards the wide flagstone patio of the yard when a tall man of about her age strolled towards her.

The two looked at each other and she wondered for a moment if she already knew him. He walked as if he knew where he was heading – straight towards her – before hovering awkwardly a few feet away, with a sports bag in his hand and another bag slung across his body. He wore a jacket, smart trousers that sat a little proud of his ankles and black lace-up shoes.

Buddy barked from the back door behind which he was ensconced.

'I . . . I knocked twice, on the front door, but no one answered.' He gestured towards the front of the house, as if she might not know where it was.

'Right.' Along with his cockney accent, she noticed his odd-ness – it was hard not to: the way he stood, the tilt to his head, his unconventional looks, but she also saw the kind crinkle at the corners of his eyes, his awkward manner and his big but brief smile, as if he was unsure of his place in the world.

And this, she understood.

'Well, sorry to keep you waiting. Is no one in the house?' She looked towards the kitchen, wondering where everyone had got to.

The man shook his head and used his index finger to loop his long fringe across his forehead and behind his left ear.

'I wasn't sure I was in the right place, but I have this.' He pulled a brown envelope from the front pocket of his satchel. 'And it says here, Waycott Farm.'

'Well, this is Waycott Farm.' She waited to see what the man wanted. Was he selling something? Or could he be their overnight guest? He didn't look much like the archetypal banker that she'd been expecting. He looked more like a trainspotter or a librarian.

The two stood, caught in a moment of silence that was excruciating. She sought through the nervous jumble in her mind and tried and failed to think of something to say.

The man looked back down the path and eventually spoke. 'I was wondering how you sort things out when they go wrong in the countryside.'

'I don't know what you mean.' She had lost the thread of the conversation.

'I was just thinking that, if I was in the wrong place, I'm not sure what to do next. The taxi dropped me and left quickly, and I was thinking that, to get help, it would be a lot more challenging here than it is in a city. I mean, if ever I get locked out of the flat I live in, I can knock on a neighbour's window. My next-door neighbour, Reggie, used to be able to open our front door with a credit card. And if I need to get anywhere in any kind of emergency, I just jump on a bus or train or the Underground. It's easy. But out here' – he plucked his phone from his pocket – 'I don't even have a phone signal.' He held the phone to face her as if she might need proof.

'No,' she concurred, thinking how very little a lack of signal impacted on her own life. 'Are you our bed-and-breakfast guest?'

'Yes.' He again held up the brown envelope.

'Mr Grayson-Potts?' His unusual name had stuck in her mind.

'Yes.' He nodded, staring at the chicken under her arm. 'I'm sorry to interrupt your . . .' He paused.

She felt the bloom of embarrassment at the fact that she might have been caught dancing with the chicken, swirling, singing and humming as she turned this way and that for the benefit of the lovely hen.

'I thought you were holding a baby in the air. At first.' He shuffled his feet, confirming that she had indeed been caught in the act.

'Oh no, no baby! This is Daphne.' She had quite forgotten she was holding the chicken and ran her finger over the soft, feathery head of the pale bird.

'Hello, Daphne.' He made eye contact with the hen and lifted his hand in greeting.

She laughed at the formality of his introduction and instantly regretted it, as his face flushed red.

'She likes me to make a bit of a fuss over her.' Hitch leaned forward and whispered to him, even though they were the only two people around. 'I'm not supposed to have favourites, of course – this is a working farm – but isn't she just the prettiest chickie you've ever seen?'

'I suppose so. Your accent is nice. Soft. It makes me think of treacle.'

Hitch smiled at the compliment and it was her turn to feel a flush on her face. There was an odd and unique gentleness to their interaction, as if they had known each other for a very long time and were comfortable in each other's company, pleased to see each other, catching up.

Buddy barked loudly, clearly keen to come and greet their guest. The man flinched.

'That's just Buddy, my dog.' She saw him exhale and swallow, as if afraid. 'You're a bit early.' Placing Daphne carefully back in the run, she wiped her hands on her thighs, as if this might be enough to remove any residue of chicken. The man grimaced a little, appearing somewhat unnerved, possibly at the thought of spores from feathers and bird dander floating in his direction. It made her smile.

Townie . . .

'What time is early?' He looked at her, as if unaware that there was a wrong or right time to arrive.

'Well . . .' She paused and placed her hands on her hips. 'Usually we say any time after three to give us a chance to get the room turned around from the previous guest, but no matter.'

The man twisted his upper body and looked back towards the path that ran around the side of the house. 'I could go for a walk, if you like, and come back later.'

'No! No, that's fine. I'll just fetch Buddy and get you settled.' She marched down the paddock and again saw him stiffen. 'Do you not like dogs?' she called over her shoulder.

'No.'

Hitch stopped walking and turned to face him.

'You don't like dogs?' She tried and failed to hide her note of disbelief, unable to imagine anything nicer than greeting her beloved each morning and burying her face in his coat. The thought of being without her beautiful boy was almost more than she could stand.

'The thing is' – he swallowed – 'I never know how you can tell if they're the friendly or snarling variety, and so they frighten me. I can only speak from experience and say that I've never met a dog that I do like.'

She stared at him, trying to figure him out.

'And have you met many dogs?' Her tone was a little softer now, as she remembered this man was, after all, their guest.

'About seven.'

Hitch laughed loudly. This time he didn't turn red but laughed too, seemingly gladdened that he could elicit this reaction but not having any clue as to why she might be laughing.

'Seven?'

'About seven,' he corrected, and having placed his bag on the ground, he used his fingers to count while looking up towards the heavens.

'Mr Riley's mongrel, Mrs O'Hanlon's boxer, Michael the postman's Staffie, Auntie Joan's poodle, the Rottweiler on the ground floor, the Westie in the newsagent's and Reggie's old girlfriend's chihuahua . . . Yes. Seven. But I say "about seven" in case I've forgotten any.'

'Okay then.'

She continued her walk towards the house, watching him step gingerly over the clods of earth in his smooth-soled, lace-up shoes that she was in no doubt were more accustomed to pounding pavements than walking over soil and grass.

'I love dogs,' she confessed, 'and I can't imagine feeling any other way – Buddy's my best friend. Why don't you like them?' she asked over her shoulder.

'They shit everywhere,' he said. 'On the stairs of the flats where I live. The pavements where I walk. I even found a shit in the lift once – my Auntie Eva said it might have been a human shit, because she saw it too, but I don't know. It's hard to tell with big dogs: their shits look a bit like human ones. She thought it might have been one of the junkies who lived on the top floor. But I thought it was a dog's.'

'So . . .' She smiled at him, trying to sift the facts from the torrent of information that came at her so quickly: he lived in a block of flats where junkies lived on the top floor; he had an Auntie Eva as well as Auntie Joan with the poodle . . . 'Just to get this straight, it's not the dogs you don't like, so much as their shit.'

Mr Grayson-Potts paused to consider this. 'Yes, that might be right. Not the actual dogs, but their shit.'

Hitch opened the back door and out bounded the tail-wagging Buddy, who scampered around the visitor with a daft look on his face that looked a lot to her like smiling.

'This is Buddy. My dog. He's definitely the friendly variety.'

Mr Grayson-Potts nodded, but kept his arms close to his body and his eye on Buddy, with a look of mistrust.

'Can I tell you a little secret?' She turned to face him.

'Sure.' He leaned in and her heart raced a little. She liked the scent of him. It was peppery and reminded her of the amber-coloured soap they used to have in the bathrooms at school. 'There isn't a person alive who likes dog shit, not one – even dog lovers, like me. So, who knows, you might be a dog lover after all and just not know it.'

The man watched Buddy running his excited laps around the yard and, if anything, seemed a little perplexed, as if this were something he hadn't considered. 'Maybe.'

'Right, let's go and get you settled.' Hitch made a clicking sound with her tongue and Buddy ran over, trotting to heel. They all three then proceeded round to the front of the house and the man followed her up the path, the scrape of his soles making a scratchy noise on the stone pathway. She was conscious in a new way of her one foot that stood on tiptoe and the way that leg dragged a little. She felt unusually bothered and wondered if he was staring at it, wishing, for reasons she could not quite fathom, that she could present perfection to him as she pushed on the heavy oak front door to reveal the dark, panelled hallway.

'You leave the front door unlocked?' he asked, aghast, apparently more interested in their security arrangements than in her dodgy foot.

'Yep, we don't really have any bother out here. There's always someone around and, besides, Mr Chops over there is a fearsome guard dog.' She nodded towards the lithesome pig that ferreted in the undergrowth.

'Guard pig,' he corrected, and again they both snickered, sharing a joke like friends. Hitch pulled the red leather-bound guest book from the writing desk and licked her finger before flicking through the pages. She saw the man wince a little.

'You might have chickeny stuff on your fingers,' he pointed out.

'I might have.' She smiled at him, with a faint shrug of indifference, before turning her eyes back to the ledger and running her bent finger over the page. 'Here we go – Mr Grayson-Potts, here for two nights and all paid for!'

'I'm here to go to a seminar – speaking at a hotel tomorrow. Organised by the brokers I work for in London, but I'm talking to people here in Bristol about how I do my job.'

'I see, and you didn't want to stay right in Bristol? We're a little way out.' She wondered if this out-of-towner had booked the farm in error.

'No.' He seemed to consider this. 'I've stayed in a hotel before, but Sherry, a girl in Accounts, said I could choose a hotel or a farm. I thought I could stay in a big hotel any time and they all look the same, but I've never stayed on a farm – so I chose the farm.'

'Right. And you've come from London?'

'Yes.'

'I've been twice.' She nodded, as if to emphasise this truth that she considered an achievement.

'To London?'

'Yes. I went to Covent Garden and Victoria Street on one trip and the next time I went to Chelsea to visit the flower show with my mum and her friend from the village, Mrs Pepper.'

'I've never been to the flower show.'

'Would you like to go?' she asked.

'No.'

Hitch stared at him for a second and wondered if he was about to elaborate in the way most people did, to justify their yes or their no, but instead he stayed silent. She wondered if this was in response to her again inadvertently doing or saying the wrong thing and felt a jolt of unease in her gut. She shut the book firmly and smiled broadly.

'I'll show you to your room. Follow me!' She walked through the low-ceilinged dining room and noted the way he stared at the fireplace, which took up a whole wall, letting his eyes linger on the smoky black shadows jumping up the bricks of the inglenook, over the wide stone mantel and up towards the ceiling.

'It smells like a bonfire and a pub and wet leaves.'

She watched him inhale deeply. 'It does.' She liked the way he phrased things, without pretension or flowery words or fear of offence. This was *exactly* what their house smelled of – bonfires, pubs and wet leaves.

'This way, Mr Grayson-Potts!' She climbed the slightly twisted, creaking wooden staircase.

'My name isn't Mr Grayson-Potts.' He stood on the bottom step and spoke loudly.

'Oh?' She turned to face him, trying to quell her rising sense of alarm, wondering at that moment where her parents were, as her eyes darted to the hallway and the front door behind him. She realised for the first time that she was maybe in a vulnerable situation with this stranger, alone in the house. Who was he then, if not the man written down in the guest book?

'I *am* Grayson Potts, but Grayson's my first name.'

'You *are* Grayson.' She breathed an obvious sigh of relief.

'Yes.'

'Right, I thought that was your surname and that my mum had made a mess of the booking on the phone. She does that, always rushing, or she doesn't hear properly. I thought it might be a double-barrelled surname, Grayson-Potts, or that she might have got it the wrong way round.'

'You thought my name might be Potts Grayson?'

'Well, when you put it like that, it sounds less likely, but I haven't heard the name Grayson before.'

'Most people think of Grayson Perry.'

She looked at him blankly, too shy to say she didn't know who he was talking about. Grayson Perry was probably a footballer, a sport about which her knowledge was zero. 'Why did your parents call you Grayson? It's unusual – are you named after someone?'

Grayson shook his head. 'I don't think so. I don't know. I might be.'

She stared at him, again a little fascinated. This was definitely the kind of thing most people knew about their own name.

'What's your name?' he asked boldly, without elaborating.

'My name's Hitch.' She looked at the floor.

'Hitch?' he queried. 'Is that your real name?'

'What, you think I was christened Hitch?'

'I . . . I don't know.'

She noted his red flare of embarrassment or confusion – hard to tell which – and she made a judgement call.

'My real name's Thomasina.'

'Thomasina,' he repeated. 'So why did you say your name is Hitch?'

Still she stared at him, and narrowed her eyes. 'Because of the hitch in my top lip. That's what people call me.' She touched the tip of her finger to it. 'I was born with a problem, a cleft palate, and I had to get it fixed, but they didn't do the best job. Nowadays the surgery is much better, neater, and you can't really tell.'

'So why don't you get it fixed again if they could do a better job now?' He held her gaze, his expression earnest, his tone enquiring but not mocking. It felt as if the question came from a place of genuine interest. In return, it was surprisingly easy to be open.

'Because . . . because I'm scared to.'

'Why are you?'

She gripped the banister and ran her free hand over her mouth, remembering what it felt like to wake with searing fire in her face and crying to be put back under, convinced she might die from the pain that felt like hot knives in her skin.

Don't cry, little 'un. Everything is okay . . .

'Because it might hurt – it hurt before. A lot,' she whispered. 'And I don't want to go through that again. I couldn't. It's worse when you know what to expect.'

He gave a stiff nod of understanding.

'Who calls you Hitch?'

She shrugged. 'Everyone.'

'I'd never call you that. I think it sounds mean.'

The way he spat the words suggested that meanness, indeed bullying, was something he not only understood but detested, and she liked him all the more for it.

'Okay.' She resumed climbing the stairs.

'I've never heard the name Thomasina, which is kind of funny, as you've never heard the name Grayson.'

'Does anyone ever shorten Grayson?'

'My dad, to Gray.'

'Gray,' she repeated, glancing back at him, and for a reason she didn't fully understand Grayson Potts looked a little overcome with emotion.

'Thom,' he suggested, and again their laughter burbled in unison. She looked up and was convinced she saw a rainbow-tinted cloud of happiness, as soft as feathers, dancing over their heads.

Hitch opened the bedroom door and showed the guest from London into the room. He was odd, for sure, yet fascinating to her – not weirdly odd, but different. She watched as he placed his bag on the chair in the corner and then walked straight over to the window. Most guests sat on the bed, or at the very least leaned on it to test its softness, or they opened the wardrobe with a hopeful expression, maybe thinking Narnia might be waiting, or they asked where the bathroom was, or for directions to the pub, the number of a local cab firm . . . but it seemed as if these things might all be secondary to him, as he stood with his hands in his pockets and stared out over the rolling fields, drinking in the view all the way down to the bend in the River Severn.

'Are there any street lights?' he asked eventually.

'Street lights?' It was a question she had not been expecting.

He nodded. 'I like street lights.'

'Er . . . no, not here on the lane, but the farm always has lights on so it's easy to find if you go out and about.'

He turned to look at her and she again took in his quirky appearance. She studied his rather odd haircut properly for the first time, a short back and sides that was quite neat, but the top and fringe . . . she wondered if the barber had given up the ghost halfway through or been called away. As if he felt her staring, he again used his index finger to scoot his fringe away from his forehead and over his left ear. It was a look that might have been incredibly trendy were it not for his clothes, which suggested anything but. Mr Grayson Potts was, she decided, a curious character; he was at once reserved, edgy and yet spoke frankly and without guile. She noticed that he looked at her hair, her eyes, seeming to take in her whole face and not doing what most people did – stare at her jagged lip or make a great show of looking somewhere else altogether. His eyes swept over her face and body without any hint of embarrassment or of trying to be subtle about it; it was more in an appraising way, and one she didn't mind at all.

'I'll leave you to get unpacked and whatnot.'

He looked at her with an expression of bewilderment. 'Thank you.'

Holding his gaze, she felt compelled to say more. 'If you're at a loose end, I'll be around the farm. Come and find me, if you like.' This wasn't something she usually offered, but she got the distinct feeling that Mr Potts was unused to being away from home alone, and she felt a certain kinship for his apparent sense of uncertainty.

'Okay.' He nodded, giving no indication as to whether this suggestion had been well received or not.

Hitch left the room quickly, racing down to the kitchen to prepare the steak pie for supper. Their guest remained in her thoughts. It was odd, as if, having started off by breaking all convention – coming to find her on the farm and not waiting on the doorstep to be shown inside – and then talking so freely, they had quickly smudged the boundaries, changed the rules a little. She felt a touch sorry for him, thinking that, for people like Mr and Mrs Silvioni, who had support and company, a break on a farm was probably great fun, but Mr Potts seemed very alone, and it bothered her.

She pulled the large china mixing bowl from the shelf above the range and set it on the sideboard. After making the pastry, she rolled it out on to the marble slab and lined the pie tin, leaving a good overhang, which she would trim later. After grabbing a handful of carrots, peas, a fat onion and two lumpy potatoes, she worked deftly, peeling and dicing the veggies and lobbing them into the heavy pan on the hotplate. Next she added the large slab of diced stewing steak from the butcher that her mum had taken delivery of earlier, leaving the meat to brown in the pan. She added seasoning to the pot, along with a handful of fresh herbs, before giving the mixture a stir and beginning the prep on the gravy. It all smelled wonderful. Finally she tipped the meat and veggie mixture into the pastry case, along with the sauce, and topped it off with a lid of pastry, which she washed with beaten egg before shoving it in the medium-hot oven, where it would turn golden brown.

'Why are you humming?'

She hadn't heard Emery come into the kitchen. She ignored him, wiping down the wooden countertop with a damp sponge and scraping the vegetable peelings into the little enamel bucket to add to the compost later.

'I said, what you sounding so happy about?'

'You didn't. You said, "Why are you humming?"'

'So you did hear me.' He ran a glass of water and sipped it noisily.

'I always hear you, Emery. I just don't always answer you.' She kept her eyes on the bucket of peelings. He finished his drink and thumped the glass down on the table.

He wiped his wet mouth on his sleeve. 'I reckon, if I took over Waycott, I'd have to make some changes, but I don't want you to worry about that just yet.'

'I don't worry about it at all, Emery. Pops would have to be crazy to leave the place to you.'

'Not if I was the only person he *could* leave it to – if, say, your golden-balls brother never comes home from Brokeback Mountain.' He watched her face closely.

'You don't fool me, Emery, and you don't scare me.' She ignored his insinuation, letting her eyes meet his briefly, hoping the loud heartbeat in her ears wasn't audible to him. Her words were assured and yet had the underlying tremor of someone not used to standing up to her bully. He jumped forward suddenly, stamping his feet as he did so and causing her to start. The bucket slipped from her hand and went clattering to the floor, its contents scattering across the flagstones.

He smiled at her and she felt her heart clatter too, within her ribs.

'I think we both know part of that's not true.' He spoke in no more than a whisper before disappearing up the stairs and, just like that, he drew the happy feeling from her soul and replaced it with something else: a deep, dark, lingering thread of sadness; an echo of a fear as to what her future might hold.

Oh, Jonathan, please come home!

◆　◆　◆

'That would be great.'

'What would be great?' She spun around, not expecting to hear the voice from the doorway. Mr Potts hovered in the hall. She saw that he'd taken off his work jacket and swapped it for a thin-knit V-necked jersey.

'You said, if I was at a loose end, I could come and find you and you'd be around the farm.'

'Yes, yes, I did say that.' She sniffed and pulled her thick hair into a messy ponytail, fastening it with the band she kept on her wrist.

'I've hung my stuff up and I wasn't sure what I should do now.' He stared at her, as if she might have the answer, his expression oddly endearing in its clarity.

'Right.' She looked him up and down, a little taken aback. This was a most unusual situation. Apart from the odd child who wanted to come and hunt for eggs or pet a pig, most guests kept themselves to themselves and let her go about her business. 'Do you want to come out on the farm with me?'

'Sure,' he offered, again with a tone of indifference that might have been annoying, were it not for his eager stride into the kitchen, usually a no-go area for guests.

She gathered the peelings into the bucket. Mr Potts hovered, as if unsure whether to help or not. The floorboards over their heads flexed under Emery's weight, before he returned downstairs. He arrived quickly in the room before she had a chance to brief their guest, not that she was sure of what she would have said.

'Afternoon,' Emery said, with a distinct smirk.

'Hello.' Grayson raised his hand in greeting.

'So you've got yourself a little friend,' Emery whispered, as he passed her by on his way back out into the yard.

Hitch looked back at Grayson, embarrassed in case he might have heard. 'That's my cousin. Ignore him.'

'Okay.'

He followed her out to the cowshed. She noticed how he seemed content to walk in silence, quite unlike most people, who might feel the need, when newly acquainted, to punctuate the air with meaning-less chit-chat or to ask questions in an attempt to get to know the other person better. She patted her thigh and ran her hand over Buddy, her boy, who walked close at her side.

'I think you might be right, you know,' he said.

'About what?' Not for the first time that day, she wondered how she'd lost the thread of the conversation.

'About me liking dogs. I quite like your dog. He seems happy.'

She smiled at his observation. 'I hope he is. I hope all our animals are. I couldn't stand it if they weren't. I think animals are so much nicer than people.' She was aware of the rare confession and felt the tingle of nerves at how it might be received.

'Do you?' He didn't laugh or snicker, and she was grateful.

'I do. I think you're right – people can be hurtful, but animals don't know how to be mean to us, not unless we're cruel to them or they're afraid or just being protective. They'll only turn on you with good reason; at least, that's what I think. Animals trust us, and looking after them feels like a privilege.'

'I suppose it is.' He reached out and gingerly ran his fingertips over Buddy's flank. 'He does feel nice, soft.'

'If you can earn the love of an animal, they will love you for their whole life.' Hitch grabbed the plastic buckets from the feed unit and tipped the milk formula into it.

'I suppose, if humans are taking their mother's milk, the calves have to be given this.' He looked on with an air of disapproval, typical of a city boy.

'Something like that,' she said with a smile. 'These are our autumn batch; they're about six weeks old now and so they have milk and water, but they'll be put to grain in another couple of weeks. A few went to market today.'

'I guess farming is just like having pets but on a bigger scale – you feed them, care for them and then they die.'

'Kind of, but they're not supposed to be like pets. They're supposed to be a commodity, but I love them all. I can't help it.'

'And you love Daphne the most because you think she's the prettiest.'

She smiled, liking the way he offered the fact without any hint of mockery. 'I do.'

'Do you name the calves too, like you have your chicken?'

She laughed. 'I've named *all* my chickens. And yes, I do name the calves, but I haven't told anyone that. They'd think I was stupid. This one is called Maisie-Moo.' She pictured Emery's mocking sneer as she pointed to the big-eyed beauty with the longest lashes.

'I don't think you're stupid.'

'You've only just met me. I might be really stupid and you just haven't seen it yet.'

She won't get any certificate of learning and she won't win any races . . .

He appeared to consider her suggestion. 'It's possible, but I think to take care of animals and care *about* them like you do is not a stupid thing. I think it's a smart thing. A really smart thing.' He picked up one of the buckets and held it at an odd angle from his body, as if the contents might be toxic.

Hitch called the calves as she walked further into the shed: 'How we doing today? I've got your milk. Come and have a drink, my lovelies!' She tipped the bucket into the long trough, watching as each barged their neighbour with their strong head, trying for a better position, gulping noisily at the milky liquid, lapping it with eager tongues and caring little that it splashed over their noses and faces.

'Tip that one in too,' she urged.

'You'll have to do it. I'll drop it.' He handed her the bucket.

The two watched as the baby cows drank their fill.

'What next?' he asked.

'I need to feed the chickens. Clean their coop out.'

Again he followed her across the yard. 'I don't think I'd want the responsibility of all these animals. I'd be worried in case I got something wrong.'

'You learn what to do, and no one knows anything without learning it, do they? Do you not have pets?' She was curious about his home life.

'No.'

'Do you have a garden?'

'No.'

'I can't imagine not having a garden.' She looked up at the endless sky, unfettered by buildings.

'I live in a flat, in a block. With my mum. I've always lived there.'

'Well, I've always lived here. I was born on the top floor, in the attic.' She pointed towards the farmhouse.

'I was born in the Royal London Hospital.'

'Does your dad not live with you?' The man who called him Gray.

'No.'

'So where does he live?'

'I don't know. I haven't seen him since I was eight. He left us.' He spoke with a look of such anguish that, had she not known the facts, she would have believed his hurt to be recent and raw.

'Oh.' She wished she hadn't asked and felt her palms clammy with embarrassment at having touched on the subject. 'I'm sorry.'

'Thank you.' He looked at her. 'I'm sorry too. I think my life would be much better with him in it.'

'In what way?'

'In every way.' He kicked at the floor. 'My mum's . . .' He paused. 'She's . . . she's quite needy and it's hard to break away.'

She looked up at him. This she could relate to, and she felt the bonds of kinship and familiarity joining her to this quirky guest.

He continued: 'I kind of promised my dad and so . . . I look after her, really.'

'Is she ill?' She felt a flame of sympathy for the woman she pictured, who might be old or housebound, and a wave of respect for this man who cared for her.

'No.' He took his time, licked his dry lips and chose his words carefully. 'Not ill, but I don't know how to describe her, really. She's preoccupied. I think she's still angry at my dad. Even after all this time.'

'Maybe she is.'

He reached out and tentatively touched Buddy again. 'I guess. She doesn't really do anything, just sits with my aunties.'

'Joan and Eva.' It was her turn to show her skills of recall, liking how he had taken on board the details of her beloved Daphne.

'Yes.' He grinned. 'They get a bit sloshed on wine and run my dad into the ground. Usually, I go to bed and leave them to it. They make so much noise. It upsets the man who lives below us with his family – Mr Waleed. He's a nice man; his wife is quite fat and she has a shiny gold tooth.' He tapped his own front tooth. 'I always dread meeting Mr Waleed after their noisy nights. Every conversation makes me feel like I'm letting him down. I try to tell him the noise and their cackling is nothing to do with me, but it's me he sees and me he shouts at.'

'What does he say?' It seemed a little unfair to her that Grayson should be shouted at by the neighbour for something that wasn't his fault. She couldn't imagine living somewhere like that, especially with junkies on the top floor and shits in the lift.

'All sorts, and I hate it. He walks towards me with his fists coiled, as if he's expecting trouble. I listen to the Waleeds of an evening. Their lounge is below my bedroom, and I hear his kids laughing; their giggles bounce up and hit the ceiling. I like the happiness.'

'What do you mean, you like the happiness?' This one phrase above all others had caught in the net of her imagination.

Grayson again took his time responding. 'I mean, I like the way they all laugh together, as if whatever they have and whatever they're doing at that moment in time is enough. I think it must be a nice way to live – happy.'

'Are you not happy then, Grayson?' She was curious, knowing exactly what it felt like to wonder about the lives of other people who had what she did not.

'I don't know.' He fixed his fringe and kept his eyes averted.

'I think,' she began cautiously, aware that, despite the ease and depth of their conversation, this man was still a guest and a stranger, 'I think if you were happy, you'd know it.'

'I suppose so. I try not to think about it too much. I just get through the day and then get through the night and then get through the day . . .' He rolled his hand as if to emphasise the infinite nature of his plan. 'Are you happy?' he countered, looking up briefly.

'There are happy moments in my day.' She recalled those moments. 'I like the first big breath I take outside, early in the morning when the rest of the world is still asleep. And I like collecting the eggs and talking to my girls and the sweep of dawn along the Severn.'

'Daphne.' He clicked his fingers.

'Yep, Daphne and the others. And I like closing the door on a room that I've finished getting ready for new guests. So yes, little bits of happiness that I string together and they help me get through the not-so-happy bits. I guess, like you, I get through the day and then I get through the night and then I get through the day . . .'

Hitch slid the door of Big Barn to fetch the wheelbarrow with the spade, bucket and yard broom.

Grayson walked over to the dog sofa and slumped down on it. Hitch looked at the clock and figured a few minutes slacking off wouldn't matter. She joined him and the two sat at either end, facing each other. It felt nice to have someone to slow her down, someone to waste time with.

'I find you very easy to talk to, Thomasina.' She got the impression that, for him, like her, this was a rare thing.

'You too. I'm having a nice time.'

'Me too.' He drummed his fingers on his bony thigh. 'My dad used to tell me it was important to find joy in the small things, as they were really the big things, and that they were what truly mattered.'

'It's good you remember the stuff he said.'

'Yep, but only up until I was eight, when he left.'

'I can't imagine not having my Pops around.' She thought again about the furrows of age he now sported and his deep sigh as he sat or stood, in direct response to the ache of bones which had known hard farm labour for more years than not.

'You're lucky.'

'I am. How did he leave, your dad?' She tried to imagine the man sneaking out and couldn't decide whether a lack of a goodbye would be the very best or the very worst thing.

'He woke me up early one morning and he was standing at the bottom of my bed. The only other time he'd done this was at Christmas to tell me that Santa had been, and I was half awake and felt really excited, like it might be Christmas and I'd forgotten, but then I noticed that his clothes looked crumpled, as if he'd slept in them, his eyes were red, as if he'd been crying, and when he kissed me goodbye, he smelled as though he hadn't cleaned his teeth.' He took a sharp breath. 'And he said, "I'm sorry, Gray," and I thought he meant he was sorry for waking me up, and I was just about to tell him it was okay, I loved seeing him any time, but then he shook his head and told me that he couldn't do it any more.'

'Couldn't do what?' she asked softly.

'Well, he didn't say back then, but I think he meant he couldn't stand living with my mum any more. He told me I was a good boy and he asked me to look after her. I told him I would, even though I was too young to know what I was fully signing up for.' He gave a small snort of laughter. 'But I have looked after her and I think I fill a lot of the gaps in her life.'

She felt a surge of empathy at his feeling that life would be better with one or two changes, one or two simple twists of fate beyond his control. He sounded a little trapped, and this she understood more than most, touching the tip of her finger briefly to her mouth.

'How would it be different, do you think, if your dad was in your life?'

'I think he would have helped me more. I struggle a bit with . . . stuff.'

'What kind of stuff?'

'The big stuff that most people find easy. I'm a bit . . .' He sighed. 'Life is . . .' Again he wrestled with the words. 'I'm okay with the detail, so I spot the small stuff most people miss, but I miss the big stuff most people spot, if that makes any sense. It can make things difficult. It *does* make things difficult. I don't usually talk about it.'

She screwed her eyes up and cocked her head. 'I don't really understand what you mean. Give me an example.'

Grayson looked up, as if trying to think of one that he was happy to share. 'A good example might be when I went out on to the walkway, just outside the front door of our flat. I saw my friend Reggie.'

'Your next-door neighbour. The one with the credit card.'

'Yes, him, I saw him, and he looked really scared. His pupils were wide and he was breathing quickly and he didn't have a top on and he was sweating, but it wasn't a warm day; in fact, it was quite cold. I smiled at him, and he looked at me as if he needed help, and I said, "Are you okay, Reggie?" And he shook his head briefly and still didn't speak, but stared at me as if he needed some help. I was watching his face, trying to figure out *how* to help him and what might be wrong, and saw him look down briefly, and when I followed his eyes I noticed he didn't have any shoes on. I thought I'd figured out what he needed, so I shouted, "Oh, your feet! Do you want me to go and find you some shoes? Your trainers? Or I can lend you my slippers?" As I said, it wasn't a warm day and I thought it couldn't be nice to be standing there in bare feet on the concrete. And then he smiled at me and, even though he didn't answer, he looked happy that I'd asked, grateful. And that was what I noticed. That's what I remember about that day. What I think about.'

He paused. 'But I think what other people might have noticed or might remember most is that the whole sky was lit with the on–off bright blue light of the sirens that coloured the darkness, or the fact that Reggie had his arms up behind his back and was being held still by two police officers in stab vests. And that there were six other police officers on the walkway. But I didn't really see them, not at first. I only saw my friend and that he was frightened and that he had no shoes on. I wanted to help him. I wanted to figure out what was wrong, like a puzzle. That's what I do for my job – I solve problems, puzzles.'

Hitch had known someone similar to this man in primary school, a boy who had extra lessons, like her, a boy who did not know why it was important to keep his clothes on in public but who could do maths. Any maths. He'd had Asperger's, she remembered. Did Grayson?

'Shit! I've never seen that many police officers. What had he done?' She sat forward on the sofa, entirely rapt.

'Oh, he killed someone.'

'He *killed* someone?' She gasped and laughed at the same time. 'Well, I wasn't expecting that!'

'Yeah, well, he says he didn't mean to, so it was an accident, really, but we have a legal system and he was found guilty by a jury.'

'How long did he get?'

'Twenty-six years.'

'Shit!' This story was as exciting as it was shocking. Mr Grayson Potts came from a whole other world.

'Yep, it's a long time. I keep thinking I should go and visit him. I've written to him, and I thought I might wait until I get a letter back before I turn up. You know how some people are about visitors.'

She paused before she answered and stared at him. 'I think you seem like a kind man, Grayson – kind and a bit weird.'

'So I've been told, especially by Liz, who sits next to me at work. She calls me the expert puzzle-solver and she thinks I'm so good at it because of my weirdness.'

Hitch laughed, and he smiled at her.

'What do you mean by "puzzle-solver" – like crosswords and things?'

'I can do those, but that's not really what I meant.'

'Rubik's cubes?' She was running out of ideas.

'No, I mean general problem-solving; it's part of my job. I can look at lines of data and spot patterns and it feels important to me. I don't know why, but I need to turn the data into a straight line in my mind and find the pattern.'

She blinked at the man. 'I have absolutely no idea what you're talking about.'

He turned to face her and his expression was pained, as if it was too hard for him to explain – and not for the first time. 'If you think about a page of facts – columns and columns of dates, prices, quantities, percentages or whatever – I can look at it and, after a period of time, I can change the way I see it in my mind until it looks like one of those puzzles where you have to guess what number comes next or what's missing. I don't know how I do it and I don't know why I do it, but I've always done it and, in my job, guessing those missing numbers, seeing the gaps, or knowing what comes next is very important because it's classed as a prediction, and that means I know before most other people what's going to happen.'

'Like magic! Like a trick!'

'Yes, I guess it is if you can't do it. But it's not a magic trick. It's just that every single line of data is like a circle, a cycle.' He drew the shape in the air with his finger. 'The only variant is how long it takes to repeat that cycle, but I open up the circle, lay it flat in my mind and, as I say, I can see a pattern and spot the gaps.'

She stared at him and hoped she was managing to disguise the crease of confusion that tried to form on her brow. He looked at her face and began again with renewed enthusiasm.

'When . . . when I look at a list or a spreadsheet, it's a bit like reading music to me. I can spot the rhythm of the numbers, like notes on a page, and just like with a piece of music, if a note is wrong, out of tune, a misplaced number, a gap, something odd or interesting . . . it jumps out at me and I can work it out from there.'

'So, you hear the numbers? Like music?' It was a difficult concept.

'No, no, I can't hear it.' He laughed softly. 'I can't hear it,' he repeated, 'but I can feel it.'

'And that's why your boss wants you to come down to Bristol and tell other people how to do your magic trick.'

'Yes, because what I can do is very valuable.'

'Can you teach other people how to do it?' She held his gaze.

'No. No, I can't. I did try to tell Mr Jenks that, but he wouldn't listen. He wants to think it's a formula or a knack, but it's more than that for me. It's how I am and how I've always been, and it's all to do with my puzzle-solving.'

'Who's Mr Jenks?'

'My boss.'

'Right, and why is it so valuable?'

'Because if you think that, with something like gold, which brokers like my firm buy and sell to make money, they buy when it's cheap and sell when it's expensive.'

'Got it so far. Like us with grain and seasonal produce.'

'Okay, yes. So if I can fill in the missing number, if I can see a pattern – which I can for everything – then I know when to buy and when to sell, or, more accurately, I can buy and sell the *option* to buy and sell. It's complicated.'

Hitch stared at him. 'D'you know, I think you might actually be the cleverest person I've ever met in my entire life, Mr Grayson Potts.'

Grayson looked at her with an expression of pure delight and she got the feeling that he only rarely got compliments. The thought filled her with warmth.

'I think words like that are the greatest kindness. Thank you. And when you say I might be the cleverest person you've met, I was wondering, have you met a lot of people?'

'Not really. But more than seven.' She liked the honesty in their exchange.

'I know that some people think the things I do are odd.' Grayson looked at his feet. 'Even my mum. But to me, they're not – to me, they're normal and so that makes them fine.'

She pictured holding her chickens, her friends, close to her chest and whispering confessions into their feathery heads. 'I know what you mean.' And she did. 'You want to go for a walk along the river?' It seemed bold to ask and yet, at the same time, almost free of risk. Hitch felt entirely confident that she could predict his answer.

Like magic.

'Sure.' Again the rather nonchalant response, but Grayson's easy smile and the way he leapt up from the sofa in eager anticipation spoke volumes.

◆ ◆ ◆

Hitch knew as they walked along the ridge of the riverbank with the wide River Severn stretching out in front of them and the low autumn sun glinting on the water that she would not forget this day.

Not ever.

It was unusual for her not to be alone, lost in her own thoughts, silently pondering and reflecting, and yet, far from finding this new situation fearful, nerve-racking, it felt surprisingly easy, ordinary, natural. And it was something she had wished for on so many occasions: to have someone here with her, someone to talk to. She found it calming being with him, as if she didn't have to overthink things and could just be. As ever, there was a clear view of the land on the other side of the water, to Wales, where people walked with their dogs along the opposite riverbank, no doubt looking back at them. She hoped they could see her and this man strolling along together like a couple. The very idea made her tummy jump.

The day felt like an adventure, a holiday even, as they combed the stretch between the two grand bridges rising like curved highways sprung straight from the water, as if raised by the gods. She hadn't felt this way since Jonathan was still at home, when the two of them had occasionally had a similar adventure.

'This is very strange for me,' Grayson began.

'Strange how?'

Grayson stopped walking and looked out over the water. 'I didn't expect this, being here in the countryside – it's as if my thoughts are freer, as if they've been lifted up in the air and can float on the breeze instead of being hemmed in, rebounding between the high walls and buildings like a ball looking for escape in a maze.'

She thought his words were like poetry and was captivated. He wasn't finished.

'I'm thinking bigger things, and everything is a little clearer, as if I can see further ahead than the next step, the next corner.'

She felt another tie of kinship, knowing that this was how she lived her life, one wobbly step at a time.

'I like being here,' he said with a sniff.

'Well, I like you being here.' She spoke to the horizon but still sensed the delight he took in her comment.

Buddy mirrored her happy state, scampering in and out of puddles and over stones, running and leaping like an adventurous pup, exuding joy, sniffing out scents, pawing at anything of interest and urinating more than she had ever seen any dog urinate before at one time.

'It's as though this is the first time he's been here,' Grayson observed.

'That's another lovely thing about dogs. They might walk the same route a thousand times, but to them it's a brand-new adventure and never the same twice. I think life would be much better if we could all learn to be a bit more like Buddy.'

'Yes.'

'There's a pub you can go to for supper later, if you want, or I can set you a place with us in the kitchen, or you can eat in the dining room. It's only pie – nothing fancy – but you'd be very welcome.'

Grayson seemed to falter and shifted awkwardly on the spot. She wondered if the suggestion seemed a little overfamiliar, despite their happy connection, and felt the sour tang of regret on her tongue. A picture of Tarran Buttermore bloomed in her mind: his smile of rejection, the way he'd high-fived Digger . . .

'I always eat alone, so I think I'd be more comfortable in the dining room, if that's okay?'

'Of course!' She exhaled her relief. 'Why don't you eat with your mum?'

'I don't know. She doesn't really eat proper meals. She's quite fat, but she mainly grazes, on salted peanuts and toast and butter. I think she overeats during the day when I'm at work. I often find empty sausage packets, chocolate wrappers and paper bags from the local shops torn open and in the bin. I saw her once put her hand in and pull out a bag to lick the frosting that was stuck to the paper. The cake long gone. She didn't know I was watching.'

'I can't imagine that. We always eat together. I do most of the cooking, and I quite like it. I don't really watch TV but, if I do, I watch cookery programmes and pick up tips. It's nice watching a handful of things from around the kitchen turn into a meal that tastes good.'

'Like magic.' He glanced at her.

'Yes, like magic! I'd like to go to other countries and learn about the food, cook somewhere where I've never heard of half the ingredients. And I want to go to New York. Have you ever been?'

'No, but we have offices there, so I could go.'

'You're so lucky.'

'I don't think anyone has ever thought I was lucky before.' He pushed his fringe from his forehead.

'So that's my thing – to travel to New York.' *That and to have a kitchen of my own where I have my own cake tins, and someone to bake for . . .* 'What would you like to do? If you could do anything?'

'I just want to be happy and be free to live my life,' he offered without guile, and her heart boomed.

Hitch wanted to pry further but, aware of the intrusive nature of her questions, instead she smiled at him and walked along slowly, with the man at her side concentrating on his footing as they walked a little further along the wide sweep of the water's edge. It was second nature to her to tread among the gently rounded boulders, kissed by the Severn's current, that littered their path, along with the smaller rocks and flattened stones, which skidded now under the smooth soles of Grayson's shoes. He walked with his arms outstretched, reminding her of a tightrope walker, teetering to the left and right in an effort to remain upright.

'You need heavy boots like these with a grippy sole.' Hitch lifted her foot.

'I only have these shoes and my trainers, which I wear if I go up the shops or anything or if I go walking, but I only walk on pavements to get from A to B and so slipping over is not really a problem.'

She tried to imagine a world where all she might need was a pair of sparkly red shoes and, even though she couldn't, not easily, she felt a flutter in her chest at the possibility, thinking it would be nice to own them.

'What's wrong with your foot?' It was his turn to be direct.

'I was born with this too. It's like a claw foot. I kind of walk on tiptoe.'

'Does it hurt?'

'Sometimes, yes, in the cold weather or at the end of the day.'

'Do you want to go back?' He pointed in the direction of the farmhouse and she was happy about his misplaced concern.

'No,' she said, laughing. 'I'm good, thank you. I was just thinking about you sitting by yourself. I can't imagine eating on my own. We eat together, my mum and dad and my pig of a cousin.'

'The one I have to ignore.'

'Yes.' She nodded at the floor. 'I have a brother too, Jonathan, but he's in America – cowboy country! He works on a ranch.'

'Oh. I don't know what you do all day on a ranch. I can't really picture any life that isn't spent travelling to and sitting in an office or a shop or a factory and then travelling home again for tea. And to answer your question, I don't know if I'd like my mum to eat with me.' It was obviously now on his mind too. 'I think it's better that she watches TV and leaves me in peace. She talks a lot. In fact, she never stops and it's' – he placed his hands briefly over his ears – 'it's terrible.'

'My mum hardly talks at all, not about anything that matters. But she constantly asks me if I'm okay, or tells me everything is okay, as though she doesn't think I'm capable of anything. It drives me crazy.' She gave a forced laugh.

Grayson looked at her with an expression that looked a lot like sadness. 'I've only known you for a few hours but I think you're the type of person who is capable of just about anything.'

She stared at this man, whose words meant more than he could ever possibly know.

The two slowed and came to a standstill on the gritty, damp bank, looking out over the water, which was moving, churning and busy. Tiny waves broke into a foamy white froth on the banks and where the currents converged in the river. Fish flipped and darted, breaking the surface with a satisfying *plop*. Birds chattered, swooped and hovered overhead, no doubt hopeful of grabbing one of the flipping, darting fish, or at the very least ogling them with watering mouths.

'I never, ever get tired of the view,' Hitch said. 'It's even different from one hour to the next. The sky changes colour from greenish grey to the clearest blue and the clouds are like brushstrokes in the sky. The water is murky or clear, moving or still. It's like a painting that's never finished. Sometimes I come and sit here of an evening and just watch: it's my favourite thing to do. The sunset at certain times of the year is orange – bright, bright orange, like you see in a film or a photo – and I always think that's the way the sun is supposed to look, like a great ball of fire, just out of reach.'

'It's quiet here.'

'I thought it was very noisy in London when I went. Is it hard for you to get to sleep? It would be for me.'

'No. I'm used to it.'

'I guess you must be.'

'In fact,' he said, swallowing, 'I sometimes find it hard to get to sleep if it's too quiet. I'm used to the sirens, dog barks, shouts, TV noises from other flats, whistles in the stairwell and the drone of traffic. It's like an urban lullaby that soothes me to sleep as surely as any nursery rhyme whispered from a rocking chair.'

There he was again with his poetry.

'I like the way you say things.'

'Thank you, Thomasina.'

Again the sound of her name on his lips almost moved her to tears. It was overwhelming, respectful and beautiful all at once.

'You want to sit down?' She coughed, pointing at a large, flat rock that looked like a table cast by nature.

'Sure.'

She nimbly trod the path and sat down on the rock, which still had some warmth to it. She ran her fingers over the soft grey surface.

'I think living in the countryside is so great because you have so many places to sit down,' Grayson said suddenly.

'What are you talking about?'

Buddy looked over in his mistress's direction, his expression quizzical, as though he were checking on her well-being.

'I mean that, in the city, the only places where I can sit are on the bus, in my flat, on my chair at work, on a bench if there's an empty spot, or maybe a wall. But here you can sit anywhere. On the grass, a hay bale, the bottom or the top of a hill, even at the side of the road. No one is going to ask you to move because you're cluttering up a verge or a rock.' Grayson patted the soft rock on which they perched. 'Can you imagine if I just sat in the middle of the pavement?'

'Actually, I can't,' Hitch said, shaking her head.

'No. Everything about the countryside is soft.'

'What do you mean?' She screwed up her face, picking up a flat pebble and holding it in her hand.

'The air tastes soft, without the dark tang of pollution. The buildings are imperfect with walls made of stones, all thick and sloping in places and irregular. You've got grass, not concrete. If the city is hard and grey, I think here it's soft, green, rounded, forgiving.'

'I suppose so.'

A man called to his son much further along the path and the boy turned and ran back to him. 'Even when people shout here, it's a long, echoey, sing-song sound, and it doesn't sound angry. Where I live, the shouts are short, sharp, aggressive, fast, as if people need to call out but know everyone is listening. Here, it's as if the person is happy to shout out across the fields or the river, letting their sound carry on the wind; they don't mind being heard.'

Hitch stood up and, with surprising force, lobbed the pebble, which skimmed the surface – one, two, three, four, five times – before disappearing beneath the water.

'I think you're right, Grayson.'

'About everywhere being softer?'

'No, what you said earlier, about you noticing some weird stuff.' She smiled at him, letting him know that her observation on this and just about every other aspect of him was something she liked very much.

He threw his head back and laughed. 'I do, I know I do, and tomorrow I get to do it in front of an audience.'

'Are you nervous?' She swung her good leg back and forth, the sole of her boot scuffing the stone-strewn path.

'No.'

'Do you like your job?' She twisted one foot beneath her, facing him, and watched his face colour under her scrutiny.

'I like getting it right.'

'But do you like getting up and going in every day to do it?' She twirled the ends of her hair around her fingers.

'What else would I do?'

'I don't know – I don't know you! A different job? Lie in bed? Go to the seaside?' Hitch raised her arms and let them fall by her side, exasperated not by the exchange but at how easy she found it to make suggestions she was too scared to implement herself.

He seemed to think about this. 'I like the routine and I like going to bed knowing what to expect the next day, so I guess it suits me. I don't think about it too much.'

'I understand that. It's a bit different for me – my job is my life and my life is my job. It's like that in farming. You can't easily see the join where one stops and the other starts.'

'So if someone asks you what your job is, what do you say?'

'I say I'm an egg collector. That's my responsibility: my girls.'

'And you like it? Don't mind getting up to do it every day?'

She saw the flicker of something in his eyes, challenging her. 'It's complicated. I love it. I love them. But living here is hard a lot of the time. There aren't many days like this when I get to chat and have a bit of time to myself. There's always something that needs doing and it's always me that needs to do it.'

'And you live here with your cousin, who I have to ignore, and with your mum and dad?'

'Yep, and casual labour in the summer months and when we're busy – mainly people we call up from the village and other farming families.'

'And has your cousin lived here all his life?'

'God, no. My cousin is horrible!' she spat, as she whipped her head around. She could see that the ferocity of her response threw him a little. She wasn't finished and her words flew from her mouth. 'He thinks he owns the place, but he doesn't! It's my mum and dad's farm and when they give it up it'll go to my brother, Jonathan.'

'And what will you do then?'

'I'll work for him, maybe, collect the eggs and carry on like I do now, but I'll probably have my own home by then. Or I might do something else altogether.'

'Like what?'

'I don't know.' She sighed and he changed the topic.

'Why don't you like your cousin?'

'Because he's disrespectful to my parents and he's teased me my whole life. Each individual thing he says doesn't bother me so much, but when I string them all together his insults are loud inside my head and it's not fair and he's not nice. Like I said, he's horrible.'

Her words changed the atmosphere, peppered their happy conversation with angry dots of frustration. The water now looked foggy and the breeze that whipped around them was no longer invigorating but instead left her feeling a little cold. She noticed the shiver to his limbs and the way he rubbed the tops of his arms, seeking warmth.

'I suppose we'd better think about getting back.' She stood and wiped the back of her jeans, whistling Buddy to heel as they began the walk home.

I know I've met someone I like.

I know Mr Grayson Potts is a little bit odd but he's also a little bit lovely.

I know he makes my stomach feel like there's a bubble of something in it, something like happiness.

I know I want to look at him and talk to him.

I know this should not be the case, as I've only just met him, but it is the case. This I know.

What I don't know is if he likes me back or if I've blown it by talking absolute nonsense.

FIVE

It was strange for her to feel the pull of concern directed at the guest who ate his supper alone on the other side of the kitchen wall – or, more accurately, concern and a little fascination. He had again declined the offer to eat with her and her family and she now pictured him sitting at the head of the dark wooden table where her great-great-grandparents had taken their wedding breakfast and wondered if he too was enjoying the steak pie with the same smacking of lips and moans of appreciation offered by her parents and Emery. Her own appetite was diminished, as subtle feelings of anticipation that she couldn't quite yet place filled her stomach. It was a rare thing to feel connected to someone she had only known for a matter of hours and yet this was exactly how it was: a connection of sorts, strings of recognition and interest threaded through the wall to Mr Grayson Potts and back again.

She pictured him in profile earlier, seated on the flat rock at the river's edge, looking around in wonder like a child who had seen the sea for the first time.

It was ridiculous, yes.

But no less true for it.

'We got a good price per head on the calves today,' her mother said, head down, moving her face to meet the spoon loaded with meat and the rich, dark gravy and not, as most people would do, lifting the spoon to her lips.

'Market busy?' Emery's voice, loud as ever, in her ears.

'Usual, really,' her mum muttered, as she reached for a chunk of bread to clean the bowl, mopping up the scraps and not wasting a lick of pie sauce. 'And how have you been, my lovely? Everything all right?' Her mum held her bread still, as if waiting for the all-clear, always expecting Hitch to be one step away from a disaster that never came. How she wished her mum would relax, so they all could.

'Yep, all good, Mum.'

'Guest settled in?'

Hitch nodded.

'More than settled in, eh, Hitch?' Emery chortled.

'We bumped into Thurston Buttermore at the market,' her dad piped up, smiling and nodding, as was his way – a kind man who treasured any and each interaction within the farming community to which he belonged.

Hitch felt her cheeks flame pink and the prickly heat of embarrassment bloom on her chest, thinking about the previous night in the pub and wondering how much Thurston's son had shared with his father.

'Oh?' Emery pricked up his ears, interested in what might have been happening over at the Buttermores' farm, the biggest in the area, with the family well known for their abundance of cash and love of any new gadgetry. They farmed within the protection of a large supermarket, the representatives of which bought their produce and cosied up to Buttermore senior at a lavish annual dinner where palms were greased, brandy was sipped and tender, tender meat was served in front of a roaring fire.

The thought of Tarran Buttermore stole the last of Hitch's appetite. She placed her fork on the table and wiped her mouth on the back of her hand. In her mind she heard the three toots of Digger Whelks's car horn and swallowed the shame that soured her tongue. Rubbing her arms, she tried to ward off the unexpected chill that snaked down her bones, and at that moment was glad that Mr Grayson Potts was on the other side of the wall.

'You done?' Emery nodded towards her food.

She nodded. Without waiting for further invitation, he reached across the table and grabbed her plate, tipping her leftover pie unceremoniously on to his own.

'You were saying you saw Thurston Buttermore?' Emery reminded her dad.

'Yes!' Her dad gave a chuckle. 'He reminded me I was getting on a bit, cheeky beggar, and said how sweet this spot is, right by the river. More or less said he'd give me a pretty price for Waycott should I ever change my mind about selling. You see, he might have the acreage and a fancy shed full of machinery, but he hasn't got our view or this beautiful old house, has he?'

'You think you might change your mind about selling, Pops?' Hitch stared at him, trying to imagine a world where this farm, this land, home to her beloved chickens, and where the Waycotts had resided for generations, came under the ownership of someone else, someone like Tarran Buttermore.

Pops looked at her briefly before turning his attention back to his pie crust. 'I used to say I'd never sell—'

'You have *always* said you'd never sell,' she interrupted him. 'You speak about it all the time: Jonathan coming home and maybe building a cottage in the lower paddock for you and Mum, just like you've always planned . . . It'd be weird, Pops, to have someone else living here.'

Her dad abandoned his fork on the plate and she shot a look at Emery, warning him to let her dad finish his food without him reaching over and helping himself to the old man's fare. Emery held her gaze.

'There's many a vegetarian starving on a desert island who would eat his beloved dog,' her dad said softly.

'What's that supposed to mean?' Hitch asked, with more aggression than she had intended, as unwanted images formed in her mind of herself and Buddy on a hot and desolate shore.

Her dad sat back in his chair. The creak of the hand-turned wooden spindles, fashioned on a lathe by her great-grandfather, rose up and filled the space above his head, warming the air before his words drifted upwards. He spoke slowly and with conviction, eloquent in a way that suggested this speech had been rehearsed in his mind, and that fact alone was enough to fan the flames of her fear.

'What it means, my little love, is that selling Waycott Farm was something I could never conceive of. Never.' He placed his roughened palm on the table. 'My father and my father's father and the one before that and before that . . . They all toiled on the soil, with some of the same tools that I use today. You and your brother were born here in the attic, and the room in which I sleep, the same room my parents slept in every night of their married life, is the room into which your mother walked as my bride and where we have lain together every night since. I've slept easy for all these years because I could see you here in your dotage and that brought me peace. This farm was built with Waycott blood and Waycott sweat. My family lie buried over yonder and there isn't a brick nor stone nor blade of grass that I don't treasure.' The unmistakable catch to his voice matched the glisten of tears in his eyes.

The other three around the table stared at him. Even Emery stopped chewing and listened.

'But here's the thing, Hitch – needs must.' The farm had not prospered as he had intended and, facing defeat, Pops raised his hands, as if this drastic solution was now a fait accompli. Hitch felt ashamed that, alongside her sorrow and unease, lay a golden sliver of joy that looked a lot like opportunity.

Her father adopted a hushed tone. 'I'm not saying now, I'm not saying soon and I'm not saying for certain, but I'm saying that, if we can't survive, then it makes no sense to starve within these glorious walls.' He reached for his handkerchief. 'Margins are tight and getting tighter and I'm tired of being so squeezed. No matter how hard, I have to think of all the possibilities.' He blew his nose. '*All* the possibilities.'

Emery finished his mouthful, and her mum sat in silence, staring at her husband with a rarely seen expression that to Hitch looked a lot like love.

With a busy mind, she slowly cleared the table and piled the dirty dishes into the sink before taking a plate of cheese and crackers into Mr Potts – Grayson. There was something heart-rending about seeing him all alone at the head of the table with the empty bowl in front of him and a napkin tucked into his shirt collar.

'How was your supper?' She knew her tone echoed with the sadness of the knowledge she now carried, but reminded herself that this man was still a guest and a stranger and she should try and summon a smile.

'Good.' He folded his hands over his stomach.

'I got you some cheese.' She popped the worn breadboard on the table and pointed to the selection of cheeses. 'This is a local goat's cheese, and this one's strong Cheddar, and—'

'I'm very sorry, Thomasina.' He stared at the offering, which she had daintily arranged with crackers and chutneys. 'I don't like cheese.'

She smiled at him, a genuine smile that she didn't have to summon, not because of his dislike of what she had prepared, but merely at the novelty of being called Thomasina.

'You don't like cheese?'

'No.' Grayson shook his head. 'I don't,' he said with a grimace.

She retrieved the board and spoke without too much forethought. 'Do you like cider?'

'To drink?'

'Yes.' She drummed her fingers on the edge of the wooden platter. 'To drink!'

'I think so.'

'Well, I don't know if you have plans this evening, but if you want, you could come with me to the flat rock where we sat earlier. The sky looks very different as the sun sets and I thought we could take some cider – only if you like. But I know I would like. I could do with a bit of cheering up.'

'Yes,' he said, looking at her. 'I'd like to.'

'Okay then. I'll meet you out at the front in about fifteen minutes?'

'Okay.' He smiled at her.

She rushed back into the kitchen, wanting to scrub the worst of the pots, wash her hands and clean her teeth before they set off. Her mum and dad, as per usual, had gone outside to do the evening rounds of the animals. Emery leaned against the sink. 'A little birdy told me you've been fraternising with the guests.' He tutted loudly.

'What, are you spying on me now?' she asked, as she wrapped the cheeseboard and popped it in the fridge before plunging the scouring pad into the suds.

'Don't need to,' he sighed. 'You're an open book. Anyone can see what you're about just by looking at you. Did you have a nice time up the Barley Mow?' He laughed. 'I heard you made a move on Tarran.'

'Why don't you leave me alone?' she asked through gritted teeth.

'Don't be like that! We're cousins!'

Hitch whipped her head in his direction. 'That's right. We're cousins. And yet the way you treat me is so mean, and I see the way you laugh at Pops, like he's stupid! You're the only one who gets properly paid and you still take advantage. It's not fair, Emery. I hate you being here!' She knew that having Grayson Potts sitting the other side of the wall gave her the strength to respond. Emery followed her gaze to the door.

'Ah, so that's it! You think that weird, lanky idiot is going to come to your rescue!' He laughed loudly. 'Christ almighty, you're so sad. You're worse than a dog, literally throwing yourself at anything with a cock. Tarran only the other night, and now that freak of nature in the dining room!'

She looked at the floor, her confidence evaporating under his quick-fire verbal assault. He wasn't done.

'You think I'm scared of him? Some dickhead banker from London?' Emery spat his words with venom.

'Just shut up! Shut up!' She slammed the plates in the sink and whirled out of the room. Buddy barked, unhappy because she was.

Hitch grabbed the cider and a rug from the rack in Big Barn and went to say goodnight to the girls. They were quiet, settled, sitting on their perches and offering no more than a barely audible occasional cluck, reminding her very much of people on the verge of sleep who couldn't find the energy or enthusiasm to chat.

'Night night, my chickies! Sweet dreams, my lovelies. See you in the morning.' She shook her head at the idea of having to say goodbye to them for good if her dad sold the farm. And therein lay her dilemma: while she dreamed of a different life, she just couldn't see one, not really, not for someone like her . . . It might be selfish, but she wanted to see the world, wanted to walk the streets of New York, knowing that Waycott Farm would be waiting for her and Jonathan, just as it always had been. She couldn't always see a future, but there was something comforting about knowing this place was full of her past.

'It'll be all right, girls, you'll see. It'll all be okay.'

Grayson stood in the middle of the lane in his trousers, navy sweater and lace-up shoes. His long fringe had fallen over his eyes. He turned to the left and right, looking out of place, like a person who had wandered off from a party of tourists or stopped to ask directions – a townie.

'I heard what your cousin said about me being a dickhead banker from London,' he said plainly.

She was a little taken aback, not only by the fact that he had heard, but also by his direct manner of speech. There was no sugar-coating his thoughts or disguising them in flowery words that might soften the message or spare them both the sharp spike of embarrassment.

'Just ignore him. I told you, he's a prick.' She began walking along the lane, confident that Mr Grayson Potts would fall into step beside her, which he did.

'You've already told me to ignore him, but I'd like to say something.'

She stopped and turned to face him. 'What?' Her brusque manner was born of nothing more than awkwardness about the topic in hand.

Grayson looked up the lane towards Waycott Farm and then back at her, as though checking that the coast was clear.

'I wanted to say that I didn't like the way he spoke to you.'

She waited to see if he had more to add. He didn't. And strangely, his words on the subject, no matter how limited, soothed the wounds where Emery's barbs had landed. She took a deep breath, grateful for this unexpected support and kindness when it was most needed.

'Thank you,' she whispered. 'I don't like it neither.'

With a shrug, she continued along the lane, her pace now slowed. The two walked in silence until they came to the path that meandered down to the river's edge and back to the rocky stretch of beach. With no one else around, the air was still, quiet, and the swollen river had calmed. Hitch made her way across the pebbles and sand to the flat rock and placed the folded blanket on the top before settling on it with her legs crossed.

'You look like a gnome on a lily pad,' he noted.

'Good.' She smiled at him. 'That's what I was going for.'

She patted the space next to her and Grayson sat down with his hands on his knees, sitting at a stiff right angle, as though waiting for a job interview.

She unscrewed the top from the bottle of cider and took a swig, letting the cold, sweet, honey-coloured liquid dance on her tongue before handing it to him.

'What do you usually do of an evening?' She was curious about life in the big city, picturing her two day-trips, when she'd been taken along by her mum, who wanted to visit Buckingham Palace, and of course their visit to the Chelsea Flower Show, where the tickets had come courtesy of Mrs Pepper, who had some vague connection, meaning the tickets came free. As darkness had drawn and they had boarded the Bristol-bound bus home, she had sat with her face pressed to the window, stealing glimpses inside flats and houses lit from within, capturing images of chandeliers, gilt-framed paintings and a woman in a turtleneck sweater dumping a grocery bag on a table. Londoners: sophisticated dwellers of this magical place where she would love nothing more than to spend the night. She had walked among the bright lights of Covent Garden, where people dined and smoked al fresco and glamorous girls, wearing the shiny, pretty, red shoes she could only dream about, walked with suited and booted boys, tripping arm in arm over the cobbles. They were to Hitch like no other species she had encountered. Neat, clean, glossy and artfully painted, with knowledge of what to wear, how to act and where to go, knowledge that was beyond her. These were not lessons she had learned in her twenty-odd years of living in Austley Morton with only her chicken girls for company and the odd evening spent up the Barley Mow.

'Nothing.'

'Nothing?' She found this most disappointing, having hoped to add to her mental repertoire with his tales, in the way she now stored an image of Mrs Silvioni and her *dawtah* on the streets of NYC.

'I don't do anything. I get home, I have my tea and I go to my room.'

'It sounds like punishment!' She laughed at this, not meaning any offence.

Grayson, however, looked at her with such anguish that she regretted the off-the-cuff remark, spoken half in jest. He took a large glug of the cider and wiped his mouth.

'It feels a bit like that too sometimes.' He drank again.

'What are you being punished for?' she asked softly, feeling a beat of compassion that resounded loudly in her chest.

'I don't know.'

She watched as he kicked the ground and let his shoulders sink.

'You never go out with your friends?'

'I don't have any friends.' He held her gaze and spoke without any edge, as if this was not what most people might consider a failing, but just a state over which he had no control.

'I don't have any friends either,' she confessed, taking the bottle and sipping the cold cider that slipped in bubbles of joy down her throat. 'I sometimes chat to Shelley up at the pub; she works behind the bar. I've known her since school, but we're not really friends.'

'I suppose I have Reggie, or at least I did.'

'Reggie the murderer?'

'Yep.' He nodded.

'I'll be your friend, Grayson.' She spoke in earnest and handed him the bottle, watching him drink eagerly, quickly.

'I'll be your friend, Thomasina.'

She put her hand out to retrieve the bottle, but instead Grayson Potts slipped from the rock and put the bottle on the ground. He walked around until he stood in front of her, quite blocking the view. She opened up her legs to let him come closer. And there they rested, she sitting and he standing so near to her.

She felt a flutter in her chest and a quickening to her breath as he stared at her.

'I'm glad you're my friend. I feel like I've known you for a very long time, as if I know you from some time before, some place I don't remember.'

Far from finding his statement comical or dismissing it as a cheap attempt to woo her, Hitch felt the intensity in his stare and his words and her heart raced accordingly.

'I think you're . . .' He looked away and swallowed, as if searching for the right words – or having found the right words, was anxious about putting them out into the universe.

'What?' she whispered.

He gazed back at her, his hands grasping at the air in front of his chest as if unsure of where he should place them. 'I think you're beautiful.'

Hitch felt the swell of tears sting the back of her throat. This was the first time in her life anyone had said this to her.

The first time ever.

His words were a sincere balm that warmed her from the inside, making her feel happy and hopeful. This man! This man who she had known for no more than a few hours. Slowly, hesitantly, Grayson leaned forward and, taking his time, allowing, she suspected, time for her to protest or refuse, he drew closer and closer, until there were mere millimetres between them. And then Mr Grayson Potts, his actions chaste and considered, did something that no person, no man, had ever done in her whole life . . . He closed his eyes and very gently touched his lips to hers.

He kissed her mouth.

And the lips she considered ugly, the mouth a little misshapen, was the very thing that connected her to him. She thought her heart might burst at this gesture that seemed so natural and easy and yet was something she had doubted she would ever experience.

And she knew she would never, ever forget it.

Never.

'Is that okay?' he asked sheepishly.

'Uh-huh,' she whispered, from a smile so wide it made speaking difficult. His soft lips against hers had left the sweetest residue, like the feel of sun on skin after the rain. 'Are you okay?' she asked, a little recovered, but still breathless, holding the moment in her heart, a thing so precious she feared that the tiniest flutter and the essence of it might slip away.

'Uh-huh.' He too beamed and leaned in again.

Hand in hand, they walked slowly back along the lane. Hitch was almost in a daze and quite lost to the memory, which raced around and around inside her head. It made her happy and it filled her right up!

They parted on the upstairs landing and she danced along the hallway to her bed with her head spinning and her soul leaping with happiness! Diving on to the duvet, she pulled her jotter from the bedside table and wrote with a flourish . . .

I know this:

he kissed my mouth . . . he kissed my mouth . . . he kissed my mouth . . . he kissed my mouth . . . he kissed my mouth . . . he kissed my mouth . . . he kissed my mouth . . . he kissed my mouth . . . he kissed my mouth . . . he kissed my mouth . . . he kissed my mouth . . . X

SIX

Hitch felt torn, wriggling back under the duvet as morning broke – keen to rush from the room and see Mr Potts again, but also a little reluctant to rise and start the day, wary of a new dawn where any experience might corrupt the happy state in which she found herself. Touching her fingers to her lips, she felt the soft, bruised imprint of his apple-flavoured kiss, the memory alone enough to fire a fully charged bolt of joy through to her very core.

She lay back on the soft bolster and looked up at the beamed ceiling. The first, hesitant kiss they had shared made the drunken, rushed coupling she had shared with Tarran Buttermore pale into insignificance. Her head ached a little and her mouth was dry, but she was smiling on the outside and on the inside. With the thought of Buddy waiting for her in the kitchen, she kicked off the heavy bedspread and walked to the deep-set leaded window, where she stared out over the fields, where grass swayed in the morning breeze. Today the landscape looked particularly beautiful.

Looking out towards the shadow of the Welsh hills on the horizon, she replayed the kiss and the ones that followed. Like an observer, she saw herself sitting on the rock; Grayson stood in front of her with his feet slipping on stones, feeling for purchase, while his mouth was fixed to hers. Her gut bunched in a feeling hitherto unknown. It was a heady combination of joy, excitement and something that was similar to the first flickering of fear, but without the dread that accompanied it, as if she was aware of the edge of the abyss at which she stood, toes curled, back and arms straight, ready to dive. How was it possible that she could be this person? It was as if, when she was with him, she could shake off the suit of the broken, as if she were no longer damaged, but a girl who a man like Grayson wanted to spend time with. No, a woman a man like Grayson wanted to kiss!

Like a toddler on Christmas morning, she ran back across the room and jumped on to the bed, landing on the mattress with a thud, where she buried her face in the pillow and let out a silent scream of pure joy.

Hitch balanced the tray loaded with cutlery and a cup of tea on her forearm and walked it into the dining room, where Grayson sat. There was a momentary flare of sickness in her gut before she saw him – supposing he regretted his actions? Her fears of rejection were immediately assuaged as his fingers twitched and reached out to touch her arm, before deciding against it. She more than understood his hesitant desire to feel the warmth of her skin, as it was the same for her. Hitch was entirely unsure of how she should navigate the morning. This was like nothing she had experienced before. She was a little fixated by the curl of his fingers around the napkin in his lap and wanted so badly for him to take her hand that her chest ached with the longing of it. The cup of tea rattled in its saucer as she placed it on the table, and she giggled.

'How did you sleep, Mr Potts?' She smiled at him, a wide, unselfconscious smile which he returned, and she knew she would tuck his almost shy expression in a pocket within her heart to carry with her when he was far away – the prospect of which was enough to catch in her throat.

'I didn't sleep very well at all,' he said honestly.

'Oh? Most people say it's one of the comfiest beds they've ever laid their head on, but you didn't sleep?' She looked at him with rising concern.

'The bed is comfortable, but I couldn't get to sleep.' He shook out the white linen napkin and tucked it into his shirt collar.

'Was it too quiet for you out here in the sticks? Maybe we could get you a recording of some sirens and some dogs barking to help you nod off tonight?' She kept a straight face.

'Ha, no need for that. It was quiet, but the reason I couldn't sleep was because I was thinking about you. I thought about you as we walked back from the flat rock and I haven't stopped thinking about you. But I like thinking about you. It makes me happy. I don't mind that I didn't sleep. I don't even feel tired.'

'Well,' she whispered, for fear of giving in to the rising bubble of joy in her gut and whooping out loud, 'knowing that makes me feel happy too.'

She liked the way he spoke so candidly, and the soft, nervous manner in which he did so made the words entirely believable.

'And how would you like your eggs today, Mr Potts?'

'I don't mind. At home I have a boiled egg.'

'A boiled egg it is then. The girls have laid especially for you today.'

'That was very kind of them.' He nodded and reached for his cup of tea. 'I do like eggs, but I always feel a little bit guilty about eating them.'

'Guilty? Why?'

He took a sip of tea and placed the cup back in the saucer. 'Well, it's all the chickens' work, isn't it? And a lot of effort, I should imagine. That little oval, carrying all their hopes and plans for the future, wishes for a family, maybe – they probably want chicks.'

'But it's not! They're just eggs. There's no cockerel. They can't ever be chicks.'

Grayson nodded. 'Yes, I know that, of course, but I don't know if the chickens do. It feels like cheating them a bit.'

She laughed. 'I don't suppose they do know that, and it's nice you're thinking about all the work they do. I know they'd appreciate your consideration.' She made a note to relay this to the girls. 'Would you like some bacon too? And toast?'

'Thank you, yes, please.'

Hitch sang as she took extra care preparing the breakfast before waltzing back into the dining room with the loaded plate.

'Can I sit with you? Would that be okay?' She sounded a little sheepish as she put his breakfast plate in front of him, remembering his preference to eat alone, but she didn't want to waste a second of his company.

'I would really like that.'

She watched with fascination as he picked up the knife and gave an expert tap to the top of the egg, before spooning out the little dome of perfection within. Sprinkling the mound with a few grains of salt, he paused before bringing it to his mouth. It was a very particular way of eating, almost a performance.

'You've done that before.'

'Once or twice.' He smiled at her and ate the top of his egg. She found it nice to sit and chat, able to think of things to say and not at all tongue-tied, here in this room, where her family history dripped from the walls and pooled in puddles of nostalgia on the flagstone floor. He followed her gaze up over the black-and-white photographs in wooden frames that lined the shelves and windowsill, and the ornaments from a bygone era sitting polished on the mantelpiece.

'This is a very grand room.' He took a bite of his toast.

'I suppose so. I'm used to it. It's a bit dark. I think it could do with brightening up, but that's not up to me.'

'Where I live isn't nearly so solid. I can see how a man could feel settled here, unafraid for the future. Everything feels safe and permanent.'

'Too permanent sometimes.' She let this trail.

'It's as though I'm in another world and I'm another person – and I like the person I am here.'

'Me too,' she whispered. 'I like him very much.'

The sound of her dad's whistling filled the kitchen on the other side of the door. Grayson coughed and she sat up straight.

'What time are you leaving to go into Bristol? There are buses that leave from the village – I can drop you up there. Or we can call you a cab, or if Pops is going into town I know he'd be happy to take you, if I asked him. If you can put up with his whistling.'

'Thank you, Thomasina, but I'm not going into Bristol.'

'You're not going?' She laid her forearms flat on the table and stared at him.

'No.' He took another sip of his tea. 'There's a lady called Liz at the bank where I work. She's really nice, very good at her job. We have cubicles that are next to each other and she told me that I should do more of what makes me happy and less of what people expect of me. I didn't really know what she meant until I woke up this morning and I knew that I didn't want to go and talk at a seminar. I want to spend the day with you. My last day, really. I go back to London just after lunch-time tomorrow and so I want to spend today with you, if that's okay?'

'It is okay.' She smiled. 'I can take a bit of time.'

'Good.'

'But won't you get into trouble?'

He seemed to consider this. 'I probably will, but if the seminar's finished, what can they do? It'll be done. Over. Plus, I've never done anything to get into trouble before, never caused even a tiny ripple. A lot of my colleagues come in and sleep off hangovers, take sick days, leave early, but not me. I work hard, and I can't explain why I think it's okay, but I don't want to waste today in a seminar, trying and failing to teach others how to do my trick. I want to be with you. It feels more important.'

'It does?'

'Yes.'

His simple words were like food that filled her up and sustained her. He wanted to be with her and that made her feel very important indeed.

'I suppose you could lie to them and say you have a tummy bug or the car broke down or something.'

Grayson stared at her. 'No, I wouldn't do that. I never tell a lie. Ever.'

The two stared at each other for a second or two.

'I believe you.' Hitch opened her mouth, about to say more on the importance of this honesty, when her mum came into the room from the kitchen. Hitch jumped up and began clearing the table of the now empty teacup and saucer.

'There you are, Hitch!' her mother tutted, as if addressing a wilful child. 'Is she annoying you? She can sometimes forget that she's here to serve breakfast and nothing else, isn't that right, my love?'

Grayson looked at her. 'No, she's not annoying me. We were just chatting. She's . . . really, really great.'

'Is she now?' Her mum spoke softly, as she pulled her head back on her shoulders and looked at their guest with her head cocked to one side.

'I don't know her very well, but if I had to say so, then, yes, I would say she is great.'

Grayson held Hitch's gaze and it was all she could do to laugh behind her palm as she busied herself with brushing crumbs from the table, aware of her mum standing with her mouth flapping, quite unsure of how to respond.

◆ ◆ ◆

Once Hitch had tidied the guest room with Grayson watching her from the chair in the corner, they stood in the field as she shook a fine powder in and around the chicken coop.

'What are you doing?' he said, wrinkling his nose.

'I have to make sure I cover all the joints between the wooden planks and their perches, anywhere the red mites might be. They're horrible little things that live in all the cracks and they come out at night and suck the girls' blood and feed on them. It can kill them. I heard on the grapevine that a woman in the next village has them and so I'm taking extra care. I put this powder down and it means that, if we get any of the little pests, they have to crawl through this to get to my girls and the powder will finish them off.'

'I've never heard of red mites.'

'Well, you've never kept chickens!'

'No, I don't think they'd fare too well on the balcony and I don't think they'd like it in the basement.'

'You have a basement?' This wasn't something she'd envisaged for a flat.

'Kind of.' He sniffed. 'Not so much a basement as an area of underground car park where each flat has a kind of cage.'

'It sounds spooky!' she said with a shudder.

'It is a bit, I suppose. The pipes leak and leave slimy, greenish puddles on the path. And it's quite dark, but I don't mind it down there. In fact, I like it. Sometimes it's preferable to listening to the incessant cackle from my mum and aunts.'

'It's good to have a refuge.'

'Do you have one?'

'Here, I suppose. This is where I come. When everything feels a bit noisy.' She clambered out of the coop and fastened the door.

They stood side by side and watched the plump-chested chicks, their feathery, crested heads pecking at the grass, listening to their *bock, bock* noise, exchanging the sound at regular intervals, which made it sound a lot as though they were chatting.

'Yes, Daphne, we see you!' Hitch tutted lovingly, as the hen came over and jutted her head back and forth. 'It's nice having someone to do chores with. My mum would kill me if she knew I was letting you help out. You're supposed to be our guest, paying for the privilege.'

'Do you let other guests help you out?'

'Nope. Never.'

'I'm glad.'

She looked him steadily in the eye and wondered if he felt the same burst of happiness she did at nothing more than the admission of this shared, special, yet mundane thing. He bent sideways, to tentatively pet Buddy's ears, and she noted the way in which her dog panted and stood close to his leg, accepting his touch.

'Are you sure this is better than being at your seminar?'

'I don't know. I don't know what the seminar would be like, but I can't imagine having a better time than this.'

'I'm glad to hear it.' She whistled and Buddy ran to her side. 'So tell me about your house.'

'It's a flat, not a house.'

'So tell me about your flat!' she tutted mockingly, but her eyes smiled.

'It's in a large block, one of six identical blocks that stand quite close together like dominoes. Everything is grey and the actual flat is small.'

'Cosy?' she asked with optimism, this one word making the whole idea more palatable, like honey in hot lemon or a spoonful of sugar after medicine. She wanted to paint a pleasant picture of his life.

'Constricted,' he corrected.

She felt the smile slip from her face.

Grayson continued, 'And you already know about the storage cages in the basement – rows of them along the outside walls, all caged in.'

'What do people keep in them?' She was having difficulty imagining the dimensions.

'All sorts. Ours is quite neat and everything fits, but some of them are overflowing with things people have shoved into every gap. I think it's because, for someone like Mr Waleed, who had to pack up his whole life and come to England, it must be hard to find a place for all the stuff inside. As I said, the flats are small.'

'What does Mr Waleed have in his cage?'

Her eyes swept the outbuildings and Big Barn, as she tried to picture such a lack of space and rooms.

'Things like rolled-up carpets, spare shoes and clothes, blankets, chairs, old beds, picture frames.'

'It sounds interesting, like a flea market.'

'It is interesting, but a bit sad too.'

'Why sad?'

Grayson looked out over the grass that bent in the breeze which whipped over it. 'There are garden tools, hoes, spades and trowels. Old-looking things with wooden handles and thin strips of faded paint, and some have clumps of mud and dirt encrusted on them. And I think about that soil, which Mr Waleed will never dig again, or likely never walk. Soil from somewhere far, far away, where it was possible for him to have a garden, a patch of outside space. And it makes me sad because I think how much better it would be for his little kids to have their laughter rising up higher and higher into a bright blue, sun-filled sky, rather than stopping short on the roughly plastered ceiling of the bedroom below mine.'

'What's in your storage cage?' she asked softly, loving his kindness as she kicked her heel against the lawn.

Grayson looked down at his lace-up shoes, as if slightly ashamed and a little embarrassed to be making the confession. He gave a small cough to clear his throat and looped his long fringe from his eyes with his fingertip, tucking it behind his left ear.

'I'm the only one who goes down there. It has my dad's stuff in it,' he whispered.

'What stuff?'

'Some of his books, some of his clothes.' He took a breath and looked up, as if picturing each item catalogued in his mind. 'His dark wedding suit, his narrow black tie for funerals, his soft woollen bathrobe with a gold rope belt, his box of cassettes. All written on in his tiny, neat script. He loved rock and roll.'

'He did?' Hitch said, smiling.

'Yep, he really did. He told me once that it reminded him of his mum and dad and when he was younger. And when I was little, on a Sunday, he used to put his tapes on, just for a few hours. The whole flat came alive, jumping with the sound of Charlie Rich's 'Midnight Blues' and Ray Harris's 'Lonely Wolf'. He and my mum used to dance, right there in the front room.'

Hitch tried and failed to picture Pops and her mum doing something similar.

'That's the only time I remember my mum being truly happy. The two of them hand in hand, bopping around the room. They'd push the coffee table to one side and stack the chairs to make space.'

'What kind of dancing was it?' Hitch leaned in, curious.

'You know, like jiving, I suppose. Standing opposite each other with their arms outstretched and their hands gripped, and he'd pull her to him like rolling a rug and then push her away again, still holding tightly on to her hand.'

Hitch couldn't help but picture herself and Grayson dancing in this way, beaming and breathless as she skipped and danced away from her man and then back to him, coming to rest briefly with her shoulder on his chest, her head beneath his chin, before the music upped tempo and off she would go again, wheeling back and forth. Bouncing on flexing knees and smiling, trotting and tripping in time and in sync, clicking their fingers and singing along with hearts beating fast, and her face flushed red, and the notes and fast beat filling the air with something that tasted like endless possibilities. And in her fantasy her bad foot was good and her fingers worked perfectly and her mouth was . . . her mouth was pretty.

'I used to like watching them in secret from the doorway.' He drew her from her imaginings. 'I felt like I was part of the celebration and it helps now to remember that it wasn't always gloomy. It wasn't all uncomfortable silences, shifting feet and deep sighs. There were these pockets of happiness that shine in my memory even now, like bright jewels, precious and gleaming.'

'It sounds like a happy house.'

'Flat.'

'Sorry, a happy flat.'

'It was at times, but not very often.'

'How old was he when he left?' She wondered how someone went from a dancing, happy man to one who felt the need to leave his wife and son.

'He was thirty-five.'

'Where did he go?'

'I don't know.'

'Have you seen him since he went?'

'No.'

The upturn in his chin and his double blink gave a hint to the hurt and anger that lay beneath this one word, offered so definitively.

'I can't imagine what that must be like.'

'It's shit,' he said.

'Would you like to see him?'

'Oh.' Grayson paused, as if surprised by the question. 'Yes, yes, I think I would. Or at least I used to think that, but as time goes on I'm not so sure. I feel quite angry and so I don't know if it would be the best thing to see him. I don't know.' He shook his head, as if the dilemma were too much to consider.

'You must still miss him.'

He looked up thoughtfully. 'I suppose it might be missing him, but it's more like I have this empty feeling in my stomach and it came on the night he went and is still there now, so I've always assumed that only he can fill it and I'd like it to be gone. It stops me eating, it stops me from feeling warm and it' – he moved his splayed fingers in the air – 'it makes everything feel unsettled.'

'Have you asked your mum where he went?'

'I did when I was younger, when he first left.'

'What did she say?' Hitch ran her finger daringly over the back of his hand.

'She said he'd gone to hell in a handcart and good fucking riddance! I know now it was just the wine talking, but it's just something we don't discuss. I try not to say anything that's going to set her off.'

'That must be hard, not being able to talk about him.' Hitch took the two steps towards him and placed her fingers on his arm. She watched his long fingers land over her hand and his touch felt incandescent on her skin, her stomach weighted with desire and the wish that he would hold her tightly against him. This longing was a new sensation and felt a lot like sickness.

Grayson again shook his head. 'It's got easier, but at first—' Again he paused. 'There are only two things that my mum and dad have ever said to me that have stuck, really stuck. Words that play like records in my head, and I think about them a lot.' He coughed to clear his throat. 'My mum said, "If you ever mention him, it will kill me. I will die. I will kill myself. I will." And my dad said, "Look after your mum for me." And so here I am, stuck in the middle. Not mentioning him for her and looking after her for him.'

There was a moment or two of silence, until she spoke, aware of the catch to her voice. She stared at him. 'And what do you want, Grayson?'

'What do I want?' He looked a little blank, wide-eyed, suggesting that the thought rarely occurred to him, and she remembered what he had said, how it was all about getting through the day and trying to get through the night and then trying to get through the day and then trying to get through the night . . .

'Yes.' She moved a little closer to him and felt the brush of her hip on his thigh, a feeling so exquisite that she felt a flare of longing that she never wanted to end. 'What do you want, Grayson?'

'I don't think too much about what I want, but since being here . . .' He paused.

'Go on,' she urged, willing him to voice all the unfeasible, impossible thoughts that rang loudly in her head.

'Since being here and meeting you . . .'

'Yesterday,' she reminded him, 'that was only yesterday.'

He looked skyward, as if sharing her utter disbelief at this indisputable fact. 'I feel like—' He paused again, drawing breath and looping his fringe from his face. 'I feel like you're the kind of person who can find the gaps, fill in the missing pieces and solve the puzzle of my happiness.'

Hitch stared at the man who had awoken something within her, and if it were not such a ridiculous notion, she would have said that it felt a lot like love. 'Maybe I can. Maybe I'm as clever as you after all, Mr Potts.'

'Maybe you are.' He leaned forward and, without the sweet encouragement of cider, he gently kissed her again on the mouth and again she saw . . . fireworks.

'Outside shithouse is blocked!' Emery yelled loudly from the yard, quite destroying the moment and making Grayson chuckle. With the spell broken, the two made their way over to Big Barn.

'Do you look like your dad?' she asked, almost casually.

'My mum says I look like her uncle, my grandad's brother, but I don't, not really. I found a photograph of my dad inside a book cover when he was younger and he looked like me. So yeah, I do look like my dad.' He smiled.

'So he was handsome then?' she said, kicking the grass and looking down at her feet in their heavy boots.

Grayson stared at her. 'Do you think I'm handsome?' he asked, not in the manner of someone who was fishing for the compliment, but rather as if this was something that had never occurred to him.

'I do.'

Grayson placed his hand on his stomach and she wondered if the empty feeling that they had been talking about only minutes before had disappeared. She hoped so. She hoped that she was able to do for him what he did for her, fill her up with the moon and stars.

'What do you want to do this afternoon, Grayson?' she almost whispered.

'I want to be with you. That's all, really.' He spoke steadily, confidently. 'You make me feel ten feet tall.'

◆ ◆ ◆

'Can I take the pickup, Dad?' Hitch called into the tractor barn as she leaned on the door, trying to keep the enquiry casual, fully aware of Emery listening while pretending to focus on the greasy nut and cloth in his hands.

''Course you can, my lovely. I reckon I'll be in here most of the day. We're not making much progress and this engine isn't going to fix itself. You off to town?'

'Uh-huh.' She deliberately kept her response vague, torn between not wanting to lie to her dad and not letting Emery know where she was heading and with whom. 'Chickens are fed and happy, washing's out and calves have had their morning milk. Guest room's been cleaned and there's cold lamb in the fridge for your lunch. Mum's put a loaf in the oven – you know where the pickles are.'

'You taking that lanky girl out with you?' her cousin said, without looking up.

'See you in a bit, Dad.' She ignored Emery, but her breath stuttered in her throat nonetheless.

Weaving along the country lanes, Hitch glanced to her left, taking in the sight of Grayson Potts with his head leaning out of the open window as the wind lifted his hair, eyes closed, shirtsleeves rolled above the elbow, and with an expression that looked something close to bliss. He reminded her of Buddy when he was allowed to travel up front. There was something about this man – and curiously, she suspected that the magical thing was how he made her feel about herself. The sensation of his mouth pressed to hers, an act committed without hesitation and with such sincerity the memory of it was enough to make her heart swell, even now.

'I'm worried you'll get into trouble for not going to your work thing. I mean, isn't that why they sent you down here in the first place?'

'Yes and yes.' He pulled his head in from the window and looked at her. 'That is why they sent me down here, and my boss Mr Jenks has already sent me lots of texts.' He didn't seem overly perturbed.

'Oh God! What do they say?' She watched as he reached into his trouser pocket and pulled out his phone, pressing in the code and scrolling through the texts with his thumb.

'I'll read them in order.' He paused and gave a small cough before reading them aloud.

ARE YOU RUNNING LATE GRAYSON? IF SO NO WORRIES, I CAN HOLD THE FORT FOR TEN MINUTES OR SO.

WHERE ARE YOU, GRAYSON?

PICK UP YOUR PHONE!

IS THERE A PROBLEM I SHOULD KNOW ABOUT? SHOULD I BE CONCERNED OR MERELY PISSED OFF!

OKAY, POTTS. CALL ME OR GET YOUR SORRY BUTT OVER HERE
IN THE NEXT TEN MINUTES OR THERE WILL BE FALLOUT. WTF?

'And finally . . .'

ARE YOU KIDDING ME RIGHT NOW?

'Oh my God! He sounds really mad! What did you say to him?' She felt
the mild rumble of guilt that she was the cause of this discord and was
at the same time absurdly flattered.

'I didn't say anything to him. I haven't called him yet. I'll go and
see him when I get back to London.'

'Might he fire you?'

'Yes,' Grayson said with a nod, 'but he probably won't.'

'God! That would be terrible if you lost your job just so we could
hang out for a day.'

'I would lose my job for less than that,' he said, looking at her, 'but
I make them a lot of money. I make myself a lot of money too, but I
make them a fortune and I don't think they would fire me because of
one day. Jenks will probably just shout at me a bit.'

'I'd hate that, knowing someone was waiting to shout at me.'

'Me too, but to be honest, an hour, five minutes, any time with you
would be worth it.'

Hitch felt the blush bloom on her cheeks. 'You say the nicest things
to me, Grayson. And tomorrow you will leave, head back to your noisy
night-times and your flat with a cage and your shouty boss who wants
to know your magic trick.'

'I don't want to think about that right now, Thomasina. I don't
want to think about work or Mr Jenks or going home. It will spoil the
day for me.'

She liked his sweet, honest way of putting things. 'I get that – it
would spoil the day for me too.'

Tomorrow . . . You will leave tomorrow, go back to your big city with its hard surfaces, nowhere soft to sit and your murderous neighbour who stands outside without shoes, and I'll be stuck here with my girls . . . and Emery.

'Where are we going?' he asked, sitting back in the seat.

'Chew Valley Lake – it's a lovely spot and we get to walk around it then have the best fish and chips you've ever tasted at Salt & Malt – are you up for that?'

'I am. I never walk for the sake of walking.'

'But you do walk?'

'Yes, but it's always walking to get somewhere or from the station to the office and back again. I never think of going for a walk in a circle just to walk.'

'I walk a lot,' Hitch said, picturing the lonely miles she covered in her heavy boots. She walked in all weathers with Buddy lumbering at her side or racing ahead as she pounded the earth, trying to sort through her jumble of thoughts. 'It helps me think.'

'What do you think about?'

She paused and tried to rank the thoughts that occupied her mind. 'Lots of things. I think about what it might be like if we lose the farm—'

'Lose it how?' he interrupted her, asking with a crease of confusion at the top of his nose.

'I mean if my dad has to sell it. Things are tough for us right now – in fact, not just right now, they've been tough for a while, and so when I walk I try to imagine a life where I wake up somewhere else, in a world where I might have to do different work and where my chickens might have to live somewhere else.'

'Can you imagine that?'

She shook her head. 'No. No, I can't.'

'You love your chickens.'

'I do, Grayson. I really do.'

He seemed to let this permeate before asking, 'What else do you think about?'

105

'Well, I think about what my life might be like if we *don't* sell the farm. I think about the time passing by faster and faster each year and I think about waking up one day and suddenly I'm the same age as my mum is now and everything is as it has always been. I'm older, but still walking the fields, feeding the animals, chatting to my chickens and clearing up shit, and nothing has changed for me. Nothing at all.' She gripped the steering wheel.

Grayson turned in his seat to look at her. 'Thomasina?'

'Yes?'

'I'm thinking about what you said and I'm not sure if losing the farm would make you sad or if staying on the farm would make you sad.'

She smiled at his accurate summary. 'The truth is, I'm not sure either.' It felt good to be able to talk this openly about the emotional subject to someone who had no vested interest either way. 'I guess I don't want to have the decision made for me about whether I stay or go. Selfishly, I suppose, I want to know the farm is there, just as it has always been. I love it,' she said with passion, 'but I don't want my parents to struggle, and it feels like they've run out of ideas or luck. And I definitely don't want to be there with Emery, and I couldn't be there alone with him after my parents . . .' She swallowed.

'After your parents have died?'

'Yes.' She cursed the sting at the back of her throat. 'And that's assuming my brother Jonathan doesn't come home. Which I hope he will.'

'Do you think he will – come home, that is?'

She shook her head, recalling the tone of his postcard: happy, settled, home . . . 'I don't know. I kid myself that he will. I talk as though he will, but truthfully, I think he's made a life in the sunshine and that's where he might choose to stay, more's the pity. I don't like the set-up at Waycott Farm right now.'

'So it's all about Emery?'

'Not all, no, but it's a lot about him. He doesn't deserve Waycott and he's such a pig to me. I see the way he laughs behind my dad's back and I could thump him!'

'Do your mum and dad know how you feel?' he asked.

Hitch closed her eyes briefly and could smell the cranberries bubbling away on the top of the range, her mum stirring the vast, blackened pot with a wooden spoon and tipping in cups of brown sugar with her spare hand. She saw her ten-year-old self twisting her good foot into the flagstones as she sought out the words.

'Mummy . . .'

'What?'

'I don't like Emery.'

'Don't be daft, little one, he's your cousin and he's not going anywhere. He'll pop up like a bad penny every Christmas, birthday, Easter, wedding and funeral, so you'd best get used to him!'

She tasted the salt of her tears, which clogged her nose and throat, speaking quickly, looking over her shoulder, lest he should be lurking.

'He's mean to me.'

'All boys are mean. Just ignore him!'

'But . . . he . . . he's really, really mean to me, Mum. He calls me names and he does an impression of my voice . . .'

'For the love of God, Hitch! Go and play nicely! He's your cousin and we don't get to choose our kin, and when all is said and done he would stand up for you, he would! I'll have a little word with him if you want . . .'

She blinked away the memory of that day when she had tried to explain just how much it hurt her to hear Emery's jibes and how every moment in his company was spent with a knot of ugly anticipation in her gut, waiting to see what he said or did next. It was one thing to hear the cruel taunts of the kids at school and strangers, but quite another to hear it from Emery, *kin*, in her home, her refuge.

'I think they know how I feel – I find it hard to lie about my feelings – but I don't think they fully know how much it bothers me.' She sighed deeply. 'I just want more, Grayson.'

'More what?'

Hitch shook her head and concentrated on the road, wary of another vehicle coming in the opposite direction, which would mean she had to pull into a lay-by or mount the verge.

'Just more. My own life. My own kitchen. It's as if my parents have set my boundaries, and I know they mean well, but . . .'

'It can be stifling.' He finished the sentence with a faraway look on his face and she wondered about his mum, who was not ill, but needy.

Quiet filled the car and, for the first time since Mr Grayson Potts had arrived, she wondered if this was a good idea – what had Emery said about 'fraternising with the guests'? What did she think was going to happen? By this time tomorrow he'd be gone and she would be alone again, walking, pacing, working and thinking, and the loss of him, this man who had all of her attention, this man she was opening up to, well, it might just be harder to live with the gap he was going to leave behind than if he had never arrived.

She swung the Subaru into the car park and jumped down from the cab. Chew Valley Lake was peaceful, even the water calm. Birds pecked for morsels in the shallows, shaking their feathers like preening ballerinas to keep dry. Gulls squawked overhead and the air was heavy with the threat of rain brewing in the clouds that gathered ominously overhead, spreading a dark bruise over the day. It threatened to further dampen the mood.

'This is incredible!' Grayson's enthusiasm rekindled the bright spark of happiness within her. There was something intoxicating about his excitement. It made her forget her maudlin reflections and enjoy the moment.

'Look – a fish just jumped! This place is brilliant.' He walked with a slight skip to his gait.

'I can't imagine not having places like this to come to when you want to clear your head. Can't imagine living in a big city. I bring Bud up here sometimes.'

'There are places to walk in the city – lakes, ponds and a path along the river. And out where I live, near the Isle of Dogs, there's been a lot of regeneration because it's where some of the Olympics were held.'

'Of course.' Hitch remembered the velodrome and the swimming events that she had watched on the small, temperamental TV in the kitchen. 'But you still don't go out walking?'

'No, I have a very different life to this usually. I keep my head down and I get on with it.'

'Same. My mum couldn't believe it when I told her I was having a couple of hours off!' She smiled at him, as thunder rolled in the distance and a fork of lightning split the dark sky, flashing bright and orange, like a brief flourish of peach flesh. 'D'you want to go and get fish and chips or carry on walking in the rain?'

He tipped his head back and looked up at the sky. 'Let's walk in the rain and then go and get fish and chips.'

'Okay.' She shrugged, tucking her hands into the pockets of her waxed jacket as the warm bullets of water started to hit her skin and hair, leaving her drenched yet happy. It felt reckless, foolhardy and all the more fun because of it. The two continued their leisurely stroll along the path, which quickly turned to mud beneath their feet. The surface of the lake danced with a million tiny ripples from the bouncing droplets.

Later, they ate fish and chips in the car with the windows steamed up, their greasy fingers reaching for piping-hot, batter-crisped fillets of cod and fat, golden chips, liberally doused in salt and malt. The food was, she thought, all the more delicious when eaten in the rain with the heater blowing warm air on to their chilly feet and with their damp bottoms sticking to the grubby leather seats of the Subaru.

'I feel as though you've been here for a very long time.' She licked her fingers clean and reached for the next chip.

'I know. I do too.'

'It's weird, isn't it?' She licked her fingers once more. 'I don't really know you, I can't. And yet . . .' She let this hang, unable even to voice the extraordinary way she felt – as though he had been parachuted into her life at her request.

'It's the same for me.' He traced a raindrop with the tip of his finger down the inside of the window.

'And I think about how exciting this is, and then I remember that this time tomorrow you'll be back in London.'

He looked across at her and swallowed his mouthful, folding the lid down on the box of fish and chips he could plainly no longer stomach.

'Oh no! We agreed not to mention it and now I've put you off your fish and chips!'

'You were right, though. It was the best fish and chips I've ever tasted.'

'But you don't want to finish it?' She looked at the scrunched-up parcel in his hands.

'I can't. I can't eat when I think too much. It's as if my stomach is connected to my brain and, if my brain has to work too hard, my stomach shrinks up and sits just about here.' He touched his fingertips to the base of his throat.

'I know what you mean.' She sighed as her own appetite faded, and she tucked in the lid of her cardboard container.

They drove home in near silence. Grayson seemed deep in thought as he scoured the hedgerows and looked up at the sky, searching for what, she did not know.

'I have some chores to do this afternoon.' She spoke a little curtly, knowing it was the best way to stop this silliness before the awkward matter of the goodbye tomorrow. It was about self-preservation and the nagging lack of self-esteem that ate away at her confidence. She knew it was probably best for them both if he simply went back to London and found a girl like himself who was sweet and nice and who lived in a domino block of flats close by, one he could see whenever the fancy took him and who didn't feel tied to a piece of muddy land on the banks of a river.

'I can help you, if you like.' He turned to look at her. His hair was plastered to his head and his face flushed with the exertion of walking in the rain. He had lost his pastiness and looked handsome.

She shook her head. 'No, that's fine, Grayson. I really should get on. I need to clean out the girls and give them their afternoon corn, and there are a few jobs my mum wants doing, and supper to cook.'

He stared at her and she watched his eyebrows rise and knit. His mouth opened a little and he looked . . . desolate, crushed, cheated, and she felt like shit. The instant change in his demeanour and the fast-paced beat of her heart at the prospect of not seeing him again was more than she could stand. Letting him down might have been the right thing to do for them both, but it was not the *easy* thing, and she knew at that moment that all she wanted was one more second of him, one more kiss, one more feeling of his palm resting on hers.

'But . . . but if you like and, as it's your last night,' she said, swallowing, 'we could go to the pub later after supper?'

His smile slowly crept back across his face. His eyes crinkled into happiness and his mouth lifted in an expression of pure joy. 'I would very much like to go to the pub later.'

He sat back in his seat, and just like that, with the equilibrium restored, the atmosphere in the pickup changed. The air was softer, the temperature warmer and she was sure that, if she looked close enough, she would see small sparkles of delight leaving Grayson with every breath he exuded. These sparkles, she was certain, flew in her direction and she inhaled them until they filled her right up.

◆　◆　◆

'Nice day, my love?' her dad asked, raising the next forkful of ham hock to his mouth.

'Yes. Nice.' She hoped he'd leave it at that, wary of the heat of Emery's occasional glare.

'The Reedleys have got red mite,' her mother announced with a sigh.

Hitch pictured the Reedleys' farm, a good six miles away over in Wattingbrook. Julie Reedley had been in her class at school, not that they were ever friends.

'I've been putting down the powder twice a day and can't see anything that's bothering me,' she said earnestly, the care of her chicken girls of vital importance to her.

'Sure you're not a bit distracted?' Her mum looked briefly at Emery and then back to her plate.

Hitch thought about their guest eating his supper, as requested, alone in the dining room next door. 'No, Mum, I'm not distracted, and even if I was, generally these distractions have a habit of disappearing after a day or two, so no harm done.' She felt the burn of anger on her cheeks. How dare he try to cause trouble, telling tales, and probably false ones at that, to her mum?

'Best keep your eye on them birds,' Emery suggested.

'I don't need you to tell me that.' She looked daggers at him.

'For the love of God, can't I have one meal without you two bickering like kids!' Her mum threw down her cutlery and rested her elbows on the table. 'Emery's only trying to help, love. He works hard here, Hitch, and you don't give him an inch! He's family, and I know he's not your brother, but he's still family!'

Hitch stared at Emery, whose smile was subtle. 'Can I take the pickup, Dad?'

'Off again?' Emery asked, almost casually.

'Drop dead, Emery!'

'Hitch, please!'

'For the love of God!'

Her mum and dad shouted at her almost simultaneously as she grabbed the car keys and her jacket and walked through to the dining room, where Mr Grayson Potts, their soon-to-be-departing guest, sat with his hands folded on the table, in front of an empty plate with the white linen napkin tucked into his shirt collar.

'Are we going to the pub or what?' she asked loudly, caring little if her family on the other side of the dining-room wall heard or not.

The Barley Mow had the usual crowd in. Hitch kept her eyes on the bar, deliberately away from Tarran Buttermore, Digger Whelks and their whole pathetic crew, who now crowded around the pool table, heckling and waiting impatiently for their turn on the cue, sipping warm, flat lager between goes and nipping outside for a smoke every now and then.

'All right, Hitch?' Shelley stood behind the bar and might have been addressing her, but her eyes were very firmly on Grayson.

'Yep, you, Shell?'

'Not bad.' She chewed her gum with her mouth open. 'Who's this?' she said, addressing Hitch but continuing to stare at Grayson.

'This is my friend Grayson.'

He gave the customary lift of his hand in greeting.

'All right?' Shelley said with a nod.

'What would you like to drink?' Hitch asked Grayson, who looked around the pub with confidence, seeming keen to take it all in.

'Whatever you're having.'

'Two ciders, please, Shell.' Hitch pulled the small fold of banknotes from her jeans pocket and paid.

She handed Grayson his pint and walked to the table in the corner, a wonky table, but the one with the clearest view of the room; she didn't want her back to anyone. Tarran's snicker was loud and her heart raced in her chest. She sidled on to the red faux-leather padded bench and shot him a look, intimidated by the way he and the boys were laughing, red-faced and with shoulders hunched, their behaviour juvenile and unbecoming. The source of their comedy, she realised, was Grayson, who walked slowly with his pint in his outstretched hand, creeping at a snail's pace with his tongue out, as if there might be a penalty for spilling even a droplet of his pint. She smiled at him and he widened his eyes in her direction, an acknowledgment of her encouragement, but still he didn't deviate from his mission.

Finally he sat down, pushing his long fringe across his forehead and behind his left ear. 'So this is your local?'

'Yep.' She sipped her drink, wondering why she had thought it a good idea to bring him here, knowing deep down it was partly to show Tarran and his shitty gang that she had a friend. The realisation now that at some level tonight she was using Grayson as collateral filled her with self-loathing. He was sweet, lovely and deserved more.

'Drink up!' she smiled, nodding at his pint. 'I think we should go somewhere else.'

'Somewhere else?' He stared at her with a small laugh on his lips, as if he had missed the point. 'We've only just sat down.'

'It's boring in here.' She drank quickly.

'We can make it less boring. We can chat.'

'What do you want to chat about?' The edge to her tone was almost instinctive and she watched him shrink back against the chair.

He shrugged. 'I don't mind.'

As she formulated the words of apology to explain that it was her anxiety talking, the door opened and her heart sank as Emery walked in.

'Hey, big man!' Tarran shouted from behind the pool table. Emery raised his hand in greeting and walked straight over to the wonky table in the corner.

'Fancy meeting you here!' he said, winking at his cousin. 'And you're our guest at Waycott Farm. Sorry I didn't get the chance to say hello properly earlier.' He held out his hand. Grayson reached up to offer his own. Hitch watched as Emery shook it with such force that, when released, Grayson sported a white imprint of the man's fingertips.

'What is it you want, Emery?' she demanded, not only dreading him mocking her in front of this man she liked, but also feeling a pulse of protection towards Grayson and wanting to get him as far away from her enemy as possible.

'Now is that any way to greet your own family?' He shook his head in mock-distress. 'That's not nice, is it, Mr . . . ?'

'Potts.'

'Mr Potts, what d'you think of that?' Emery jerked his head towards Hitch. 'Anyone listening would think she doesn't like me!'

'I don't think she does like you.' Grayson took a sip of his pint.

Emery laughed loudly. 'Is that right?' he said, running his tongue under his top lip and around his gums. 'That's the funny thing, because all I've done is help out – you'd think she'd be more grateful! Saving her dad's sorry butt. He'd be on his knees by now, what with Jonathan golden-balls sodding gone off to play cowboys.'

Grayson looked from Hitch to Emery, and she wished he hadn't been drawn into this, certain that he would now be glad to get back to his needy mum and tiny flat tomorrow. *Tomorrow . . . It will be here soon enough and yet here we are, wasting time in the bloody pub . . .*

Emery continued, 'I don't think she's ever liked me.'

'Because you've always been a dickhead,' she spat.

Tard . . . Fuckwit . . . Rabbitmouth . . . Whassamatta, Hitch, going to cry?

Emery ignored her. 'But I'll tell you who she does like – she likes Tarran, don't you, cuz?' He pointed at the pool table, pausing and holding her gaze, while she silently implored him to shut his horrible mouth.

'Come on, Grayson, we're going.' She drained her glass and thumped it hard on the table.

Grayson drank a couple of mouthfuls and stood.

'Surely you're not going without buying me a pint?' Emery placed his hand on his chest, suggesting that this wounded him.

'Oh!'

She watched as sweet Grayson Potts put his hand in his pocket and pulled out a small, stiff, brown, horseshoe-shaped leather pouch. He tilted it and coins dropped into the leather lip with a satisfying *plink*. 'How much is a pint here?' he asked out loud.

His kindness and sweet nature again lit the flame of shame in her chest. She had brought him here and now she had to get him out.

'You'll get a little bit of change out of four quid,' Shelley called out from behind the bar.

Grayson smiled at her and counted out four pound coins and placed them in a neat tower on the sticky tabletop. 'There you go.'

Emery stared at the pile of money. 'What the fuck is that thing in your hand?' he said, pointing.

Grayson lifted the brown leather pouch. 'Oh, it's my change purse. It was my grandad's.'

Emery could barely contain the laughter that escaped his pursed wet lips. 'Change purse!' he repeated with a titter, as he walked forward and gathered the coins into his hand before giving them back to Grayson. 'You keep this, son. Is it from your paper round?'

'No, I haven't got a paper round.' Grayson held the money in his palm, seemingly unsure of what to do with it.

'Come on, Grayson!' Hitch held the door open and walked briskly out into the cool evening air.

'I'm not sure what that was all about.' He peered over his shoulder, looking back at the pub with confusion.

'What it's all about is that my cousin is a shit and the people in that pub are shits and I don't want to spend my last ever evening with you in their company. I'd rather go somewhere we can be alone and kiss some more without being disturbed. How about that?' She threw the car keys into the air and caught them. Her relief at being out of the threatening environment of the pub was sweet and instant.

'Okay.' He smiled at her and climbed into the cab of the pickup. 'What's wrong with my change purse? Or the term "change purse", for that matter?' he mused.

'Nothing. There's nothing wrong with it, but there's plenty wrong with them idiots.' She revved the car and swung it across the uneven surface of the car park. The gear stick felt the full force of her frustrations.

'Do you really think that?'

'Think what?' she kept her eyes on the road.

'That this will be our last ever evening together?' Disappointment dripped from his words and she understood, feeling it too.

'I think yes, it probably is.' She took a deep breath, feeling the cold creep of reality wrap itself around her. 'I mean, you live in London and I live here and we have such different lives. I can't see the point at which they cross over, can you?'

She glanced at him as he apparently considered this.

'No.' He shook his head. 'I guess I can't. I wish I could, but I can't, not really.'

'Me neither. If I was someone who caught your bus or you worked on a farm in the area, well, then I'd see you every day!' she beamed, 'and I would really, really like that, but I'm not on your bus and you're not working on a farm and so that's that.'

'So that's that,' he repeated, his tone so melancholic that it made her want to weep.

'So let's just enjoy right now, okay?' She found brightness and lavished it on her words.

'Okay,' he whispered without conviction. 'Where are we going?'

'Back to my place.' She smiled at him with false conviction and put her foot down.

◆　◆　◆

Hitch cut the engine and switched off the lights, letting the Subaru idle down the last of the hill before coming to rest on the verge at the foot of the driveway. She quietly ratcheted up the handbrake and silently climbed from the cab. Looking at Grayson, she held her finger over her lips, indicating to him to keep quiet. The last thing she wanted was her mum and dad coming out and disturbing their peace. He nodded, watching as she reached into the back of the pickup for the tartan rug they had placed on the flat rock earlier and the bottle of cider she had taken from the larder, just in case. Keeping close to the hedgerow, with her phone flashlight showing the way, and with the bottle under her arm, she walked soundlessly along the paddock boundary with Grayson following closely behind. He too shone his phone at the ground. She felt him stumble a couple of times in the dark behind her and they both giggled softly into the night air. She found his ineptitude when standing on anything other than a flat, grey paving slab quite endearing, and the irony wasn't lost on her that it was he with his two good feet who couldn't remain upright. With expert precision and showing off a little, she kicked her leg up to climb over a sturdy stile and waited for him to do likewise, smiling at his cumbersome execution of a task so familiar to her.

Finally they walked on the stone-strewn path to the edge of the lower paddock, out of earshot of the farmhouse.

'That's some sky, huh?' She looked up at the large full moon which striped the grass and surrounding woodland with its silver glare, the clear indigo, starry cape of the heavens providing a dazzling backdrop to this, their last adventure. She breathed in the cool night air and felt the ball of tension that had appeared in the pub ease in her gut.

'It is.' He nodded. 'When I was little, if I looked up with one eye closed out of a certain part of the window behind my bed, I could see a slice of the moon, and I liked the fact it was the same moon that my dad could see wherever he was.'

Her heart shredded at the image of Grayson as a small boy, so thoroughly abandoned. 'I used to look at the moon and try to understand how it was the same moon that people all over the world could see. People in places I wanted to go to – America, Norway, India.' *Places I still want to go to. One day, maybe . . .*

'Well, I used to wonder if my dad was looking at it too, thinking about me.'

'I'm sure he was.' She offered the salve. 'Don't you think?' It was hard for her to imagine adults parenting differently to her mum and dad, who loved her, loved her unequivocally.

'I'm not so sure,' he said thoughtfully. 'I think, if he thought about me at all, then he would have contacted me or come to see me. Don't you?'

She hated the note of desperation in his question. 'Not necessarily. I don't know – maybe it was hard for him. I obviously don't know much about it, but by the sounds of it you only have a little bit of the story. You only know what you saw and heard, but you were just a little kid, so there were probably lots of things going on that you didn't know about, adult stuff. And maybe that made it hard for him to come back or keep in touch.' She put forward the thin rationale in an effort to ease his pain.

'I guess.' Grayson walked by her side and she heard his deep, slow intake of breath, as if what came next might require courage. 'I haven't said this out loud before, but I understand why he went.'

'You do?' It was a startling insight and one she felt flattered to be the recipient of.

He nodded. 'My mum, she's' – he paused – 'she's hard work.'

'In what way?'

'I meant what I said before, about her being needy – she doesn't shut up, ever, she just goes on and on and on, spouting the same nonsense on repeat, and I always feel she's having a go at me, digging away. And so I don't talk any more.'

'What do you mean, you don't talk?' Hitch gave a small laugh at the very concept.

'I mean, when I'm at home, she goes on so much that I can't get my words out. I'm quiet. I think a lot more than I say and it's a habit that's hard to get out of. It's been a long time since I spoke properly, like I do with you.'

'How long?' She stopped walking and turned to face him.

'About twenty-four years, since my dad left. I used to be able to talk to him.'

'And he left you.' She regretted her earlier laugh. There was nothing funny about this, nothing at all.

'Yes, he left me, and then there was no one to listen, and no one around with anything to say that I really wanted to hear. My mum got louder and louder. It's a strange thing; my home became deafening and silent at the same time.'

She blinked at him. 'And yet you can talk to me?'

'Yes,' he said, shrugging as if this required no further explanation, 'but I don't talk to anyone else.'

'What, not even at work?' In her imagination, working in an office or a shop was the way she saw it in any film – it meant an instant social life, where chatting between buddies only halted when you had to get on with the job in hand. It was one of the things she thought she missed out on most in farm life.

Grayson shook his head. 'Not really. I have the odd chat with Liz, who sits next to me – she's nice – but I don't speak to anyone else about anything significant, and never about what matters to me . . .'

'Why not?'

As he began to speak, she heard the hesitant air of embarrassment in his tone and concentrated on listening hard, sensing that whatever revelation might follow represented a risky moment of openness on his part.

'I've always felt a bit different. Always. I don't know why and I don't know how, but somehow, when I was a kid, I knew that all the things that made the other boys "normal" seemed to have passed me by.' He paused, and she sensed that this was no easy admission. 'I mean, even now, in my early thirties, I know I'm not like other men. It's not only the big detail and small detail stuff I told you about, it's more than that . . . It's like, when the things were being handed out to make a successful life, I got barged out of the line.' He snorted briefly with laughter, an act she recognised as one she deployed herself in moments of embarrassment.

'What kind of things?' She turned her head towards his outline in the darkness.

'Confidence. Awareness. Conversation. Humour. Drive. Muscles. And a basic understanding of the offside rule.'

I know you . . . I'm the same . . . I know what this feels like . . .

'I tried to talk to Reggie about it once, tried explaining how it felt like everyone was happy to barge me out of the way because I just don't count. Like everyone got the joke, apart from me. But it was hard for him to understand, and even he got impatient; he had to be somewhere.'

'You do count, Grayson. It's true I don't really know you, but in some ways I feel like I know you inside out, and you do count.' *To me.*

'Yes, and it feels different here, but in the real world I just don't know how to be the same as everyone else. I don't know what to wear, how to walk, what music to listen to, what to say. I just don't.'

'Maybe you don't have to, maybe you worry too much about fitting in and being like everyone else. And trust me, I know what that feels like.' She touched the coiled fingers of her right hand. 'I also know it's a waste of life, really, and this *is* the real world here, Grayson. Not the world you're used to, but a real world nonetheless. It's my world.'

'I find it easy to talk to you. I don't know why, but it feels like a relief.'

'And I find it easy to talk to you.' Reaching back, she felt for his hand in the dark and, taking it into her own, where it fit most neatly, the two walked on in silence until they came to the lower slope on a bend, further up the river where the mighty Severn meandered, providing water for the farms on the lower plain.

There was the gentle sound of the water lapping the bank and the occasional flip and dip of fish that breached the moon-dappled surface of the river. Hitch laid the blanket on the soft, grassy bank and sat down, pulling Grayson with her.

And just like that, he again kissed her mouth, as if he'd been doing it for a lifetime. She felt the pull of longing deep in her gut, lost to this man who didn't push her head away from his face, didn't avoid looking at or touching her and didn't hesitate when it came to kissing her misshapen lips.

She'd had only one brief sexual encounter, with Tarran Buttermore, an unhappy, unsatisfying collision that darkened her thoughts and had left her with a feeling of emptiness, the exact opposite of what she had sought in that quick, cold, casual tryst that had lacked intimacy in every way.

Now this man was lying on top of her, kissing her with confidence, and the yearning she felt for him was an awakening. Pulling away, she whispered in his ear as she helped unfasten his belt, 'Have you . . . have you done this before?' She wondered if his oddness and his lack of friends and social life might be a factor.

'Yes,' he murmured, smoothing her hair from her face, 'but it didn't feel like this.' He kissed her again. 'Nothing feels like this. It's brand new.'

From anyone else, she knew this would be a line to be snickered at, no more than chat, but not only did it feel true, she knew that Grayson Potts did not lie. Hitch closed her eyes and laid her cheek against his. He was right; it was brand new. This feeling was tinged with sadness at the fact that this was a one-time thing. Grayson Potts was a kind and gentle soul who would tomorrow go back to the big city, while her life was here, helping her parents. She shook the intrusive thoughts from her mind, trying not to think too far ahead and concentrating on the now, the glorious, exquisite now.

Grayson eased his clothes from his body. She felt him reach down and he gasped before bringing his hand up towards his face. She could see in the beam of light from the phone set on the ground that it was covered in blood, dark red, glossy and bright in the moonlight.

'Oh God! Oh no! Grayson!' She felt her pulse quicken and her face blush. 'I'm sorry, I . . .'

He shook his head and kissed her. 'It's part of you. It's all part of you. And every part of you is perfect.'

Hitch knew his words would line her gut with warmth on the coldest of mornings and send a smile to her face when her muscles ached from shovelling shit. He thought every part of her was perfect. Every. Single. Part.

Gently, he leaned forward and again kissed her mouth. Hitch clung to him with shaking arms, unable to stem the tears that fell and quite overcome by the sweet, sweet sensation of being held for the first time with love.

I know I feel different.

I know I'm different.

I know it's because of him.

I feel like a woman.

I feel happy when I'm with him.

I know that, if I could feel like this every day, then I would wake up happy.

I know that life can give you the most beautiful and unexpected gifts when you least expect them.

SEVEN

Hitch woke slowly and spread her arms wide over her head. Her head felt slightly fuzzy as, in a dreamlike state, she played the movie in her mind from the night before: remembering the feel of lying in Grayson's arms, his fingers running through her hair, which lay spilled across the tartan rug; the way he ran his finger lightly down her cheek, now wet with tears . . . And afterwards, lying huddled together, a jumble of arms and legs, wrapped in the edges of the rug with clothes scattered there on the riverbank in the moonlight.

She rose now and showered quickly, stepping into her jeans and feeling so full and satisfied she could barely face breakfast. Making her way across the landing, she hesitated outside the guest bedroom and, having looked both ways along the landing to make sure the coast was clear, she knocked quietly and popped her smiling face inside the door.

Grayson sat up and looked around for his shirt, a little more self-conscious of his nakedness in the cold light of day.

'You're awake.' She beamed at him.

'I am,' he said, nodding, and the sight of him was enough to fire a bolt of longing right through her. 'I was just thinking about you.' He patted the duvet.

'And I was just thinking about you.' She walked forward and perched on the edge of the bed, planting a chaste kiss on his face. 'My mum would kill me if she knew I was in here with you.'

'Don't worry, I won't tell her,' he whispered.

She laughed, and he took her hand. 'It's a wonder to me that I can make you laugh like that. It feels like a superpower.'

Hitch kissed their joined hands. 'You go home today.' She addressed the elephant in the room.

'I do.'

'How do you feel about that?' she asked softly, watching as his face seemed to lose a little colour as he looked towards the window, where sunbeams filtered through the branches of the trees.

'I feel like someone is about to take a large stone and smash my happiness beneath it.'

'You have a lovely way of saying things, Grayson.'

'I don't normally.'

'And that's how I feel too. I don't know what to say and I don't know what to do.'

'I'm trying not to think about it,' he confided.

'Do you want some breakfast?'

He ran his finger over her face, and with the thought that he would not be within reach tomorrow, it was as if he had cut her.

'I don't want any breakfast.' He spoke from a throat croaky with barely contained emotion.

'Do you want to come and see my chickens with me?'

He nodded. 'I'd like that very much.'

'I'll meet you outside.' She kissed him and slipped from the bed, lingering in the doorway to catch one more glimpse of him while she could.

◆ ◆ ◆

'Are you ready for your formal introduction?' Hitch called out from the paddock as he strode across the yard, just as he had only a couple of days ago, with his bag in his hand and his brown envelope within reach.

'I guess.' Grayson wiped the sweat from his palms on his trousers.

'Well, come on then!' She beckoned him forward before bending over to chuckle at him.

'What are you laughing at?'

'You! The way you're creeping forward, scared of approaching Daphne. She's such a sweet bird – she won't hurt you!'

He looked warily at the fat hen. 'It's not that I'm afraid of her, more afraid of doing the wrong thing. And not just doing the wrong thing, but the wrong thing in front of you.'

'She's tough. She won't be scared. Just bend down and say hello,' she said, coaxing from the sidelines, watching as Grayson straightened his shoulders and spoke clearly.

'Good morning, Daphne. Hello.' Hitch roared with laughter and he spun around. 'Why is that funny?' he asked, with his arms spread.

'Because!' she managed. 'You sound so formal – she's a chicken, not the Lord Mayor! Although she's very grand, I'll give you that.'

'It's harder for me with you watching!'

She decided to intervene. Picking Daphne up, she cradled her to her chest.

'You're my beautiful girl, yes, you are. This is Mr Potts and he's come to say hello to you. And I know what you mean about being watched.' A wide smile split her face. 'When I was about nine, up in the top field, I was desperate to drive a tractor—'

'At nine?' he interrupted. 'That sounds a little young. I think at nine I was all gangly legs and reading chess books by torchlight under the duvet.'

'This is a working farm, Grayson! Nine is nothing to be driving a tractor. If anything, I was coming a little late to the party. Anyway . . .' She drew breath. That wasn't really the point of her story. 'I couldn't get the hang of it. It was hard, with my leg not doing what I wanted it to. And what I really wanted was to be left alone to figure it out, but my dad and brother insisted on calling instructions from the edge of the field. It was only when they fell silent and I forgot they were there that I cracked it, and my dad sounded so proud, yelling, "You've got this, Hitch! Look at you! You're driving all by yourself!" Oh my God, it felt wonderful. I felt so powerful, like I could put my foot down and keep going, smashing through fences, fields and across rivers, just keep on going, in charge of my own destiny, free to go wherever the fancy took me. I've never forgotten it – it was the most free I've ever felt. I don't know why I should think of it now. But it felt good to be in control.'

'I don't think I've ever felt like that.' Grayson blinked at Daphne, who now made a clucking noise. Hitch placed her gently back in the run.

'Here.' She pulled grain from her pocket and tipped the tiny granules into his palm. 'Feed her this.'

Grayson bent down and held out his flattened hand.

'Look, Daphne, look what Grayson's got for you!' she coaxed.

'Morning, Daphne,' he said with a smile, stretching out his arm. To his obvious surprise and delight, Daphne took a hesitant step in his direction, looking left and right, as if scoping out the scene, checking out this stranger who sat patiently with the gift of grain. Eventually, she came close enough to peck from his hand.

Hitch clapped and squealed. 'She loves you! She loves you!'

The words left her mouth like a song and Grayson looked up at her. There was a beat of quiet while he straightened to face her and the morning sun lit him from behind like a halo. Hitch captured the image like a photograph and stored it in her mind, there for perfect recall when she was walking alone down by the river or driving the lanes in the dark.

'Does she?' he blinked.

'Yes.' She nodded. 'I think she does.'

The two stared at each other in silence for a moment or two.

'I think I'm going to miss you, Grayson.' She spoke softly, her throat tight with emotion.

He nodded. 'Me too.'

'I feel as if I've been in a clothes dryer and everything is a bit upside down and my stomach is churning, and I like it, but I don't know what happens next and that feels scary.' She bit her lip, hoping he might take the initiative, clear a path for the future. His words when they came left her cloaked in disappointment.

'I've written my address and number on a piece of paper and left it by the side of the bed. If you need anything, if you want to come and visit or if you're ever passing . . .'

She gave a nasal laugh of derision. 'If I'm ever passing? Okay. I don't even go into Bristol, so that isn't going to happen, is it? But thank you.' She wasn't sure if leaving his address was an invitation or a kind dismissal.

'I guess I could . . . I could come back and—'

'When?' She jumped in, thankful for the bolt of optimism that fired through her, thinking that to make a date gave them a foundation on which they could build.

'I don't know,' he confessed with a look of confusion. 'I have to go to work and—'

'It's okay, Grayson. I get it. Maybe it would only make it harder, having to say goodbye again – or worse, making a plan that you can't stick to. I mean, it's a bit crazy, isn't it? I've only known you for a couple of days and it's been nice, so nice. I can't tell you how low I was until you arrived.' She paused. 'But maybe now it's time to get back on with real life again.'

I can say this easily enough, but my heart is aching and the words cut my throat like glass . . . I want you to want me. I want you to say you want me! I feel desperate at the thought that this is all we've got! I want more, Grayson – I want more of you!

'Do you mean that?' His breath came quickly and he looked pained.

'Well, of course I mean that! I don't want you to make a promise you can't keep and I don't want to think we're heading in one direction when we might be heading in another. That's not fair on you or me.' She stared at him, cursing the tears that gathered at the back of her throat.

'You're such a good person, Thomasina. And I don't want to make you a promise I can't keep, no matter how much I want to.'

She folded her arms across her chest, as if this stance could deflect the verbal blows of disappointment. 'I like your honesty and the fact that you never tell a lie. And I don't regret anything.' She spoke with a wobble to her voice. It was important he knew this, as again the picture of them on the riverbank in the moonlight sprang into her mind.

'I don't regret anything either, quite the opposite. I don't only think you're a good person, I also think you're smart and beautiful.'

'God, Grayson, you don't see me how other people do!' she said, laughing.

He stared at her. 'Well, that's good. I don't want anyone to see you how I do because they might just be slicker than me, less weird, and that means you might choose to be with them. Someone who knows how to dress and stuff.'

'Someone who understands the offside rule?' she joked painfully, trying to raise a smile.

'Exactly.'

With the back of her hand, she wiped the tears that had finally found their way to the surface. 'I don't feel as if I get to choose anything right now.'

'I guess not,' he said softly, 'but it's not that straightforward, is it? It's life. It's geography and it's circumstance and, until I can figure all that out . . .'

He let this hang, but she took little comfort from the thin sliver of hope he cast in her direction.

'Or until *I* can figure all that out . . .' she said, matching his senti-ment, reminding him that this was a two-way thing, tired of the feeling that her parents steered her own ship of fate, as surely as if they were on the high seas in a boat crafted from the timbers that held up the roof of the farm. It was, she realised, maybe about time she became the captain of her own vessel, forged her own future. After all, if she was, as Grayson said, a good person, smart and beautiful, what was to stop her?

'Can I ask you to do something?' he said, with a catch to his voice.

'What?'

He held her gaze and reached for both of her hands. 'Tell people not to call you Hitch – tell them your name is Thomasina.'

'Why?' She freed one hand to swipe the tears defiantly from the top of her cheekbone with her fingertips and then placed her fingers back in his palm.

'Because it's important.'

She laughed and shook her head. 'But it's not important, Grayson, not really.'

'It is to me. And it should be to you.' He gazed deep into her eyes, as if thinking about what else he wanted to say, his parting words. He thumbed the skin on the back of her hands. 'I feel sick, sick and sad. I can't help it. I want more of you, Thomasina, more time, more sex, more everything. You are amazing,' he whispered now, leaning forward to kiss her again on the mouth and run his fingers through her long hair. 'I can't think that I won't see you again.'

'Well, you must. It's for the best – like you said, it's not straight-forward. It's life, it's geography and circumstance . . .' she paraphrased.

'Goodbye, Thom.' He let go of her hands and walked slowly back towards the farmhouse, where he would gather his bag and climb into a wretched taxi that would carry him away from their fairy tale.

'Goodbye, Gray,' she whispered into the ether, as the chickens clucked and the cattle lowed, as if they too sensed a shift in the air, picking up on the fact that, suddenly, all was not right in their world.

I know I have a pain in my chest and my heart.

I know I feel a little lost.

I now know that the phrase I have heard since my childhood is a big fat lie.

I know it is not better to have loved and lost than never to have loved at all, because I now know what I'm missing and what I'm missing is Grayson Potts.

EIGHT

Grayson Potts left, and Hitch felt down in the days following. But this was different from her usual lows – she felt sadder and more lonely than before she ever knew of his existence. Changing the bed linen now in readiness for a new guest, she slowly ran her fingers over the pillow on which he had laid his clever head and pictured him swiping his long fringe with his finger and tucking it behind his ear.

'I've written my address on a piece of paper and left it by the side of the bed.' She practised her cockney accent. 'If you need anything, if you want to come and visit or if you're ever passing . . . as if I'd ever be passing! What d'you think, Grayson, that I just click my heels and, hey presto?' She shook her head.

'Who are you talking to, darlin'?' Her mum's voice took her by surprise.

'Myself,' she admitted.

Her mum stared at her from the doorway with her hands on her hips and a duster in her hand. 'You do that a lot, my love.' Her tone was at best accusatory, at worst suspicious, undercut with a cloying note of pity that made Hitch want to scream.

'I do.' She laughed. 'I have no one else to talk to.'

'You have me and your dad and Emery.'

Hitch rolled her eyes. 'As if I'd want to talk to Emery about anything, and you and Dad are too busy to talk about anything that matters . . .' She let this trail.

'What is it you want to talk about that matters?'

'Lots of things!' she fired.

'Like what?' Her mum looked a little perplexed.

'Well, I don't know!' she shouted. Her mum again stared at her with a quizzical lift to her eyebrow.

'Is this about that young man who stayed?'

'Partly.'

And partly because I want to make plans and I don't know where to start, and partly because I have big ideas. I want to travel, but if I stay here, I can't earn enough money to make any changes. And partly because I'm done with it all!

'For the love of God, Hitch, you only knew him for five minutes! He probably does it all over the country: goes and stays somewhere, chats up the ladies, and then on to the next! And I'm not saying you shouldn't have fun – I think you should – but you can't put any stock in it.'

'I don't think he's like that, Mum.' She pictured his earnest expression, his lack of guile, his unsuitable footwear and the sight of him bending low, trying to make friends with Daphne. 'Not him. He was different.'

'Well, if you say so, and when you figure out what it is you want to talk about that's so important, come and find me. Everything is going to be okay, I promise.'

She smiled at her mum's sweet, if irritating, cliché and would have found this invitation to confide in her heartening, were it not for the slow shake of her mum's head that again suggested her exasperation.

Hitch flopped down on the bed and stared at the ceiling.

'I liked you being here, Grayson.' She reached for the square of paper in her jeans pocket with his address on it, signed with a single kiss. 'I liked being near you and I liked talking to you,' she whispered into the atmosphere.

'Hitch?' her mum shouted from the bottom of the stairs.

'What?' She sighed, closing her eyes and wishing she could take a few more minutes to reflect on the man she missed and the exquisite feeling of his mouth on hers . . .

'There's something up with the chickens.'

She jumped up from the bed as if scalded and raced down the narrow staircase. She might lack the energy and enthusiasm for much else, but where her girls were concerned, she had rocket fuel in her feet and a devotion that was sky-high.

'What's up with them?' she asked, a little breathless, as she fastened her fleece jacket. Her mind ran riot with all the possibilities – another raid by a fox, sickness or escapees.

'One of them is sitting on the eggs, proper broody,' said her mum, waiting in the kitchen.

'Oh no, which one?' Hitch asked, as she held the back door open.

'How should I know? Dad's gone back up to the coop.'

Hitch whistled for Buddy to come as she trotted across the yard, out over the back grass and towards the paddock. If a hen got broody, it was bad news. Broody hens wanted to sit on eggs and raise a clutch of chicks; what they didn't want to do was lay other eggs.

She saw her dad pulling a small crate to the edge of the run.

'I've separated her from the others, love, but she's pulled out some of her chest feathers to line her nest. Gave me a right pecking, she did, when I had to move her.'

'Which one is it?' She bent low and peered through the gaps in the crate at Daphne. 'Oh, Daph, my poor love.' She looked up at her dad. 'That's not like her. She's not aggressive – none of them are.'

'No, but if she thinks I'm going to harm her little 'uns . . .' He sighed. 'She was warm and so I've given her water. It's important she stays hydrated. There were a few eggs under her, Hitch. Have you been collecting as regularly as you should?' he asked softly.

'I think so, maybe missed once or twice while I was, erm, while I was . . .' She struggled to think of how to phrase her preoccupation.

'While you took a shine to that London chap?'

'Yes.' She bit the inside of her cheek. The idea that her girls might have suffered because of something she might have done or not done was more than she could stand.

'It can just happen, love, whether you collect regular or not,' he said, smiling at her, her sweet dad. 'Trouble is, it can be contagious – one broody hen can lead to two and then three, and they sit on all the eggs and stop laying, and then they're not layers, not paying their keep, and they're just costing us time and money.' He shook his head.

'That won't happen.' She tried to hide her note of panic, knowing the consequence for a chicken that did not lay. 'Daphne's smart. She'll figure it out, get back on track.'

'I'm sure you're right.' He winked at her.

'Poor little thing, it's not much to ask, is it? To be allowed to have a little one of your own, to live in your own house and to be a mum, especially when that's all we ask of her, to lay eggs.'

'It's the nature of it, darlin'.' He patted the crate. 'Was he nice then, that London chap?'

Hitch nodded. 'He was. Really nice.'

'Might he come back again?'

She shook her head. 'I don't think so. He works for a kind of bank, he's busy and he's far away.'

'Well, even people who work in kind of banks and live far away need holidays!'

His attempt to cheer her had the opposite effect. She felt her tears pool.

'I liked him, Pops.'

'I could tell – you carried the scent of joy with you, and it was lovely. Well, if it's meant to be, it's meant to be.' He walked over and ruffled the top of her hair, like he had when she was a child.

'Do you think Jonathan might come home soon?' She sniffed. On top of everything else, she missed her brother, wishing he were here and cursing the moment she had asked the question, knowing that to put her brother's absence in her dad's mind was unfair.

What is wrong with you, Thomasina?

Her dad took his time in replying, letting his eyes sweep across the land over which he was king. 'I don't know. I think he's happy and he likes life in the sunshine, and who knows – maybe there'll be nothing for him to come home to?'

'Please don't say that!' She cursed the tears that fell, crying for several reasons.

'Truth is, I've had an enquiry, a very generous enquiry, via a lawyer chap in Bristol. He phoned me yesterday. As I've said, I have to think of all the options.'

'Them bloody Buttermores, chucking their money at us – well, we are not for sale! We are not!' she hissed, balling her fingers into fists.

'We might not have any choice, my little love,' he offered solemnly. 'Besides, we don't know it's the Buttermores.'

'Who else would it be?' She stared at the crate in which her little hen clucked forlornly. 'I feel like everything's unravelling, Pops, and I don't know what to do.'

'You'll be fine, and we'll be fine, you'll see.' He pulled her into his arms and held her close – her dad, the only man in the world she trusted to tell her the truth and to treat her right. Unbidden, an image of Grayson rose in her mind and her tears fell afresh.

◆ ◆ ◆

Plunging the large serving spoon into the hotpot casserole, she heard the satisfying crack of crisped golden potatoes on top of the rich meat and gravy as she heaped a portion on to the plate, alongside buttered peas and hot steamed cabbage.

'Smells good.' Her dad smacked his lips. 'Where's Emery? Not like him to be late for supper.'

Her mum shrugged. 'No matter, his plate'll keep in the warming oven.' She lifted her own cutlery in readiness for her food. Hitch placed the bowls in front of her parents and went back to the range to serve her own.

'Anything important you want to talk about tonight, my lovely?' her mum asked flatly, and Hitch couldn't tell if she was taking her earlier request seriously.

'Actually, yes,' she said with a cough. 'There is something.'

'Well, we are all ears!' Her mum smiled at her husband across the table and she felt a warm stir of memory that this was what life had been like before Emery had pitched up permanently. How she had missed it!

She coughed again to clear her throat, attempting to give her announcement gravitas. 'I don't want you to call me Hitch any more. I want you to call me Thomasina.' She spoke with as much authority as she could muster, turning to face them with her portion of hotpot in her hands, taking her seat at the table and smiling as she tucked in.

'Ooh, this is good!' She chewed the soft lumps of meat and forked a number of peas in for good measure.

'But *everyone* calls you Hitch!' Her mum stared at her. 'They always have.'

'I know, and now I want *everyone* to call me by my name, Thomasina. The name you gave me!' she reminded them both.

'Do you know, you're right, love, you are absolutely right.' Her dad chuckled and her mum followed suit. 'Thomasina it is.'

'Reckon I might forget while I'm getting used to it.'

'That's okay, Mum, as long as we get there in the end.'

'This is a lovely hotpot. Thank you, Thomasina,' her mum said with a smile.

'It really is – one of the best, Thomasina,' said her dad, joining in.

'Could you pass the salt please, Thomasina,' her mum said with a giggle.

'And I'll take the pepper, Thomasina,' her dad snickered.

'All right, you two – pack it in!' Thomasina laughed – at least she had got her message across.

She and her beloved mum and dad sat around the table, the legs of which had worn wells in the flagstones over the years, as generations of Waycotts before them did likewise. Buddy slept by the hearth, and with bowls of good food in front of them it was as near perfect an evening as they had had in a while.

The back door opened suddenly with force, slamming against the wall as if taken by the wind.

Emery stood in the doorway, the great hulking brute, with his fat, pale face and his hands of ham. Without uttering a single word, he sucked all the warmth and joy from the room. Thomasina felt her smile fade and discomfort return to her gut.

'You're late.' Her mum nodded at the clock. 'There's a plate of hotpot in the warming oven.'

Emery nodded and walked in, closing the door behind him. 'I'm afraid I have some bad news.'

He spoke slowly, sincerely, and the words would have seemed innocuous to anyone other than Thomasina, who knew enough of him to recognise the slight twinkle in his eye and the almost imperceptible lift to his top lip, as if something had greatly amused him.

'What's that, son?' Her dad let his spoon drop into the bowl and all three turned to face her cousin.

'I found this.'

Thomasina looked up almost casually, expecting to see a broken piece of fence post, part of a breached pen or a discarded tractor bolt, the usual rusted, soiled or fractured detritus of farm life. Instead her heart boomed in her chest as the wail left her throat. In his big hand lay the limp body of a chicken – and not just any chicken, but her lovely Daphne, the little broody hen who had spent the day in a crate, away from her feathery friends, dreaming fruitlessly of motherhood.

'No! No!' she shouted, as she jumped up from the table, abandoning supper. 'What did you do to her?' She grabbed the hen from his grip and cradled her to her chest, and the feel of her tiny head lolling over her thumb was almost more than she could bear. 'I said, what did you do? You pig!' She couldn't control her rage.

'I didn't do anything!' He spoke with an underlying hint of laughter that sent a spike of anger through her.

'I don't believe you! You did this to her!' she yelled.

'For God's sake, calm down, it's only one hen!'

'Only one hen?' she screamed at her cousin. 'How can you say that? They're more than just hens to me! Much more.' She turned to her mum, pointing at her cousin as her tears fell. 'I know he did it on purpose! I just know it!'

'Why would I do it on purpose?' Again he laughed and she launched herself at him, punching him with the free hand that didn't cradle Daphne.

'I fucking hate you! I hate you! I hate you!' she screamed, until her voice was hoarse.

'Jesus Christ! Enough, Hitch! Enough!' Her dad jumped up and stood between her and Emery.

With a racing pulse and her heart hammering in her chest, she turned to her dad, 'I told you, my name is Thomasina!'

'Thomasina . . .' Her dad spoke gently, as if calling to her.

She shook her head and rubbed the little feathered breast that lay in her palm. 'I can't do it any more, Dad. I can't. I'm so fed up. I want more, more time, more everything. I'm stuck! And I understand that all Daphne wanted was a chick of her own, I get it, but how can she, when no one thinks she's capable of anything other than changing the beds and cooking a bloody hotpot!'

She saw her mum and dad exchange a quizzical look and then lower their eyes to the floor, as they tried to piece together the words of her outburst and the muddle of her mind.

'I'm going out,' she sniffed. Grabbing her wallet and phone, she made for the back door and ran up to the coop. Crouching down with Daphne in her arms, she spoke to the rest of the birds, who were unsettled, their behaviour a little odd. Daisy Duke had pecked some of her own feathers and Little Darling was squawking with her chest pushed out.

'It's okay, it's okay, girls. I know you're scared, but it's all going to be okay. You have nothing to be scared of. It will all be fine. You'll see.'

With Daphne in her hands, Thomasina jogged back across the yard, past the house, and turned right at the bottom of the yard, through the five-bar gate and up the narrow lane.

She carried on walking as dusk began to bite. With her tears subsiding and Daphne now cool in her hand, she made it to the pub. Her plan was to get very drunk. She immediately cried at the thought of her last pub visit with Grayson by her side, her gut folded in longing as she pictured the lanky, long-fringed man who lived in a domino flat far, far away.

She pushed on the door and walked to the bar. Some of the boys were playing pool and a few older farmers were sitting in their usual spots with caps on their heads, gripping warm pints in calloused hands with dirty fingernails.

Shelley looked up. 'Jesus, Hitch, you look like shit!'

'Good,' she said, wiping her nose on the back of her hand. 'I feel like shit.'

'What's that?' Shelley nodded at the feathery mass in her hand.

'It's Daphne. My chicken. She's dead. Emery killed her.'

Shelley walked slowly from behind the bar and put her arm around her. Thomasina cried again, angered and embarrassed by the seemingly never-ending stream of tears and touched by Shelley's display of kindness; it felt a lot like friendship. She heard the coughs of embarrassment from some of the men who looked on. Not that she gave a damn what they or anyone else thought.

'You can't bring a dead chicken in here, lovey. Come on, let's take her outside.'

With Shelley as her guide, Thomasina let herself be steered back out into the car park.

'Where's Change Purse tonight?' one of the lads at the pool table shouted, as she left the pub.

'Get lost, Des! Leave her alone!' Shelley shouted on her behalf, and Thomasina was grateful.

She sat on the wall of the car park while Shelley smoked, cuddling her much-loved hen.

'I know Emery did this on purpose, Shell. He's a shit.'

'He's a shit. No mistake there,' the other girl concurred as she exhaled a long plume of blue smoke up into the air.

'I'm not going back to Waycott, not tonight. I can't.'

'Where are you going to go?'

'I don't know,' she admitted, feeling pathetic that she had no grand plan. She thought about sneaking back to Big Barn and crashing on the dog sofa, maybe.

'You want to sleep on the couch upstairs?' Shelley crushed the butt of the cigarette under the heel of her boot and jerked her head towards the top rooms of the Barley Mow. 'I mean, it's not very grand up there, hardly five star, but you're more than welcome. I have spare blankets.'

Thomasina stared at the girl who was showing her such kindness and she wondered for the first time what it actually meant to be a friend. Shelley had been around her whole life and wasn't mean to her like some of the others, and now this kind offer. Could it be that she might actually have had a friend close by all along?

'Thank you, Shell. Can I bring Daphne?' She lifted the little corpse in her hands.

Shelley pulled a face and twisted her mouth. 'If you have to.'

Thomasina sat on the sagging sofa, listening to the sounds of the pub, which, like the smell of beer, drifted up through the floorboards. The chuckles of laughter, shouts of delight and roars of disagreement, all punctuated by the bang of darts in the dartboard, the calls for drinks and the general hum of conversation. She felt it suited her perfectly, sitting up here listening to life, close to but not part of it, a self-imposed exile, where she, who wasn't capable of getting a certificate of learning and was never going to win a race, kept herself to herself. It summed things up for her. The question was *how* to change? How to break out of the rut into which she had fallen? She pulled out her jotter and tapped the pen against the pad. Tonight, the words were slow in coming . . . So much for steering her own ship.

She considered going back down to the bar and drinking vodka until she fell asleep, but even the thought of that made her cry. What she really wanted was to feel the way she had on the riverbank, when Grayson Potts had taken her in his arms and told her she was beautiful.

Eventually, once her tears had subsided, she fired off a text to Pops so he wouldn't worry and made herself a large mug of tea in the tiny galley kitchen. She thought about texting Grayson, but to say what? He hadn't made contact and she now wondered if her mum was right. Was she simply a conquest? Did he go up and down the country spinning the same line?

Nursing the hot drink, she tried not to look at the forlorn lump of Daphne, who lay on a plastic bag placed on a cushion on the floor. She wondered now if it were sanitary to have her anywhere near Shelley's soft furnishings.

The television helped her pass the time, first a cookery show where Mary Berry showed her how to fillet a salmon, whip up a hollandaise sauce and poach a pear, followed by a DIY programme where an expert went in to sort stuff out for people whose houses were nearly falling down because they were too lazy or stupid to sort things out for themselves.

Shelley came up the stairs at a little after midnight.

'Thanks for letting me stay here, Shell.'

'S'all right.' Shelley lit a cigarette and sat back in the floppy armchair with her boots up on the coffee table. 'It's not much, but at least it's warm.'

'It is.'

Shelley snickered and looked up at the ceiling. 'Jonathan used to tell me all about the farmhouse and the land and the paddock up where you live, and I thought it sounded like a little slice of heaven. I can't imagine having places to roam, big rooms to wander in and space.'

It was the first time Thomasina had thought about how her life might seem to others; compared to Shelley's existence here in the pub, it was a very lucky life. But still, not enough for her, not now.

'What are you going to do?' Shelley drew her from her thoughts.

'I don't know.' Thomasina spoke the truth. 'I need to make a plan, but starting feels like the hardest part. I keep looking far ahead, but that doesn't help with the right now.'

'So don't look too far ahead. Start with right now, tomorrow, baby steps. I hate to see you like this. You seemed happy the other night when you were in here with that tall man. Happiest I'd ever seen you, kind of settled and confident. Like you knew where you were heading.'

Thomasina pictured lying with Grayson on the grassy bank later that same evening, and the way he had looked at her, the way it had felt to be grabbing life and running with it. *That* was what she wanted more of, that feeling . . .

'I *was* happy. I really like him. But it was also about how he made me feel about myself.' She felt the loss of his company and the yearning for him like a punch to the chest.

'How did he make you feel?'

'He made me feel like . . . like the kind of girl who might own a pair of sparkly red shoes and travel to New York!'

'So why don't you go and find Change Purse and be happy with him?'

'Grayson, his name's Grayson.'

'Yeah, so why don't you go and find him? Time is passing, Hitch, and life isn't going to come to you, love, not around here. You have to go and chase it. Go to New York. Buy the red shoes!'

'You make it sound so easy.'

'I was speaking metaphorically, but at the very least go and knock on his door, say you were just passing and see what he has to say for himself.' Shelley took a drag on her cigarette and Thomasina laughed at her choice of words.

'What you laughing at?' Shelley giggled.

'Just passing!' Thomasina threw her head back on the sofa. 'That's so funny!' She waited for her laughter to ebb and tried to picture herself knocking on his door. 'Supposing he doesn't want me there? Supposing I go all that way and he just stares at me blankly? My mum said I might be reading too much into it – I did only know him for five minutes. Supposing he's the type of man who has girls up and down the country? I'd feel like such an idiot. An idiot a long way from home!'

Shelley sat forward in the chair. 'Darlin', three things. First, he didn't strike me as the kind of ladies' man who has a girl in every town.' She giggled, as if the very idea were amusing. 'And second, I saw the way he looked at you in the bar – like you'd just fallen from Planet Fantastic! I'd bet my entire New Tits Fund that he'd welcome you with open arms.'

Thomasina smiled. 'Did he really look at me like that?'

Her friend nodded. 'He really did.'

Thomasina considered this, grateful for the jolt of excitement that fired through her. 'What's the third thing?'

Shelley sat forward, as if what she was about to impart was of importance. 'Third, if he does turn out to be a dickhead, just say, "I only came to tell you that you're dumped, because I'm worth more!" Then turn on your heel and strut away, head held high, and don't look back!'

'Okay.' She tried to picture herself doing just this. 'How much have you got in your New Tits Fund?' She was curious.

'About sixty-five quid, give or take.'

'Why do you want new tits?' Thomasina looked at her friend's perfectly adequate bosom.

'New tits, more tips.' Shelley winked at her.

'I remember at school, Shell, you were always so good at art. You used to draw such wonderful things and they were brilliant. You should paint, not work behind the bar – or maybe do both until you've built up your business. I'd definitely buy your paintings.'

'Would you?'

'Yes, I really would. I'd have a really big one over the fireplace.'

'I did use to love it. I could just escape when I painted, but it always felt out of my reach. So here I am!' Shelley smiled and seemed to consider her words. 'You never . . .' She paused.

'I never what?'

Shelley took a drag and crossed her legs at the ankles on the table. 'You never really joined in, Thomasina.'

'What d'you mean?'

'I mean, at school, you always kind of hung back and kept your barriers up, as if you expected the worst from everyone.'

'I did expect the worst from everyone. Kids can be horrible – they were to me anyway.' She thought of Emery.

'Yeah, but not all of us. You had friends, you know – you just didn't commit.'

Thomasina thought about the terrible ache of loneliness she had carried throughout her school years and the desperation she had felt at being excluded. 'I thought I was a burden to any social group. I couldn't run or keep up very well and I was never going to help lure the boys in.' She passed her hand over her mouth.

'Yes, but that's not what we thought, certainly not what I thought, only what you did.' Shelley spoke softly and met her gaze.

'I think I was conditioned to think like that, not anyone's fault, not really, but my mum and dad always made me feel a bit different. They were overprotective and told me what I couldn't do and that I had to stay close, stay safe, and I guess I just . . .'

'Went with it because you're a good daughter and it was easier, safer?' Shelley filled in the blanks.

'I guess so. It's only now that I'm shaking off my armour, breaking free a bit.'

'Well, that's good. That's really good. Because it's true what I said – life doesn't come to you, you have to chase it.'

Thomasina nodded. This had never felt truer than now.

'Where's that dead bird, Hitch?'

'She's in the bath now. I moved her off the cushion. I didn't know what to do with her.' Again the reminder of poor, dead Daphne was enough to make her tears bloom.

'So you put her in my bath?' Shelley shook her head. 'For the love of God, go and see Grayskull, or whatever his bloody name is, and take that sodding dead bird with you!'

'I just might.' She pictured herself running into his arms. 'Can I ask you to do something?'

'Sure, what?' Shelley stubbed her cigarette out and stared at her, all ears.

'Can you call me Thomasina?'

Shelley nodded. 'Yes – yes, I can. Thomasina! Now *that's* what I'm talking about!'

The two girls laughed as they sat in the top rooms of the shitty pub that was their whole social life. They laughed because they motivated each other in the way that friends did, with nothing more than their words of positivity, and in those moments everything felt possible.

Thomasina lay on the sofa and again picked up her pen.

I know Shelley is right. I need to find the courage to chase the life I want.

I know I need to find the courage to chase the life I deserve.

I know what I experienced with Grayson felt true.

I know I have never felt as happy as when I was with him.

I know he made me feel brand new.

I know, if he's not the man I thought he was, I'll be crushed.

I know I can rely on Shelley.

I know I can't think about Daphne without crying.

I know I'll miss her.

And I know that this is my turning point. I know I need to stop looking at all the reasons I can't and start thinking of all the reasons I can. And I know that if anyone tells me I can't, I'll tell them I'm worth more and turn on my heel and strut away with my head held high and without looking back!

NINE

Paddington Station was busy, scarily busy, but undercutting her fear was a thrilling sensation of adventure. Here she was in London. The Big Smoke. Alone. There was no Mum reminding her to keep a hand on her bag and no Mrs Pepper hollering over her shoulder in any crowd, 'Stay close! Stay close!'

Thomasina noticed that everyone apart from herself seemed to know where they were going. With her mum's instruction now echoing in her mind, she held her bag close to her chest and studied the Tube map on the wall. People rushed by and there was constant movement and a ricochet of sound that assaulted her senses. She looked around left and right, as if newly stepped from a merry-go-round at the fair, a little dazed and trying to figure out how to stay upright.

The plan had seemed so straightforward in her head. She would confront Grayson and ask him outright if he had felt the same way or whether she had badly misread the situation and he was indeed capable of telling a lie. The outcome would then be one of two things. If he had been telling the truth and did feel the same way, they would make a plan, find a way to navigate life, geography and circumstance . . . because life without him was not half as wonderful as life with him in it. It really was that simple.

If, on the other hand, he *was* a liar, she would stop pining for him and walk away with her head held high, leaving him in his shitty flat and wishing he too might fall down a well, preferably one with Emery already in it, and she would do as Shelley had suggested: not think too far ahead, but grab life and run with it.

Despite such brave and empowering thoughts, her heart raced at the prospect of their reunion with a mixture of excitement and naked fear, and it would be happening sooner rather than later.

'Bakerloo line to Baker Street, then the Jubilee line from Baker Street to Canary Wharf, then I can walk the rest.' She locked this in her mind and descended the stairs that would take her down to the Underground. It felt like the most unnatural thing in the world to be leaving the sunlight and heading beneath the city like a mole or a rat.

'It's okay, don't be scared. You can do this.' She whispered the self-soothing mantra under her breath. The Tube was crowded, dirty, and she knew that, no matter how exciting, this was a life she would find hard to get used to, instantly missing the fresh air and being able to look up at the big sky. The tiled walls of the station were grimy and the carriage itself felt claustrophobic. She more than understood why her fellow commuters all looked so miserable, if this was how they were forced to spend large chunks of their day. The only positive was that, because no one looked up from their phone, newspaper, book or Kindle, they didn't stare at her mouth and it felt nice to be just another face in the crowd.

By the time she emerged from the station, she felt dirty in a way she never did when covered in farm muck. There was something quite unpleasant about breathing second-hand air, and the thought of sharing the cramped space with so many other people all squished together like sardines in the hot, confined carriage was gross. She had hated the Underground and, looking around now, was sorry to admit that she hated what sat above the ground too. This was absolutely nothing like the dazzling Covent Garden or the Chelsea Flower Show, the sanitised face of the capital, scrubbed clean and beribboned for tourists and visitors alike. Her eyes were drawn to the graffiti-covered walls, the litter, the grey concrete and the corrugated iron, ugly buildings, the soot-filled kerbs and the trucks that hurtled by. And she saw in sharp outline all the hard corners, spikes and jagged edges.

Grayson was right: if the countryside was soft, then this place was hard – and too fast-paced for a girl who had spent her entire life in the green and gentle world of Austley Morton. Here in the big city it felt as though life moved to a different rhythm. People hopped up and down the kerbs, skirting around each other, slowing down or speeding up to match the swell of feet in front of them, or jumping to the left or right to dodge obstacles. Everyone seemed well rehearsed in a dance that was new to her and she felt as if she missed a beat with every step she took. Her foot ached and it was rare for her to feel sorry for herself or overly consider her physical difficulties, but as she trod the hard, grey pavement the discomfort threatened to overwhelm her rather. She didn't want to be limping slowly up to his front door, but instead wanted to appear sprightly, appealing, and to make a good impression on his mother. It felt important.

Backing up against the wall, she lifted her foot and rotated her ankle as best she could before smoothing the crumpled square of paper from her jeans pocket and reciting the flat number. Armed with the knowledge that he got home from work at six thirty, she had deliberately timed her journey, knowing she did not want to be hovering in the walkway outside the murderer's home, all alone. It was now a little after a quarter to seven as she slowly trod the ugly concrete stairs of Grayson's tower block. The going was cumbersome with her foot, but the stairs, she had decided, no matter how much a chore, were still preferable if it meant she could avoid the lift, where she knew a large shit had once lurked. Dog or human? The jury was still out.

The reek of urine invaded her nostrils and she spotted discarded syringes gathered in the odd dark corner, no doubt courtesy of the junkies who apparently lived on the top floor. Cautiously, she made her way along the gangway, trying not to look down to the car park below, where vans and cars were tightly parked, or pay attention to the harsh shouts, sirens and the seemingly continual banging of doors that put the fear of God into her.

Nerves began to bite, along with a reluctance to knock at the door, as her earlier courage slipped from her and trickled over the edge of the balcony. She looked back along the path she had trodden and for a second considered leaving quickly and hoping she hadn't been seen, not sure this was worth it. As quickly as the question rose in her mind, it was suffocated with an image of him leaning in as they dawdled by the riverbank and kissing her mouth . . .

Standing outside the half-glazed front door, Thomasina looked to the right, towards the wide picture window that separated this flat from the one next door. She took in the grubby net curtains and the hazy flickering light of a TV, which pooled on to the walkway as dusk now gave way to darkness. A worn coconut mat sat on the floor with three cigarette butts lodged under the side. She took a deep breath and rang the tinny doorbell before taking a step backwards and waiting. As she wondered for the first time who might answer and exactly how she might introduce herself to Mrs Potts, she heard a loud shout from within, so loud she took another step backwards until she rested against the balcony wall. It was a woman's voice, not only loud, but also rather angry.

'Tell them to go away! Disturbing our evening! It'll be bloody Jehovahwhatshisnames. Tell them I gave up my faith when my husband abandoned his marriage vows, ruining my life and destroying my belief in God! That father of yours made a mockery of my promise to the Almighty!'

Thomasina had very little time to digest the shout or react to the naked fear that leapt in her gut when the door opened and suddenly everything felt okay . . . There he was!

Grayson.

Her heart flipped at the sight of him and she felt her face break into a smile that was almost involuntary.

Standing in a white shirt with a tie loosened at his neck and clutching a red cotton napkin in his hand, he stared at her with an expression of disbelief. She felt her legs sway beneath her and her tongue stick to the dry roof of her mouth. It was a relief to find that the excitement he evoked in her had not diminished.

He pushed his long fringe behind his ear and blinked, looking lost for words, and she understood, sharing this mute sense of shock and wonder. She felt a similar collision of fear and joy swirling through her veins, leaving her limbs trembling.

Tentatively, he walked forward and stared at her, as if unable to process that she was here, standing on the very spot, no doubt, where Reggie the murderer had stood without his shoes as the flashing blue lights filled the night sky.

'Hurry up, boy! You're letting all the heat out!' Again the woman's voice hollered from within.

'Sorry.' Thomasina swallowed. 'No message about Jesus. I was just passing.' She watched, as he reached out his fingertips and brushed the side of her face, as though he needed the contact to confirm she was real.

'Thomasina.' He smiled at the sound of her name, as if to utter it brought nothing but sweet relief, which again she understood. She felt a little light-headed and at the same time so happy she wanted to shout out loud!

'The very same.'

'Is this the point at which our two worlds cross over?' he asked quietly, looking briefly over his shoulder, clearly wary of being heard by the shouty lady inside.

'It would appear so. We need to talk, Grayson – we need to talk about stuff.'

'Yes, yes, we do.' He swallowed.

She smiled a little sheepishly, comforted by his agreement and happy that it seemed she was not going to have to employ option three and turn on her heel, mainly because, at this time of night and having climbed several flights of stairs, her foot ached far too much for an effective strut. She too now looked over his shoulder.

'Are you going to invite me in, or do we have to do our talking out here?'

Grayson looked briefly from her back to the door, and she saw the blush of discomfort spread over his face and neck, as if making a judgement call. It made her stomach shrink.

'Please, come in.'

He stood back and, as she passed him in the narrow corridor, the gentle brush of his thigh against her hip was intoxicating. She took in the narrow hallway, where doors painted in yellowing white gloss presumably led off to bedrooms. The carpet was patterned with black and red swirls and coats, jackets and an umbrella were slung on a row of hooks over the radiator.

'Come and eat your bloody tea! There's lemon meringue for afters.'

It was the first time Thomasina noticed the slur to the woman's shouts. She popped her head around the door and looked at the lady to whom the voice belonged: a large woman with thinning hair and a florid complexion who looked a little shoehorned into her narrow seat.

Grayson's mother.

She watched as Mrs Potts, parked in one of two chairs in front of the television, slugged the remaining liquid in her tumbler and immediately reached for the bottle sitting within reach on the floor, with the same eagerness a child might feel for its dummy. She was drunk, was possibly *a* drunk, and this was a surprise to Thomasina and something Grayson had only touched on briefly.

My mum's . . . quite needy and it's hard to break away . . . She's not ill, but I don't know how to describe her, really . . .

There was so much about the cramped room that drew her eye – it was hard to know what to look at first. A small Formica-topped table was pushed up against the wall with a place set for one; a plate with foil partially peeled away revealed a fillet of flaky yellow fish with some kind of pale scum on it and some rather grey-looking runner beans.

A small alcove led through to a kitchenette, while on the wall sat an electric fire with two bars glowing red. A large carriage clock took pride of place on the mantel, *tick-tick-tick*ing loudly. Grayson folded the napkin in his hand and placed it on the table next to his plate.

Mrs Potts looked up from her chair and did a double-take. 'What's going on here, and who might you be?' Her voice was gravelly and on the verge of aggressive.

Thomasina's gut flipped and it took all her courage not to turn and trip right back out of the door. Grayson stepped forward and stood by her side and, when he spoke, she cursed the warble in his voice; it did little to give her confidence. If he was this nervous, what hope was there for her? Mrs Potts hauled herself upright in her chair, staring at her.

'Mum, this is Thomasina. My friend.'

'Your *friend*?' Mrs Potts spoke with an underlying hint of humour, as if such a thing were not possible, pulling her head back on her shoulders before again sipping her wine.

'Yes! We met when Grayson came to stay at my parents' farm just outside Bristol. I'm sure he told you about it,' Thomasina chirped, thinking it might be easier for her to jump in and try to break down any barriers. She remembered Pops's words and figured that, by engaging with his mother, she might be able to spread the joy she carried with her like a scent, hoping at some level to rid the space of the pungent, acrid sting of cigarette smoke and milk-poached haddock.

'Oh, you're *sure* of that, are you?'

Mrs Potts eyed Thomasina suspiciously, and again she felt her confidence shrink into an icy little ball and slip down into her bowel. She could not in a million years imagine her parents greeting anyone in this way, let alone a guest. She felt pity for Grayson, sensing the unease coming off him in waves, an almost tangible thing. The atmosphere was tense, to say the least.

Grayson's mum slurped her wine and narrowed her eyes. 'Well, for your information, he ain't told me nothing! Just sits there like a useless lump. *Friend . . .*' She shook her head.

His mum had spoken so disparagingly and eyed her with a look so close to hatred that Thomasina now gathered herself and dusted off her armour. 'Well, he certainly told me all about you.'

'Did he now?' His mum nodded and twisted her jaw, shifting in her seat as if she were squaring up for battle.

'Yes! He told me about you and his aunties, Eva and Joan, and said that you like a chat, and I thought that was good because I like a chat too. Can I sit down?' She pointed at the empty chair.

'If y'like.' His mum watched her with hawk eyes.

Thomasina sat down, her heart beating somewhere at the base of her throat, as Grayson hovered by the dining table.

'Eva and Joan are my sisters. Joan trained as a hairdresser up west – she's the only person to ever cut Grayson's hair – but she never finished the course, had a baby and that put paid to that. My dad chucked her out, but he was a lovely dad really!' The woman gave her first smile of genuine happiness. 'Different days then, but lovely days. Grandad Arty, Grandma Noella and Betty next door – oh, she was a character. One day Grandma Noella got her leg stuck in the fence between her and Betty's house!' She wheezed with laughter. 'And Betty was screaming, "Get her orf my fence!" And Grandma Noella – she was a fierce old bird, let me tell you – she screamed back, "I can't, I've got me bleeding leg caught!" And then Grandad Arty got mixed up in it all . . . Oh my days!' She wiped her eyes. 'All gone now. All of them, all gone.'

The following silence was sharp and seemed to ring like a bell. Thomasina tried to fill the quiet and build a verbal bridge.

'I like your ornaments.' She ran her eyes over the dusty clutter packed on to the shelves and mantelpiece and, briefly catching Grayson's eye, saw him smile at her act of simple kindness. 'We have a lot of ornaments at home too – most of them were my grandma's. I like to think that I look at the same things she did every day while I'm cleaning or pottering.'

'What's the matter with your mouth?' His mum lifted her half-empty tumbler in the direction of Thomasina's face, lest there be any doubt as to which mouth it was she referred to.

'Oh!' The direct question was a little shocking, but actually Thomasina found it preferable to the whispers behind cupped hands and the stolen glimpses of those who shied away from such questioning. She took a breath, steeling herself. 'I was born with a cleft palate and lip problems, and a few other wonky bits and pieces, and the surgeon who fixed me didn't do the best job, as you can see. It's very different nowadays. I've seen kids born the same as me and you'd never know – they end up with a tiny fine line, hardly noticeable, but I wasn't so lucky. I got this.' She touched her fingers to her own mouth.

'Can you eat and drink all right with that then?' Mrs Potts knew no shame. The path of her words oiled with the liberal application of alcohol meant the query was presented unadorned with pleasantry or politeness.

'Are you kidding me – have you seen these hips of mine?' Thomasina laughed. 'Eating and drinking is definitely not a problem for me.'

'Want some wine?' Grayson's mum lifted the bottle towards her and Thomasina greeted the gesture with a mixture of dread and relief.

'That would be lovely. Thank you.'

'Get her a glass!' Mrs Potts shouted the instruction in her son's direction.

Thomasina watched as he went dutifully to the kitchen and lifted another tumbler from the draining board by the sink, coming back and handing it to her with a certain resignation. Her stomach bunched at the barely perceptible wink he gave her. She watched as Mrs Potts poured a big slug of wine into the glass and handed it to her. Thomasina took a sip of the noxious sweet liquor and smiled sweetly.

'And you've come from Bristol, you say?'

'Yes, on the train.'

'What you come all this way for, this time of night?'

'Actually, I came to see Grayson.'

'Did you now? What for?'

'Because we need to talk about some stuff.' She looked up at him and was glad to see that a little colour had returned to his face.

Mrs Potts gripped the arm of her chair with her free hand and sank back into it. 'Well, good luck getting him to talk to you. I don't get a bloody word out of him – do I?' This last she addressed to her son, as she struggled to keep her eyelids open and her head lolled. 'Goes off to his little job . . . I deserve to hear where he's been and what he's been up to! Bristol!' She drank again. 'What's so bloody important in bloody Bristol and took up so much of his precious time that he couldn't pick up the phone to his old mum or answer a bloody text message!'

'I did reply to you, Mum.' He sighed, and his mother ignored him.

'Just like his bloody father – too busy to chat about his day, leaving me here to sit on me tod, no idea if he's dead or alive! If I didn't have your aunties, I wouldn't've seen a soul for days!'

'I was only in Bristol.'

'Don't I know it – Bristol! Bloody Bristol!' She sat back heavily in her armchair and reached once more for her bottle of wine. 'Might as well have been the Bahamas or Borneo, no damned contact . . . What, don't you have phones in Bristol? Is it a different time zone?' This she addressed directly to Thomasina.

'We do have phones, but where I live we don't always have a phone signal.'

'Charming. Bloody charming!' Mrs Potts shook her head and emptied the bottle into her glass. 'And where, if you don't mind me asking, are you thinking of staying?'

Thomasina stared at Grayson, wondering what came next and already casting her mind as to where she might go and whether it would be possible for him to go with her.

'Well, I was hoping that, if it was all right with you, I could sleep here, but if that's too cheeky then I can go and find a hotel.'

She watched the woman consider this, knocking back the wine as she eyed her up, slipping further and further down in her chair until she looked positively slumped and could barely keep her eyes open. She now roused herself enough, however, to continue shouting, albeit with less coherency.

'You can stay if y'like. There's a blow-up bed of his dad's somewhere. He was an arsehole! *What* an arsehole! Walked out on us, he did, like we was nothing . . . Chucked away, no longer wanted! Just up and went, without so much as a by-your-leave! Snuck out in the dead of night! Coward. You heard the like of it?' She drained her glass again. 'He left me and the boy – just went!' she shouted, slurring her words. 'Bastard!'

Thomasina snuck Grayson a look and closed her eyes in a slow blink, knowing that to hear his dad spoken about in such terms could not be easy.

'Well, how lucky was Grayson to have you, staying put and looking after him. You must have been both a mum and a dad to him.'

'I was!' His mum suddenly beamed, clearly delighted by the compliment. 'I am!'

'Well, there we go.' Thomasina sipped the wine again and pulled a face at Grayson as the less than palatable brew clung to her tongue.

'So, what d'you want to talk to him about? What do you want to tell . . . to tell him?' Mrs Potts hiccupped.

'Oh, lots of things,' Thomasina began. 'I wanted to tell him about one of my chickens.'

His mum slapped the arm of her chair. 'A chicken?'

'Yep, Daphne, one of my hens – a chicken.'

'To eat?' Mrs Potts screwed her face up.

Thomasina shook her head. 'No, not to eat. I had to bury her. In the car park of the pub. She was killed by my cousin Emery.'

'Oh no!' Grayson spoke with a tone of sorrow, as if he knew how much this would mean to her, and she was glad.

'Yes, I'm afraid so.' She smiled sweetly at him over the rim of her glass, trying to be brave, and the look of understanding he gave her was enough to make her heart flex. All she wanted was to remove herself from this pantomime and lie in his arms while he quietly held her tight.

'You took a chicken to the pub?' his mum shouted.

'Yes.' Even she snickered at the absurdity of the statement.

'His dad was an arsehole!' Mrs Potts yelled, as if Thomasina's tale was of no interest and she was desperate to get her message across.

◆　◆　◆

Thomasina stood next to Grayson and the two cleaned their teeth. It felt lovely, performing this intimate task side by side. She sat on the edge of the bathtub while he changed into his striped pyjamas, and they acted without embarrassment, as if they'd been doing this for years.

'I'm sorry about Daphne,' he whispered. 'I know how much she meant to you, that pretty little hen.'

'Thank you.' She swallowed the lump in her throat.

She glanced at Mrs Potts as she crossed the narrow hallway, his mum now snoring noisily in her chair, head back and slack-mouthed.

'Should we move her into her room?' She looked to Grayson for guidance, concerned for the woman's welfare. 'I can help you, if you like.'

He made a kind of *tsk* sound and shook his head. 'She does this most nights. She'll be okay. She's never still there in the morning.'

Thomasina understood that this was normality for him and slipped into his room, closing the door behind her.

'You're right, this is a very small bedroom.'

'With a very small bed.' They both looked at the narrow mattress.

'Well, I seem to remember, not so many nights ago, we fell asleep on a rug on the side of a river in the dark. We should consider a bed a rare treat. No matter how small.' She thought about that wonderful, wonderful night.

'I guess. I couldn't imagine you being here, not when I compared it to that lovely room at Waycott Farm.'

'And yet here I am.' She shrugged.

'Yes, here you are. I can't believe it.'

'When I saw my little Daphne dead, I just wanted to see you. I knew you'd get it, how awful it is.' She bit her bottom lip. 'Although I felt a lot better the moment I set out for London. I feel brave.'

'You are brave. And it is awful, about Daphne.' He was silent for a second or two in reverence.

'Your mum, she seems . . . Is she . . .'

'She's an alcoholic,' he interjected. 'I don't know why I didn't tell you. Actually, I do know,' he corrected himself. 'I shied away from it because when she's drunk she's unpleasant and when she isn't drunk she's marginally less unpleasant.'

'It can't be easy for you.' She leaned back on a walnut-coloured chest of drawers.

'I'm used to it.' He picked at a loose thread on the collar of his pyjamas.

'Does anyone help you? Do you have anyone to talk to about it?' She hated the thought of the burden falling on his narrow, kindly shoulders.

'Not really. I've spoken to my aunts about it in the past, but they don't really help. They drink with her and then leave me to clear up the mess. I think they find it funny, but it isn't. Liz at work once told me I should call my mum's bluff and move out. She said it might force her to take control, to confront the situation, and so I did.' He paused.

'What happened?' She liked Liz, despite having never met her. The woman's advice and logic seemed sound.

He gave a deep sigh that sounded like defeat. 'I moved out, rented a flat near work, and she was furious. She didn't think I'd go through with it, and then, when I did, she got drunk and burned herself quite badly – fell on to the electric fire.'

'Oh God!'

'Yep, and a short while later, a couple of days, she knocked on all the neighbours' doors in the early hours and was ranting, and they had to call the police, who called me. And another time she fell in the bathroom and knocked her tooth out, and another she nearly set fire to the chair with a cigarette.' He looked skyward and let his arms rise and fall. 'You name it, she did it, and I kept getting the calls late into the night and early morning, which was wearing and stressful, and when I didn't get calls it was wearing and stressful, as I couldn't imagine what was going on, and I was on edge, waiting for the calls. So I gave up, came back home and here we are.'

'You should have told me what it was like for you, told me about your life here.'

'I don't really tell anyone. It's shameful and it's not the life I wanted.'

Thomasina looked at him in earnest. 'No, no, Grayson, it's not shameful. It's quite amazing how much you do for her to keep her well and how selfless you are. There aren't many who would. And you do it because you're a good son and because, in the end, it feels easier, safer . . .'

'I guess so.' He looked down, as if weary.

'But the truth is, Grayson, time is passing and life doesn't come to you – you have to chase it.'

'Or sometimes it does come to you, because here you are.' His face brightened. 'I've thought so much about all the things I want to say to you and what it might feel like to have you here, and now that you are I feel a bit tongue-tied.'

'That's okay. You don't have to say anything and you don't have to feel nervous. Everything is okay. Your mum's asleep and I have no intention of rooting around to find your dad's blow-up bed.'

He nodded. 'He wasn't an arsehole.' He kept his voice low, picking at the button on his pyjama top.

'I know.' She placed her hand on his arm and he laid his palm over it, anchoring her to him. Her heart pulsed.

'And he didn't sneak out in the dead of night. He spoke to me, told me he was sorry.'

'He must have felt so torn.'

He nodded. 'I'm sorry about the way she spoke to you.'

'That's okay. She's just lonely and probably a bit scared, and alcoholism is a horrible sickness.'

'What do you think she's scared of?' He looked a little perplexed.

'That you might run out on her, like your dad did. That she might be left alone. That she might lose you.'

'I guess so. I can't pretend my sympathy hasn't worn thin over the years, because it has. Ironically, it's the way she behaves that might make me run out on her. I'm sick of it, and yet I love her, feel responsible for her. It's complicated.'

'Families always are.' She thought of the pull of the farm and how she and her parents leaned on each other.

'I'm happy you're here, Thomasina.'

'Me too. I didn't want to force you to see me, in case you didn't feel the same, but I had this . . .' She faltered.

'This what?'

162

She placed her hand on her stomach. 'This horrible ache. Like I'd lost something and I needed to find it. I felt sad, really lonely – and I missed you. Does that make any sense?' She twisted her face upwards to look at him.

'It does. It makes complete sense.'

'Did . . . did you miss me at all, Grayson?' She felt dry-mouthed with nerves at asking. But this was bold! This was chasing life!

'Every second.' He nodded. 'I missed you every second. I thought about you all the time and I couldn't get to sleep for thinking about you, and I thought about you from the moment I woke up until the moment I went back to sleep.'

Thomasina reached out and took his hand. The feel of his dry palm against hers was life-affirming, warm and wonderful. 'Really?'

'Really. You are the best person, smart and beautiful.' He ran his fingers over the side of her face.

'You make me feel beautiful.'

'You make me feel beautiful.' He spoke sincerely, easily, the truth. 'Thank you for coming to find me.'

'I didn't feel like I had any choice. I wanted to see you, Grayson, to make sure you were the man I thought you were. I couldn't understand why we didn't make more of a plan, but I get it now, now I've seen . . .' She nodded her head in the direction of the lounge, where his mum was sleeping off the drink.

'I want to be the man you think I am. I want to be the man you make me think I can be.'

'And I want you to feel about me the way I feel about you.' She reached up and kissed his face.

'I do.' He kissed her in return. 'I do.'

Grayson let go of her hand and pulled back the duvet before lying down on his side. He lay watching her, propped up on his elbow in the half-light as she shrugged off boots and jeans, leaving them in a crumpled pile on the carpet. The feel of his skin as she slid in next to him was a moment she knew she would never, ever forget. It was as if all the spaces were suddenly filled – those aching voids of loneliness, the crevices that had turned into canyons over the years, levered open ever wider by self-doubt until she was almost entirely comprised of hollow pockets of emptiness. She felt whole with a warmth that started in her stomach and spread throughout her limbs, and at that precise second she knew what it felt like to be one of those neat, clean, glossy and artfully painted girls with knowledge of what to wear, how to act and where to go – knowledge that was now hers too, because here she was with a man as wonderful as Grayson Potts.

And it felt as if the whole wide world and all it had to offer lay in the palm of her hand.

I know he's the man I thought he was.

I know he's more than the man I thought he was.

I know what pure happiness feels like.

I know I'm going to carry on being brave and making things happen!

I know I absolutely hate Liebfraumilch.

TEN

Thomasina opened her eyes slowly and was happy to find herself wrapped in Grayson's arms. It was the dead of night, and she looked around in the darkness at the wooden furniture with its air of utilitarian functionality, along with the map on the wall, the shiny brown curtains and the apricot wallpaper. It was a dated and depressing room, despite the bubble of joy in which they nestled.

'Are you awake?' he whispered into her hair.

'I might be. Are you?' She giggled, sliding down the bed and turning dexterously until her face rested against his chest. 'I can't sleep.'

'Because it's so cramped.'

'No, Grayson, because I'm happy! Excited! And I don't want to waste a second of being with you.'

He kissed the top of her head and combed her hair with his fingers. 'What are you thinking?'

'Oh.' She considered lying, but instead told him plainly, 'I was thinking that your bedroom is sad. There's no colour here and nothing pretty.'

'I know. When my dad left, I remember sitting in here and thinking it felt like a safe place to be, the last place I saw him and where I could picture him, hear his words. But then, as I got older, I could see that it was as miserable as the slow beat of a solitary drum – you know, the way that sound goes right through your chest and drags grieving from you, lays it bare.'

Thomasina nodded. She understood what he meant and again appreciated the beautiful eloquence of his words.

'So, I put more stuff in it: the wall map, the books.' He took a breath and looked at her briefly. 'But it still feels like a sad place, a prison. So when I'm here, I spend a lot of my time looking out of the window. Looking down on the world and the strings of lights that shine brightly in the rain and punch holes in the dark.'

His eyes twinkled, and she liked the look of him when he spoke like this, animated and happy. She was so very intrigued by anything to do with him.

'My dad told me once that the tower blocks where we live are ugly – "Ugly on the outside, ugly on the inside, but there's magic if you know where to look for it." That's what he told me and he was right. I didn't always know what he meant, but he used to say we had a rich man's view: we get to see something quite remarkable – London from way up high. And we get it for free!'

'I'm afraid I don't really know what you mean.' She felt a little foolish for having completely lost the thread.

'I like to rest my elbows on the windowsill and look at all the lights twinkling in the dusk. It's wonderful. It makes the city look otherworldly and strangely beautiful, and yes, like magic – the way the ugly, bland, square, mismatched, unloved concrete buildings that during the day reek of deprivation by night become almost a single thing. And it's a beautiful thing, a community almost, unified by the street lights that line the routes, looping in every direction and joining the dots. They're a dazzling carpet of lights, shining brightly from windows and headlamps, a clear sparkle against the inky sky.'

'I remember you asked if we had any street lamps when you arrived at Waycott Farm. I thought it was a strange question!'

'It probably was. Come and look at this.' He raised his knees and scrabbled out from under the duvet. Leaning against the headboard, he threw the heavy red curtains open wide and placed his elbows on the windowsill. Thomasina took up position in the small space to his left, the mattress creaking under their combined weight, and she too leaned on her elbows on the windowsill.

He pointed down towards the industrial area and the housing estate and the tower blocks beyond. 'Look, you can see for miles and miles from here.'

'Yes, you can!'

She leaned closer to the glass, aware he was studying her profile, and it felt nice to be able to share one of his favourite things.

'It's like,' she began, 'it's like looking at the stars, all those blurry dots of light as far as your eye can see, but upside down, like a mirror of the night sky. It's beautiful.'

'I'm glad you think so.'

'Now show me the slice of moon you can see through the window!' She wriggled out from the bed and stood in the narrow gap of floor between the bed and the wardrobe.

'Okay.' He laid his head back on the pillow. 'You have to tip your head back and close your right eye.'

She jumped back into bed and copied his pose and, sure enough, there in the top corner of the window was a slice of the moon.

'I see it!' She kicked her legs against him in excitement. They laughed, remaining still until their breathing had settled. Thomasina shifted until her cheek again lay on his chest. He placed his arm around her and pulled her to him, kissing the top of her head.

'Can I ask you something, Grayson?'

'Yes, anything.'

'When I asked if you had been with anyone before and you said yes, who was it, or have there been lots of people?' She wanted to understand the measure of him, learn the Grayson before they met.

'Oh!' He swallowed nervously. 'Not lots, no. It was only one time, with a girl called Melinda Liebermann. An American intern who was leaving the trading floor at the bank, and we had to go out. Everyone was invited and we all got very drunk. And it was then.' He shrugged, suggesting at worst disappointment and at best indifference to what clearly should have been a moment of great note. 'I didn't see her again after that night. I can't really remember her face. What . . . what about you?' he asked nervously.

She answered honestly in spirit with his own directness. 'I'm telling you because I remember what you said, and I never want to lie to you either. I don't want anyone knowing something about me that you don't.'

'I appreciate that. I've always thought that if my parents had been able to talk openly about everything then there might have been a different solution other than him running out on us.'

'That might be true.' She drew on all her courage. 'I had sex with Tarran Buttermore, one of the local farmers. Now, he *is* an idiot!' She watched him closely, trying to gauge his reaction.

'Did you think he was an idiot before you had sex with him?'

She gave an inappropriate snort of laughter, wondering how to explain her simultaneous revulsion and attraction for a boy she knew at an intimate level and yet who was still a stranger in so many ways. 'I did, yes, but I didn't care at the time. I just wanted someone to want me . . . and he kind of did for a little while, a few minutes. But not really . . .' she whispered, thinking of her recent humiliation in the car park.

'I want you.'

'You do?' She kissed his face.

'I do, and before I couldn't see how we could make it work, not with things how they are here and you so far away, but then not seeing you . . .' He shook his head. 'That's not going to work either. I hated it.'

'I hated it too. There are lots of things I want to do, Grayson. I want to see the world, try a new life, and I want to do it with you.'

Grayson leaned forward and kissed her. 'I'd like that. And as for Tarran, we can't change or worry about what has gone on before, that would be completely pointless. We are brand new, remember?'

'We are, Grayson. We are brand new.'

◆　◆　◆

In the morning, as the sun rose over the city, Thomasina reflected on the extraordinary night, quite something in this very ordinary room in which seemingly nothing out of the ordinary ever happened. Grayson hummed a tune of his own composition.

'I don't know how many thousands of nights I've spent in this room, but I know I'll always remember this one. Will you be okay while I go and shower?'

'Yes,' she said, nodding, his concern touching.

He took his time in the shower, and she sat listening to him sing, unable to wipe the happy smile from her face and yet equally anxious about the next hour or so of her life, when she would again have to face his mum, whom she could hear rattling around in the kitchen. Her skin was suddenly covered in goose bumps and she shivered at the prospect of coming face to face with the sober version of his mother. Thomasina sat on the bed and took deep breaths, consoling herself with the thought that, when drunk, the woman lost her filter and was more than a little mean, but this morning she was probably regretting last night's outburst and might be all sweetness and light to compensate. Thomasina certainly hoped so, feeling a sudden flash of homesickness for the cosy kitchen table in front of the range and the feel of Buddy's muzzle against her cheek in greeting.

The door opened and in walked Grayson, newly shaven with wet hair, and apart from his long fringe hanging down to the tip of his nose, he looked smart in his freshly ironed shirt and trousers.

'Breakfast is on the table!' she heard his mum call.

Thomasina leaned back against the headboard with her knees up and her arms clasping her shins. It was the first time he'd seen her in daylight in a state of undress and with her hair all messy. He sat on the edge of the bed and gathered a section of it, running his fingers over the ends as if fascinated by the cascade of hair that spilled over her shoulder. 'It's not one colour, but a thousand shades of brown and, where the light catches it, it's almost gold.'

'I like the way you see me, Grayson.'

'You hair is one of the most beautiful things I've ever seen.'

'Good Lord, give me strength, do you want this bloody breakfast or not?' his mother shrieked, interrupting the moment.

'I'm coming!' he called towards the door. 'Did you get any sleep?' he now asked Thomasina.

'Not much. Did you?'

'Not much.'

They giggled.

'How's your mum this morning? I'm a bit scared to go out there.' She pulled a face.

He looked at the floor. 'Haven't seen her yet. But it'll be okay.' He spoke with reticence and she wasn't sure whom he was trying to reassure. 'Do you want to shower?'

'Yes, please.'

Thomasina showered quickly and stepped from the bathroom into the lounge with a sick feeling in her gut.

This was it. Time to pull on her big-girl pants and go and face the music.

His mum was back in her chair, nursing a mug of tea and staring out of the window. The TV was off and the sound of Grayson chewing on his boiled egg seemed especially loud.

'Morning!' Thomasina's sweet, happy greeting was alien in this environment, like putting ribbons on a dark rock or seeing a rainbow rise over the city dump.

'You'd best get a move on.' Mrs Potts spoke between sips of her tea. 'Don't want to miss your bus, son.' The woman ignored Thomasina's greeting, and it was so awkward it left her feeling cold.

'Grayson, you'll miss your bloody bus at this rate!' his mum hollered from the chair.

'Okay. Okay.'

'You don't want to get into trouble with your little job, do you?' she yelled.

'Nope.' Grayson rolled his eyes at Thomasina. 'Would you like a cup of tea?' He blushed, clearly embarrassed at his mother's snub.

Thomasina scanned the table and glanced at his mum, who still sat with her back turned. There was no place set for her, no table mat and certainly no teacup.

'No, no, that's fine, thank you. I can grab one later.' She smiled and sat at the table next to him.

His mum turned slowly, her expression one Thomasina could only describe as thunderous. 'Blow-up mattress comfy enough for you, was it?'

'Oh! I didn't . . . erm . . . we didn't . . .' Thomasina faltered.

'Thomasina slept in my bed,' Grayson said levelly, and she admired him for it, knowing it was better not to deceive his mum, while at the same time rather hoping the specifics of the previous night would not be broached. She watched as Mrs Potts stood and pulled the crumpled tunic down over her stomach. 'I know she did!' she spat. 'Think I was born yesterday?'

Grayson laid his spoon by the side of his plate and pulled the red napkin from his neck. Clearly, he was finished.

His mum, however, was not. She drew breath, seemingly reloading for her next verbal assault. 'This is *my* flat, *my* home. And you think you can bring any old floozy here, day or night, like it's some kind of whorehouse?'

'Please don't talk like that.' Grayson looked at Thomasina and shook his head. This whole exchange was terrible! As humiliating as it was unnecessary.

'I'll talk how I please under my own roof!' she shouted.

'Actually, Mum, it's my roof too.' He spoke softly.

'What did you say?' She jerked her head forward.

'I said it's my roof too.'

'Is that right?' His mother cackled in a way that, when used to bookend something she clearly didn't think was funny, was nothing short of sinister. 'If you think she's shacking up in your room another night, you've got another think coming.'

'I have no intention of staying another night,' Thomasina began. 'I—'

'Who rattled your cage? And what did he tell you? Did he tell you I was a drinker? Because I'm not!'

It was his mum's unfounded aggression that took Thomasina by surprise. She had expected a sore head, hoped for contrition, but this was something else.

Grayson stood abruptly. 'I need to leave now. I need to get to work.'

'See what you've done?' his mum shouted at Thomasina. 'You've upset him, and you've upset me! Coming all that way and sliding into his bed – what sort of girl does that?'

'Please don't talk to her like that, Mum!' Grayson's voice rose.

'And I told you that I'll talk any way I damn well please in my own flat!'

'It's okay, Grayson. I need to go anyway.' Thomasina's cheeks were aflame and she wanted to be anywhere else, anywhere other than here.

'You don't have to go,' he said, swallowing.

'What you talking about?' his mum yelled. ''Course she's got to go! This is my home!'

'Mum! For God's sake!' He clenched his fists. 'Just stop! I don't want to hear you talking the way you do, I don't want you to be so angry about everything, and I don't want you to be so rude to Thomasina!'

'It's okay, I—'

'No, Thomasina!' Grayson fired back. 'I mean it. It's not okay!'

'You kidding me?' His mum leaned on the back of a dining chair. 'You're taking the side of this little madam you've known five minutes? Who turns up on my doorstep in the dead of night and thinks nothing of sinning under my own roof!'

'Since when did you care about sin?' he asked.

'Don't you cheek me!' Her face was puce and her mouth quivered, Thomasina suspected, with equal measures of fear and all the poisonous retorts she still had left to fly.

'Come on, Thomasina.' Grayson took her hand and led her back to the bedroom, where he picked up his satchel and watched as she pulled on a boot, lacing it over her foot, which still carried the residual ache of yesterday.

Back in the living room, Thomasina couldn't help but raise her hand in a small wave, thinking it would be impolite to leave without any gesture, but Grayson closed the front door behind them without saying goodbye to his mum.

Thomasina walked ahead, scanning the concrete walkway, looking for junkie shit or needles.

'I bet you wish you'd never come down here.'

'No, Grayson, the very opposite. I wish I had come sooner.' She drew a breath. 'I don't like how you live. I don't like how your mum treats you, and I know it's not my place to say, but that's how I feel.'

'I don't like it either.' He kicked at the floor and tucked his fringe behind his ear.

'So . . .' she began. 'So why don't you do something about it? Change it?'

He held her gaze and spoke with the glint of tears in his eyes. 'Because I promised.' He bit his lip. 'I promised my dad. And I don't know what she'd do.'

'But you know, Grayson . . .' She framed her thoughts carefully. 'Your dad was wrong to hand that burden to you. You were just a little boy! He couldn't hack it, he did a runner, no matter how calmly, and yet he expected you to pick up the slack, and that's very selfish. Plus, he might have just said it like a casual goodbye or to give you something to focus on after he'd gone, but I'm sure he didn't mean for you to be holed up here, trapped, looking after her instead of living your own life.'

'That's more or less what Liz said.'

'Well, for what it's worth, I think Liz is right. I also think that your mum needs help, but it's not help that you can give her, necessarily. She needs to see someone who understands about her illness.'

He laughed. 'That's the trouble. You heard her – she can't admit that she drinks' – he gestured towards the flat – 'let alone understand that she has an illness.'

'I'll help you, Grayson, if you want me to. There must be information available. You can't be the first person in this situation. Plus, I can be the person you talk to. I don't know if I'll always say the right thing, but just talking things through can make it feel better sometimes.' She thought about her own situation and resolved to try harder to find a solution to all the things that bothered her about life on the farm. Maybe she should talk to Emery directly, have it out? And as for selling Waycott, she decided to get more involved, either to help ease the process for everyone or at the very least so she fully understood the situation. Knowledge, she decided, was how she would best find the answers to everything that irked her. She figured it would be the same for Grayson and his ghastly mother.

'Yes, please.' He took her hand in his and kissed her knuckles.

She walked down the stairs full of hope, with a new lightness to her spirits and clarity to her thoughts. With Grayson by her side, she hardly noticed the smell of urine, the piles of takeaway wrappers littering the steps or the new graffiti across the wooden door at the bottom of the stairwell – a spray-painted image of a smoking gun.

'Oh no!' She felt his hand stiffen.

'What's the matter?'

'It's Mr Waleed, by the bins!'

She looked over at the little bull of a man lobbing full, knotted black bin bags into the dark abyss. He lifted them with ease, this man who used to be a wrestler. Grayson waved to him in greeting.

'Your mother!' he shouted, by way of response. 'She laugh so loudly, Grayson, she shout, she stamp her feet! What in the name of God is she doing up there! Is she dancing? Because I have to tell you that I don't feel like dancing, not with her up above me, *bang, bang, bang!* My kids moan, my wife moans – and now my mother-in-law, she is learning English so she can moan at me in three different languages!'

'I'm sorry, Mr Waleed.'

'It's not you, Grayson. You're good man. But your mother?' He shook his head. 'Maybe you take after your father.'

Despite the fraught exchange, Thomasina saw the small creep of a happy smile on Grayson's face, as if this were the first time it might have occurred to him: the idea that he not only carried some of his father with him, but also that he was not like his shouting mother, who liked to stamp her feet.

'Yes, I think I might.'

'Well, I go talk to her again! Have a nice day!' Mr Waleed raised his hand in a wave as they crossed the main road.

Thomasina blinked. 'I'm sorry if I've caused trouble for you with your mum.'

'You haven't. The trouble has been there for a while, probably for-ever, and don't apologise about coming to find me. It's the best thing that's ever happened to me.'

She leaned up and kissed his face and knew the novelty of that one act would never dull for her, the joy would never diminish. 'What are you going to do? Go back and talk to her now?'

'No.' He shook his head. 'I need to get to work, plus, she'll have calmed down by tonight, but I know things need to change.'

'I feel the same,' she said, scuffing her toe on the pavement. 'I know things need to change for me too. I need to step out from under my mum and dad's wings. I need to find my own way, sleep under my own roof and have my own cake tins, start living . . .'

He squeezed her hand. 'It's scary, but exciting too, isn't it?'

'It is. I'll walk you to the bus stop, Grayson, and then make my way to Paddington to get the train back home to Bristol, but we can make a plan of how and when we'll see each other again, if you like . . .' She let this trail.

'I do like. Of course I like!' This time it was his turn to bend down and kiss her. 'I shall come and stay and you can come and . . .' He floundered.

'I can come to London and meet you somewhere that isn't your flat!' She laughed.

'Yes, something like that. We'll make it happen, Thomasina.'

'Yes, we will,' she agreed, with something like fireworks exploding in her gut.

'I can't believe Emery did that to Daphne.'

'I believe it. Nothing surprises me about him. He's so nasty,' she whispered.

'He didn't seem that nasty to me. But you've known him longer,' he conceded.

'Trust me, he's a shit.'

'And we don't like shits.'

'We don't. Not in the lift, not from a dog, and not the human variety like Emery.'

They laughed. It felt nice to have an in-joke.

'Will you be okay?' He held her hand.

'I'll be fine. Can I call you?'

'Yes, call me. Call me any evening – in fact, call me any time if ever you need anything, anything at all, and I'll try and help, or at least listen. I want you to know that I will always, always, try to make your life the best it can be. If I can do anything to help you, then I will, because that's what you deserve, Thomasina. You are amazing, that much I know. And I can't wait for the day that you own your own cake tins, if that's important to you!'

She beamed at him. 'That means the world to me, Grayson.'

He reluctantly let go of her hand and climbed on to the waiting bus. Thomasina watched him settle into his seat and, in that moment, as the bus pulled away, he blew her a kiss and she felt like the most beautiful girl in the world.

I know for the first time that I don't feel afraid for my future.

I know that I want to rescue Grayson and I know that he will rescue me.

I know what being in love feels like!

I know that I've found someone who is kind and good.

I know I don't want to live in London. A day trip to Covent Garden is all right, but to live here among the tower blocks and be too afraid to dance in case Mr Waleed shouts at you by the bins? No, thank you.

ELEVEN

With a mixture of relief and disappointment, Thomasina walked into the kitchen of the farmhouse. Buddy leapt up from his basket like a pup and pawed at her thigh, panting, his tail wagging and an expression that was as close to a smile as he could manage. She bent low and kissed his muzzle, running her hands over his handsome face and whispering her affectionate greeting. Her parents' reaction to her homecoming after two days of absence was a little more muted. It wasn't that she wanted an altercation, having stormed out, and she certainly wasn't in the mood for celebratory fireworks on her return, but their quiet acceptance of her dramatic flounce, almost an indifference, made her feel, at best, a little foolish. Her dad looked up from reading the *Gazette* and winked, returning to the article that was, apparently, gripping him. Her mum paused from stirring the soup in the pot on the range and looked at her briefly.

'There's a cup of tea in the pot, Thomasina. Welcome home, darlin'.'

She liked the way her mum used her name, as requested, and used it with ease. It meant a lot.

'Thank you. Did you miss me?'

'Well, it was quiet!' her dad quipped.

'How are my girls doing?' she asked, grabbing a mug from the drainer and collecting the teapot from the trivet.

'They're all good. A little unsettled at night, no doubt missing their friend.'

'Daphne.' Thomasina looked briefly at her mum, who rolled her eyes, but with a crinkle of understanding around her crow's feet. 'Daphne . . .' she muttered under her breath.

'I was proper worried until you texted,' her dad said with a sigh. 'I went running up the paddock to find you and you'd disappeared! Fancy walking to the pub. I'd have run you in – it's no good for your foot, all that walking.'

'I wanted to walk, Pops. Help clear my head.'

'I can understand that.' He smiled. 'So you stayed at the pub for a couple of nights?' He finally closed the paper. 'Did you hear anything on the grapevine about the offer for the farm? I expect it's what people are talking about – can't keep nothing secret around here.'

She spun around. 'Is it common knowledge then, the offer?' She felt a little anxious at how fast things seemed to be moving.

'Well, I don't know about common knowledge, but it's moving forward, for sure. The lawyer in Bristol called me, told me it's the Buttermores who made the approach.'

'Well, that's no surprise.' She sighed. 'But no, I didn't hear anything about it, Pops. Is it a serious offer, is it what you were expecting?'

''Bout as serious as they come.' He tweaked the edge of the newspaper.

'Anyway, I didn't really hang about in the pub.' She took a breath and spoke with confidence. 'I was only there for one night. I went to London.'

'London?'

'London!'

Her parents shouted in unison. It made her laugh.

'Yes, London! Christ, it's not the moon!'

'Yes, but London.' Her dad tutted. 'Terrible place, full of crowds and noise, where folk scuttle like mole rats underground – t'ain't natural!'

'It's London, only a couple of hours away, really.' She smiled, thinking of the stinky stairwell, Grayson's narrow bed and his awful, awful mother.

'Well, get you, Miss Cosmopolitan!' her mum said, chuckling. 'London! I don't know, whatever next? New York?'

'Oh God, I do hope so!' Thomasina took a chair at the table, a little pleased now that the atmosphere was conciliatory and that Emery was nowhere to be seen.

'So where did you stay, as if we need ask?' Her mum mumbled the last bit.

'Yes, I stayed with Grayson. And it was lovely to see him again.'

'Did his people make you welcome?'

Thomasina snorted. 'Not exactly. He lives with his mum and she's . . .' She blew out through pursed lips, recalling the woman's venomous manner. 'She's a proper handful.'

'Really, and him being so quiet?'

'I know. I reckon it's because he can't get a word in edgeways!' In her jest lay more than a kernel of truth.

'But it went well, did it, love? He was nice to you, was he?'

Her mum's pained expression tugged at Thomasina's heart strings. It was nice to be loved and, having spent time with Ma Potts, she knew just how much, but still she felt the weight of the suffocating blanket of love around her shoulders, and she'd only been home for a few minutes . . .

'We spoke to Jonathan yesterday,' her dad said, steering the conversation in a different direction. 'Had a long chat about everything.'

'How is he?' She took a chair at the table, grateful for the immediate and familiar cup of tea in her hands. Buddy lay across her feet, anchoring her to the place, as if asking her never to leave him again. She touched his ears.

'He was thoughtful, you know, quiet – it's a lot to take in – but he listened to what I had to say and he agreed,' her dad offered in summary.

She was confused. 'Agreed to what?'

He shifted in the chair. 'Are you not listening to me, Thomasina? I told him about the call from the lawyer. The offer! What d'you think I called him for, to talk about the weather?'

'Sorry, Pops. I didn't realise we were at "offer-accepting" stage. I feel like it's happening a bit fast.' She sat up straight. 'And you know, I'd like to talk about it too. I want to be fully informed. It's not just Jonathan's life that will change.'

'We know that, lovey,' her mum interjected.

'But also, I don't want you and Mum to be rushed or feel pressured. You *are* going to think about it all carefully?'

'It's all I can think about, love.' He bit his lip. 'Yes, it's all moving quite fast, and you're right, you should know what's going on and the situation we're in. After all, you're a grown woman.'

She felt the bloom of something warm in her gut. These words from her dad felt a lot like progress, an acceptance that she'd quietly yearned for.

He tapped the table with his working man's fingers. 'The truth is, things are . . . things are tough. More so maybe than your mum and I have let on.' He glanced at his wife and Thomasina felt her presence as an intrusion to the current of intimacy that flowed between them. It made her think of Grayson and she felt a burst of longing for him.

'How tough exactly?' She took a sip of the strong brew in her mug and pushed the soles of her boots against the flagstones, steeling herself. It wasn't easy to hear that her beloved parents might be suffering.

Her dad swallowed and looked towards the window, then the door – anywhere, she noticed, other than her face.

'We are . . . we are struggling, love, and I can't . . .' He stopped and sighed, as if the words carried a physical weight he did not have the strength to bear. 'I'm tired. Your mum is tired, and it would be one thing to work as hard as we do and enjoy the rewards, but there are no rewards. It's never-ending. The early starts in all weathers, the late finishes . . . I've lived with one eye on the clock my whole life – my whole life,' he said, letting this sink in, 'always alert to the next task waiting for me, and now I want a rest.' He nodded, as if this was it in summary, the point of the discussion. 'I want a rest and I want to be able to buy your mum a new frock.'

She thought about the shiny red shoes that lived in her mind and a wave of sadness threatened to engulf her. It was such a sweet and simple desire from a man who had worked so very hard yet was struggling to buy his wife this one simple thing.

'I don't need a new frock! Never go anywhere to wear a new frock!' her mum offered affectionately, her eyes on the soup.

'That's not the point!'

He spoke a little more forcefully than Thomasina was used to, and it jarred, reminding her that, however hard the whole idea of giving up the family farm might be for her and her brother, for her dad, it was a whole lot more painful. And her heart flexed for him.

He continued, quieter now. 'I want choices. I want a holiday! I want change.' It didn't seem like much to ask.

Thomasina put her mug on the table. The theme of change seemed to be a recurring one, and she understood. 'How much are they offering?' She couldn't believe they were getting down to the detail, making it real, and yet here they were.

'Enough for us to sell the farmhouse and most of the land and to retain a couple of acres we can build a bungalow on.'

'A bungalow?' She tried to picture her mum and dad in a new house – well-nigh impossible when she'd always thought of them as part of the fabric of this old building. A bit like the legend of the ravens deserting the Tower of London foretelling doom and disaster, she wondered what might happen if the Waycotts left.

'Yes,' her mum said, picking up the thread. 'A little place with straight walls, central heating, hot water on demand from an efficient boiler, new carpet, double-glazed windows that keep out the draughts and don't rattle at the first breath of wind, and new furniture – things from Ikea!'

'Ikea!' Thomasina rubbed her face, trying to picture this compact, glossy, neat, square world her parents were trying to paint.

'It means we can retire happy, safe and warm without worry. Can you imagine what that would feel like, not to have the worry?' Again her father looked at his wife.

Thomasina realised that they deserved this reward for all the hard physical labour over the years. But no matter that this was what she told herself, the thought of handing over the keys that had jangled in the pocket of her great-grandmother's apron – and handing them over to the Buttermores, no less – was enough to bring a swirl of nausea to her gut. She pictured Tarran swinging a hammer on this rickety kitchen, radio blaring as he set to work replacing the worn wooden cupboard doors and ancient range with something sharp, modern and shiny. It was almost unthinkable, and yet it was on the verge of happening.

'And I could get my own place . . .' She spoke with a hard-summoned nod of enthusiasm that she did not feel.

'A place of your own? You daft thing, you'd be with us, of course!' her mum tutted, as if nothing else could be a possibility.

'You know, I'd be all right on my own. I've just travelled to London and back and I managed just fine. I—'

'But supposing you had a bad fall,' her mum interrupted breathlessly, 'like you did when you slipped on the top stair – that was terrible! I won't ever forget the sight of you lying on the flagstones with your leg all bruised and your face bleeding!'

'I was twelve, Mum!'

'Or supposing you had another turn with your heart? I'm the one who has to give you your pills and keep an eye on you!' She bit her lip.

'But, Mum, I'm not a kid any more. You don't need to keep an eye on me. I can take my own pills. I need to spread my wings . . . get my own bloody cake tins!' A torrent of frustration and sadness flooded through her. Her dad might now regard her as a fully grown woman, but her mum clearly still had a little catching up to do.

Her parents stared at her open-mouthed, as if she'd lost the plot.

Thomasina tried to picture herself in a new house, away from her square room with the saggy mattress on the brass bed and the damp patch on the ceiling that in certain lights looked like a map of Australia. Her childhood bookshelves crammed with Anna Sewell, Enid Blyton and Joyce Lankester Brisley, each page glued together with dust – particles of her whole lifetime. The secret space behind the chest of drawers where she'd written *I hate Jonathan*, aged about six, and then tried to colour it over with red felt-tip. She smiled at the thought of her evil deed being revealed after all these years. And yes, it would mean walking away from her childhood home, her history, but this was a new chapter. She remembered the tractor pedal beneath her feet and the wide steering wheel in her hands when she was nine and that feeling, as if she could put her foot down and keep going, smashing through fences, fields and across rivers, just keep on going, in charge of her own destiny, free to go wherever the fancy took her . . .

'I can't lie – it breaks my heart, the thought of seeing another family, especially one like the Buttermores, living in our house, but I can see that it's not worth it, not worth carrying on when you can have a different life, a better life for you now. You deserve a rest, Pops, you do. And you, Mum, you deserve a new frock.'

Her dad nodded and took her hand in his across the table. 'Thank you, Thomasina.'

There was the unmistakable sound of sniffing from the range: her mum, showing a rare flash of emotion at this most emotive of subjects.

'Who wants soup?' she asked, a little more aggressively than was necessary, banging the ladle down on top of the range as if this might counteract the sentimental display.

◆ ◆ ◆

Thomasina finished up the vacuuming and stripped the bed in the guest room. She flopped down then on to the wide mattress, sinking into the springs and staring up at the ceiling, remembering how she had lain with Grayson on his narrow bed, and how it had felt safe, warm and secure to fall asleep with her head on his chest and his arms wrapped around her in a wonderful bubble of their own making. The conversation with her parents and the realisation that things were moving at pace left her feeling the very opposite: insecure and unsettled. It was the first time in her life she could not picture her immediate future. Where would she live, exactly, and what work would she find? She was still battling with her parents to be allowed to spread her wings, but now she exhorted herself to *think* – *t*hink of how to make things work, how to make things better.

'What on earth is wrong with you, Thomasina?' her mum shouted from the doorway. 'I'm going to have to put a rocket up your backside if you're not careful! Christ alive, with you wandering around all dreamy-eyed, everything's going to take twice as long!'

'I can't help it, Mum. I can't stop thinking.'

'What you thinking about?'

'The future, Grayson, lots of things.'

'I reckon you've got it bad, my little 'un.' Her mum looked at her with a knowing expression and a small smile of understanding lifted the corners of her mouth.

'I have. I sort of feel that, if I'm with him, I can do anything. He makes me see myself differently.' Thomasina jumped up off the mattress and gathered the dirty sheets from where she'd dumped them on the floor.

'And you're sure he feels the same? I don't want you to get hurt, darlin'.'

Thomasina nodded. 'He does.'

'Well, it might not be the bungalow for you then. It might be that you live all that way away in London with your tall man, his funny haircut and his proper handful of a mother!'

Her words were a step in the right direction, confirmation that Thomasina would one day go, and she was grateful. 'I don't think so. I can't imagine me living there, not at all, especially not with her. But then I can't see me in the bungalow with you and Dad either.'

'So where *do* you see yourself, my girl?'

'I don't know exactly, Mum. But I know that Austley Morton isn't big enough to contain all the thoughts and dreams I have. I think I want to travel, try new things.' She took a deep breath, a little embarrassed by her statement of intent and pre-empting her mum's next question. 'And I don't know what "new things", but something completely different! And that thought doesn't scare me – in fact, the opposite. I feel excited – alive! And yet a little afraid at the same time. I guess I always thought I could wander as far as I wanted but still have the farm to come home to: a base, a beacon to guide me back again . . .'

'I understand that,' her mum said with a sigh. 'It's not easy for any of us. My little girl is finding her feet.'

The two stared at each other, Thomasina a little overcome by her mother's acknowledgement.

Seconds later her mother coughed and shifted on the spot. 'Well, that all sounds very interesting, but right now you need to stop daydreaming. There are a dozen calves glad you're not doing something completely different right now, as they're waiting to have their shit picked up, so you'd best crack on!' She winked at her.

Thomasina fed the calves and mucked them out, scooping their waste into the wheelbarrow and carting it away before setting to on the cement floor with a hot-water pressure hose, detergent and a stiff brush, and finally topping it off with fresh bedding and straw. She didn't mind the labour, thinking ahead now to a time when this might be someone else's chore and how she would miss the interaction with these beautiful beasts. She remembered her gran saying to her once, "Be careful what you wish for!" It had always struck her as the oddest of phrases, but now, at the prospect of Waycott Farm passing into Buttermore hands, she understood it in a way. Countless were the times she'd wished to be anywhere but on the farm, bemoaning the work and the long, long hours and yet now, in the light of it all coming to an end, she could only look upon each task with sweet nostalgia and a worrying sense that she might be losing more than she would gain.

'There we are, my darlings, a lovely clean house for you all!' She felt a fine film of sweat across her brow and ran her hand over the smooth, hard back of Maisie-Moo. 'Can't imagine you in an Ikea bungalow, not at all.' She liked the feel of the animal beneath her palm. 'At least not until you learn to control that flow of shite and can aim it at a toilet!'

As she and Buddy walked out towards the chicken coop, she checked her phone, hoping for a message from Grayson. There wasn't one. A charge of disappointment exploded in her gut. 'Don't be ridiculous, Thomasina. He works all day, and not how you work – he's in an office on a computer. He can't just whip out his phone and call you up for a chat any old time.' She pictured the moment she'd left him, as he jumped on the bus with his long fringe flopped over his eyes and his satchel over his shoulder – a long, odd fringe, because Auntie Joan had never finished her hairdressing course, stopping to have a baby and get chucked out by her dad . . .

'*Call me any time,*' that's what he'd said, '*if ever you need anything, anything at all, and I will always, always, try to make your life the best it can be. If I can do anything to help you, then I will, because that's what you deserve, Thomasina.*' The thought that there was someone thinking about her, there for her, no matter that he was all that way off in London, made her smile.

But also she remembered that, no matter how grand his words or his intentions, he would still have to navigate his mother's moods to make anything happen in actual fact. She wished things were different for her and for him, wished he would do the right thing and jump ship – and this thought brought her back to the very beginning: how she could so easily make the suggestion and yet struggle to act on it herself.

'It's complicated, Buddy boy! That's what it is!'

The hens enjoyed their afternoon corn and were perky, seemingly not missing Daphne a jot. In fact, if anything, Little Darling seemed to have found her voice and was walking around like queen of the coop now that the competition for prettiest hen had taken a step in her favour.

Poor little Daphne . . . Thomasina felt guilty that her hen had had a rather crude burial in the back of the pub car park. Shelley had stood at her side, smoking a cigarette, as she laid Daphne in a shallow grave. It was hardly the fitting end she'd envisaged for the beautiful bird.

Calmer but no less forgiving, she was relieved not to have seen Emery since she'd got back. He was apparently out with the tractor, cutting the hedgerows back on the lower fields. Thomasina walked back to Big Barn to get the dry bedding from the tumble dryer. As she looked up towards the yard she saw the unmistakable shine of Tarran Buttermore's sleek new black Range Rover pull in through the gates. Ordinarily, she would have rushed to a mirror to fix her hair, splash her face and wash the animal shit from under her fingernails, but today she could only recall the way he and his moronic friends had heckled Grayson and didn't think twice about what she might look like. He wasn't the one who made her feel beautiful; he never had.

Tarran jumped down from the car and walked in a determined stride with his hands on his hips, looking up at the farmhouse and then down over the field. His stance irritated her beyond belief. He didn't own the bloody place, not yet.

'Emery still not back?'

As usual when sober, he addressed her in this businesslike, matter-of-fact manner, as if they were strangers or she were of no consequence. His cool delivery always made her feel grubby, turning their brief shared history into something even more sordid, if that were possible. Not that it mattered now; she'd found something so much better.

She'd found Grayson Potts.

'No, he's not.'

'He's borrowed our flail arm for cutting and we need it.'

'As I said, he's not back.' She stood firm, taking in the confident, almost cocky swagger of the boy, who thought he was the bee's knees, all because he was blessed with a pretty face, a pocketful of cash and drove a fancy car.

'Anything else, Tarran? Or can we both get on?'

He smiled at her, a crooked smile that managed to convey the fact that he was both insincere and irritated. 'Tell Emery I'll see him later.'

She had no intention of playing messenger and said nothing. He looked her up and down.

'Shelley told me you were freaking out over a hen. Is that right, Hitch?' He laughed now. 'Just wanted to say you should get your facts right. Lots of birds dropping down dead for no reason all over the county. The Reedleys have had to get rid of their whole brood of hens, and I don't reckon your cousin is killing them all, do you?'

'My name is Thomasina.'

'What?' He looked at her quizzically.

'I said my name is Thomasina. I don't want people to call me Hitch any more.'

'Is that right?' He shook his head, laughing to himself, and climbed up into the car, slamming the door before roaring off up the lane.

'Arsehole!' she called out as his licence plate disappeared from view.

'Who's an arsehole?' her mum asked, head down, as she trotted by on her way to the compost with her little enamel bucket full of vegetable scraps.

'Tarran Buttermore.'

'Oh yes, he is,' her mum said, heading off up the yard. 'A proper arsehole.'

The walk along the riverbank with Buddy restored her calm. It was not only beautiful, the sky clear and the water lively, but every step reminded her of being there with Grayson. She liked to think about his mannerisms, his scent and the way his hand felt in hers. She took her time on the flat rock, throwing stones out into the current.

'I was just thinking that we can still come down here, Bud, when-ever we want. It's public land. We might not own the farm in the future, but nothing's going to stop me coming down to the edge of the water and chucking in stones. I've been doing it since before I can remember. It's our special place, isn't it?' She pictured herself and Grayson, holding each other close on the tartan rug.

Buddy made a groaning sound.

'It won't be the same, I know, but the flat rock will still be here and no Buttermore dickhead can stop me coming to sit on it.'

She checked her phone intermittently for a text message. Doubt crept up on her, loud and destructive over her thoughts. What if Grayson didn't call? What if he was just being kind when he said those things? What if his terrible mother had put her foot down again and he'd listened to her horrible words, like 'floozy'? It was not going to be easy, this long-distance relationship, especially when one of them worked rigid hours in an office environment and the other lived on a farm with the crappiest phone signal in the whole wide world.

With a swirl of resolve in her gut, Thomasina painted a picture in her mind of herself standing tall in a pair of sparkly red shoes. She was going to have to fasten her armour, determined that, even if things with Grayson did not turn out as she hoped, the wheels she'd set in motion would carry her forward to a different future, one in which she smashed through those fences and kept on going.

'*Dawtah . . . cworfee . . .*' she practised out loud.

Buddy began to run in circles in and out of the shallows; he didn't want to sit still. 'You want to keep walking, boy? All right then.' She jumped down from the flat rock and dusted off the seat of her jeans. The day was slipping away and she wanted to make the most of the light, suddenly troubled by the realisation that there would be paths and lanes barred to her once the farm was no longer Waycott property. The idea was almost unthinkable for a woman used to roaming so freely and brought a lump to her throat that sat like glass. She'd reluctantly envisaged the farmhouse changing hands, but this particular thought had not yet occurred to her: that she would not be free to wander the land on which her family had toiled for generations, that she would have to use the roads and byways like any other person and that she would have to go the long way around. Her foot ached at the prospect. She called Buddy to heel and, with her spirits a little sunken, made her way home.

The sight of her message icon flashing when she woke the next morning meant she was smiling within seconds of opening her eyes.

SORRY. LOST MY PHONE. FOUND IT! THINKING ABOUT YOU. SHALL WE CHAT LATER?

She let her thumbs dance over the letters, firing off a reply as quickly as she could, with sweet relief and excitement in her veins.

YES! YES! YES! LET'S CHAT LATER. I'M THINKING ABOUT YOU TOO, ALL THE TIME. WENT TO THE FLAT ROCK. NOT THE SAME WITHOUT YOU . . . X

She felt bold adding the kiss, but hoped it conveyed what was in her mind, that she wanted nothing more than to kiss him and for him to kiss her in his own beautiful way.

He replied with:

X

Thomasina practically leapt from the bed, performing an elaborate dance in her pyjamas, her head nodding, feet tapping and arms flapping to music only she could hear in her head. This was what he did to her! And she liked it. She jumped into the shower with a spring in her step and a smile on her face.

◆　◆　◆

'Humming now!' Addressing his wife, her dad jerked his thumb in her direction as Thomasina fried the bacon, enough slices for the lovely couple from Glasgow currently sitting in the dining room, as well as their own family.

'Yep, and singing earlier. Dancing too. I heard her thumping around, thought she was going to drop down into the parlour through that rotted joist in the floor!' Her mum joined in the ribbing.

'Bloody racket is what it is! Think I preferred it when she was away in London.' Emery did his best to draw the happiness from the room, but this morning he failed. It was a strange thing. They were inching closer every day to losing the farm and yet there was what could only best be described as a lift in the atmosphere of the place. She disliked the Buttermores, but the thought of them owning Waycott Farm was preferable to her cousin snaffling it from under Jonathan's nose. Her mum and dad too were more relaxed than she'd seen in an age. It was as if they felt nothing but relief now that the thing they had feared and railed against for so long was actually underway. Without the fear of it, without the worry of uncertainty, there was room for the beginnings of peace and the chance to make a plan. Thomasina too felt a sense of calm. It was as if shackles were being unlocked and a whole new world of possibilities was opening its arms in welcome.

'I'm off to market today,' her mum said, slurping her tea.

'Reckon I might come with you, love. I could do with nipping into Bristol on the way back. Hopefully, the trailer will be empty, if the calves go as planned.'

'What d'you need in Bristol?' Emery looked up.

'I need to go and see the lawyer; the office is in the town centre. Just to talk a few things through. The farm valuation has come back and things seem to be moving on apace.' He coughed.

'When did they value the farm?' Emery asked indignantly, and it bothered her, the way Emery assumed he could talk to her dad like that, as if he had any right to question him in that way. Who did he think he was? He wasn't Jonathan!

'Couple of days ago, while Thomasina was away in London. A man came round with a clipboard and I walked him over the farm and he took a look over the house and asked a few questions and whatnot. I had to fill out some forms.'

Thomasina liked the look of surprise on Emery's face, a reminder to him that the three of them were a unit long before he pitched up.

'What will you do if the Buttermores take over, Emery?' She kept the questioning casual. 'Reckon you'll like working for Tarran? Sleeping in the shed? Doubt they'll let you have a room in the house. Maybe we should leave the dog sofa in Big Barn for you?'

He stared at her, choosing not to answer.

She plated up the bacon and eggs, black pudding, fried bread and beans and whisked them into the dining room.

'Good morning, Mr and Mrs Arbuckle. Did you sleep well?'

'We did, dear, thank you. Like logs. Mind you, David and I can sleep on a clothes line. This is such a lovely place. We've been out early this morning, chatting to a very handsome pig over the road!'

'Ah, that'll be Mr Chops, guard pig extraordinaire!' It made her smile, thinking of how Grayson had said this first.

'I loved him!' The petite, dark-haired Mrs Arbuckle beamed, and continued, in her beautiful Glaswegian accent as she cut into her bacon, 'Such a smart, noble creature!'

'Can we book ahead for next year?' Mr Arbuckle enquired hopefully. 'We'd like to bring the grandkids – we have quite a clutch!'

'Actually, I'm not sure.' The reality of the farm sale flared in her stomach. 'The farm might be for sale and I don't know if bed and breakfast will be on offer, but I can keep your details and either pass them on or let you know?'

'That would be grand, thank you. How can you stand to leave this beautiful place?' he asked.

Thomasina looked around at the ornaments and bric-a-brac gathered over the years by the women in her family. While leaving would be hard, maybe the bungalow for her parents wouldn't be so bad, not when Thomasina would be living a different life, one she'd chosen and not one she'd been born into. For the first time ever, it felt within reach.

'Life moves on, I guess,' she said with a smile.

'I guess it does,' Mrs Arbuckle acknowledged, loading up her fork.

Swishing back into the kitchen, Thomasina put plates of bacon and eggs on the table for her parents and Emery before resuming her humming as she began doing the dishes.

◆　◆　◆

The lovely Arbuckles had left a little while ago and the room had been stripped and cleaned. Her day was flying by fast. The animals were fed and mucked out and the vegetable beds weeded and mulched. She decided to forgo lunch and instead make a start on supper – one less job for later. With a steady hand and a song in her heart, she piped the top of the shepherd's pie with creamy mashed potato and set the Pyrex dish on top of the range, ready to be browned.

'What's for lunch?'

She turned sharply, not having heard Emery come in.

'Whatever you find in the fridge, I guess.' She was damned if she was going to cook just for him. She stacked the saucepan and utensils into the deep sink and ran the hot tap.

'I work hard for this family, and the way you treat me—'

'The way I treat you?' She spun around, cutting him off with passion in her words. 'Jesus Christ, Emery! You might have Mum and Pops fooled, but I'm on to you.' Her words and reaction were offered without the filter of self-protection that normally shaded her exchanges with him. On this occasion she spoke her mind with her guard down and her confidence high.

'Is that right?' He laughed.

'Yes! You think the way you treat me is funny, but it's not. I'm not here for your sport.'

'No, but you're game – or so Tarran was telling everyone in the pub the other night. He said you were well up for it.'

'There you go again!' She paused to draw breath. 'Only you make me this feel this way and it's not fair. I hear you coming into a room and I get a sick feeling in my stomach. How is that right?'

'You need to be less sensitive.' He reached for the milk jug from the fridge and poured himself a glass, quaffing it quickly.

'No, you need to lay off! I don't even ask that you're nice to me – we are way past that. I just want you to leave me alone.'

'Get over yourself, Hitch. I don't give a shit about you or what you want!'

She shook her head at the case in point and found her voice. 'Do you know, Emery, you've been so horrible to me my whole life! Every memory

I have of you is one where you're calling me names, teasing me,' she said, swiping furiously at her falling tears. The last thing she wanted to do was cry in front of him and yet here she was, her weeping almost overwhelming now in response to those memories. 'Nanny and Grandpa were only in the snug and you called me Tard, Fuckwit and . . . and Rabbitmouth.' It was hard for her to say it out loud. She saw the smile slip from his face. 'And them names have stayed with me. I think about them in every new situation – when I have to face someone, when I go into a shop or walk down a street. You don't think it was hard enough being me without you giving me horrible names to think about? The farm was my refuge, but whenever you were around I lost that, and here you are! And you cosy up to Mum and Pops because you think you can get control of the farm.'

'Well, it's not like your golden-balls brother is going to be around, is it? He's not coming back and so what's your Pops going to do? Leave it to you?'

'No, Emery. No, he isn't. As he said, he's going to sell it to the Buttermores and they will finally have this house, and you know what? I'd rather they had it than you. At least it will just be business, fair and square, but you' – she straightened her shoulders as her tears subsided – 'you don't deserve it. You've been a total shit to me and I *never* deserved it. I was just a little girl! A little girl with way enough on her plate!' They came again, those darn tears.

As if in tune with her distress, Buddy came in from the dining room and barked loudly, then began to growl: a low, deep, rumbling sound that suggested he was primed and ready to defend the girl he loved.

Emery looked at the dog, slammed the glass on to the table and turned on his heel.

Thomasina felt her strength leave her. It had taken a lot to confront her bully of a cousin. Buddy barked again.

'It's okay, boy, it's okay. Come on, let's go and get some fresh air.'

Without stopping to look back at the farm, she set off down the lane with Buddy following behind her. When she reached the riverbank she slowed and bent forward with her hands on her thighs, fighting for breath and trying to stem her flow of tears and still the frightened heart that boomed in her chest. Buddy barked, offering comfort in the only way he knew how.

'It's okay, Bud, it's okay, boy.' She dropped to her haunches and held his head in her hands, kissing his nose. She made her way to the flat rock and sat down. Her legs had stopped shaking and her breathing found a normal rhythm. Through the fog of her distress came clarity and with it a new and glorious sensation. She had stood up to Emery, confronted him after carrying around the hurt he had caused her for all these years. What she felt was strength. And it felt good.

Thomasina pulled her phone from her jeans pocket and dialled.

'Thomasina!'

'Grayson.' She smiled with happiness at the sound of his voice. 'I . . . I wasn't sure you'd pick up. I thought you might not have your phone on at work.'

'Well, here I am.'

'Yes, there you are.' She sniffed.

'Are you crying? What's the matter?' His concerned tone was comforting.

Thomasina closed her eyes. 'I *have* been crying, but I'm not any more. I just wanted to hear your voice. Can you talk now, or can you at least listen?'

'Yes, I'm in my cubicle, but it's quiet – lunchtime. Liz is getting me a sandwich and most people are out. I can listen. What is it, Thomasina?'

'Nothing important. I just wanted to tell you that my life is infinitely better because you're in it. Every little bit of it feels brighter and happier because of you. And I like the way this feels. I feel . . . excited! For the future, for everything!'

'I like the way it feels too,' he whispered, and she could tell by the shape of his words that he was smiling. 'And actually, I think that's very important.'

'I'm here now by the river at the flat rock. I had a bit of a row with Emery and I'm not going back up to the farm until Mum and Dad are home.'

'Are you okay? What did you row about?'

'I've never really had the courage before, but I told him how he makes me feel – how he has always made me feel. He was so horrible to me when I was little and is still so mean to me now. It's like he finds it funny, but it's not funny.'

She looked out at the water.

'How is he mean to you now?'

'He calls me names, he puts me down, he imitates my voice, my limp.'

Grayson listened in silence while she gathered herself. It felt uncomfortable to be highlighting these imperfections; she had hoped at some level that, by not mentioning them to him, he might not notice. Ridiculous, of course.

She drew breath. 'When I was about six, he came to stay at Waycott for the summer and I was in the meadow just running around with the dog we had then – Daisy, she was called. It was a perfect day, and it sticks in my mind because up until then' – she paused – 'I'd always thought I was pretty, because that's what Mum and Pops told me. They told me all the time, "You're pretty and you're wonderful – our special girl," and I believed them.

'I saw Emery and some of the local boys smoking and mucking about in the top field and I waved. I thought he'd wave back, but he' – she coughed – 'he stood up and raised his elbow with his hand curled against his chin and he turned in one of his feet and pulled this terrible face, like . . . like Quasimodo' – somehow she got the words out – 'and the boys he was with were laughing, and I'll never forget how I felt, how it made me feel.' She gripped the phone in her hands, treasuring the con- nection with him across the miles. 'He made this awful, wailing noise and shouted out, "My name is Hitch. I'm a tard and a fuckwit and I have a rabbitmouth," then he shuffled around on the grass, and the boys he was with were laughing so hard they were bent over with their hands on their stomachs, and I felt' – she paused – 'I felt like less than a person.

'The thing is that, as I got older, I heard those words above all others, as if Mum's words weren't as strong. It massively affected my confidence. I have always felt less than a person, Grayson, until you came along.' She took a breath. It had taken a lot of courage to speak so openly. She waited to hear his response, aching for some kind of note that he'd understood or was on her side. Her comments were met with silence that made her feel uneasy until she could stand it no longer. Swallowing her confusion, she asked, 'Are you . . . are you still there?'

'Yes,' he answered, with a steely undertone to his voice, 'I'm still here.'

Thomasina wondered if her earlier assumption had been right and wished she hadn't highlighted her imperfections. She wanted nothing more than to see his face, knowing this would give the true measure of how he had received her words. And not for the first time she thought how much easier it would be if she was someone who caught his bus or he was someone who worked on a farm in the area, and she could get to see him every day . . .

I know I feel better for saying the words out loud, as if I don't own them any more, as if they've been sent out into the universe.

I know the farm will go and I know we'll all survive, because, after all, it's only bricks and animal shit.

I know that I stood up to Emery and, if I stood up to him, I can stand up to just about anything.

I know I will forge a different life.

I know I'm strong enough!

TWELVE

Thomasina closed the chicken run and stood watching her girls, who were about to settle down for the night. They seemed a little morose and she more than understood. The weather on this gloomy evening suited her own mood perfectly, with a dark bruise of a cloud spitting fat droplets of rain like watery bullets that danced on the flagstones and cobbles. It had irked her that her confession to Grayson, summoned from a place where words did not come easily, had been met with silence. It was the opposite of what she thought a boyfriend would do and the disappointment rankled – another sharp reminder that this love business was all well and good but, ultimately, the only person she could really rely on was herself. And Buddy, but he didn't really count.

Her phone rang in her pocket as she pulled up the collar of her Barbour and shivered at the encroaching chill. It was Grayson.

'Hello, you.' She spoke with as much enthusiasm as she could muster.

'Hey, Thomasina.'

'I'm glad you've called. I've felt a bit . . .' She struggled with how to phrase the complex knot of thoughts that bothered her.

'A bit what?'

'I don't know. But thank you for listening earlier. I feel better that I told you all that stuff, I really do, and it's okay that you don't feel the need to comment. I get it – it's not a pleasant topic, and I'm fine, or at least I will be.'

'That's good.' He paused. 'I wanted to ask you something.'

'Ask away!' She hated the mock-enthusiasm she used; it felt shallow, insincere. And she hated even more the fact that it was Grayson whom she was trying to convince that everything was 'absolutely fine'.

'Does Emery *still* call you names?' He spoke slowly and with a gravitas that removed the smile from her face. 'Because when he said those things he was no more than a kid himself, really, and that's no excuse, but it might help explain it – ignorance, fear, trying to impress his friends . . . I don't know, Thomasina, I really don't, but what I'm trying to understand is if he has been any kinder to you over the years since?'

'Not really,' she replied bluntly. 'It's as if he set a pattern of behaviour that he doesn't know how to break free from.' She remembered when he'd come down the stairs in the morning with the words, '*Morning, ugly dog. Morning, Buddy!*' 'I think he might find it funny, but I don't.'

'Because it's not funny and it's not okay. I hate bullies,' he spat.

'Me too,' she whispered, thankful for his show of emotion at last, which felt a lot like support. 'It's cold here, grey and miserable.'

'Yes. At least you've got your Barbour on, but a hat wouldn't go amiss.'

'How do you know I've got my . . .' Before she had a chance to finish her sentence, she looked up towards the yard. Her heart booming with a fierce mixture of happiness and excitement, she saw Grayson leaning casually against a wall with his satchel over his chest, chatting on the phone.

Thomasina ran to him and, in those seconds, it didn't matter that it was raining or that the sky was a dull, dull grey – she felt full of sunshine!

'Oh my God!' She jumped up and flung her arms around his neck. 'What are you doing here?' she squealed, before smothering his face with kisses.

'I wanted to see you.'

Thomasina let her arms slide from his neck. 'You wanted to see me?'

'Yep.' He nodded, as if it really were that simple. 'I wanted to see you and hold you in my arms and tell you that I hate what Emery and his friends said and did and that you're not to give them one more day, not one. Put it out of your head, because you're perfect. Perfect for me.'

Reaching up, she smoothed his wonkily cut, overly long fringe from his forehead. 'You have no idea, Grayson. It means the world that you came all this way.' She felt quite overwhelmed at his gesture. 'Come on, let's go inside. I'm wet through.'

She led him by the hand across the path towards the house. The kitchen was empty. They left their wet boots and coats by the door next to Buddy's basket, who now beat his tail on the floor to greet his new friend. She liked how Grayson bent to pet his head without the reticence that had initially bordered on fear. The two went into the dusty snug with its lingering scent of a real fire and an abundance of squashed cushions and discarded newspapers. Thomasina struck a match to the fire Pops had laid and they settled back on the tapestry-covered sofa that was older than she was – another relic of family history, part of the fabric of life on Waycott Farm. Again she felt the bite of nostalgia, missing every bit of the place before it was even sold. As the flames took hold, the kindling fizzed and the logs began to crack and pop, the two stretched their toes towards the flames and Thomasina leaned her head on Grayson's shoulder, sighing with a deep and new-found sense of well-being.

'You left work to come here?'

'Yes.'

'Did they mind?'

Grayson gave a soft burst of laughter. 'I think they're getting used to me not doing as I'm told any more. I said I had to go and see a girl.' He kissed her on the head. 'My boss was annoyed, but then, as I left, he patted me on the shoulder and said he'd had to go and see about a girl once too.'

'And you've left your mum?' She blinked, still a little embarrassed to raise the topic.

'Auntie Eva is checking on her. I still feel so bad about the way she treated you. It was awful. I wanted to fall through the floor and disappear.'

'Not sure Mr Waleed would have been too happy about that.' She pictured the man by the bins.

'God, can you imagine?' He sighed.

'I don't want you to feel awful, Grayson. It wasn't that bad, and she was drunk – not in her normal state.' She gave the excuse she didn't really believe, wanting to rid him of the embarrassment.

'I think that more or less is her normal state.' He gave her a knowing look, as if aware that she was offering a verbal balm, which he accepted gratefully.

'Either way, I'm very glad you're here. I like it when our paths cross.'

'I can't stand the things Emery said to you. I hate bullies.'

She felt his arm twitch beneath her head. 'Have you been bullied?' she asked softly.

'My whole life,' he answered, without hesitation but with an underlying air of sadness, no matter how resigned. 'At school, at work . . . everywhere.'

'I know what that feels like.' She snuggled more closely into him.

'I just never seemed to . . .' he murmured, as if he couldn't quite explain why he didn't fit in. 'Even when I was little, I remember feeling like I was the only one who didn't get what was going on, as if everyone was speaking a foreign language, and they'd get angry with me because I didn't get the most basic things.'

'Like what?' Thomasina was curious.

'One time – I must have been about six – my teacher, Mrs Collier, asked us all what we wanted to be when we grew up, and she got all the usual answers. Gregory wanted to be a footballer and play for West Ham.'

'Of course!' she smiled.

'Liam said he wanted to be a cabbie, like his dad. Tanzeela said a doctor, and then it came to me and Mrs Collier asked what I wanted to be and' – he took a deep breath – 'I shouted it out because I thought it was the right answer because it was *my* truth. I shouted, "I want to be happy!" The class roared, but it wasn't nice, supportive laughter, it was loud and collective and sharp. It was this and moments like it that anchored me in my weirdness. My odd ideas rooted me forever in a particular time and place. I was encased by all the things I had ever said or done that others considered strange, and they'd laugh just to see me in the corridor or if I was out shopping with my mum, as if the memory or the tale of what I'd done or said lingered like an echo and was enough to start them off.' He sniffed and wiped his face with his hand.

Thomasina didn't know what to say to make it better. She knew how it felt to be at the mercy of words that cut you on the inside and over which you had no control. It was the worst feeling.

Grayson raised his voice, his tone quite passionate. 'And it was always me – always! Me who sent Mallory Davies a Valentine's Day card and wrote "I love you" and signed it Grayson Potts by accident. Me who was sick on the bus to Canvey Island and the driver insisted on turning back, and so no one got to go to the beach and the whole class threw apples and scrunched-up crisp packets from their lunches at me, and they'd shout, "Happy? You want to be 'Happy!'" randomly whenever they saw me, as though this was as ridiculous as saying I wanted to be an astronaut!'

'I think wanting to be happy is an admirable thing to want to be. It's everything, really. I'd rather be a happy egg collector than a miserable astronaut,' Thomasina offered sincerely, but for some reason it struck them both as hilarious and they laughed with ease, releasing the tension that had built up within the room.

'Thomasina? Where are you, little one?' her mum now called, her voice getting closer and louder with increasing urgency. 'Where are you, love?'

'I'm in the snug, Mum!' she hollered towards the door, rolling her eyes at her guest.

'Oh, thank God, I was having a bit of a panic. Didn't know where you were! I thought you might have fallen or come over faint! My heart was thumping nineteen to the dozen! I was just saying to Pops . . . Oh!' Her mum stopped talking when she walked into the snug and saw that her daughter was not alone. 'Oh!' she uttered again, fanning her face with her dishcloth, as if a little overcome, as well as lost for words. 'Mr Potts!'

He stood up and faced her. 'I came to see Thomasina.'

'Well, that's lovely – lovely!' she said, smiling at him and then at her daughter, who enjoyed watching their interaction. It felt a lot like building the bridges she knew would be necessary for a happy future. 'I'll set you a place for supper – you will be staying for supper, won't you?'

'If that's okay?' His voice was quiet, and she guessed that he, like her, was thinking how very different her mum's greeting was in comparison to the welcome, or rather lack of one, that she had received from his mother.

'Of course! Emery's not home yet. He had to go down to Exeter to pick up some parts, so he's missing supper, I think. It'll be lovely to have you at our table. It's nice to see you, Mr Potts.'

'Grayson,' he offered.

'Yes. Grayson.'

Thomasina liked the way her mum looked at him; this boded very well. 'We'll have a cup of tea if you're making, Mum!' she called as her mother made to leave the room.

'Cheek of it!' her mum called over her shoulder. 'And a biscuit too?'

'Go on then!' Thomasina smiled and curled her feet up on to the sofa against Grayson's thigh. The fire now raged and the warm heat filled the room, tinting everything with an attractive orange glow.

'You're lucky, you know.' He watched her mum leave the room.

'I know, but it's not perfect living here. You heard how she was panicking just because I was out of sight for a bit. It can be suffocating sometimes.'

'I know how that feels.' He held her hand again. 'We're like two peas who have found their way back to their pod.'

She laughed, understanding exactly what he meant and liking the analogy.

'I love you, Thomasina.'

His words were unexpected, although no less welcome for that. With a lump in her throat, she twisted to face him on the sofa. 'You . . . you love me?' she asked shyly.

'I do. I really do. I have never felt it before but it's kind of how I imagined it would feel.'

'How does it feel?' she whispered, barely able to suppress the whoop of joy that sat in her chest.

'As if . . . as if I'm full up on something better than food or drink, something you could never have too much of, and as if I have nothing to feel scared of because nothing scares me if I know I can be with you. You make everything feel okay for me. It's as if nothing else matters.'

'I know. As though nothing else matters.'

'You make me so happy!' he grinned.

'Me too.' She could only agree. 'You make me so very happy too.'

Thomasina exchanged a look with Grayson across the kitchen table. He looked a little grey, his top lip clammy; he was nervous. She crinkled her eyes at him and hoped he felt the support she mentally set sail across the red-and-white gingham tablecloth. His new admission of love was still fresh and bloomed like something warm and beautiful in her chest. She watched as he lifted his hand to sip at the glass of water in front of him before looking back down into his lap. She noticed for the first time the extraordinary length of his eyelashes. They were lovely. A reminder that it was early in their relationship and that she was still learning him piece by piece. His awkwardness, she knew, was partly due to the fact that this was the first time he had sat at the family table in the kitchen and not as a guest on the other side of the door. She also knew it was rare for him to sit and eat with other people, picturing the forlorn single setting at the small table behind his mother's chair where he tucked a red linen napkin into his collar. Her own mum now carved the leg of lamb she had pulled from the oven and lay soft, juicy slices on to the warmed plates with extra-crispy roast potatoes, rosemary-roasted carrots and a whole ladleful of glossy red-wine sauce. She had obviously decided to treat them and put Thomasina's shepherd's pie in the freezer for another day.

'Here you go, love.' Her mum placed the plate in front of Grayson.

'This looks . . . amazing! Thank you very much.'

She saw the genuine look of delight in his eyes and shuddered at the thought of his poached haddock, curling forlornly under tinfoil.

'So, Grayson, you work in a bank then?'

'In a way.' He made eye contact with her dad and her heart pulsed at how badly she knew he wanted to make a good impression. 'It's a broker's, really, but in banking, yes. It's not that interesting.' He reached for his water glass.

'Funny, isn't it, that no matter what your job, what someone else does always seems interesting. I mean, I can't think anyone would be interested in taking soil samples or testing milk or mucking out, but there we go,' her dad said with a chuckle, reaching to take his plate of food from his wife's outstretched hands. 'Ooh, look at that! Thank you, my darlin'. This looks wonderful.'

She saw how Grayson watched the interaction between her mum and dad with something close to fascination, and wondered if he, like her, was thinking of the times when his parents had danced in the little space in the flat, in a time when they seemed happy . . .

'And no brothers or sisters?' her mum asked, lifting her cutlery to signal that the feast could now begin.

Grayson shook his head. 'Just me.'

'You'd love our Jonathan.' Her dad nodded in his direction as he forked a spud into his mouth. 'He's a lovely lad! In America, no less, working with a friend he made at college. He has a degree in agriculture and farming, our clever boy.'

Thomasina was glad they were chatting but wondered, as she sometimes did, just how different her life might have been if her parents had not decided so early on that there would be no certificate of learning for her. It was part of her awakening, her growing confidence, that, along with this consideration, came the flicker of frustration in her gut: *Why not me?*

'And your clever girl too.' Grayson eyed her across the table, as if reading her thoughts. 'Did you not want to go to college, Thomasina?'

'Not really. I didn't do too well at school.'

'Well, no, lots of people don't, but then they pick up education later in life, when they're ready.'

She was aware of the current of heightened awareness that now flowed between her parents and knew it was possible they might take his candid observation as a slight on the choices they had made on her behalf.

'Maybe I haven't been ready until now.' She spoke softly, letting the suggestion creep over all assembled like warm water on ice, allowing the slow thaw of realisation that things for her were changing.

'Maybe you haven't,' Grayson acknowledged.

'Jonathan was born ready, wasn't he, Pops? We all miss him.' She steered the topic into less choppy waters but, in truth, Grayson's words had planted a seed in her thoughts.

'I look forward to meeting him,' Grayson replied, and her heart soared. This meant a plan: someday when he would meet her brother.

The back door now banged open against the wall. In walked Emery in an oversized parka, wet with rain, a grubby cap on his head. He filled the space with his presence and his bulk, carrying the scent of dirt and diesel, enough to put a large dent in Thomasina's appetite. She watched as he shrugged himself free of the coat, caring little that he showered droplets over the floor and sideboard. He lobbed his cap on the side, scratching his scalp with his fingernails as he turned to look over the table.

'Well, this looks nice. A little dinner party. Not interrupting, am I?'

''Course not, lad!' Her dad, sweet as ever, smiled and shifted his chair to one side. 'Go and fetch an extra seat from the parlour and come and eat!'

Her mum stood, grabbed a plate from the rack above the sink and began loading it up with slices of lamb and all the trimmings.

'Mr Potts! Didn't expect to see you back so soon. Couldn't keep away, eh?' Emery asked with an air of sarcasm as he went to fetch the stool.

Grayson gave a brief nod and did not invite the man to call him by his first name. Thomasina noticed the change in atmosphere and felt her stomach shrink. She wished this meal could continue with the chat and warmth, as before. She knew her dad and Grayson would have bonded over a beer while the excitement for all that lay ahead bubbled beneath the questions and the storytelling.

And now her cousin had spoiled it.

Emery came back, thumped the seat down next to her dad and sat down hard, as her mum put the plate in front of him.

'I don't know – leave for five minutes and someone's in my seat!' he almost shouted, but without the smile or laugh that suggested this was in jest.

'Now you know how my brother feels,' Thomasina muttered.

Her dad gave her a stern look, while her mum asked quickly, 'More gravy, anyone?' as if this sauce-led diversion might be enough to quash the exchange that threatened.

'Oh, still having a go at me, are you?' This time Emery did laugh.

'Come on now, you two!' her mum tutted playfully, as if she were addressing kids. Thomasina wouldn't have been surprised if she'd threatened to bang their heads together, and her mum's manner irritated her.

'I'm not having a go at you, Emery, just speaking the truth.'

'This lamb is lovely,' her dad said, wrinkling his eyes at his wife in a kindly smile.

Emery chewed his food. 'Seems like the dog has found her bark, or should I say the rabbit her squeak.'

Thomasina winced at his deliberate and cruel rabbit reference and felt her pulse race as her face coloured.

Her dad put his cutlery down hard and stared challengingly at his nephew, chewing his food quickly, seemingly trying to finish his mouthful so he could speak, but it was Grayson who spoke up first. He laid his cutlery across his plate.

'Please don't speak to her like that.'

'What?' Emery held his fork still.

'I said, please don't speak to her like that.'

'Oh, I see what's happening: the dweebs are forming a tag team. Change Purse and Hitch – sounds like a bad country-and-western duo.' He laughed again.

'I'd . . . I'd rather you didn't call me Change Purse, and I know Thomasina wants to be called by her real name. Everyone else seems to manage it.'

'How about I couldn't give a shit what you do or don't want!' Emery flashed, and she saw her dad sit back in his chair, his jaw tense and his eyes narrow.

Her mum froze.

'All right, Emery. That's quite enough – you don't talk like that, not to anyone in this house! This is the dinner table and a lovely meal has been prepared and I will not have it spoiled.' Mr Waycott banged the table.

'Don't tell me that, tell him,' Emery said, jabbing his fork in Grayson's direction. 'That lanky moron . . .' he muttered under his breath.

'I said, enough!' Pops yelled.

Grayson stood suddenly and the table jarred, the water glasses slopping their contents and gravy sloshing from the edge of the plates.

'Good Lord!' her mum gasped, raising her hand to her throat.

'I think you and I need to go and talk outside,' Grayson said.

Emery laughed loudly. 'Oh yes, please!' he grinned. 'I could talk to you outside all day long!' He too stood, and balled a fist.

'Stop it! Just stop it!' Thomasina yelled. This was not how she had seen the lovely meal ending.

'Yes, just stop it, Change Purse!' Emery pretended to lunge at Grayson across the table and he flinched.

'You're a bastard, Emery!' he yelled. 'I know how you've taunted her throughout her whole life, and it stops now! I *know* how shit it feels to listen to the crap people like you spout, just because it makes you feel a bit better, but I also know I'd rather be on the receiving end than have your brain and your nature. You are nothing!'

'Is that right? Look at you – who the fuck *are* you?' Emery fired.

'Language, Emery!' her dad yelled again, a little louder this time. 'I will not have it in my house!'

The younger men ignored her dad and Thomasina felt rooted to the spot.

'I know who I am, faults and all, and I know I am someone who would never taunt a person with words so cruel they cut her. That's what you did to her!' Grayson again spoke directly.

'You'd better watch your back, mister.' Emery snorted like a bull.

'I'm not scared of you,' Grayson said, looking him in the eye. 'And if I'm not scared of you, what do you have left?'

Without warning, Emery grabbed his plate and hurled it towards Grayson, who ducked, leaving the plate free to hurtle through the air and land with an ear-splitting crack against the tiled wall behind the range. All five watched, shocked and with hearts hammering, as shards of floral china, meat, veggies and thick gravy slid down the wall, landing with a hiss near the hotplate.

'Oh no!' Mrs Waycott whimpered.

Thomasina yelled out, 'Holy shit!'

'What in the name of God is going on here?' Her dad stood and drew himself up to his full height. 'This is my home! My dinner table! And this is not how you behave! It's not fair and I will not tolerate it!' It was an uncharacteristic outburst from this usually most demure of men. 'How dare you two argue like this, and how dare you throw food, break china in this kitchen! It's a disgrace! *You* are a disgrace!' His voice shook with an unfamiliar undercurrent of rage.

'Grayson's right, Pops – he *is* a bastard, and I wish I'd told him that years ago!' Thomasina piped up. 'It's my home too and there have been many times, because of him' – she pointed at Emery – 'that I wanted to be anywhere else, and that's not bloody fair!'

Emery looked from her to Grayson with a smirk. 'I'm leaving before I do something we'll all regret! But this isn't over, you freak – not by a long shot!' Emery spat the words at Grayson and glared at Thomasina before reaching for his coat and cap and heading back out into the darkness, slamming the door on the way out.

Grayson pushed his plate away and she knew that, as with her, his appetite was now non-existent. Her mum rinsed out a cloth and tended to the sticky brown splash on the wall.

Her dad stumbled back into his seat, a little overwhelmed by the exertion. 'What in hell just happened? Good Lord, I have never known the like!'

Thomasina wasn't sure if he was addressing her or Grayson. Both of them, probably.

Grayson looked at her dad and her heart flexed for him. 'I'm sorry I shouted at your nephew in your kitchen.' He looked at the barely touched plate of food in front of him. 'I was just so angry.'

'So I noticed.'

'It's not his fault, Pops,' Thomasina said in his defence.

'I think everyone just needs to calm down,' her mum added from the range, looking at her husband over her shoulder in concern, trying to calm the situation.

Thomasina saw Grayson examine his hands and curl his fingers, in an effort to steady them, she thought. He then sat up straight in his seat.

'Well, I'm not sorry,' she stated, all eyes now on her. 'I'm not sorry I stood up to him. And I'm not sorry that Grayson wants to stand up for me.'

'Are you hearing this?' her dad said in exasperation, addressing his wife and daughter. 'I don't understand: one minute we're having a nice dinner and the next . . .' He shook his head.

'You know, Pops, Emery has upset me, impersonated me, laughed at me. He's said and done some really terrible things, and I mean it, it's not bloody fair.'

'But' – her lovely dad was struggling with the information – 'he's your cousin! Known you his whole life, like another brother.'

'He is *not* like another brother!' she corrected, thinking of Jonathan. 'Not at all.'

'But he's been living here under our roof . . . Is it true, Hitch – Thomasina?' he corrected himself, looking from his wife to his daughter and back again, as if hoping someone was going to help him figure out the puzzle, understand what in hell was going on. 'Has he been mean to you?'

'It's true, Pops.' She kept her voice steady, her stance firm. 'He's been disgusting to me. It's not the gentle ribbing you think it is, not like with me and Jonathan, who love each other. Emery makes me feel like less than a person.'

'How does he do that, love?' Her mum stopped scrubbing and leaned on the range, giving her daughter her full attention.

She looked at her parents and she whispered the word still shameful on her tongue. 'Since I was six, he has called me rabbitmouth and other things . . .'

Her dad made a small sound, as if he'd been winded, and again there were a few seconds before he spoke. 'Oh, love. Why – why didn't you tell us? Why didn't you say something?'

Thomasina looked back into her lap and her voice was soft. 'Because, as you say, he's kin, and I know things are hard enough. I know you need the extra pair of hands and—'

'Extra pair of hands?' Her dad's voice had gone up an octave. 'I'd rather let the whole bloody place go to rot than let anyone treat you badly. Your mum and I have done all in our power to protect you, to look after you, and he comes into our home and is *horrible* to you? I feel so stupid – I *did* think it was just affectionate ribbing between the two of you. I mean, I know you used to bicker, but . . .'

He looked at his wife, who shook her head, as if lost for words.

'Me too,' admitted Thomasina's mum. 'The way you moaned about him, I thought it was the way you always told a tale on Jonathan. Of course I would have listened if I'd known it was anything more! You should have said something.'

'I did say something. I told Grayson.' Thomasina spoke plainly.

'Yes, you did.' Her dad sat back in the chair. 'And here we are.'

'I love her,' Grayson announced, reaching for her hand across the table. 'I think she's pretty perfect.'

'Is that right?' Her dad smiled at them both briefly before rising slowly from his chair.

Thomasina watched as he walked around the table to place his hand on Grayson's shoulder. It was a moment of tenderness she would never forget, a shoot of something good growing up through the dark soil of new beginnings.

'You know what, Mr Potts?'

'What?' Grayson asked a little sheepishly, looking up at the older man.

'I like the way you care for my daughter and, for the record, I happen to agree with you. I think she's pretty perfect too.'

◆ ◆ ◆

She slept fitfully in his arms. Adrenaline from the previous day and a jump of joy in her limbs meant she watched the sun rise through the window she'd cleaned countless times while Grayson ran his fingers through her hair. She knew that this was the most perfect way to spend any night: by his side and in his arms while the tall cedar tree tapped its nosy spikes on the windowpane and the sun filtered through its wide branches.

'I'm in this bed with you.' She spoke dreamily, her head on his chest and her arms about his waist.

'You are.'

'I think it would be nice to wake up like this every day.'

'Me too.'

She felt the inevitable bolt of joy at hearing him echo her own thoughts and marvelled at how easy it was to be in this other world, where life felt kinder and every thought was tinted rose with optimism.

'How are you feeling today?' she said with a yawn.

'Surprisingly good. A little embarrassed by the scene we caused, but I think your parents have forgiven me.'

'They have.' She kissed him. 'And I've been thinking about what you said, about maybe it being the right time for me to think about education.'

'What would you like to do?' he asked, with such solemnity it only reinforced her thoughts that this could actually be possible.

'I don't know exactly, but I was thinking of something to do with chickens.'

'Chickens?' This time there was a hint of levity in his tone.

'Yes! What do I love the most? Chickens! Who do I spend most of my time with? Chickens! I'm a bit of an expert.'

Grayson twisted free of her grip and lay facing her now, with his head propped up on his arm. 'Of course, there's another way of looking at things.'

'What do you mean?'

'I mean, you're right in what you say – you *are* an expert, so instead of learning more about chickens, how about you teach other people about chickens?'

'Me? A teacher!' She laughed, partly at the absurdity of the suggestion, but also with joy at the very idea. 'Who would I teach?'

'I don't know.' He seemed to consider this. 'But you have a love of them and a lot of knowledge to pass on. There'll be a way . . .'

She lifted her head and looked at him. His words were so simple and yet so heavy with the possibility of a new and different life that could be hers. She just needed to figure out how . . .

'Did Emery come back to the farm last night?' His voice was now not quite so assured.

'I didn't hear him, but even if he did, I feel as if I can stand up to him now and so I don't really care.'

'That's right. We won't let him get away with anything.'

'We . . .' she smiled. 'I am part of a "we"!' She rolled on top of him, kissing him on the face and burying her head in the space beneath his chin. 'You're going to get in trouble again, Grayson, aren't you, missing work because of me?'

'Probably, but if you look at the wider picture, it's only the fourth day I've taken off ever. I'm never sick. I think the issue might be that

I've disappeared again without notice. They like things to be planned, requested. But life doesn't always work like that, does it?'

'It really doesn't.' She considered this. 'How are things going to work out for us, Grayson? How do I get to wake every day by your side when you're based in London and your mum is so . . .' She didn't have the words. 'And even if she didn't hate me, I can't imagine living in that little flat with you both.'

She felt him shift beneath her as he moved up the bed and leaned back against the headboard. 'Things need to change for me – for us.'

'They do,' she agreed, knowing that recognition of this was half the battle. 'What was it like with your mum after I'd gone? Did she say anything?'

'She said lots of things. Not that I paid any attention.' He pushed his long fringe behind his ear.

'She hates me.'

'She hates everyone, just about. She hates the wicked world that has done her wrong. It's all nonsense, of course. She's just a mess and she drinks too much to see things clearly. And the alcohol and her distorted view are the linchpin to everything.' His sigh was loud and came from a place deep within.

'I don't know what the solution is, Grayson, but I know we have to find one, because I'm not going to be satisfied with anything other than this every day. This in tandem with me branching out – who knows, even teaching!' she said with a laugh. 'This is what will make me happy and I want it all! And the big difference is, for the first time ever, I actually feel that I can have it.' She reached up to kiss his face and, as the two sank down on the soft, soft mattress, she again felt herself slip into another world where nothing mattered more in that moment than the feel of this man's skin and his mouth kissing hers.

◆ ◆ ◆

Grayson sat at the table while Thomasina fried eggs and bacon. She noted the soft slant to his shoulders as he read the *Gazette*, and the way he hummed as if all was right in his world, and she understood, feeling a lot like humming and singing herself with the overwhelming sense of relief.

'I think today we should spend a bit of time with the girls – they'd love to see you – and then we could walk to the flat rock with Buddy, hang out, maybe take a picnic lunch, some warm soup in a Thermos? Would you like that?'

'I would,' he said, looking up from the newspaper.

'Look at us, planning a picnic before we've even had breakfast,' she said, laughing.

The back door opened and her mum came in. She took up a seat at the table, smiling at her daughter briefly then looking away, as if the knowledge they shared was almost too much.

'Morning, my lovelies. How did you sleep?' Her manner was a little flustered.

'Good, thank you.' Thomasina felt her chest flutter with embarrassment, figuring her mother was probably aware that Grayson had been by her side, although, at some level, she was glad. For her it was a clear and open statement that she was no longer the child they often treated her as: she was a young woman, with a future that might just lurk outside the walls of Waycott Farm, and with a man like Grayson Potts by her side. *Me, a teacher – an expert!*

'Well, I'm glad someone slept well. Pops and I stayed up talking until God knows when, chasing things around and around, trying to make sense of it all, working out how we go forward, talking about the sale of the farm and the things you said about Emery. It doesn't feel nice knowing there's a split in the family.' She gave a weary sigh. 'And I keep thinking of how I used to run back and forth from the school if we even got a sniff of someone being mean to you.'

Thomasina looked up sharply; this was something she'd not been fully aware of.

Her mum continued, 'And we would nip it in the bud, and yet, all the time, my own nephew, the boy we have tried to help . . . We feel like we've let you down.'

'No, you didn't, Mum.' Thomasina walked over and crouched down by her mother's side, kissing her gently on the cheek. 'You and Pops are and always have been great with me. I love you both.'

'Oh, my girl, you wonderful woman – how we love you.'

To be called a woman meant more than Thomasina could express. It was an admission, a recognition of all the changes that had recently taken place within her.

Grayson stood and took her spot at the range, using the abandoned spatula to turn the crisping bacon and push the mushrooms deeper into the shiny fat.

'You're a good man, Grayson.'

She watched him turn to smile at her mum, who, in her roundabout way, had just given him her blessing.

'You say that' – he smiled – 'but I think I've made a bit of a mess of this.'

Her mum stood to look at Grayson, who held the skillet with the burnt bacon in it out for examination.

'We'll make a farmer of you yet, son,' her mum chuckled, 'and the first thing you need to learn is how to cook bacon.'

It was a golden day, one Thomasina would remember; the air tasted full of possibilities. It started with Grayson having his cookery lesson at the range as her mum taught him the intricacies of frying in an aged skillet: the importance of fat temperature, heat control and moving things around the pan. He seemed to really enjoy it, and Thomasina could see it was not only the actual lesson but the feeling that he was being entrusted with something – understanding, as she did, that to be welcomed into this country kitchen, the beating heart of Waycott Farm, was akin to being welcomed into the family.

◆ ◆ ◆

The breakfast things were scrubbed and put away and the bed turned down, and now, with the basket packed in readiness for their promised picnic at the flat rock, Thomasina raced outside to meet her beau. She watched him idle on the flint wall as he tapped his phone against his palm. It was nice to watch him unobserved, see the tension gone from his shoulders and the way he jerked his head to flick his long fringe. Gone was the nervous finger push through his hair. He breathed deeply, throwing his head back and taking in great lungfuls of the clean air under the big, clear sky. Having spent time as one of the 'mole rats' in the grubby Underground, she understood his need to do so. He even clicked his fingers, calling to Mr Chops, who, as usual, patrolled the lane, snuffling around in the grass verge. She liked the fact that Grayson Potts was within reach on this cold yet sun-filled day. What more did she need?

He was right: they could not be satisfied with anything other than this, every day. It sounded so straightforward when she thought about the big picture, but the truth was that any change would need careful planning on both their parts. She was more than ready for the challenge, knowing the reward was great. Only that very morning while she packed the picnic basket, she had had one brilliant idea of how to start bringing her dreams to fulfilment . . . She patted the card she'd written out that morning; it lay in her pocket like a precious thing.

'What are you thinking about?' she called out. 'You look miles away.'

Grayson looked up sharply, as if he hadn't heard her approach, and hopped down from the wall. 'I was.'

Buddy skittered to a halt in front of him and pushed his muzzle into his leg, demanding the affection his mistress gave so freely. Grayson petted him.

'I think you rather like that dog of mine!' she teased.

'I have to admit, the whole shit thing aside, he's a lovely dog.'

'That makes me happy,' she admitted, noting the look of tension that crossed his brow, an unwelcome addition to this perfect day. 'So, come on, what are you thinking about?' she pushed.

'Lots of things.'

'Don't give me too much detail there, Grayson!'

He raised his arms and let them fall. 'Literally, my head is full. I'm still thinking about yesterday and rowing with Emery at the table. I can't believe he smashed a plate and made that mess . . . I'm embarrassed, and I don't want your parents to think I do stuff like that.'

'They do know that. Apparently, Emery *did* come back last night, but late. Mum heard him pack a bag and leave, and he hasn't turned up to work today.'

'I didn't know I was capable of speaking up like that. I've never fought back, not really.'

'I think it's the dawn of a new age for you – for us.'

He nodded, biting his lip as if vexed.

'What else are you thinking about, Grayson?'

He picked a long straw of grass from the verge and wound it around his fingers, fidgeting. 'I'm thinking about my job and how happy you make me, how much I enjoyed this morning . . .' He blew out slowly through pursed lips.

'Wow! You weren't joking – lots of things!' Thomasina beamed up at him. 'It was nice for me to see you cooking. It made things feel a bit permanent – not that I'm suggesting . . . Not at all. I mean, I'm not . . .' She stopped talking, flushed hot, and reached for Buddy.

'I know what you mean: me too. I have never cooked in the flat.'

'Never?' she asked incredulously.

'It's not that I don't want to,' he began, 'but you've been there . . .'

'Yes, I have.' She blinked quickly, trying to imagine cooking in the kitchenette under his mother's watchful gaze.

'What did you think of the place? I'm interested. You're the only non-family member to have spent time within its walls.'

'What, no one over for tea? No birthday party? Nothing?' The very thought saddened her.

'Nothing,' he confirmed. 'I have never had a birthday party.'

'Well, I thought it was small,' she said, 'but then I know most people don't live with as much space as we have here. We're lucky.' She nodded over the wall at the ramshackle farmhouse, where any one room shared the proportions of the entire surface area of his London home.

'Hmmm . . . small, not cosy.' He recalled their conversation the day after their first meeting, which now felt like an age ago.

'Constricted,' she said, reminding him of his earlier, more accurate, assessment and holding his gaze. With this one word she told him that she understood. 'Although, having said all that, for a long time now I've often felt hemmed in here, trapped, no matter how much space we have.'

'And so what are you going to do about it?' he asked straight out, stopping abruptly in the lane to look down at her.

'Move away, I guess, teach, learn, all the things we talked about – and I think I might have figured out a way to get started. Something that'll help me save and set me on the right track. It'll build my confidence.'

'Sounds intriguing!'

'Can I show you something?' She bit her lip.

He nodded and she peeled the postcard from her pocket, holding it up so he could read it. Written in a block print, neat and not too fussy, were the words:

THINKING OF KEEPING CHICKENS BUT DON'T KNOW WHERE TO START?

NEED A CHICKEN-SITTER WHILE YOU'RE AWAY?

CALL THOMASINA WAYCOTT, 'THE CHICKEN EXPERT'

REASONABLE RATES.

'This is brilliant!' he enthused.

'Is it?' She pulled a face.

'Yes, it's great – a really good idea, and, as you say, it'll get you started.'

'That's what I thought, and while we still have the farm I can work here, help out, like always, but also it's like starting my own business, doing something for myself. I was thinking, one day, I could even get a van!'

'You could! Where are you going to put the card?' he queried.

'I know just the place,' she said with a smile. 'Plus, it's where we're heading anyway.'

'The flat rock?' He looked at her quizzically.

'The flat rock eventually, but first I want to buy you a present, Grayson.'

'I don't need a present!' he protested, while his tone and the way he almost jumped up and down on the spot suggested he might be more than a little thrilled at the prospect. She suspected that a present was a rare and lovely thing – especially for a boy who had never had a birthday party.

'Why do you want to buy me a present? What's the occasion?'

'No reason and no occasion. It's a "just because" present.'

'I don't think I need a "just because" present,' he said, beaming.

'Well, that's too bad, because I'm getting you one anyway. Don't you want to know what it is?'

He shrugged, embarrassed.

'It's a pair of wellingtons,' she said, putting him out of his misery. 'We can't have you tramping all over the farm in your fancy lace-up London pavement shoes now, can we?'

◆　◆　◆

Thomasina and Grayson drove over to the country store on the outskirts of Thornbury to stock up on chicken feed, place her card on the wanted-ads board and purchase a new pair of wellington boots for him. These were not only new, but his first adult pair, apparently, and ridiculously exciting.

'My very own pair of puddle-jumpers. That's what my dad used to call them. I could only have been about three, but I can see myself holding my dad's big hand and him swinging me by the arm along the path in the park, making sure I landed with a splash in the shallow puddles.' He looked at her and laughed, and she loved that he was sharing his childhood with her. 'I quickly sussed the game and tried to jump down hard, feet first in my little yellow wellingtons.'

'I'm picturing you doing just that.' She glanced across at him and smiled.

'It's these memories that are confusing for me,' he said, and paused. 'Such lovely moments, and I remember feeling loved, yet this was the man who ran away. Who just left, and that was it, all I got.' He coughed. 'I'd liked to have introduced him to you.'

'I'd have liked that too,' she said sincerely in return.

She swung the Subaru into the roughly paved car park. No sooner had they jumped down from the cab than she espied one of Thurston Buttermore's contemporaries, loading sacks into the back of a van and wearing the khaki-and-mustard uniform of the country set.

He called out across the yard, 'How's things, Hitch? Heard you had a bit of trouble at home yesterday evening?'

'No,' she said, shaking her head, 'no trouble, Randall. But thanks for asking.'

That would be down to Emery, the blabbermouth!

'Righto. Well, give my best to your dad,' he offered, his gaze lingering on Grayson before he jumped into the van.

Grayson caught up to walk alongside her. 'How do people know what happened yesterday? It happened in the kitchen and we haven't seen anyone!'

'Welcome to country life. Everyone knows everything. If a farmer shits in Chepstow, we get the scent of it over in Austley Morton before he's had a chance to wipe his backside.'

He laughed at her delicate turn of phrase.

Thomasina liked this place, had been coming here since she was a small child with her dad, and it always felt like a bit of an adventure. The store was actually more of a warehouse, with a concrete floor and metal roof, crammed with shelves and racks stacked high with plastic sacks of farm feed, compost, sawdust, tools, wooden stakes, fencing, wire, country attire and all manner of paraphernalia. It smelled like a cross between a garden centre and a sawmill. Thomasina watched Grayson taking it all in. 'A bit different to your local corner shop, eh, Grayson?'

'Just a bit.' He smiled. 'No crisps, magazines or energy drinks!'

She watched with something close to fascination as he ran his fingers over the long counter where gardening gloves, bolts, locks and, surprisingly, Kendal Mint Cake were on display – and then caught sight of Tarran leaning on one elbow, chatting to the girl behind the till.

Shit! Shit! Shit!

'So, Hitch?' he called out when he saw them, straightening with a look of glee on his face. It was the kind of smile given by someone who took joy in the misfortune of others and she felt a wave of dislike for this man and his despicable nature. 'I heard Emery's been chucked out?'

'Did you now?' she called back dismissively and, with her back to him, as she ran her fingers over the rack of wellington boots, some with fancy tartan lining, others in wild shades of grape and blue. 'What size are you, Grayson?'

He smiled as he told her, seeming to like the way she took control, choosing something for him as if they'd known each other for years and she knew his taste. Thomasina concentrated on the job in hand, just as if they were any old couple.

Apparently, Tarran didn't like being ignored and strode over. She felt her heart race.

'All right?' he said, nodding confidently at Grayson.

'Yes, thank you.' Grayson looked briefly at Thomasina and she knew he recognised the man from the pub, the one she had confessed to having slept with. Her mouth felt dry.

'Come on, Hitch, what happened? Don't be shy – that's not like you. I heard you got your cousin thrown off his own farm in the dead of night, in the rain. Now that's not something that happens every day.'

'Well, Tarran, firstly it's not "his own farm", it's my dad's, as well you know, and secondly, you shouldn't believe everything you hear. He wasn't thrown out. I think, more accurately, he went to the pub for the evening and then came back and packed his bag. Sorry there's nothing more dramatic to add.'

'Is that right?' Tarran eyed Grayson with thinly veiled dislike, no doubt having been fed a line by Emery.

'Yes, that's right.' She smiled sweetly, with a feeling close to triumph at how she felt able to stand up to him.

'And I heard you were involved in the hostilities?' Tarran now addressed Grayson directly.

'In a way.' Grayson nodded, giving the most succinct and harmless response he could.

'What d'you mean, "in a way"?' Tarran pushed.

'I mean, I did tell him what I thought of him because I don't like him – more specifically, I don't like the way he treats Thomasina.'

Tarran's smile faded and he bit the inside of his cheek. 'I see. You don't like the way he treats Thomasina,' he repeated, with the hint of a mocking chuckle. 'You do that a lot, do you? Throw your weight around when there's someone you don't like?'

'Well, I wouldn't be hostile to someone I did like, would I?'

Now it was Thomasina's turn to laugh.

'You trying to be funny?' Tarran jerked his head forward.

Grayson shook his head but held his gaze steady. 'No.'

'You like guns?' Tarran folded his arms across his chest.

'No.'

'You ever fired a gun?'

'No.'

'Because we're big on guns around here, air rifles and shotguns. We like to go out and let off a bit of steam, practise our aim.'

Grayson narrowed his eyes in confusion, as if he could not tell if the man was trying to make polite conversation or was threatening him. 'I've never had a gun, never held a gun, but my next-door neighbour had one.'

'Oh, yeah?' Tarran hooked his thumbs into his belt loops and looked for all the world like a gunslinger in the Wild West with Stetson cocked and a muzzle resting in a fancy leather holster against his thigh. She wondered how Grayson, the novice, would fare in a duel. Not very well, she suspected. 'What does your next-door neighbour shoot – clays? Targets? Rabbits?'

'Erm, people, mainly. Well, one person for sure. He got twenty-six years, which is a very long time.'

She saw the swagger disappear from Tarran's stance, along with the smirk on his face.

'How about these?' Thomasina held up a tiny pair of green wellingtons with little frog-eyes sticking up on the front.

'Perfect.' He smiled at her, his girl.

'His face!' Thomasina squealed with laughter as they drove back along the lanes with Grayson's new wellingtons – a plain green pair without frog-eyes – nestling on the rear seat of the pickup.

'I only told him the truth!'

'Like you always do, Grayson.'

'Like I always do.'

The atmosphere was charged with their joy and a tone of hope and new beginnings.

'Think I'll get any calls?' Thomasina pictured her postcard, pinned centrally amid the advertisements for farm equipment for sale and leaf-lets inviting entries for the county show in all manner of categories.

'I think you will.' He looked out of the window.

'I love being with you.'

He snatched her compliment from the air and returned it: 'I love being with you, and I'm thinking about how to make it happen, how to be here with you every day.'

'There are banks in Bristol, you know.' She grinned as excitement rose within her like a fountain.

'There are, and maybe that's the answer, but I don't know.'

'Are you fed up with your puzzle-solving?'

'Something like that. I need a change of scenery. I want to climb off the conveyor belt that carries me straight back to that flat every night. I'd certainly get to do that in Bristol – for some people, it might as well be the Bahamas or Borneo!'

'So I've heard.' She chuckled.

'I don't know – I like this fresh air!' he said with a shrug, and she wished he could better articulate his thoughts.

'Well,' she sighed, 'if my dad takes the Buttermores' offer and sells the farm, we'll all be doing something different. But I don't fear it; in fact, I'm starting to think it might be quite exciting.'

'The Buttermores?'

'Yep, Tarran and his dad with their flash farm and flashier cars. Idiots, the lot of them, as you just saw. They're the ones who've made the approach to buy Waycott. They've been sniffing around for years, and we're running out of options. I think not having Emery around to work with my dad might be the final straw. But d'you know what, Grayson?' She took a deep breath, like someone galvanising herself for the battle ahead. 'Getting rid of him and gaining freedom from worry for every-one, as well as giving me the chance to do my own thing – it just might be worth losing the farm. And I never thought I'd hear myself say that.'

She parked in the yard and reached over, plucking the wellingtons from the rear seat. 'Here you are, Mr Potts, your very own boots – bet-ter than those lace-ups.'

'Thank you. I love them – I really do.'

'You all right, Grayson?'

'Yes,' he said, swallowing. 'I'm just thinking of how to start. I want to say something, but I want to get it right.'

She placed her hand on her heart. 'Just tell me – it's nothing bad, is it?'

'I don't think so.'

'You're scaring me a bit,' she whispered. 'I think the world of you and I still can't believe you like me back. I keep thinking that, at any minute, you will see me like everyone else does and run away, and even the thought of that makes my heart hurt. I picture you by my side, in my chicken-expert van!' she added, in an effort to lighten the mood.

'I want to be by your side in the chicken-expert van.' He smiled at her and she felt her insides leap with joy!

They jumped down from the cab and Grayson stepped into his wellington boots, leaving his shoes in the footwell. He stood taller and walked with confidence, reaching out for her free hand. They now walked along the lane with the picnic basket, tripping along the twists and turns of the rutted path as they made their way down to where the River Severn bordered the land.

'The thing is, Thomasina . . .' he began.

'The thing is what?' She giggled nervously, still thinking, in spite of his reassurances, that this state of happiness was too good to be true. She was waiting for the sting in the tail, the dark consequence, the sledgehammer to fall, which would shatter their happy state into fragments of regret.

It turned out that neither of them had to wait too long.

As he opened his mouth to speak, the phone in his pocket rang.

He glanced at the screen. 'It's my mum.' Seemingly in no mood to talk to her, he ignored the call. With peace restored, he again reached for her hand.

'The thing is, I want to ask you—' The phone again broke the peace.

She looked towards his pocket. 'Maybe you should get it?'

'No. She'll only want to shout or cry or both, and I don't want her voice and her demands to dilute this.'

Again the phone fell silent and he smiled at her. Her heart beat quickly and she sensed that what might be coming was a proposal. Her spirits lifted at the very thought.

'I want to ask you—'

The third ring in succession made them both jump.

'Shit!' he cursed, and let go of her hand.

'It's okay,' she soothed, as he brought the phone to his ear.

She could hear the high and low notes of a woman's voice, a lot like his mum's but with the slightly deeper rasp of a roll-up addiction giving each word a sandpaper-like quality.

'Auntie Joan, what's wrong? It's okay – calm down. You've got me now. What's happened?'

Thomasina watched the rise and fall of his chest as he held the phone. The colour drained from his face as he stood with her on the banks of the river in their special place.

'I'm . . .' He looked up at Thomasina, who had heard, if not the details of the exchange, then certainly the tone of it. She stood with her knuckles pressed into her mouth.

'I'm on my way. Try to stay calm. I'm on my way.'

He looked down at his feet, encased in his new wellington boots, which had taken no more than a hundred steps. 'I'm on my way.'

I know I feel mentally free of Emery.

I know that Grayson Potts loves me.

I know that I love Grayson Potts.

I know we are heading to London, as his mum is very ill.

I know it doesn't make me a very nice person, but I keep thinking how angry I am at her for robbing us of this happy time. We are just getting started with so many plans — and now this.

I know I will never tell that to a living soul.

I know these thoughts make me feel quite ashamed.

THIRTEEN

Grayson seemed to be operating on autopilot, distracted and tense from the moment they jumped down from the Subaru at Bristol Parkway.

She had kissed her dad.

'Bye, Pops. And thank you . . .'

'Keep us posted, little love, and take care.'

And then, gripping her man's hand, she had stumbled once or twice on her twisted foot as he strode purposefully through the throng of people, all oblivious to the urgency he felt. He was preoccupied, understandably so, but still, this felt a lot like returning to reality, coming up for air, as if they had been living underwater in a bubble of rural perfection where they made protestations of love, put cards up in the farm wholesale store, planned for the future and reached for each other's hand. It was a shock to her system – noisy, sharp and cold. The sea change unnerved her.

Grayson, leaning on the table in the chair opposite hers, rubbed his forehead. As the carriage rocked along the tracks, he kicked out a couple of times, as if the leg room were inadequate, running his finger under the collar of his shirt, suggesting that the carriage temperature was too hot and progress a lot, lot slower than he was happy with.

'We'll get there as soon as we can, Grayson. Try to take a deep breath.'

He nodded, breathing in through his nose and out through his mouth. And for a second, peace seemed to come over him, before his leg started jumping and his fingers fidgeted with the edge of the train ticket, flicking the corner back and forth, back and forth.

'I just want to get there.'

'I know.'

According to his sobbing Auntie Joan, his mum had had a heart attack, been whisked to Barts Hospital and was on the brink, hooked up to tubes and wires and machines . . . It intrigued Thomasina that the embarrassing exchange of a few weeks earlier no longer mattered in the light of this new crisis. Nothing did. As is often the case in an emergency, everything was forgiven, the slate wiped clean, and all that did matter was getting Grayson to his mum, either to reassure her or to say goodbye. And Thomasina would be there by his side, offering support, should the worst happen.

'I've thought about my mum dying,' he said as the train hurtled past Swindon.

'I think everyone does that,' she said, to console him. 'It's how we try to cope with the scary stuff before it actually happens, like an emotional trial run.'

'I suppose so. I think what it will be like afterwards – my aunts so sad, drinking, no doubt. And I think about what the flat might be like, plunged into silence. And I know it sounds terrible, Thomasina, but I think about that life of quiet, without the trickle of words from my mum, on constant send, voicing her interior monologue like the man on the radio giving the shipping news.' He gave her a brief smile. 'I'm ashamed to say that the idea of that quiet used to fill me with a little relief.'

'I don't think that's terrible.' She again pictured Mrs Potts's anger and her spiky turns of phrase. 'Not at all.'

'And yet now there's a very real chance of her not making it, and I don't feel relief at all. My heart's racing and I feel guilty.'

'Why do you feel guilty?' she asked softly.

'Because she didn't ever want me to leave her, and now, whatever has happened to her, she had to face it alone.'

'You'll have a chance to make it up to her, I'm sure of it,' Thomasina offered, forcing a smile. This was not the time to voice her opinion that he deserved some respite from the chaotic and demanding life in which his mother had ensnared him.

◆　◆　◆

The hospital was hectic and she hated the smell, the bright, bright lights and the glimpses of the sick and injured. She was no stranger to hospitals, and it was impossible for her to walk the pastel-painted corridors without recalling the many operations on her gut, foot, heart and the painful, painful ones on her mouth when she was a kid. She felt a surge of sickness at the memory.

Grayson ran around, misreading signs and in a state close to panic as he tried to find the ward, the details of which he'd written down on a piece of paper and on the palm of his hand, lest he should forget. Still holding tightly on to his hand, as his flat-soled shoes squeaked on the highly polished floors when he rounded the corners, it was all Thomasina could do to keep up. With his satchel clutched to his chest, his fright seemed to cloud his sense of where he was. Eventually, he put a call in to his Auntie Joan, who gave them directions towards the ward. She and Eva were huddled over cigarettes outside the building, without any hint of how inappropriate this was.

'Can I come in?' Grayson pressed the buzzer and spoke to the kindly, slightly robotic voice on the other end of the line.

'Patient's name?'

'Mrs Ida Potts, but I don't know why she still calls herself Mrs Potts – she's been single for far more years than she was ever married.' Nervous energy took over his tongue, and Thomasina kissed his hand.

'Everything is going to be okay.' She liked the way her mum's mantra sounded at this moment, understanding now how this warm and comfortable platitude was a little like emotional cotton wool to stuff into the edges of one's mind when emotional turmoil left gaps.

The door unclicked slowly open.

She felt a sudden wave of unease, as if she should be elsewhere, as Grayson walked briskly along the ward, peeping into rooms where the doors were ajar and hovering outside curtained beds, until a noise or a voice told him it was not his mum loitering within its flowery confines. A fat nurse with a fixed smile and an iPad approached him.

'Can I help you two? Who is it we are looking for tonight?'

'My mum. Ida Potts.'

'Ah, yes,' she said, nodding along the corridor. 'Second bed from the end on the left.' She turned and pointed with her arm extended, her hand flicking at the wrist like a flight attendant in the middle of the safety briefing.

They ran then, and as the adrenaline that had fuelled him since he first took the call from his Auntie Joan a few hours before began to ebb, he began to shake with fatigue, lines of worry etched upon his face. Thomasina rubbed his arm and again kissed his shoulder when they arrived, tiny gestures designed not to intrude but to let him know she was close.

The two stared at the woman in the bed. Thomasina noticed that she was smaller than when she pictured her curled into her chair at home, and she also looked older – small and old, with fear and tension shading her furrowed brow even as she slept.

She heard the gasp of distress from Grayson as he sat down on the plastic chair by the side of the bed and placed his satchel on his knees, watching his mother sleep. His shoulders sloped in relief at finally being with her.

Gently, Thomasina placed her hand on his shoulder, and he jumped, as if he'd quite forgotten she was there. 'Do you want me to leave you alone?'

He shook his head. 'I feel like I should take her hand and whisper words of comfort, but we're just not that kind of people.'

'This isn't a film. There's no blueprint, Grayson. You do whatever you feel is right,' she said, gently rubbing his back.

He nodded again and gave a small smile. She stood by his side, both of them watching as his mother drifted in and out of dreams, head back, mouth a little slack, the oxygen coming from somewhere overhead, filling her lungs through a snug-fitting mask over her mouth and nose. Despite the intimacy of the situation, Mrs Potts was still very much a stranger and Thomasina felt her presence to be a little intrusive. But as Grayson reached back and took her hand in his, she felt all doubt diminish, knowing she was where she should be.

Their breathing slowed and the atmosphere grew a little calmer as she and Grayson settled into the environment. Their new-found peace, however, was shattered when his aunts came bustling on to the ward, carrying with them a fug of cigarette smoke that seemed even more repulsive in this sterile environment. The two women, almost carbon copies of their sister, were crying loudly, disturbingly so, as they approached the cubicle, dabbing at their eyes with damp bits of tissue and linking arms, as if this mutual physical support were necessary for them to remain upright. Thomasina couldn't help but think that there was an element of performance in their manner.

'Frightened us half to death, she did!'

'I thought she was a goner!'

'Called us and was all wheezy, breathless . . .'

'By the time we got there she was on the floor – *the floor*!'

'Shouting out for you, she was, but you're here now.'

'Yes.' They more or less barged Thomasina out of the way in their eagerness to squeeze and pat their nephew's flesh beneath their pudgy fingers. 'He's here now.'

'Is she going to be okay, do you think?' he asked softly, as if wary of triggering another wave of distress from his aunts.

'They said she was lucky.'

'Very lucky.'

'She's always been lucky.'

'Except for picking that bastard – she wasn't so lucky then.'

'True.'

'Fancy running out on your wife and child . . . Who does that?'

'Bastard.'

'Bastard.'

Thomasina saw Grayson sit up straight, as if their words were a slap across his cheek, and she wished they would either shut up or leave but was not in a position to request either.

'This . . . this is Thomasina.' He gestured towards her before turning his attention back to his mother.

She felt the gawp of the women graze her skin. It was a look that managed to be both disapproving and judgemental, leaving her in no doubt that they had been thoroughly briefed by their sister and already held fully formed opinions on her, *the floozy*!

'Hi.'

They lifted their chins briefly in response.

She pictured driving along earlier on this very same day with Grayson's new puddle-jumpers nestling on the back seat, her confidence high at having confronted Emery and the whole day feeling like sunshine . . . Now it felt like a lifetime ago.

The minutes ticked by and turned into an hour, which slipped into two. The aunts hovered around the bed, took turns at sitting in the chair on the opposite side from Grayson, rubbing their sister's arm or crying into their soggy bits of tissue, which they rolled between their impatient fingers. Twice, at his insistence, Thomasina sat on Grayson's vacated chair until the ache in her foot subsided, or she walked to the waiting room and back, aware of the silence of the women when she returned, as if she'd interrupted a delicate conversation. And, the way they greeted her with a semi-scowl, she suspected that the topic was herself.

'I could do with a cup of tea.'

'I could do with a cup of tea,' the other echoed, parrot-fashion.

It might have been the mention of tea but, as the word left their mouths, Mrs Potts's eyes flickered open.

'There she is!'

'Hello, darlin'!'

'Don't you worry, we're all here, all of us!'

'Welcome back!'

Her sisters crowded over her. But it was the sight of her son that made her tears pool. She pawed at the plastic mask that covered her nose and mouth, pulling it down to her chest, gasping for breath. 'My boy . . . I knew you'd come. I knew you would. I knew . . .' Her breaths were quick and shallow.

'It's okay, Mum. Just sleep – rest now.'

'I was . . . I was so frightened,' she cried again, her words coasting on stuttered, distress-fuelled breaths.

''Course you were!' Joan boomed.

'Lying there all alone on the floor like that, 'course you were frightened!' Eva shot Thomasina a look, as if it were her fault that he had been otherwise engaged.

She watched as Grayson seemed to shrink in their presence. It was as if their words, reminders of his abandonment, were a blanket that smothered him, leaving him gasping for breath and wordless. It was as ridiculous as it was bloody unfair.

Mrs Potts looked at her briefly and her eyes narrowed in the way she remembered. Thomasina felt torn. Part of her wanted to turn and run, all the way back to her soft bed in Austley Morton, the bed with a dip in the middle and the creaky springs, and part of her wanted to pull Grayson to her, to get him away from these women and never let him go.

◆　◆　◆

It was late when they got back to the flat in the domino block, odd to find it in darkness and so quiet. She didn't notice the graffiti or the wee smell on the stairs, or even the syringes. Tiredness and an aching body meant she didn't notice much, other than the empty chair by the window with the empty wine bottles gathered around it, standing guard in a row. Thomasina and Grayson went straight to bed, forgoing the opportunity to fry something up in the kitchen. His lesson at the farmhouse range that morning was now nothing more than a dim and distant memory, and to mention it, something so frivolous as eating supper, felt churlish in the face of what was occurring.

Thomasina's stomach rumbled nonetheless.

Overcome with fatigue, they fell awkwardly on to the narrow mattress in his sad bedroom. Grayson buried his head in the pillow and reached out to smooth the soft length of her hair as though it were a comfort blanket for him, and she liked it, liked his need of her. It made her smile.

'I don't know how my mum will cope in hospital overnight. She was pretty upset when we left.' He slurred his words like a drunk.

'She's in the best hands,' she mumbled, yawning.

Thomasina pictured the woman's tearful face, pleading for him to return first thing in the morning. He had, of course, promised. And she'd felt a jolt of nausea at just how much Mrs Potts controlled him, this followed by a sharp mental rebuke: *For goodness' sake, Thomasina — the woman is very ill!*

'Oh shit!' Grayson lumbered into a sitting position. 'I need to tell work. I only had another day as planned absence, but I think I might need more.' He fired a text off to his boss.

MR JENKS. MY MUM IN HOSPITAL. HER HEART. WILL TAKE FORMAL LEAVE. THANK YOU. GRAYSON.

The reply was immediate and unexpected.

SORRY TO HEAR THAT. TAKE ALL THE TIME YOU NEED. SENDING
YOU OUR VERY BEST.

The words were a relief and the final incentive he needed to fall asleep.
They lay spooning, his arm over her stomach anchoring her to him and
with the welcome weight of his thigh over her leg. She paid no heed to
the heckling shouts to flats above and below from the concrete car park
or the wail of sirens . . . Grayson was right: it was an urban lullaby – this
was her last thought before she fell into a deep, deep sleep . . .

◆ ◆ ◆

'How's Grayson's ma?' her dad asked with a note of concern.

'Well, she's awake, and so that's something,' Thomasina informed
him as she knelt on Grayson's bed and looked out of the window at the
little train creeping along the bend of a track in the distance like a toy.

'Good, good, and how's the boy himself doing?'

'He's bearing up, Pops. It's hard for him, but we were so tired last
night we slept like logs. Should know more this morning. We're heading
off to the hospital in a minute.'

'Righto, righto. Well, rest assured, all is okay here. Thurston
Buttermore called me to say he's taken Emery on as labour, just wanted
to let me know, which was decent of him, and Mrs Reedley has popped
up to lend a hand this morning and your chickens are all fine. I told
them you'd had an emergency. And Buddy is right here, aren't you, boy?'

She felt a flash of love for her birds and her pup.

'I'll be home soon as I can, Pops – love you . . .'

◆ ◆ ◆

Standing at the end of Mrs Potts's bed when they arrived was a young
doctor in an open-necked shirt and with the confident handshake of a

person certain of their place in the world. In that respect, he reminded her of Jonathan.

'Your mum has been telling me all about you. I'm just glad my mother isn't here, or I'd be in trouble – you're setting the bar way too high.'

'I'm not sure about that.' Grayson looked at Thomasina, knowing that she'd borne witness to his mother's dismissal of him and her sniping, which left him feeling worthless.

His mum beamed, as if complimented.

'You have a bit more colour in your cheeks, Mum.'

'Yes, a lot better today. Did you stay over last night?' she asked Thomasina directly, with an undercurrent of disapproval that was strong for one so close to death's door.

She nodded. 'Yes, thank you. I didn't think Grayson should be on his own.'

'I was just telling your mum that this was a warning.' The doctor spoke earnestly. 'A minor heart attack, but she does need to change some of her habits to give herself the best chance going forward. The heart is a muscle just like any other and needs exercise and the right environment to thrive.'

'I'm going to change, Doctor.' Mrs Potts closed her eyes briefly, as if in prayer. 'I ain't going to go through that again. Thought I was going to wake up dead.' She shook her head.

'Well, as I say,' the young doctor said, jollying the chat along, 'it was a warning, Mrs Potts, and you were lucky, but no alcohol, no cigarettes and regular exercise. These would be the kindest changes you could make for your body.'

'As God is my witness, I'll exercise every day and give up the cigarettes and the booze. Not that I drink that much, not compared to some.'

Grayson again looked at Thomasina and rolled his eyes, suggesting that he, like her, was trying to think of anyone who might drink more than his mum.

'You're going to need some looking after, at least until you're properly back on your feet. Plenty of rest until you feel able to get back to your normal routine.'

'I'll be fine. I've got my boy.' She nodded in his direction.

Grayson stayed mute, but Thomasina felt the shout in her head like a bang. It was the sound of every door of opportunity through which she had tantalisingly glimpsed closing all at once. Was this it? Their great 'make life happen' plan – was this how it stalled, because Grayson would be reeled in by his mother, caught on a hook made of duty, attached to a line fashioned from guilt? The very thought made her feel a little nauseous, as well as reflective. She too had felt the twitch of haste in her heels at the sound of her dad's voice, with the news that Emery was over at the Buttermores. She knew Waycott Farm was a pair of hands short and she felt the pull in her gut that she needed to be there to help.

'Okay.' The doctor patted the bed. 'Well, the occupational therapy team will be around in a day or so to go through your convalescence plan and what you might need and how best to approach it.'

'We'll be all right, won't we, son?'

The doctor walked along to the next patient. Thomasina watched as Grayson slipped down into the chair by the side of her bed as if his limbs were leaden, looking at her with a look of such sorrow it pained her. Thomasina was certain that, if she altered her view, she might actually see the bonds that tethered him. And as much as she resented it, she thought about the pile of shit that would be waiting to be shovelled from the yard and she understood.

'I didn't sleep a wink,' his mum said with a sigh, chattering and oblivious. 'Bloody noises and beeps from machines and people coming and going at all hours, and then a nurse woke me up to ask if I needed something to help me sleep – have you ever heard anything like it! I told him outright, I *was* a-bloody-sleep!'

'I guess they're only doing their job,' Thomasina suggested. Grayson and his mother ignored her.

All three sat quietly for a second or two until his mum spoke, her words coasting on great, gulping tears.

'I was worried I was going to die and not see you again. It was my worst nightmare come true – you running orf to God knows where.'

'Just outside Bristol,' he explained.

'Yeah, there. And me not seeing you.' Mrs Potts bit her lip and her tears fell. 'I reckon it was you going orf what caused the whole thing. Got myself in a proper state.'

Thomasina saw the way Grayson stared at his mother, as if feeling the punch of guilt in his gut. His mum had had a heart attack and been forced to lie on the floor of the flat until help came, and Thomasina got the feeling that Grayson would think it was all his fault because rather than be on call, he'd been out shopping for wellingtons and searching for how to be happy.

Mrs Potts wasn't done. 'But I forgive you, Grayson, because I love you and I know you won't leave me, will you, son? You're a good boy. I know I can rely on you. Just you and me, together against the world, just like it's always been. I told that doctor you'd look after me. I knew it. We don't need no one else, do we?'

Whether accurate or not, Thomasina took this as a message sent directly to her. She looked around the walls of this London hospital, glanced at the sick woman in the bed whom she had only met twice before, and not for the first time wondered what in hell she was doing there, when there were fields that needed attention and animals to be fed and watered.

'I could do with a cup of tea.' Mrs Potts wriggled a little up the bed, wincing as she did so. Thomasina watched the widespread wobble of fat on the woman's arms as she supported herself until she was comfortable.

'Would you like me to go and get you one?' Grayson offered.

'Oh, go on then!' his mother said with a smile, looking him up and down. 'And we need to get you a haircut, mister.'

Grayson used his finger to loop his long fringe over his forehead and behind his ear before grabbing Thomasina's hand as the two went off in search of a cup of tea for his mum.

'She seems a bit better,' he said as they inched along the corridor, aching to spend time together and reluctant to return to the ward.

'She does. And I was thinking that maybe . . . maybe I should go home, Grayson. I didn't want you to be on your own or travel alone and I had no idea what awaited you, but . . .' She chose her words carefully. 'I feel like a bit of a spare part, and there's so much work to do at home, and I think the last thing your mum needs is me staring at her! I seem to make her agitated, and that can't be good for her heart.' She waited, hoping he might reassure her.

Grayson stood still and took a deep breath. 'I'm so glad you came with me. And I'll keep you posted on how she's doing.'

It wasn't the plea for her to stay by his side that she had, at some level, hoped for. In fact, it was at best accepting and at worst spoken with no small measure of relief. He pulled her towards him and held her against his chest. Running her hand over the front of his shirt, she inhaled the scent of him and imprinted the feel of his arms across her back. Arms she knew could only carry so much and, right now, it felt for all the world as if she might be the weight he cast aside.

'I love you, Grayson.' Her mouth twitched with all she wanted to say, but she knew this was not the time or place.

'I love you too.'

◆ ◆ ◆

With her sleeves rolled up and her breath sending plumes of smoke up into the cold autumn sky, Thomasina toiled hard all week, humping hay, driving the tractor and guiding the cows from one field to another along unwieldy tracks where briars bothered them and small pebbles made them hesitant. She liked the extra responsibility, but the ache in her limbs at the end of the day and the throb in her foot more than wiped out any joy.

Peeling off her fleece top and beanie, she took a seat at the table in the kitchen opposite her dad while her mum brewed tea.

'How's Grayson's ma faring?' her dad enquired, as he smoothed the pages of the *Gazette*.

'She's coming home, actually.'

'They didn't keep her in long!' her mum added, as she placed a welcome steaming mug in front of her.

'Four days.' She sipped the hot tea, which slipped down her throat like nectar. 'Thanks for my tea.'

'And how's Grayson doing?' Her mum asked this with a downward slope to her mouth, as if to add, *the poor boy* . . .

Thomasina recalled their conversation earlier in the day. It had left her feeling low.

'How's things?' She hated the banality of her words when what she wanted to do was talk earnestly, fearing they had gone a little off track, unable to feel the same vibe from him as she had when they were nestled side by side on the old sofa in the snug. Thinking of that moment on the path when she had felt sure that a proposal had been imminent, knowing that she would have shouted without hesitation, '*Yes!*' Now, though, she wasn't so certain. She didn't want to come second to Ida Potts and was not about to give up on her own ideas and her desire to travel just to play second fiddle to his demanding mother, watching from the sidelines in their shitty flat.

'Okay, I guess. Auntie Joan and Auntie Eva came in while I was at the hospital and ran the vacuum cleaner over, dusted and changed my mum's bed linen. They've put milk in the fridge and we have plenty of tea bags. So we're all set. We even have a vase of yellow carnations on the table.'

'That's good.' She didn't know what to say next.

She could hear the hum of expectation in the pauses, felt the pulse of longing in the silent spaces between the spoken words and sensed his reluctance to open up more. They kept the tone general and uninteresting, frustratingly swapping titbits about their day, and when he said goodbye it left her with an aching, unsatisfied void in her gut. The rest of their communication that day had taken place via text message. Grayson explained he was often travelling underground without a signal, or was in the hospital, where phone use was barred, but she feared the truth was something more straightforward: he was trying to back away a little.

Thomasina felt physically sick and so overcome with doubt that it left her feeling a little light-headed. It felt easier not to think about it, to encase her emotions in a thin veneer of forced indifference and go about her day ignoring the gnawing feeling in her gut that felt a lot like hunger but was nothing to do with food.

'Piece of cake, darlin'?' Her mum held out one of her Grandma Mimi's tins, and her tears finally came at the sight of the once gilded cake tin with its faded imprint of blue and pink roses – a tin she still had no hope of filling with sweet confections baked for the man she loved. She dropped her head on her arms at the table as her mum palmed circles on her back.

'It's okay, my little 'un. Everything is going to be okay . . .'

Grayson's texts slowed and Thomasina galvanised herself against the increasing disappointment, until, only a week later, his communiqués had declined to one a day. She felt a combination of anger and distress, in direct proportion to the decrease in contact.

Her mood was further hampered by the fact that she was yet to receive an enquiry from her 'Chicken Expert' postcard, which had been on the board at the farm wholesale store for a couple of weeks now. She remembered the excited anticipation with which she had pinned the card up, afterwards keeping her phone within reach and waiting for the calls to come flooding in from chicken novices across the county, all seeking out her know-how, but this was not quite how it had panned out, and, in truth, she felt stupid for thinking it might have been otherwise. Frustration kicked at her shins and made her restless, which only added to her general malaise. If this little business didn't take off, she wasn't going to be able to afford a ticket for the Bristol bus, let alone to anywhere further afield. She had decided to redouble her efforts and maybe place a proper ad in a proper magazine, like *Practical Poultry*, but that would cost money, which she didn't have, and couldn't earn unless her venture took off . . . and with these thoughts she was back to square one.

'You need to call him,' Shelley told her plainly when they bumped into each other in the lane by the pub. 'You need to call him and tell him how you're feeling because, right now, it's like you're . . .'

'In limbo.' Thomasina finished the sentence.

'Yep, you're right there. And you look like total shit.'

'Thanks, Shelley. I feel like total shit.'

'You look like you did that night when you turned up with your dead chicken and put her in my bath!'

It was testament to her friend's good humour that Thomasina managed to raise a smile. Shelley took a long drag on her cigarette. 'Call him and get this sorted one way or another.'

'Maybe I will.' She found it hard to explain her reluctance, how she felt torn. She knew at some level that she did not want to have the conversation that might change them, end them – didn't want to have to admit that to have this half-hearted, semi-interested boyfriend might actually be better than not having him at all, because she loved him. But at the same time the fire in her belly grew, and with the sale of the farm creeping ever closer, change, whether she liked it or not, was afoot.

'Maybe you should. You're worth more, Thom.'

She smiled at the affectionate nickname. *Friends.*

'You're worth more,' Shelley reiterated, 'and if he can't see it, then he's a dick.'

'He's not a dick, not really, just a bit weak.'

'Aren't they all? Which then begs the question, do you actually want to be with someone like that?' Shelley trod the butt of her cigarette under the heel of her boot. 'Oh, and by the way, I took your advice.'

'What advice?'

'About my painting. You were right – I *am* brilliant at art. I'm drawing wonderful things, and just doing it makes me feel happy!'

Thomasina saw the way Shelley's face came alive, and she envied the bubbles of joy that fizzed from her, knowing this was how she felt when she pictured a future with herself in the driving seat. Shelley was right: she was worth more!

◆　◆　◆

Standing in the paddock, she cradled Little Darling to her chest, cooing as she stroked the hen's soft, feathery head with her finger. 'What d'you think, little birdie? Should I call him?' Little Darling wriggled and tried to flap her wings. Thomasina placed her gently back in the run and took it as a sign. She walked to Big Barn and sat on the sofa, where Buddy lay sprawled. Easing his head to make a gap, she sat down and liked how her pup placed his muzzle on her thigh.

'Okay, Buddy, I'm going to do this.' He closed his eyes in supreme indifference as she picked up her phone and tapped out the number. She exhaled sharply, like an athlete preparing for the final push.

'Thomasina.'

It spoke volumes that she was equally delighted and unnerved that he had answered. It was hard from the one word to guess his mood, but she did not feel the flutter of yearning at the sound of him longingly uttering her name, not like she used to. She knew that, when she first met him, Hitch would have crumbled at the thought that he might be a little indifferent, but Thomasina, with her new-found strength, who knew she was worth more – well, she was as much irritated as upset.

'Hello, Grayson.' She cursed the rise of a lump in her throat that made it hard to speak. 'I wanted to talk to you. Is now a good time?' She tried to keep her voice steady.

'Yes. I'm lying on my bed looking at the ceiling.'

The image of the two of them smiling and kneeling beneath the roughly plastered ceiling as they looked at the city lights below brought a crushing pain to her chest. It had felt so perfect, as though they could take on the world, and of all the futures she had envisaged for them, this separation and coolness was the furthest from her imaginings.

'How's your mum doing?'

'Good. I'm back to work and she managed today with no problems. She's napping now.'

'Good.' Again that gaping, loud pause. She felt the quake of nerves. Her tongue stuck to the roof of her mouth and again she tussled with the thought that maybe it was better to let things drift, to keep an iron in the fire, just in case . . . But then she thought about Pops, who very soon was going to hand over the keys of his beloved farm to the Buttermores, and she sat up straight, knowing that sometimes, no matter how hard, it was right to take a stand, to make a choice and go with it. 'This is hard for me to say, Grayson, but I will do my best. I think this might be the last time I contact you. I can take a hint.'

'No, don't say that,' he said urgently. 'It's not that—'

'I . . . I don't understand what's happened.' She cut him short, knowing she needed to keep talking or her confidence would evaporate. 'I keep thinking how things were so lovely, and then after your mum got ill everything changed, and I thought it would all blow over, that the world would spring back into shape, but it hasn't.'

'It's not that easy for me. You know that. She's demanding, and she—'

'Yes, yes, I know all of that.' She was unwilling to listen to what sounded more like excuses than reasons. 'But there comes a time, Grayson, when you have to make a stand, make a decision. You have to chase life, and you said to me on the lane, when I told you about wanting change – you said, what are you going to do about it? And I guess I'm asking you the same question now – what are *you* going to do? I feel as if we're slipping, and I believed you when you said we were solid, but I don't want to hang around like this, feeling like an afterthought. I'm worth more.' She borrowed Shelley's phrase.

'I feel so torn. I hate feeling like this.'

Having expected, hoped even, that he might rush in with words of reassurance and reconciliation, his fractured speech and awkward whispers suggested he was hesitant, unsure, and it snipped the last of the fragile stays that kept her heart strings connected to the man she loved.

'Welcome to my world,' she offered a little bluntly, as anger now fanned the hurt and her defence mechanism kicked in.

'My mum is an alcoholic and she's a danger to herself and she hasn't got anyone else.'

'She has her sisters!'

He gave a dry laugh. 'They're fucking useless!' he snapped, and she knew this frustration was not necessarily directed at her. 'They drink and they encourage her to drink and they talk utter nonsense the whole time, just burbling away with their soundtrack of anecdotes and shit memories, washed down with milky tea and wine. I can't . . . I can't rely on them. There's only me.'

'So' – she tried to think ahead – 'so why don't you get a nurse? Or send her to a facility – rehab?'

'She won't go! How can I make her? And we had a nurse who walked out after a week because my mum was just too much.'

'Well, that's her fault. She's keeping you hostage, keeping you away from me, and I honestly . . .' She swallowed. 'I honestly thought you'd put your foot down and not let this happen. You need to think about what you really want and be brave, Gray.'

'Be brave?' He gave a dry laugh. 'You say that so easily, Thomasina, and yet you haven't been brave! You stay at the farm and give a million reasons about duty, but you're not so different. You've never really tried to break free, and I get why – it's safe. It's the same when you talk about further surgery, which would make you feel better, give you confidence, and yet you hide behind excuses about the pain, and I think actually you use your disfigurement to keep people away so you don't have to feel so guilty about hiding.'

His words hurt, largely for the element of truth they carried. 'You have no fucking idea, Grayson! None at all! You have no idea what it's like being me and, apart from anything else, I can't just up sticks and go! Financially, things are hard; my choices are limited.'

'Maybe I don't have any idea, but if we have any kind of future together we need to be able to say everything.'

With anger colouring her immediate reaction, she snorted in derision at the likelihood of that ever happening, not now. 'Yeah, and you know what, not calling or contacting me, going silent, is not the best way to achieve that!' she yelled.

They were quiet for a beat or two. This felt like the beginning of the end, and it was painful. Buddy put his head on his paws as if he didn't like the sound of their row, not one bit.

It was Grayson who spoke first, his tone now softer, and with the loss of his hard edge came another wave of regret and longing for all that this relationship had promised and just how happy that promise had made her.

'I don't want to argue with you. But I need you to put yourself in my shoes, Thomasina. If this was your mum or Pops, if you felt you had no choice, would you leave them?'

'I don't know,' she answered truthfully, calming now and weighed down by the reality of their situation. It felt hopeless.

'If they had absolutely no one else who was going to take care of them, keep them from harm, if they had always stuck around for you, would you walk when they were most vulnerable?'

She thought of the day Jonathan left and that sensation in her throat as though she were being strangled, as if her brother's adventure came at the cost of her own aspirations. She stayed silent and they both drew breath until Grayson again broke the ice.

'I'm lying here staring at the blobs on the ceiling. When I was a kid I used to imagine they were mountain peaks where tiny, tiny people anchored ropes and hammered nails just to get a foothold. I understood this need to gain purchase. That was my whole life, trying to keep upright. But here I am in my mid-twenties and it feels just the same. I feel as if I'm sliding backwards into that life of nothingness, back into the hamster wheel where I ran for years, grabbing for anything solid, stationary, to hold on to, but it was always just out of reach . . .' She heard him swallow. 'And then you came along and you changed everything.'

'Yes.' She spoke calmly but resolutely. 'Well, you're not a kid any more, Grayson. And I might not ever have climbed a mountain, but I know that to do so takes courage. It's not only about anchoring ropes and hammering in nails to get a foothold; it's about the belief that you can do it, or are at least trying to.'

She knew this applied to her too. It was all about finding the courage to make the change.

'And you're right, Thomasina, beautiful, beautiful Thomasina: you deserve more. You deserve better than to be caught up in this bloody pantomime. The truth is, I don't know how to break free. I don't know if I can. But truthfully' – he took a second – 'I don't know if you can either.'

She wiped her nose on her sleeve and tried to control the tears that threatened. It was one thing to imagine the two of them ending, but quite another to feel it. Despite her mantra that it was for the best, trying to mirror Pops's bravery, the words made no allowance for the fact that it hurt. It hurt a lot. 'I . . . I want to, Grayson, more than you know. I want to, and I have to believe I will. I just need to find a way.' She looked down at Buddy, her boy, who now placed his big paw on her thigh. 'And I want you to know that I will always be grateful for how wonderful you made me feel. You made me feel beautiful for the first time ever, and that has changed me. I wish you well, and nothing but good things, because that's what you deserve. Because you *are* wonderful.' Her voice cracked and she bowed her head, letting fat tears run down her cheeks and over the misshapen mouth that he had kissed. 'Never forget that. And the time we had together was the very best in my whole life. You made me feel like a different person, a person I want to be – a person who can achieve more. These are the things I know. I love you. I do. I love you. Goodbye, Grayson Potts.'

The sound of his crying became their wordless farewell.

She was unsure how long she sat on the sofa in quiet thought, but it was long enough for her tears to wane, the ache in her chest to subside and her thoughts to calm. She wiped her palms on her jeans and sniffed, placing the phone in her pocket. With one hand on Buddy's head, she rubbed her sore eyes.

'Enough tears now, Buddy. Enough. I don't need tears. I need plans. I need to figure out what to do next.'

These are the things I know . . .

I know my name is Thomasina Waycott.

I know I'm not like everyone else.

I know I was born a little bit different, as if someone held the instructions upside down or lost a part when they opened the box.

I also know that words are powerful things and they have weight.

I know certain words have sat in my stomach for as long as I can remember and weighed so much that when I was in a crowd or I met someone new they pulled my shoulders down and made my head hang forward so I could only look at the floor.

Tard.

Fuckwit.

Rabbitmouth.

But not any more.

I know I want to see other countries.

I know I want a boyfriend.

I know I want my own kitchen.

I know I want to paint my nails instead of having them caked in mud.

I know I want to own clothes that are pretty.

I know I want to own sparkly red shoes that I will never get to wear but I can look at whenever I want . . .

What I don't know is how different I am, and I also don't know how I can find this out.

And I know that some days I'm happy and on other days I'm sad, but that's the same for everyone, isn't it?

FOURTEEN

It hadn't felt much like Christmas. Their last one at Waycott Farm, as the sale drew nearer, and the second one without Jonathan at the table. Her brother's gift-wrapped scent bottle had arrived, and she had been grateful for it. The decorations on the tree and the cut boughs of holly that traditionally sat on top of the mantelpieces brought her no joy. Carols on the radio did no more than irritate. In truth, it all felt a little pointless. She had got drunk with Shelley and both had ended up crying on the sofa in the flat above the pub, drinking vodka cocktails until they were sick in the tub where Daphne had once laid her feathery head. Yes, Christmas this year was no more than a red-ringed date on the calendar. There was no flutter of anticipation the night before the big day at the prospect of the fat, bearded man squeezing down the fire-place and leaving her new slippers, bath salts, thick socks and chocolate. Even the prospect of overeating and then pausing only to walk to the kitchen to re-stock and eat some more held no allure. But then, for the last few weeks, seven weeks to be precise, since that last phone call with Grayson, Thomasina had felt as if the joy had been sucked out of just about everything.

And it was all because she was stuck.

Her dreams of travel were, she realised, near impossible without the cold hard cash for a ticket, and her ideas for a chicken-focussed business felt a little foolish in the light of no enquiries and without the money to tell the world she was here. She struggled to think of a plan B, but her cogs kept turning, knowing a solution was out there somewhere.

For the first time in her life she found it hard to fall asleep and even harder to stay asleep. The problem was threefold. Firstly, her parents were on edge, worrying now about her mental as well as her physical condition, in a state of agitation she could never have envisaged for them in their own home. If they realised she had caught one of their furtive glances, they would break instantly into false and crooked smiles, as if this lifting of the lips might make everything feel better, reassure her that *everything was going to be okay* . . . It might have worked when she was little, but right now it had the opposite effect. The three of them were reticent, unusually polite with each other and a little ill at ease.

Secondly, life was tough without Emery's labour in the cold winter, when the ground was hard and unforgiving; frost turned the softest mud to iron and darkness fell ever earlier in the cold bite of a sharp wind. The Waycotts were worked to the bone. The chores took longer, work was harder, the lifting heavier. Thomasina's time with her chickens was minimal – it was all about getting through her list of jobs without the luxury of being able to linger with them or, God forbid, have a dance. She suspected that her parents, like herself, fell face down on to their mattress at night in a state of near collapse, only to be woken what felt like a short time later by the pipping of the alarm that was set a little ahead of the needs of the animals. And in her case, she was lucky if sleep was possible at all.

Thirdly, and finally, Thomasina was in a state of grief, bewildered by the longing she felt for Grayson Potts. Her thoughts whirred on an endless loop about all the things they might have done differently. Again and again she saw herself saying goodbye to him at the entrance of Barts Hospital, unbeknownst to her the last time she would see him; holding him tightly, kissing his face and reassuring him that his mum would be fine, that it would all blow over quickly, and he would soon be hotfooting it back to Austley Morton, where they would continue to get to know each other in a state of bliss. And although a little distracted, he had held her tightly, and she could still remember the feel of his arms around her, his fingers digging in. She had clung to him, happy in the knowledge that their parting was not a chosen thing but a forced thing, he was simply doing his duty, and still she had believed, deep down, that their future was rosy. She had, in spite of the serious nature of his mother's condition, sung loudly all the way back to Waycott Farm from Bristol Parkway Station with a kernel of happiness in the centre of her gut.

It was a funny thing, but that evening after she had arrived home, as she stood in the lower paddock with her hens, it was as if a black shadow crossed her mind, as surely as a dark cloud blotting out the sun. She had had a bad feeling and time had made it come true. She was once again alone and struggling with how to find a way out. Her loneliness now was topped with rejection and the fact that Mr Grayson Potts was not the man she had hoped he would be. Her thoughts ran rampant and she wondered if he might have met another girl – someone like bloody Melinda Liebermann, a girl with a pretty mouth who deserved a good man like him. Maybe a girl his mother actually liked . . .

'You got the supplement for the cows, my lovely?' her mum asked, blowing out clouds with every breath into the chill morning air. She rolled up the sleeves of her coveralls as she prepared to haul the wheelbarrow full of shit and straw to the other side of the yard.

'Yes.' Thomasina held up the wide plastic bottle, ready to shake the contents into their mash.

'How long, Thomasina?'

The question caught her off guard. 'How long what?'

'How long are you going to stay morose, fed up and lost in thought?'

'Probably forever,' she answered quickly, without any hint of irony.

'Oh good. Well, at least I've got that to look forward to.'

'I can't help it, Mum. I feel as though everything is unravelling. I'm making plans in my head, but they all feel a little soured when I think that Grayson won't be here to share them with me, by my side.' She hated the spring of tears that seemed to be on tap these days. 'I'm so disappointed. I really liked him.'

'I know, love, and I don't know if it helps, but Pops and I really liked him too. I got the feeling he would have benefitted from being part of this bonkers family.'

Thomasina nodded. 'It's true. I thought I loved him, and I thought he loved me too.'

'Maybe he did. Maybe it's not that simple.'

'Yes, Mum – that's why he's chosen to stay in that shitty life in that shitty flat with his shitty mother! It's such a waste, and so selfish of her. She's robbing him of these years and he just can't see it. And I'm supposed to carry on as if nothing has happened?' She wiped at her tears, which now flowed freely. 'I'm not hanging around for someone like that.'

'It is a waste, my girl, but you're also very tired and that makes everything feel ten times worse.'

'We're all tired!' Thomasina sniffed.

'True enough.' Her mum paused. 'I can't wait for the sale to go through and then I think I'll sleep for a thousand years, but there's always the chance it won't go through – things can and do go wrong, and if we've let things slide we'll be in a worse position than before, so we plough on, literally.'

'Yep.' Thomasina sniffed again and rattled the supplement bottle in her hand.

'Pops and I have been thinking, my love, and we agreed not to say anything, in case it all falls through – didn't want to get your hopes up – but I think it might be good for you to know, might bolster your spirits.' She paused again.

'Good to know what?' Thomasina was confused.

'I never want you to think that we have taken *your* years.'

'I know that.' *It's just how it is, the lines between this job and this life are blurred . . .*

Her mum continued. 'And I know I need to let go and not worry about you so much. And so, if and when the sale on the farm completes, Pops and I want to buy you a ticket. It's only with money you could have earned if things had been different, so think of it as though we've been saving it for you, but that's what we're going to do.'

'I don't get it, you're going to do what?' Thomasina had heard the word 'ticket' and her heart leapt accordingly, but she needed it restated in case she'd misunderstood.

'We're going to buy you a ticket, love, so you can go and see that big wide world beyond these fields and on the other side of the river.'

Thomasina felt the bubble of emotion fill her right up. 'Are you being serious right now?' She felt her pulse race and a smile split her face. It wasn't only the thought of travelling that brought her such joy but the fact that her mum was encouraging her to go.

'Deadly.' Her mum held her gaze. 'It's what you want and it's what you deserve.'

'Oh my God! Mum! I don't know what to say!' She walked forward and took her mother in her arms, her mind racing and her heart thumping with joy. The news was enough to invigorate her tired limbs. 'I can't believe it, I can't! Thank you!'

'You deserve it, Thomasina: you have always worked so hard. Any idea where you might go?' her mum whispered into her hair.

'New York,' she answered without hesitation. 'I'm going to go to New York.'

'Well, there's a surprise.'

Thomasina laughed. 'I'm going to go to New York, Mum! I'll visit the sights, eat the food, walk in Central Park! I can't wait! And then, when I come back, I can set up my business.' This reminder that wonderful things lay ahead was the shot in the arm to get her fired up, and it felt good.

'I'm happy you're happy, but I don't want you to get carried away. We need to secure the sale first, and there's a danger—'

'I know, I know,' said Thomasina, cutting her short. 'There's a danger it might all fall through, but if it does, when the warmer weather comes and things are a little easier on the farm, I'll set up my business and advertise it in Bristol. There are loads of people wanting to keep chickens in their backyard – I read about it. I can start up my business in the city. I don't even need premises, just a van – and then I can save up while I get cheap digs somewhere.'

'Sounds as if you have a plan.'

'I do, Mum. I can set people up and teach them the basics and, no matter what you say, I've already got carried away!' she whooped. 'I've looked at the prices for my services and I can set an hourly fee but also buy all the equipment they might need, like a starter kit, and I can get it wholesale, with even more knocked off if I buy in bulk, and then I can charge my clients the retail price so I make money on that too. I'm also going to do the same with feed, bedding, medicines – everything! I shall print shopping lists and my customers can order from me, and I can deliver it regularly, making money on the products and on the delivery!'

'Well, I was right about one thing. It's certainly perked you up!'

'It has.' Thomasina smiled at the thought that this was the stepping stone she had been waiting for. A break in New York for a few weeks was the best thing she could imagine and, even if it didn't work out, if there was no ticket from her parents, talking it out with her mum had given her the confidence that travel might be possible! And the irony was, it might be happening sooner than she figured because of Buttermore money – all thanks to greedy, envious Thurston and his idiot of a son,

Tarran, and she had never loved them more. She laughed, wishing she could share this irony with Grayson, and then instantly missed him. It wouldn't make losing the farm any easier, but it would sure be one hell of a diversion. For her, it was so much more than the holiday of a lifetime. It was a marker, the realisation of a dream, quite some achievement . . . for a girl like her.

'What's so funny?'

'Nothing, Mum. It's exhaustion – it does strange things to you.'

Her mum closed her eyes and ran her hand over her face. 'It does. I don't know how much longer Pops can keep going. I'm just waiting to hear that the sale is nearly finalised. I'm worried about him.'

This was the first time her mum had ever directly expressed such a concern and it fired a fearful bolt of dread right through her.

'Is he sick?' Her smile faded. This was her worst fear: something happening to her beloved dad before he had a chance to retire, to get some time to himself and to rest his weary bones. She wanted more for him than a life of hard toil ending in death. There had to be a period of rest in between; otherwise, it all felt a bit bloody pointless. She felt an uncomfortable and uncharacteristic flare of anger at her brother, picturing him riding his horse towards that mountain-lined horizon with the sun on his back and a fat steak awaitin' on the barbecue. It wasn't fair.

'Your father's not sick.'

Thomasina's relief at her mum's words was instant.

'But I can't lie. He's under enormous pressure – financial stress, as well as exhaustion and having to deal with—' Her mum stopped short and clamped her mouth shut. The physical expression of her vocal slip-up would have been comical, were it not that she, Thomasina, was the cause.

'Having to deal with losing Emery's labour on the farm . . .' Thomasina finished for her.

'Yes, but it's not your fault, love, and neither Pops nor I would have it any other way. We would rather work ourselves into the mud than have him around being so foul to you. And we could barely afford him anyway, always robbing Peter to pay Paul. You're not to worry about it or feel guilty about it.' Her tone was harsh, insistent. And it meant the world. 'And as for that Mr Potts, you didn't know him, Thomasina. Not really. You might have thought you did, but soft, sweet words have been spoken by many a man to get his way. You weren't the first to fall for it and you won't be the last. As I say, we liked him, we really did, but spending a few weeks in a whirlwind of lust and promises is very different from knowing in your heart that a person is for you, through the good and the bad, no matter what. That's real, Thomasina. Nearly crying when it's time to haul your weary bones out of bed for another day but knowing you wouldn't have it any other way because you get to do it next to the man you love. That's real.'

She watched her mum look down towards the river, where her dad was dumping rubble from the tractor, shoring up the defence of their boundary, and she felt almost like an intruder on the beautiful moment of admission. She had truly thought this was the relationship she and Grayson might have enjoyed, that enviable closeness, the glue that kept her parents together through the good times and the very bad. But she'd been wrong and it was time to let it go. Her moody reflection over what might have been did no one any favours, least of all herself.

'You should have more faith in yourself, Thomasina, more confidence. You have a lot to offer the right person. You're lovely. And I think New York will be a wonderful adventure. You will take the city by storm, my girl.'

Her mum's rare compliment was as beautiful as it was heartfelt, confirmation that she was letting Thomasina spread her wings, sending her off with her blessing, and it felt like a gift.

'Thank you, Mum.'

'Do you think you might bump into Jonathan? Both my babies in America – what a thing!'

'I don't think so. Wyoming and New York aren't close on the map. I did look.'

'Well, Pops and I will be here, living it up in our new home, God willing. Life goes on, eh, my little love? Life goes on.' It was her mum's turn to well up. 'Anyway, that supplement's not going to get into those cows with you stood there snivelling! Do I have to do everything myself?' her mum yelled with vigour as she made her way across the yard.

'I do love you, Mum,' Thomasina called out. Her mum ignored her, lifting her hand, as if catching the words. Thomasina smiled after her. She was right, of course. It was time to let go and move on.

Life goes on . . .

◆　◆　◆

The lights in the mall at Cribbs Causeway were bright, the shop windows shiny. It was like another world, where everything was glossy and clean and everyone had neat hair and wore make-up, a million miles away from the mud and grime of farm life. This wasn't the first time she and her friend had ventured here. On their first trip she'd acquired a bottle of plum-coloured nail polish and on their second a rich velvety hand cream that helped rid her hands of calluses and which had the most glorious scent of gardenias. She was getting her hands 'holiday ready', not wanting to step off the plane with cow shit under her fingernails.

'What will you do first when you get to New York?' Shelley asked, holding up a slinky dress with sparkles down one side.

Thomasina shook her head. 'Ew, no – I'm not going to any discos. I'd never wear it!'

Shelley put the dress back on the rack as Thomasina considered her question.

'I'm not sure what I'll do when I get there. Probably walk for miles and miles and look at everything: the pavements – or should I say sidewalks – the skyscrapers, the "walk"/"don't walk" signs, the stores, Broadway! And

I'll eat hotdogs and giant pretzels and drink *cworfee* as I stroll through Central Park. Ooh, and I have to jump in a yellow cab and cross Brooklyn Bridge and ride the subway and take the Staten Island Ferry and salute Lady Liberty. And when it's dark I'll go to the top of the Empire State Building and throw wishes off the top. It'll be like living in a film! All the things I've seen in films and on the TV, and I will *actually* be there!'

'Not that you've given it much thought,' Shelley offered sarcastically, and the two giggled.

'I can't help it, Shell! A million images keep whizzing around my mind! I feel sick, I feel excited, happy, nervous, scared, you name it, but most of all . . .'

'Most of all what?' her friend prompted.

'Most of all, I feel like me. The me I'm supposed to be.'

'Your mum and dad are going to miss you.'

'I know, but it's only for six weeks, and missing me I can cope with. At least with the farm gone they won't *need* me, and that makes it a hell of a lot easier to go.' She thought of Grayson, as she did from time to time – about ten times a day, if she were being honest.

'And they're going to build on the land they hold back?' Shelley was trying to keep up.

'Yes. They're retiring, but keeping a couple of acres where they can build a bungalow.'

'That'll be really weird when you come home and Tarran's living in your house!'

'It will be, a bit, but the thing is, Shelley, I've wanted change for so long in my life and this feels like my chance! I shall come back renewed and ready to start up my little venture. And I'm bloody hungry for it!'

'You crack me up.' Shelley laughed. 'I'm bloody hungry now – fancy cake and a coffee?'

Thomasina nodded, and they abandoned their clothes shopping, or rather pretend clothes shopping, as neither had the funds right now for anything new, and headed to the food court in search of a bun.

'Oh my God!' Thomasina stopped in front of a window, drawn to the most exquisite pair of shoes she had ever seen. Her eyes drank in the sparkly toffee-apple-red fabric, bedecked with sequins, the neatly curved kitten heel, and with a bow no less, sitting on the front. They were the beautiful shoes of her imagination. Shoes that would never fit a foot like hers, but she loved them nonetheless.

'Oh my God, Shelley, will you look at them?'

'They'd be no good for mucking out the cows, but I *can* see you walking down Fifth Avenue in them.'

'Oh, I wouldn't want to wear them, no matter where I was. I'd just love to own them, and I'd have them on a special shelf, on display like art!'

'Well, that I understand,' her friend said, laughing, peering closer at the price tag. 'Holy moly! They're nearly five hundred quid!'

'As I say, art!' Thomasina giggled and took a picture on her phone so she could look at the pair of beauties whenever the urge took her.

'I can probably get you a few shifts at the pub if you like, before you go?'

'Oh, that might be good. Thank you!'

'If nothing else, it's the only way to meet fellas where we live. Not that you're going to need any introductions – they'll go mad for your accent over there.'

Thomasina felt her smile slip as she tried to imagine walking in that strange city with her head held high, avoiding eye contact with anyone who stared, and she wondered again if Grayson was right. Had she been hiding? Was now the time to get her mouth properly fixed? She covered her lips with her hand, almost in reflex.

'You still missing Grayskull?'

'Yes, a bit.'

'You need to get back out there. I mean, look at me,' Shelley said with a sigh. 'I was gutted when your Jonathan left. We were getting on great. I felt like we had a real connection – he's lovely. And then, just like that' – she snapped her fingers – 'he'd taken off for bloody America!

What is it with your family and me? We get close and, before I know it, you're applying for visas! Don't let me meet Pops, or the next thing you know he'll be heading for Chicago and your mum to Florida!'

Thomasina stopped and stared at her. 'I didn't know that you and Jonathan, that he and you . . .' She felt at a loss for words.

'Oh, nothing happened, but you know when you both know that something might and it's so exciting!' She beamed and bit her lip. 'We were at that stage.'

Thomasina remembered a conversation about Shelley before her brother left.

'*You like Shelley?*'

'*Kind of . . . I would never want to be mean to her – she's fabulous!*'

'I had no idea.' She thought of how different things might have been if her brother had stayed at home and settled down with this girl, who was indeed a bit fabulous. *Home.* It was a moment of realisation that the Waycotts had farmed the area for generations and yet, in a couple of weeks, it would all come to an end. She wondered what Great-Grandma Mimi and Great-Grandpa Walter would make of that.

'You look miles away. What are you thinking?'

'I'm thinking I'm ready for that coffee and cake!' she lied, linking her arm through Shelley's and swallowing the nostalgic bloom at the back of her throat. Just a few weeks, and that would be it: a different surname on the deeds. She placed her hand on her chest and tried to ease the sting where the realisation of what was about to happen had pierced her heart. She pictured the Big Apple and the wonderful adventure that beckoned and, not for the first time, she felt torn.

Thomasina fed the cattle, cleaned out the chickens and, with Buddy on the front seat, she drove around the lower lanes to find Bonnie and Clyde, the two ducks that had gone AWOL. Again. This time, she found them in a muddy, shallow puddle, looking rather pleased with themselves.

As she pulled back around to the front of the farmhouse with the ducks in the rear, a taxi pulled up at the front of the house – a rare thing now that there were no bed-and-breakfast bookings, not with them so close to completing the sale, which would happen only next month. She drove past the vehicle and pulled into the yard and, as she did so, the breath caught in her throat, her legs turned to jelly and she felt sick.

There in the back seat of the cab sat none other than Grayson Potts. *Shit! Shit! Shit! Shit! Ohmygod! Ohmygod! Grayson!*

Her first thought was to hide, her second to run away.

She had, in the first weeks since she'd seen him, longed for him to turn up, imagined the sweet joy of reunion, jumping out of her bed and looking out of the window at the slightest squeak of a brake or the whirr of an engine, but this was nothing like that. Things were different now: she had started to prepare for New York and her bedroom was packed away into boxes. At the sight of him, she felt the spread of panic as her heart beat fast and her mouth went dry. She wasn't sure if it was excitement, anger or anticipation at the thought of seeing him again – possibly, a combination of all three – but whatever it was, she felt light-headed and more than a little nauseous. Her thoughts raged: Why had he come back? Had she brushed her hair? Was she covered in cow shit? She wasn't sure she wanted to hear whatever it was he had to say – her hurt had been visceral and the wounds still smarted. These thoughts, however, were all underpinned by an internal whoop of joy over which she had no control.

She turned her attention to Bonnie and Clyde, the escapee ducks.

'Come on! Come down, you two! You can't be wandering off wherever you like. You'll cause your mum and dad no end of worry!' She scolded the birds, trying to keep her voice steady and ignoring the wide flap of their wings and squawks of protest as she thrust them into the yard, shooing them towards the inner pond and their awaiting family.

She was aware of Grayson walking up the side path, recognising the lope of his gait, the scrape of the soles on his lace-up London shoes and the outline shape of him, his height, his quiet calm . . . all from no more than an awareness in her peripheral vision. Buddy, the traitor, ran over and pushed his muzzle into his hand. She heard the enthusiastic welcome and the small laugh that underpinned his words, coming from this man who was no dog lover, apparently.

'Thomasina!' he called to her.

'What?' she answered, still concentrating on driving the ducks towards the pond and closing the iron gate behind them, not giving Grayson the courtesy of turning around to face him.

'I'm here!'

'So I gathered.' She leaned on the gate and closed her eyes, knowing she was going to have to turn around and look at him at some point, steeling herself for the moment. He sounded happy to be there, his tone sincere and open, and she cursed the confusion this caused in her muddled brain. It was a fight between self-preservation and giving in to her heart, which, whether she liked it or not, ached for him.

You can't turn up like this and mess with my head. I have plans! I'm leaving – going on my big adventure! And I can't let you hurt me again . . . It's too painful and takes too long to fix . . . but, oh my God, just the sound of you!

'I missed Buddy.'

She turned to squint at his attempt at humour and the first thing she noticed was that he'd cut off his hair. He looked younger and handsome, so handsome. His large eyes were now clearly visible and gone was the curtain of hair that half-hid his face.

'And you got a haircut.'

'D'you like it?' He ran his hand over his head and his expression was desperate.

She nodded. 'I do, actually,' she whispered.

'I went to the barber!'

'Like a big boy.'

'Yes,' he chuckled wryly, 'like a big boy.'

He took a step forward and she saw for the first time the bag that he'd dumped by the wall. A bag large enough to contain the odds and ends of someone who might be intent on staying for a while. The idea both thrilled and alarmed her. How was it possible that the thought of his staying felt both like a glorious new beginning and the ending of something wonderful before it had begun?

'What is it you want, Grayson?' she asked flatly.

He licked his dry lips and put his hands in his pockets, looking over her head. 'There's so much I want to say to you, it's hard to pick a few words that might help me begin.'

She stayed quiet, knowing it was up to him to find those words and not down to her to help him out. He drew breath and looked steadily at her. 'It's been so hard for me, missing you, that it felt easier not to think about you – does that make any sense?'

It made complete sense, not that she was going to tell him that. She felt her shoulders straighten as she stood tall, thinking of the girl who was willing to sleep with Tarran Buttermore just because she wanted to be wanted, and here she was, standing down this wonderful man because, finally, she knew her worth.

He coughed. 'I've always been a bit slow in realising things that others seem to jump to in an instant. It takes me a little longer.' He paused. 'I knew I needed to sort the facts from the fog in my mind, and I've done that. I spoke to Liz and I thought about all the wonderful things you said to me and all the promises we made, all the ideas better than anything I've ever had or known.' He looked again over her head. 'I thought I didn't deserve you, not really, because you're so wonderful and I'm just me, and I know I've no right to ask you to consider having me back in your life, but I give you my word that things have changed. I know what you said is right: I need to take control, make it happen, and that's what I'm doing. And if you decide you don't want to take a chance on me, I'll understand. But it'll kill me, and I will regret it for always but, as I say, I understand, Thomasina, if—'

'No, you don't understand,' she interrupted, shaking her head and matching his stare. 'Not even a little bit. You ran out on me. You gave up on us! You made it clear that you couldn't have your life in London with all that self-imposed pressure *and* your life with me. You made your decision, Grayson, and even though I respected it, it crushed me!' She placed her hand on her chest. 'I thought I must have imagined everything that happened between us, and I figured the way I felt was not the way you felt, because if you did, then you wouldn't have . . . you couldn't have—'

'I did! I did! I do!' It was his turn to interrupt. 'You didn't imagine it, and the way I feel about you is off the chart! It's sky-high!' He made his arm into a rocket and zoomed it up over his head.

'So if that's true, what happened? How come it was so easy to cut me off?' Thomasina kicked the toe of her boots against the ground and waited.

'It just took me a while to figure it all out, to catch up. After you left the hospital, I fell back into the web.'

'What web?'

Grayson sighed. 'You know what web! My aunties, my mum, the guilt at the thought of her lying on the floor on her own, her heart being weak . . . a million things. And I knew, I knew I couldn't do both – couldn't give you what you want, what you deserve and live that life with those women, trapped.'

'So I still don't understand – why are you here now?' She folded her arms across her chest, a protection of sorts.

'To tell you I'm sorry and to try to explain, if you'll listen. A lot has happened.'

'A lot has happened here too.'

He nodded, before gazing wearily skyward, and she felt a flash of love at his desperate expression. 'I've been run ragged, and unhappy. I came back from work a couple of nights ago and walked into the lounge, and my aunties and my mum were sitting with sheets of grease-stained white paper spread over their laps; they were eating battered sausage and chips in pools of salt and vinegar. Knocking back measures of wine between mouthfuls and then lighting up cigarettes.' He swallowed, painting a picture so vivid that she felt she was witnessing the scene, could hear their incessant babble and smell the sharp tang of the food and the acrid smoke. 'I reminded my mum that she'd told the doctor she'd stop smoking, that her heart attack was a warning and that she needed to change things if it wasn't going to happen again. And she . . .'

'She what, Grayson?' Taking a step closer to him, she could smell his glorious scent, which still reminded her of the amber-coloured soap they had had in the bathrooms at school, spicy and warm.

'She snarled at me. She said that what she did was none of my business. She said I was a fucking idiot, like him. And then she told me . . .' He paused, as if even the memory of the words was still enough to cause pain. 'She told me that she hoped my dad's floozy and his shitty new family . . . she hoped they'd all rot in hell! Two little girls, apparently. My aunts went quiet, as if she'd gone too far, and Auntie Eva choked on her chip.'

'He has another *family*?' Thomasina was trying to keep up.

Grayson nodded. 'And she knew. She always knew. I remember scrawling him notes when I was little and being too afraid to ask her where to post them, so I'd throw them off the roof of our block, thinking they might float to him. And she told me that she wrote to him, telling him not to make contact with me. I tried to tell her how much of a difference it would have made to me just to have a Christmas card or a birthday card – anything! It would have made all the difference in the world to know that he hadn't just disappeared into thin air.'

'Oh my God, that's huge!'

'It is. All this time, she knew where he was, she knew all about him. And I'm not laying the blame solely at her door. I mean, my dad didn't exactly fight for me, did he? He didn't try. He never made contact, but she made it easy for him, really. But I realised that you're right, Thomasina. There comes a time when you have to make a stand, make a decision. And

I'm done with both of them. I need to start thinking about me and about you, and that's why I'm here, chasing life. I'm chasing you.'

'Because it doesn't come to you.' She smiled at him, feeling the warm spread of desire through her limbs. How she'd missed him!

'That's right, because it doesn't come to you.'

'And yet here you are,' she whispered.

'Yep, here I am.'

She stepped closer and placed her hand on his arm, and to be in contact felt wonderfully familiar. She stared at him, feeling a flicker of joy rise up through the cruel embers of rejection.

'I'm glad you came, Grayson, but—'

'But what?' he asked, his expression pained.

'Things are different now. *I* am different. I have set goals and I've taken control and it feels good!'

Grayson took a deep breath. 'Have you met someone else? You're not with that Buttermore chap?'

'No.' She shook her head, finding the very idea laughable and noting his expression of relief. 'There's no one else. But the farm is being sold and I'm going to New York for a long holiday.'

'Wow! You're really going?'

'I am,' she replied, with a certain smug satisfaction, a recognition of how far she had come and how far she intended to go. 'I figured it's not that much different jumping on a plane to New York as it is jumping on a train to London. As long as I have a map and a tongue in my head, I'll be fine.'

'Can I come with you?'

'What?' His question threw her off course.

'Can I come with you?'

She avoided answering him. Grayson had not figured in her plans for New York and she wasn't sure she wanted to alter the image of herself walking solo around the city that never slept. 'When I come back, I'm going to set up my business – properly set up my business.'

'That sounds great. I know you can make it work.'

'I think so too.' She looked over towards the chicken coop.

'I quit my job.'

'You quit your job? Oh my God!' She knew that this too was big news, aware that going each day to fulfil his role as number magician was not only a routine he thrived on but that the place was also a refuge of sorts. There, and in the basement beneath the flats where the storage cages lurked. She watched as Grayson reached for her hands and she liked the pulse of his warm palms beneath her fingers on this cold, cold day. There was something about being this close to him with their hands touching. It eroded a little of her resolve and it was almost instinctive, her need to stand closer and feel his skin against hers.

'You're the missing piece of my puzzle, Thomasina. And it's the only puzzle I have to figure out: how to be happy. And the answer is you – you're what makes me happy. You're where I've been heading, always. This I know.'

His words were sweet and sincerely offered and caused a ricochet of happiness within her. She thought of all the years before Grayson, when kind words, confidence and being desired were short on supply. 'That's a lovely thing to say to me—'

'I mean it!' he cut in.

'I believe you, but things are a little uncertain for me, Grayson, and I'm not sure what my future looks like.'

'Who's sure?' He laughed. 'No one! I've quit my job – left London! Who'd have thought that one seminar invitation to Bristol that I nearly didn't accept could change my whole life? Could you change yours?'

'Yes, but this farm is all we've ever known, and it's going to belong to someone else, and the closer it gets, the more the hugeness of that hits me. So yes, I'm looking forward to my trip, but at the same time, all of this' – she threw her arm around in an arc – 'when I come back it will be private property and to set foot on it will be considered trespassing. Can you imagine? Trespassing on the land that my dad, my grandad, great-grandad and great-great-grandad have worked on every day of their lives! It was supposed to be Jonathan's, and I thought' – she drew breath now, about to make a confession that had only previously lived silently in her mind – 'I thought that, if ever I had children, they would have the run of the place, like I did. I thought they'd learn to drive a tractor when they were considered too young, play in Big Barn and have a dog like Buddy.' She hated the catch to her voice, unable to control the sadness that underpinned her words. 'It's a lot.'

'It is a lot.' He too looked down towards the water, across the green pastures of Waycott Farm. 'What does Jonathan say about it all?'

'He's gutted. We text and stuff, but it's hard to tell him exactly how I feel and how I think it will affect us all when I don't really have an alternative to offer. I know it will just make him feel as bad as I do, and what's the point of that?'

'I must say that, for someone who's planning her own business, setting goals and taking control, you seem to be letting the place slip through your fingers a little more easily than I would have expected. I know that, if my dad had wanted to, he'd have fought for me. And if you really wanted to keep Waycott, you'd fight for it too.'

She stared at him, feeling a flare of defence at his words, which were both direct and hurtful, but they also stirred something within her. 'Well, that's easy for an outsider to say. And just by saying it shows me you don't understand the situation. Not at all!'

'Well, I don't want to be an outsider and maybe I understand it more than you think. Maybe you're just riled that you say you're in control but, actually, you're not. Maybe going to New York is a diversion from what really matters – maybe you're looking for happiness in the wrong place?'

As Thomasina caught her breath, considering his words, her mum yelled from Big Barn, 'Hey, Mr Potts! You'd better get these on!'

She turned to see her mum holding up Grayson's wellington boots, the ones without the frog-eyes.

'It's all very well standing there chatting away, but there's work to be done! Chickens are knee-deep in shit!' her mum said, tutting, and threw the wellingtons on the ground.

Thomasina watched as Grayson went off to retrieve the present she'd bought him, just because.

How do I fight for it? How can I do that? The questions raced around and around in her mind. The answers, however, were a bit slow in arriving.

◆　◆　◆

'Do chickens have knees?' Grayson asked as he leaned on the wall of Big Barn and put the boots on his feet.

The sound of the tractor came over the field and into the paddock, and her dad came to a halt. 'Hello there, Mr Potts! Just in time for a cup of tea, and a slice of cake if we're very lucky.' He spoke matter-of-factly, as if they had last seen each other yesterday. 'And I'm very glad you're here – I have news!' he said with a wink.

Pops jumped down from the tractor cab in an almost sprightly fashion, and the four made their way into the kitchen. Thomasina couldn't deny that it was lovely to have Grayson here again, in the heart of the home where he'd learned to cook bacon. It reminded her of the comfort that lay in being part of a couple, something she'd almost forgotten. She liked the way her parents welcomed him in with ease, as though he'd never been away, as though he was part of the family . . .

With mugs of tea in their hands and crumbs of fruit cake littering the table, Pops coughed to clear his throat.

'The lawyer chap called when I was down on the riverbank.'

'Oh?' Her mum sat forward with her hand at her mouth, knowing this was either confirmation that the sale was nearly done or that something disastrous had happened.

The anticipation was almost unbearable. Thomasina held her breath.

'He told me that all the paperwork had been received and there were no further queries and we'll sign over the farm in four weeks' time.' She watched as her dad reached across the table and took his wife's hand in his. 'And then, my lovely, we'll go to Ikea and look at all the things we might want for our new home, and on the way back we'll stop off at that Cribbs Causeway mall and we'll get you a new frock!'

'I don't need a new frock,' she said, shaking her head, her face contorted with barely contained emotion, 'especially if we're moving into a caravan while the new house is being built – but I wouldn't say no to a couple of new cake tins.' She beamed. 'Thought I might pass the old ones on to you, Thomasina. For safekeeping.'

Thomasina smiled at her mum, knowing that the gesture was so much greater than the mere handing over of some slightly rusting cake tins.

'Is it . . . is it too late, Pops?' she said quietly, unsure of what she needed to say or how to say it.

'Is what too late, my darlin'?'

'Is it a done deal with the Buttermores, or can we still pull out?'

Her dad laughed and sat back in the chair with a wrinkle to his brow, as if he were unable to think of a single reason why, at this late stage, they might want to. 'Well, it's not too late until I sign to exchange the contracts, and that'll happen next week, God willing.'

'Can you give me a few days, Pops?'

'A few days for what, love?' her mum queried.

'I'm not sure,' she levelled with them. 'I just want a few days to think about everything, and I need to know you won't sign or move things forward while I do that. Is that possible?' She fixed her eyes on her dad.

He nodded and looked helplessly from her to his wife and Grayson, as if he were the only one who might not understand what was going on. Thomasina noted that her mum shared the same vexed expression, but not Grayson. Grayson gazed at her calmly with something that seemed a lot like pride.

'It's possible, Thomasina. A few days to think. That doesn't sound unreasonable.' He winked at her, her lovely dad.

The sudden bang of the back door against the wall took them all by surprise, shattering the calm. Her cousin Emery stood in the doorway, with his knack for ruining the loveliest of moments. She saw Grayson stiffen and her mum put her cup firmly on the table. Thomasina had forgotten just how much she disliked the very sight of him.

'What can we do for you, Emery?' Pops asked calmly. It seemed that nothing could spoil his day.

'I just heard from Thurston that the farm is nearly theirs.'

'That's right,' her dad said. 'Nearly, in a few weeks, give or take.'

'So I thought I'd come and . . .' Emery swallowed, his confidence seemingly evaporated.

All four stared at him.

'We . . . we are family,' he managed.

'Yes, Emery,' Pops said with a nod, 'we are family. And you are a Waycott and have contributed your own blood and sweat to keeping this farm running in some of its darkest times. And I appreciate all your hard work – it's not an easy life, not at all – but how *dare* you call my little girl names? How dare you make her feel scared or sad in her own home? You think that's what family does? You think that's nice or fair?'

She had never heard her dad so threatening or so earnest and her heart flexed with love for him.

Emery shook his head and looked at the floor. 'I'm sorry, Thomasina.'

She stared at him, unable to forgive him, not when the hurt still ran deep, and chose to say nothing.

'I've been up at the Buttermores' for a while now, and it's . . . it's different.' His voice was uncharacteristically small, his shoulders hunched.

'What's different?' her dad asked, a little more settled now.

'I'm an outsider, not family, and now I'll be coming back to Waycott but working for them, and it's made me think that my great-great-grandparents built this house.'

She looked at the brute, amazed he was on her wavelength, but not liking him any more for it. Maybe spending time with another family had made Emery realise just how good he had had it here.

'Yes, they did' – her dad paused – 'but it's only bricks and stones, Emery. Home is where your family is, and it'll be good for you working here with all the investment the Buttermores can make. Remember, lad, this building and this land will be here long after we have all gone.'

Emery nodded. 'And I wanted to say I'm sorry, Change Pur—'

'Grayson!'

'My name's Grayson.'

She and Grayson spoke in unison and they smiled briefly at each other.

'Yeah,' Emery said, nodding. 'I'm sorry, Grayson, for all the things I said.' He hesitated for a moment and had clearly not finished. 'And, Thomasina, I shouldn't have taken your postcard off the wall at the farm store. Tarran said that was a shitty thing to do.'

Well, no wonder I didn't get a single bloody call! Thomasina swallowed her response, not wanting to give him any satisfaction and glad that Tarran had apparently spoken up in her defence. It meant a lot and lessened some of her embarrassment when she thought of him.

'And also . . .' Emery swallowed, and she wondered what else he had done – this was turning into quite a list. 'I wanted to tell you that, on my life . . .' He now placed his hand on his heart. 'I didn't kill Daphne. I found her like that.'

'Right.' She was relieved that Daphne more than likely had lain her little head down and fallen asleep and not met the grisly, fearful end she had suspected. Slowly, Thomasina stood up from the table and nodded briefly. 'Do you want a cup of tea, Emery?'

'Yes, please.' He walked sheepishly around the table and took the seat she had recently vacated, as was the way in this kitchen.

'And a slice of cake?'

Emery let a small, hesitant smile form. 'Yes, yes, please. I tell you what – the Buttermores might have all that flash equipment and loads of money, but they're right stingy with their cake.'

Thomasina petted Buddy's ears as she made her way to the stove and filled the kettle, placing it on the hotplate, waiting for it to whistle. She looked over her shoulder at the four people sitting around the kitchen table and smiled. It was funny how things turned out. When she had woken up this morning she could not in a million years have envisaged the day ending with a scene like this.

◆ ◆ ◆

With the tea things cleared away and the Skype call connected, she and Grayson sat at the dining-room table.

'Your text sounded pretty urgent. Are Mum and Pops okay?'

'They're fine, Jonathan.'

'Thank God for that!' he said, exhaling deeply.

'I just need to talk to you, and we don't have a lot of time. A few days at most.'

'I'm all ears! Ah, and you must be the infamous Mr Potts my sister's told me about,' he said, pointing.

'Hi!' Grayson raised his hand and peered at the screen.

'You mess her around and you have me to deal with!' Jonathan let out a loud laugh, but Grayson, sitting stony-faced, clearly wasn't sure he was joking.

'I . . . I won't.' He held her hand beneath the table.

'So come on, what's going on?' Jonathan clapped his hands and sat forward smiling, with his familiar confidence of a man who lived a happy life with a glass half full.

'I keep thinking about the sale of the farm.' She watched the smile slip from his face.

'I can't . . .' he interjected, shaking his head and looking off-screen. 'I can't even think about it. I mean, I get it, I know it's happening and I understand why. I tell Pops it's all okay, because I don't want to make him feel bad, but I can't believe it. I didn't realise we would run out of time.'

'What do you mean, run out of time?' she asked.

He took a deep breath. 'I thought it would always be there, and some of the things I'm learning here . . . I figured I'd become proficient in new things, better ways to farm, and one day I'd come back and implement them.'

'And there was me thinking you were just having fun . . .' She let this trail.

'Oh, I'm having fun, but I miss home. It's . . . home!' She noted the lump in his throat.

'What if we try to fight for it, Jonathan? What if we really try to think of anything we might do to keep it in Waycott hands?' *So my children can run in the paddock and chase Bonnie and Clyde.* 'I have a couple of ideas.'

'Me too.' He peered more closely into the camera.

'What kind of things?' Now he'd piqued her interest.

'So much! Bringing farming into the twenty-first century, compared to how we run Waycott now – upping the pace, working smarter. I know how I can bring higher yields, things like cover crops, better rotation and complete diversification in other areas.'

'Yes!' she said, picking up the verbal baton. 'Glamping, agricultural experiences, a farm store, barn rentals for creative spaces, weddings, workshops on things like caring for poultry, or growing cutting flowers for supply.'

'Yes, exactly!' Jonathan sounded excited. 'That's exactly it! We need to get every acre and every square inch of brick making us money, and I know we could do it if we just had time and investment. I feel that, between us, sis, we could turn the fortunes of the farm, but as I say, it all needs investment, and that's the hard bit.'

'Not necessarily.' Grayson coughed. 'Thomasina and I have been talking, and I would be willing to invest in the farm.'

She thought about their whispered conversation earlier as they had tidied the cups and saucers from the table. 'There's something I don't know if I've made clear, Thomasina.'

'What's that?' She had studied his hesitant expression and her heart had skipped at what other revelations might be forthcoming today, unsure how much more she could cope with.

Grayson had held her grandma's cake tin, running his finger over the dented lid. 'I earn a considerable amount, the most at our brokers, and I have saved it all. I never really had anything to spend it on.'

'A proper haircut wouldn't have gone amiss.' She had broken the tension and he'd given her a half-smile.

'You're probably right, but I have an idea – why not let me invest in the farm? Why not let me become a partner? I know nothing about farming, but I know a lot about money.'

'Because that's your magic trick.'

'Because that's my magic trick.' He had then leaned forward and kissed her.

Thomasina now returned her attention to Jonathan on the screen.

'You would like to invest in Waycott?' His look was one of suspicion.

'Yes.'

'Sorry to be so blunt, Grayson, but can you afford it?'

'Yes. I have a lot of money.'

'Right.' It was Jonathan's turn to sit in silence.

'Plus, I want to ask your sister to marry me, and it makes sense. It all makes sense, really.'

She looked at Grayson, this wonderful man whom she loved, liking the way he spoke so plainly, as if anything other than hitching his wagon to hers was unthinkable. 'Is that some kind of proposal, Mr Potts?' she asked, thinking back to that day on the lane when instinct told her he'd been about to ask.

'Well, not really.' Grayson shifted in the chair. 'I do want to do it, but not in front of your brother – no offence!' he said, turning to the screen.

'None taken.' Jonathan beamed.

'Although,' Grayson coughed, 'if that *were* a proposal, what do you think you might have said?'

She looked at her man and smiled, agreeing with him that everything made sense – when she was with him.

'I would have said, "I'll think about it and I'll let you know when I get back from New York."'

'Hitch – you're coming to New York?' Jonathan asked, aghast.

'I am,' she said, nodding, 'and for the record, Jonathan, my name is Thomasina.'

I know that you never know what's around the corner, even if you think you do.

I know that the Buttermores might have a lot of money, but who wants to live in a house where they're stingy with cake?

I know that Emery isn't as much of an arsehole as I have always believed.

I know that Mum and Pops are going to enjoy the retirement they deserve.

I know my brother is coming home.

And I know that I'm going to New York, where I will drink cwor-fee, and then I'll come back to this farm, and to the man I love.

I know I will give him my answer on the question of marriage and I know I will be Mrs Grayson Potts and life will be . . . It will be wonderful.

EPILOGUE

Grayson stood in front of the flat rock in his heavy work boots and threw stones, trying to skim the surface of the water, which shone with the diamonds cast by the warm summer sun.

'You're really terrible at that, Gray,' Thomasina said, laughing.

'I know, but practice makes perfect!' He lobbed another round pebble, which sank straight down.

'But you've been practising for nearly two years and you're not getting any better.'

'Stop with all the encouragement!' He laughed and took up his place on the folded tartan rug by her side.

'I just tried to cross my legs and assume the gnome-on-a-lily-pad pose to make you laugh, but there's no chance,' she said with a sigh.

He reached over and ran the flat of his hand over her enormous bump. 'I can see why – you're a pregnant gnome on a lily pad.'

'I'm an *enormous* pregnant gnome on a lily pad!' she yelled.

'So come on – names!' he said, kissing her stomach.

'Oh God! Not the names conversation again!' She let her head flop forward. 'I think we should wait and see what it looks like and whether it's a boy or a girl.'

'Okay, but we should at least have a vague plan. How about Reggie?' he suggested brightly.

'As in Reggie, the shoeless murderer?'

'Yes.'

'No, no way!' she shrieked. 'Definitely not. How about Eva or Joan?'

'No, no way!' His reply was instantaneous.

'Actually, talking of which, we ought to be getting back. It's nearly two.' She pulled a face and he nodded with a reluctant sigh.

'Don't be nervous.'

'I can't help it.'

He joined hands with her and kissed her palm. This was what they did for each other: they provided safe harbour and confidence. 'Come on, Buddy! There's a good boy!' he called out, and their faithful dog leapt to heel.

'Sometimes I think you love that dog more than you love me!' She beamed.

'Not true. I love you equally,' he joked as they made their way up the twisting lane, past the paddock, towards the field where her parents were now happily ensconced in their brand-new cottage, complete with wood-burning stove and, of all things, a large jacuzzi that took up most of their bathroom. The new building sat neatly on its generous plot within a drystone wall, lovingly constructed from rocks gathered by Waycott hands of generations past – a link to their ancestors and the farm they held dear.

Jonathan, as farm manager, lived with Shelley in a similar cottage on the other side of the wall when they were not abroad, touring with her latest exhibition. Thomasina could only think of Shelley's art with enormous pride. Soon to be her sister-in-law, her globetrotting friend and her fabulous new tits dashed from country to country, with Jonathan in tow when the farming calendar allowed. A whole wide world away from pulling pints behind the sticky-topped bar of the Barley Mow . . .

Thomasina laughed, recalling a conversation with her mum, who had explained that Shelley's work wasn't quite to her taste.

'I mean, I don't know why she doesn't paint something pretty like a flower or a cow, something I can actually recognise! I know they sell for a lot of money, but Pops and I put her pictures in the closet and then, when she and Jonathan visit, we swap out our Ikea prints and put hers up in their place.'

'What would you do if they just turned up one day, Mum, and you weren't expecting them?'

'Oh good Lord!' Her mum seemed unsettled by the thought. 'I'd have to shut the front door and tell them to hang on a minute while I made the switch!'

It made her laugh. Her parents had certainly taken life down a gear but, despite having retired, they could still be found weeding flowerbeds or feeding animals, just at a slower pace and with the freedom to slope off for a soak in the jacuzzi when the fancy took them. The other difference was that her mum now often wore a nice frock over her jeans and work boots.

She, Jonathan and Grayson had made sweeping changes in the two years since they had taken over the farm. There was now an on-site farm store selling fresh produce and meat, as well as flowers, poultry supplies and local crafts. There was also a café and a wedding barn. The newly built studio within sight of the river was where Thomasina held workshops on chicken rearing, and beyond the paddock sat an encampment of luxury yurts. Further along still lay the glamping fields, just as they had done in her imagination for a number of years. This was where repeat guests such as the Arbuckles came to stay each year with their ever-expanding brood, who liked to make a fuss of Mr Chops, the guard pig, who still roamed the lane, and marvelled at the sights of the early morning when the sun hit the wide, sweeping bend of the River Severn and it looked for a second as though the water was on fire.

Waycott Farm was thriving, owing largely to the investment from Grayson and an incredible team which included Mrs Reedley and her daughter, Julie, who with a small army of helpers ran the kitchen garden, café and store. It was also down to Jonathan, who had a knack of knowing where to invest on the farm. True to his word, yields had increased. Thomasina also took pride in knowing she played her part, working as hard as ever, but also certain that, if she hadn't found her voice, it would be a Buttermore sitting in front of the fire in the snug of an evening. The very idea was unthinkable.

Emery worked for them with a new-found energy, which had seen him promoted with a handsome raise, meaning he was able to put the deposit down on a little cottage in the village. Thomasina was grateful for his hard work and liked the civility that now existed between them but knew that she and Grayson would never be close to her cousin. Too much water had flowed under the bridge and too many words had cut too deep.

It was testament to how much she had grown that she now felt able to work with Emery – in fact, she felt differently about a lot of things. As if a reminder were needed of just how much, she touched her fingers to her rebuilt lip, still more than a little amazed at the incredible job her surgeon had done. It wasn't so much with vanity but in wonder that she stared at her reflection, smiling, pouting and taking such joy from the pretty mouth that made her feel brand new.

Now, as they neared the house, Thomasina saw the car parked in the immaculate block-paved yard in front of the farm store and café.

'Oh my God, Gray, they're early!' She sped up, walking as fast as she could, and he followed in her lumbering wake. Turning back, she saw the twitch of nerves on his face. 'You've got this, my love.'

'I just don't know why you asked them.'

'Because they're family. Family.' She cradled her stomach.

There was a deafening wail of greeting from Grayson's aunties as they drew close. She waved as the women leapt from the car and embraced first her and then Grayson, smiling as Eva and Joan rubbed her bump.

'Oh god! You look beautiful!'

'You sure there ain't two in there? You're bloody huge!'

'I know!' she sighed.

She now walked to the car and opened the door on the passenger side. 'Hello, you!' she said, bending down to kiss her mother-in-law on the cheek. 'Come on – come and see how enormous I am.'

His mum nodded slowly and stepped gingerly from the car. Mrs Potts was coming up for a whole year sober and was as quiet and reflective as she had been on her last visit. She carried with her a melancholy air of regret, tinged with disapproval that sobriety meant she chose not to voice – and that was fine with Thomasina, preferable, in fact.

'How was your journey?' she asked softly.

'Fine,' her mother-in-law whispered.

'You look well.' She spoke the truth – weight loss and a healthy diet had worked wonders for Grayson's mum.

'And you do too. It suits you.' Mrs Potts looked at her burgeoning bump and then let her gaze linger on Thomasina's new mouth. She said nothing.

'Grayson's looking forward to seeing you!'

'Is he?' Her mother-in-law looked at her with such hope it was almost painful.

'He is.'

Having managed to extricate himself from his aunts' grappling hugs, Grayson walked over to his mother. 'Hey, Mum,' he said, reaching down and taking her loosely in his arms, holding his wife's gaze over her shoulder. She gave him a slow blink of support and love.

'Right, I'm sure you're all in need of tea and cake and a visit to the bathroom, and not necessarily in that order!' Thomasina marched ahead with the troop following behind. She smiled and ushered their guests into the farmhouse kitchen. 'There's fruit cake or lemon drizzle. I made both!' she said with a smile, as she pictured her grandparents' cake tins, full of fine fare, baked with love for the man she adored.

Life was good.

'Both for me,' Eva replied. 'Well, it'd be rude not to!'

'And when we've had our cake, I brought my hairdressing scissors, case you wanted a little trim!' Joan made a chopping sign at Grayson with her fingers and they all laughed. 'Anyway, I've packed it in.'

Thomasina and Grayson exchanged a mutual look of relief.

'Tell them about your new hobby, Joan,' Eva encouraged.

'I'm a tattoo artist!'

Thomasina roared with laughter as Grayson choked in shock. She knew a dodgy tattoo would be a lot harder for him to shift than a wonky fringe.

They walked via the dining room.

'Blimey!' Eva stopped to admire the very large abstract painting over the fireplace. 'Would you look at that!' She stared up at the vibrant clash of colours that brightened the room.

'My friend painted it. She's engaged to my brother, actually. We were at school together. She has exhibitions everywhere, even in New York!' Thomasina smiled at her husband, thinking of how she had got to drink *cworfee* on Fifth Avenue . . . The memories of that trip would last her a lifetime. It wasn't only what she had seen that had amazed her, but how she had felt as she travelled alone, as if she could take on the world and win.

It was a lovely afternoon spent catching up. Grayson's aunts regaled them with familiar stories, about how Great-Grandma Noella had got her leg stuck in the fence between her own and the neighbour Betty's house on a perfect sunny day.

'Betty was screaming, and it sounded like a right old bother!'

She watched as Grayson finally relaxed, as if the more time he spent with his new and sober mum, the more he was convinced there would be no more scenes or nastiness. That woman had left the building, and this lady, while not exactly approving of how he had upped sticks and relocated to the back of beyond, was doing her best to build bridges wherever she could.

After a tour of Waycott Farm, a quick introduction to Daisy Duke V, Mrs Cluck VII, Helga III, and presenting his mother and aunts with a box of freshly packed eggs each to take home, Thomasina and Grayson kissed them all goodbye and waved them off as night began to fall.

Mr and Mrs Potts got ready for bed, jostling for space at the sink as they cleaned their teeth.

'I've had the loveliest time. I hope they come again. It wasn't so bad, was it?'

'Not so bad at all.' He beamed. 'Thank you, Mrs Potts.'

'Any time,' Thomasina answered casually as she pulled her night-gown over her head. 'I gave your mum a copy of the scan,' she offered softly.

He nodded. 'Good.'

'I wasn't sure if . . .' she began.

'Wasn't sure if what?' He looked up at her.

'If I should send a copy to your dad too? Now that we have his address. I thought it might make him think about stuff.' She knew it was still a delicate subject and thought about Henry Potts, who had replied to Grayson's letter of introduction with page after page of detail about his life, his family, his job and made no reference at all to the life he had led before. The life with Grayson in it. She knew it was a lot for her husband to deal with as he tried to reconcile the person with whom he was now free to correspond and the man who had stood at the foot of his bed all those years ago. Grayson was still figuring out how to reply or indeed whether he should reply at all. She knew that his dad's letter had made him question whether contact was a good idea – such was his disappointment at reading about a life that seemingly had no space for him in it.

'I'm not sure,' he said with a sigh. 'I suppose, if he can't relate to me, then he might relate to his grandchild. I'm just not sure I want him to – not sure if he deserves that chance.'

'Only you can decide, and I will, of course, support you either way.'

'Do you think he'll come to visit, Thom? Ever come here to see our baby, our life?' His tone was now neutral and not full of hope, as she knew it would have been in the early days.

She climbed beneath the covers of the rickety brass bed and patted the space next to her on the soft and saggy mattress.

Buddy curled into his basket by the door.

'I don't know.' Thomasina, like her husband, knew it was always better, easier, to tell the truth.

He climbed in next to her and took her in his arms. 'I don't know either, but you know it's funny – I don't mind so much. Not any more. It's like you and our life here, and this baby . . . you have filled up all the gaps I had inside me. I have everything I ever wanted. I've been thinking a lot about Mr Waleed, who lived in the flat below with his kids, wife and mother-in-law, and their garden implements lying in the basement storage cage where they had no use.'

'I remember him shouting at you by the bins.' She snuggled down.

'The sound of his happiness floating up to the ceiling of my bedroom fascinated me, and I couldn't understand how he could be so happy, but I get it now. He had the people he loved around him and that was everything. That *is* everything.'

'It is everything,' she agreed as sleep pawed at her. Being pregnant was exhausting.

She thought about the sparkly toffee-apple-red shoes, bedecked with sequins, and their neatly curved kitten heels, with a bow no less, now sitting in a special box in her closet. Shoes that she would never get to wear, shoes not designed for a foot like hers, but which she could look at whenever she wanted.

Thomasina wriggled to get comfortable as her husband smoothed her long hair over his chest. She smiled as she felt the pull of sleep, confident that the sun would rise tomorrow and that she, Thomasina Potts, would idle in her own kitchen and make breakfast for the man she loved. She might get her nails painted a pretty shade of pink and put on a dress with flowers on it. And she would spend the day talking to her baby and preparing to meet them, telling her child that it was okay to be born a little bit different, okay not to be like everyone else. And even if you sometimes felt as if the instructions had been upside down when you were made, or maybe they had lost a part when they opened the box – that was okay too. Because life was all about courage, about making the changes that would make you happy, and taking chances, recognising opportunities and being the kind of person who just bought the damn shoes.

These were the things she knew.

ABOUT THE AUTHOR

Photo © 2012 Paul Smith of Paul Smith Photography at
www.paulsmithphotography.info

Amanda Prowse likens her own life story to those she writes about in her books. After self-publishing her debut novel, *Poppy Day*, in 2011, she has gone on to author twenty-one novels and six novellas. Her books have been translated into a dozen languages and she regularly tops bestseller charts all over the world. Remaining true to her ethos, Amanda writes stories of ordinary women and their families who find their strength, courage and love tested in ways they never imagined. The most prolific female contemporary-fiction writer in the UK, with a legion of loyal readers, she goes from strength to strength. Being crowned 'queen of domestic drama' by the *Daily Mail* was one of her finest moments. Amanda is a regular contributor on TV and radio but her first love is, and will always be, writing.

You can find her online at www.amandaprowse.com, on Twitter @MrsAmandaProwse, and on Facebook at www.facebook.com/AmandaProwseAuthor.